The Curious Book
of Sherlock Holmes
Characters

Michael J. Foy

ISBN 9781787056763

Published by MX Publishing
335 Princess Park Manor, Royal Drive,
London, N11 3GX
www.mxpublishing.com

Cover design by Brian Belanger

I am indebted to Alexis Barquin, curator of *The Arthur Conan Doyle Encyclopedia*
(arthur-conan-doyle.com), for source material and help in the writing of this book, many of his illustrations do not
appear anywhere else on the internet.

Table of Contents

A is for Abbey Grange

1st Earl of Balfour   [MAZA]   Male Alive   See Arthur James Balfour

A

Abernetty, Family   [SIXN]   Holmes mentions this family, to demonstrate to Lestrade that there was no such thing as a trivial case and how the Dreadful Business of the Abernetty Family, was brought to Sherlock Holmes' notice by the depth which the parsley had sunk into the butter upon a hot day.

Abrahams, Mr.   [LADY]   Male Alive   Holmes told Watson that he couldn't leave London while old Abrahams was in such mortal terror of his life, Instead he sent Watson to Europe to find out what happened to Lady Francis Carfax.

Achmet the Merchant   [SIGN]   Male dead   A little, fat, round fellow, with a great yellow turban, and a bundle in his hand, done up in a shawl. All in a quiver with fear, for his hands twitched as if he had the ague, and his head kept turning to left and right with two bright little twinkling eyes. Gave a little chirrup of joy when he thought he was safe upon entering the fort at Agra. He said he had travelled across Rajpootana. Carried the iron box containing the Agra treasure.* Very fast on his feet for a fat man, running like the wind. Tripped up by Jonathan Small by the latter putting his flintlock between the man's legs as he ran past and he rolled twice over like a shot rabbit before the Giant Dost Akbar was upon him. Killed by 'The Four'.

*There were ;

- One hundred and forty-three diamonds of the first water, including one which had been called, 'the Great Mogul' and was said to be the second largest stone in existence.
- Ninety-seven very fine emeralds.
- One hundred and seventy rubies, some of which, however, were small.
- Forty carbuncles.
- Two hundred and ten sapphires.
- Sixty-one agates.
- A great quantity of beryls, onyxes, cats'-eyes, turquoises, and other stones, Three hundred very fine pearls, twelve of which were set in a gold coronet.

F. H. Townsend   *Herbert Denman*

Acton, Mr.   [REIG]   Male Alive A little elderly gentleman Old Acton was a
magnate living near Reigate. His house was Burgled by the Cunninghams. Items
stolen were an odd volume of Pope's 'Homer,' two plated candlesticks, an ivory
letter-weight, a small oak barometer, and a ball of twine. He had some claim on
half Cunningham's estate, and the lawyers have been at it with both hands.

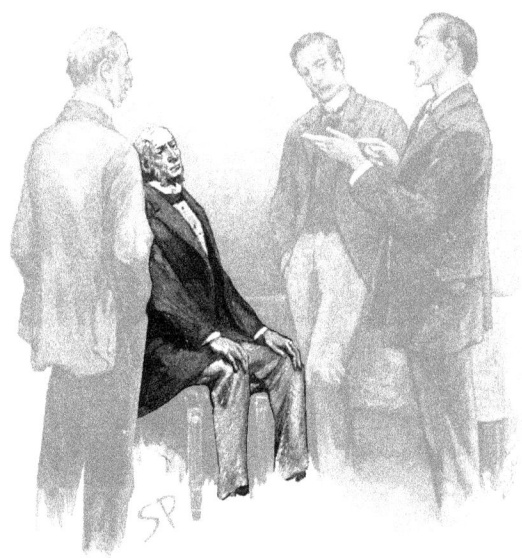

Sidney Paget

Adair, Hilda [EMPT] Female Alive . Hilda Adair was the sister of Ronald Adair, Daughter of the Earl and lady of Maynooth. Together with her mother, they discovered the dead body of Ronald Adair, shot through the head by a revolver bullet.

Address : 427 Park Lane

Adair, Hon. Ronald [EMPT] Male dead   The Honourable Ronald Adair was the second son of the Earl of Maynooth, at that time Governor of one of the Australian Colonies. He was living with his mother and sister Hilda at 427 Park Lane. He had no enemies, and no particular vices. He had been engaged to Miss Edith Woodley, of Carstairs, but the engagement had been broken off by mutual consent some months before, and there was no sign that it had left any very profound feeling behind it. For the rest, the man's life moved in a narrow and conventional circle, for his habits were quiet and his nature unemotional. Yet it was upon this easy-going young aristocrat that death came in most strange and unexpected form between the hours of ten and eleven twenty on the night of 30th March, 1894. He was fond of cards, playing continually, but never for such stakes as would hurt him. He was a member of the Baldwin, the Cavendish, and the Bagatelle Card Clubs. On the day of his death he had played a rubber of whist at the Bagatelle Card Club. He had also played there in the afternoon. The evidence coming from those who had played with him—Mr. Murray, Sir John Hardy, and Colonel Moran On the evening of his death, he returned from the club exactly at ten, a fire was lit and the window opened to allow the smoke to leave. His body was discovered in the locked front room in the Second floor of 427 Park Lane at around eleven-twenty. He had been shot with an expanding revolver bullet, but no weapon of any sort was to be found in the room. He was murdered by colonel Sebastian Moran using his special airgun rifle because Adair had discovered that Moran had been cheating at cards.

Address : 427 Park Lane

Stanley E. Armstrong

Adams, (the culprit) **[GREE]** Adams was the culprit in The Manor House Case, solved by Holmes. Mycroft thought that his brother Sherlock might have needed help from him to solve the case. Said to Sherlock "I thought you might be a little out of your depth."

Addleton Tragedy **[GOLD]** At the start of this story, while Watson is looking at all of Holmes' cases in 1894, he mentions the Addleton tragedy, but decides instead to write about the Golden pince-nez.

Adler, Irene **[SCAN]** **Female alive** Daintiest thing under a bonnet on this planet Soul of Steel Face of the most beautiful of women. Mind of the most resolute of men Superb Figure **[SCAN]** To Sherlock Holmes, she was always THE WOMAN. Well-known adventuress Contralto -La Scala- Prima Donna Imperial Opera of Warsaw Retired from operatic stage Blackmailer Former lover of Wilhelm Gottsreich Sigismond von Ormstein Grand Duke of Cassel-Felstein and King of Bohemia. Married at The Church of St. Monica just before noon. It was not a happy break-up with the King of Bohemia and she resolved to end his later engagement with Clotilde Lothman von Saxe-Meningen, second daughter of the King of Scandinavia by releasing a photograph that had the king and her together. Five times the king had attempted to recover the photograph and had failed, so he called on Holmes. Holmes dressed up as an amiable and simple-minded Nonconformist clergyman, who was injured as he tried to stop a fight breaking out when Adler came back one evening. She had him brought into her house and when Watson threw in a plumber's smoke rocket and smoke filled the air, Irene went to a concealed sliding recess, thereby showing Holmes where she had hidden the photograph. Holmes elected not the take the photograph then and there, but allow the King to get it himself the next day. However on the following morning, Irene is gone, as is the photograph, but there was a letter addressed to Holmes that read

MY DEAR MR. SHERLOCK HOLMES, - You really did it very well. You took me in completely. Until after the alarm of fire, I had not a suspicion. But then, when I found how I had betrayed myself, I began to think. I had been warned against you months ago. I had been told that if the King employed an agent, it would certainly be you. And your address had been given me. Yet, with all this, you made me reveal what you wanted to know. Even after I became suspicious, I found it hard to think evil of such a dear, kind old clergyman. But, you know, I have been trained as an actress myself. Male costume is nothing new to me. I often take advantage of the freedom which it gives. I sent John, the coachman, to watch you, ran upstairs, got into my walking clothes, as I call them, and came down just as you departed. Well, I followed you to your door, and so made sure that I was really an object of interest to the celebrated Mr. Sherlock Holmes. Then I, rather imprudently, wished you good night, and started for the Temple to see my husband. We both thought the best resource was flight when pursued by so formidable an antagonist; so you will find the nest empty when you call tomorrow. As to the photograph, your client may rest in peace. I love and am loved by a better man than he. The King may do what he will without hindrance from one whom he has cruelly wronged. I keep it only to safeguard myself, and to preserve a weapon which will always secure me from any steps which he might take in the future. I leave a photograph which he might care to possess; and I remain, dear Mr. Sherlock Holmes, very truly yours,

IRENE NORTON, née ADLER.

Holmes kept this photograph in his drawer. [BLUE] Mentioned in the Blue Carbuncle when Watson makes Holmes allude to his attempt to recover the Irene Adler papers, to the singular case of Miss Mary Sutherland, and to the adventure of the man with the twisted lip, all of which were entirely free of any legal crime. [IDEN] Watson says "Once only had I known him to fail, in the case of the King of Bohemia and of the Irene Adler photograph."

Sherlock Holmes Quotes :[SCAN] "I only caught a glimpse of her at the moment, but she was a lovely woman, with a face that a man might die for."
[LAST] "It was I who brought about the separation between Irene Adler and the late King of Bohemia when your cousin Heinrich was the Imperial Envoy. It was I

also who saved from murder, by the Nihilist Klopman, Count Von und Zu Grafenstein, who was your mother's elder brother. It was I– –"

Address : Briony Lodge, Serpentine Avenue, St.

Sidney Paget   *The Inter Ocean*

Agar, Dr. Moore [DEVI] Male Alive   Dr. Moore Agar was a physician in Harley Street. He gave positive injunctions that the famous private agent lay aside all his cases and surrender himself to complete rest if he wished to avert an absolute breakdown and so Holmes and Watson went down to stay in a small cottage near Poldhu Bay, at the further extremity of the Cornish peninsula, where the Devil's foot case unfolded.

Address : Harley Street.

Agatha, (Milverton's housemaid) [CHAS] Female Alive   She was the housemaid of Charles Augustus Milverton. Sherlock Holmes became engaged to Agatha in order to acquire information about Milverton. Holmes Poses as Escott, a plumber with a rising business. She would lock up the dog, so that Holmes as Escott could visit. She did, however have another man, who would step in after Escott disappears. She reported to Holmes "it is a joke in the servants' hall that it's impossible to wake the master."

Ainstree, Dr. [DYIN] Male Alive   According to Dr. Watson, Dr. Ainstree was the greatest living authority upon tropical disease and was currently in London.

Holmes would not allow Watson to examine him, so Watson suggested that he could fetch this doctor, but as Watson left to fetch him, Holmes made a dash for the door to stop him leaving.

Akbar, Dost [SIGN] Male in prison An enormous Sikh, with a black beard which swept nearly down to his cummerbund. One of the Four. Bounding like a tiger after Achmet the Merchant with knife in his hand and buried his knife twice in his side. Was charged with murder of Achmet the Merchant, was found guilty and given penal servitude for life along with the other members of the four Mahomet Singh, Abdullah Khan & Jonathan Small.

Dost Akbar   *F. H. Townsend*

Akers-Douglas, Aretas [MAZA] Male Alive Real Person (1851-1926)
Although not implicitly named in the story, it was said that the Home Secretary visited Holmes along with the Prime Minister, also not named but he was Arthur Balfour. Aretas was the Home Secretary from 12 July 1902 until 5 December 1905 under Arthur Balfour. 1st Viscount Chilston About the Prime Minster and Home Secretary, Billy the page says "Mr. Holmes was very nice to them. He soon put them at their ease and promised he would do all he could." Billy also says that the Home Secretary seemed a civil, obliging sort of man.

Albert, Prince Francis Albert Augustus Charles Emmanuel [STUD] Male Dead (Real Person 1819 – 1861) Husband of Queen Victoria, there is a reference to an albert chain that was on the watch owned by Enoch J. Drebber. This referrers to a style of watch chain Prince Albert wore during the Victorian period. Traditionally the chain has a bar on one end used to affix the chain to a vest button hole.

Prince Albert

Aldrige, Mr   [CARD]   Male   Jim Browner was said to resemble Aldrige. He was a big, powerful chap, clean-shaven, and very swarthy He helped Holmes and Lestrade in the bogus laundry affair.

Alexis, Mr   [GOLD]   Male in prison   He was noble, unselfish, loving. He hated violence and tried to dissuade his fellow reformers against violence. Was a reformers—revolutionists—Nihilists. Was sent to Siberia as a convict on false evidence given by Professor Coram and even now, he worked in a salt mine. Coram had a diary and papers that proved his innocence. Anna Coram handed over a package of papers to Holmes for him to deliver to the Russian Embassy, that would get his release.

Algar, Policeman   [CARD]   Male Alive   Friend of Holmes who worked for the Liverpool police force. Holmes sent him a telegram asked him to find out if Mrs. Browner was at home, or if Browner had departed in the May Day . He sent his answer to police station saying that Mrs. Browner's house had been closed for more than three days, and the neighbours were of opinion that she had gone south to see her relatives. It had been ascertained at the shipping offices that Browner had left aboard of the May Day.

Alice, (Hatty Doran's Maid   [NOBL]Female Alive   American and came from California. A confidential servant. Lord St. Simon thought "It seemed to me that her mistress allowed her to take great liberties. Still, of course, in America they look upon these things in a different way." She Helped her mistress, Hatty Doran to change before leaving the Wedding celebrations.

Alison, Mr   [SIGN]   Male   Owner of Alison's Boxing rooms, where McMurdo and Holmes fought together on the night of McMurdo's benefit. The fight took place in 1884. Holmes Showed himself, quite a fighter and impressed McMurdo who said "how could I have mistook you? If instead o' standin' there so quiet you had just stepped up and given me that cross-hit of yours under the jaw, I'd ha' known you without a question. Ah, you're one that has wasted your gifts, you have! You might have aimed high, if you had joined the fancy."

Allan Brothers [WIST] Male Alive Brothers who owned a property management firm and were the chief land agents in Esher. They rented Wisteria Lodge to Aloysius Garcia. They sent a telegram to Holmes when he made enquiries regarding large houses in the area. The Telegram said

- LORD HARRINGBY, THE DINGLE;
- SIR GEORGE FFOLLIOTT, OXSHOTT TOWERS;
- MR. HYNES HYNES, J.P., PURDLEY PLACE;
- MR. JAMES BAKER WILLIAMS, FORTON OLD HALL;
- MR. HENDERSON, HIGH GABLE;
- REV. JOSHUA STONE, NETHER WALSLING.

Allardyce, Butcher [BLAC] Male Alive Holmes must have been on good terms with this person, because he allowed Holmes to use a Harpoon to transfix a dead pig with a single blow in the back of the shop or a least tried to.

Allen, Mrs [VALL] Female Alive A buxom and cheerful person, who relieved the lady of some of her household cares. Housekeeper at Birlstone, On the evening of the death of John Douglas, she arrived after the event and escorted Mrs. Douglas away and stayed with her most of the night in the lady's bedroom. When interviewed, it was found that "The housekeeper's room was rather nearer to the front of the house than the pantry in which Ames had been working. She was preparing to go to bed when the loud ringing of the bell had attracted her attention. She was a little hard of hearing. Perhaps that was why she had not heard the shot; but in any case the study was a long way off. She remembered hearing some sound which she imagined to be the slamming of a door. That was a good deal earlier—half an hour at least before the ringing of the bell. When Mr. Ames ran to the front she went with him. She saw Mr. Barker, very pale and excited, come out of the study. He intercepted Mrs. Douglas, who was coming down the stairs. He entreated her to go back, and she answered him, but what she said could not be heard."

Address : Birlstone Manor House

Altamont, Mr. [LAST] Male Alive (See Sherlock Holmes) Was an Irish-American. He was a tall, gaunt man of sixty, with long limbs, had clear-cut features and a small goatee beard which gave him a general resemblance to the caricatures of Uncle Sam. A half-smoked, sodden cigar hung from the corner of his mouth. Holmes in disguise. Sent the message to Von Bork "Will come without fail tonight and bring new sparking plugs. ALTAMONT." He posed as a motor expert and Von Bork kept a full garage. They used a code for everything likely to come up as some spare part. If they talked of a radiator it was a battleship, of an oil pump a cruiser, and so on. Sparking plugs were naval signals." Altamont payment for the naval signals was five hundred pounds. Altamont was said to be Irish-American and a touchy fellow. Altamont had a nice taste in wines, and he had taken a fancy to Von Bork's Tokay.

R. W. Wallace

Amati, Andrea   [STUD]   Male dead   (Real person 1505 – 1576) Holmes prattled away about Cremona fiddles, and the difference between a Stradivarius and an Amati. Credited with making the first modern day violin.

Amberley, Josiah   [RETI]   Male In a mental ward of a hospital   A pathetic, futile, broken and miserable creature. A man who was literally bowed down by care. His back was curved as though he carried a heavy burden. His shoulders and chest had the framework of a giant, though his figure tapers away into a pair of spindled legs. Left shoe wrinkled, right one smooth because he had an artificial limb. Snaky locks of grizzled hair. His had deeply lined features. He was junior partner of Brickfall and Amberley, who were manufacturers of artistic materials. You would see their names upon paint-boxes. He made his little pile, retired from business, in 1896 at the age of sixty-one, bought a house at Lewisham. and settled down to rest after a life of ceaseless grind. In early in 1897 he married a woman twenty years younger than himself—a good-looking woman, too. He said that his fickle wife had run off with a treacherous friend, taking his deed-box, containing a good part of his life's savings with them. Asked Holmes to find the lady and recover his money. He said that he had one hobby in life and that was chess and not far away was a young doctor, called Dr. Ray Ernest, who he used to invite to his house to play chess. He declared that Dr. Ernest was frequently in the house, and an intimacy between him and Mrs. Amberley was a natural sequence. The couple went off together last week—destination untraced. Holmes was not able to investigate himself, having the case of the two Coptic Patriarchs to attend to, so he sent Watson to learn more. Complained to Watson, about how he was disappointed that Holmes hadn't attended, how his wife was so pampered, how he had treated the doctor like a son and how it was such a dreadful, dreadful world!

He went on to explaining that he had purchased two tickets for the upper circle seats at the Haymarket theatre, and showed thicket B31 that he declared, was the unused ticket of his wife, because he had gone on his own. (making his seat either B30 or B32) When Holmes checked with the Haymarket Theatre, neither B30 nor B32 were occupied. He showed Watson his strong-room, just like a Bank's one, with iron door and shutter, burglar-proof. He said that his wife had a duplicate key and had carried off seven thousand pounds worth of cash and securities. There was a strong smell of paint throughout the house, since he had started painting this room and also the passage. Received a telegram that read;

"COME AT ONCE WITHOUT FAIL. CAN GIVE YOU INFORMATION AS TO YOUR RECENT LOSS. ELMAN. THE VICARAGE."

Which was dispatched at 2:10 from Little Purlington in Essex, close to Frinton. Watson and Amberley travel to see the Vicar leaving at 5:20 from Liverpool Street station, but it's a wasted trip and they end up spending a night probably at the little Railway Arms in Purlington. When Amberley returns the following day, he finds that Holmes and a Mr Barker are waiting for him in his house and ask him what he had done with the Bodies. Amberley tries to take poison, but Holmes leaps forward and a white pellet falls out of his mouth.

Address : The Haven, Lewisham

Frederic Dorr Steele   *Frank Wiles*

Amberley, Mrs. **[RETI]** **Female dead** A good-looking woman Was said to have run away with Amberley's close friend Dr. Ray Ernest and seven thousand pounds in cash and securities. Was actually gassed and buried, along with the doctor, in a disused well, cleverly concealed by a dog-kennel.

Address : The Haven, Lewisham

Ames, Butler **[VALL]** **Male Alive** A quaint, gnarled, dried-up person. He Was white and quivering from the shock. Butler at Birlstone Manor House. Prim, respectable, and capable. Stated that the Drawbridge was normally raised at sunset, but because Mrs. Douglas had had visitors to tea, it had been raised at nearly six o'clock on the night of the incident. He had worked for ten years with Sir Charles Chandos—as solid as a rock. He has been with Douglas ever since he took the Manor House five years ago. Confirmed that the branding on the arm of the dead body had been frequently seen by him on John Douglas. Confirmed that the small piece of plaster at the angle of Mr. Douglas's jaw was due to him cutting himself while shaving yesterday morning . In fact had Holmes removed the plaster he would have found no cut underneath. He stated that Mr. Douglas had been a little restless and excited during the day. Knew about the hidden room, but it never entered his head to connect it with this matter.

Address : Birlstone Manor House

Frank Wiles

Anderson, Constable [LION] Male Alive A big, ginger-moustached man of the slow, solid Sussex breed—a breed which covers much good sense under a heavy, silent exterior. Was fetched by Ian Murdoch to the dead body of Fitzroy McPherson. He said that he would be glad of Holmes' advice, and that this was a big thing for him to handle and he would get into trouble with Lewes if he did anything wrong. Holmes suggested he got in touch with his immediate superior and the case was taken over by Inspector Bardle of the Sussex Constabulary. Holmes found a note on McPherson's body, which was handed over to the Constable, it read "I will be there, you may be sure.— MAUDIE."

Anderson, murders in North Carolina [HOUN] Anderson murders in North Carolina We don't know if this was the name of the victims or the murderer. Alluded to by Holmes.

Sherlock Holmes Quote : "I shall soon be in the position of being able to put into a single connected narrative one of the most singular and sensational crimes of modern times. Students of criminology will remember the analogous incidents in Godno, in Little Russia, in the year '66, and of course there are the Anderson murders in North Carolina, but this case possesses some features which are entirely its own. Even now we have no clear case against this very wily man. But I shall be very much surprised if it is not clear enough before we go to bed this night."

Anderson, Soldier [BLAN] Male dead Was a member of B squadron of the Middlesex Corps. Was in the morning fight at Buffelsspruit (Buffelspruit), outside Pretoria with Godfrey Emsworth and Baldy Simpson. They became separated from the others because it was very broken country near Diamond Hill. They were clearing brother Boer, but he was shot and killed along with Simpson and only Emsworth managed to escape on horse.

Andrews, Brother [VALL] Male Alive He was little more than a boy, frank-faced and cheerful, with the breezy manner of one who is out for a holiday and means to enjoy every minute of it. He was a total abstainer, and behaved in all ways as exemplary member of the society. One of the two Assassins sent over to kill Josiah H. Dunn at Crow Hill. He had carried out three previous missions of murder. He had often proved themselves to be most capable instruments for this association of murder. Arriving at the mine, had shot Josiah H. Dunn in the stomach. Then shot Menzies, the Scotchman, in the face. As some of the miners surged forward, he had emptied his six-shooters over the heads of the crowd, and they broke and scattered, some of them rushing wildly back to their homes in Vermissa. He escaped.

Frank Wiles

Angel, Hosmer   [IDEN]   Male Alive   See James Windibank

Anne, Queen   [3GAR,REIG]   Female dead   (Real Person 1665 – 1714)
Queen of Great Britain and Ireland between 1702 to 1714 English Baroque
architectural style developed around the time of Queen Anne, 1702 - 1714
[3GAR] Holmes asked Nathan Garrideb about his home, whether it was Queen
Anne or Georgian period. (Period between 1714 and 1830, covering the reigns
from George l, ll, lll, lV and William lV, Clearly there would be a higher
probability that it was Georgian since this was almost ten times longer.) [REIG]
William Kirwan lived in a pretty cottage and the fine old Queen Anne house was
reached by walking up an oak-lined avenue The date on the lintel of the door of
the house was that of the battle of Malplaquet. (1709)

Sherlock Holmes Quote : "I am a bit of an archaeologist myself when it comes to
houses, I was wondering

Anstruther, Dr. [BOSC] Male Alive Doctor who was prepared to take over Watson's practice if asked. When considering whether to accompany Holmes on the case, Watson's wife (Mary Morstan) suggested that Anstruther would cover for him as locum.

Anthonio, (Merripit's Manservant [HOUN] Male Alive See Anthony below, (Merripit House's Manservant)

Anthony, (Merripit's Manservant) [HOUN] Male Alive There was an old manservant at Merripit House, whose name was Anthony. His connection with the Stapletons could be traced for several years, as far back as the school-mastering days, so that he must have been aware that his master and mistress were really husband and wife. This man disappeared and escaped from the country when Stapleton's schemes fell apart. It is suggestive that Anthony was not a common name in England, while Antonio is so in all Spanish or Spanish-American countries. The man, like Mrs. Stapleton herself, spoke good English, but with a curious lisping accent. Holmes had seen this old man cross the Grimpen Mire by the path which Stapleton had marked out. It is very probable, therefore, that in the absence of his master it was he who cared for the hound, though he may never have known the purpose for which the beast was used.

Appledore, Edith [PRIO] Female Alive See Holdernesse, Duchess Edith of

Appledore, Sir Charles [PRIO] Male Unknown Father of Edith Appledore, who married the Duke of Holdernesse and had one son called Lord Saltire "

Armitage, James   [GLOR]   Male dead   See Trevor, Justice of the Peace

Armitage, Mr.   [SPEC]   Male Alive   Father of Percy Armitage, who proposed to Helen Stoner in February/March 1883. Percy was his second son.

Address : Crane Water, near Reading

Armitage, Percy   [SPEC]   Male Alive   Proposed to Helen Stoner in February/March 1883. Second Son. Proposed to Helen Stoner in February/March 1883. The second son of Mr. Armitage.

 Address : Crane Water, near Reading r Reading.

Armstrong, Dr. Leslie   [MISS]   Male Alive   One could not fail to be impressed by a mere glance at the man, the square, massive face, the brooding eyes under the thatched brows, and the granite moulding of the inflexible jaw. A man of deep character, a man with an alert mind, grim, ascetic, self-contained, formidable He was not only one of the heads of the medical school of the University, but a thinker of European reputation in more than one branch of science. Was not really a doctor in practice. He was a lecturer and a consultant, but he did not care for general practice, which distracted him from his literary work.

Sherlock Holmes Quote : "Dr. Leslie Armstrong is certainly a man of energy and character, I have not seen a man who, if he turned his talents that way, was more calculated to fill the gap left by the illustrious Moriarty."

Address : Somewhere in Cambridge City

Frederic Dorr Steele

Sidney Paget

Athene, Goddess [CHAS] Female Alive A marble bust of the Goddess Athene was to be found on the top of a large bookcase in Appledore Towers belonging to Charles Augustus Milverton. Athene was the goddess associated with wisdom, handicraft, and warfare.

Lourve

Atkinson, Brothers [SCAN] Male unknown Referenced only in Scandal in Bohemia Holmes cleared up the singular Tragedy of the Atkinson Brothers at Trincomalee. Trincomalee also known as Gokanna/Gokarna, is the administrative headquarters of the Trincomalee District and major resort port city of Eastern Province Sri Lanka (former Ceylon).

Address : Trincomalee, Sri Lanka (former Ceylon).

Atwood, Mr. [VALL] Male Alive Owner of an Ironworks in Vermissa Valley, who was forced to sell his business because of threats from the Scowrers. He sold it to West Gilmerton General Mining Company.

Aveling, (the mathematical master [PRIO] Male Alive The mathematical master at the Priory School. Told Holmes that he was certain that Heidegger's bicycle had Palmer tyres.

Address : Priory School

B is for Boscombe Valley Mystery

B

Backwater, Lord   [SILV, NOBL]   Male Alive   [SILV] Owner of the Horse Desborough, which came in second place at the Wessex Plate. Employs Silas Brown as manager of his stables at Mapleton. **[NOBL]** Recommended Holmes to Lord St. Simon, saying that Holmes had judgement and discretion. Full quote is "'MY DEAR MR. SHERLOCK HOLMES: —"Lord Backwater tells me that I may place implicit reliance upon your judgement and discretion. I have determined, therefore, to call upon you and to consult you in reference to the very painful event which has occurred in connection with my wedding. Mr. Lestrade, of Scotland Yard, is acting already in the matter, but he assures me that he sees no objection to your co-operation, and that he even thinks that it might be of some assistance. I will call at four o'clock in the afternoon, and, should you have any other engagement at that time, I hope that you will postpone it, as this matter is of paramount importance. Yours faithfully, ST. SIMON.' Lord Backwater's place, near Petersfield. was going to be used by Lord St. Simon for his honeymoon. Attended Lord St. Simon and Hatty Doran's Wedding.

Address : Mapleton training establishment.

Backwater 's (Lord) Dog   [SILV]Alive Whereas most dogs are famous for reporting that little Timmy was trapped at the bottom of the well, or that there were burglars about, this one is famous for his lack of any effort. As Holmes remarked when asked if there was any point to which he wished to draw attention to, "To the curious incident of the dog in the night-time.", when told that "The dog did nothing in the night-time.", he responded "That was the curious incident."

Leo O'Mealia

Bain, Sandy   [SHOS]   Male Alive   Jockey at Shoscombe Old Place jockey Was given Lady Beatrice's pet dog and told to take it to Old Josiah Barnes at the Green Dragon.

Address : Shoscombe Old Place

Baker, Henry   [BLUE]   Male Alive   From his battered Bowler, Holmes inferred that; The man was highly intellectual. He was fairly well-to-do within the last three years, although he had now fallen upon evil days. He had foresight, but had less now than formerly, pointing to a moral retrogression, which, when taken with the decline of his fortunes, seems to indicate some evil influence, probably drink, at work upon him. This may account also for the obvious fact that his wife had ceased to love him. He had retained some degree of self-respect. He was a man who leads a sedentary life, goes out little, was out of training entirely, was middle-aged, had grizzled hair which he had cut within the last few days, and which he anointed with lime-cream. Finally it was extremely improbable that he had gas laid on in his house. He was a large man with rounded shoulders, a massive head, and a broad, intelligent face, sloping down to a pointed beard of grizzled brown. A touch of red in nose and cheeks, with a slight tremor of his extended hand, recalled Holmes' surmise as to his habits. His rusty black frock-coat was buttoned right up in front, with the collar turned up, and his lank wrists protruded from his sleeves without a sign of cuff or shirt. He spoke in a slow staccato fashion, choosing his words with care, and gave the impression generally of a man of learning and letters who had had ill-usage at the hands of fortune. Wore a Scotch Bonnet. He was married. The goose was a peace-offering for his wife. Was attacked by a knot of roughs on the corner of Goodge street. Accidentally broke a window during attack and ran away when approached by Commissioner Peterson, leaving his bowler hat and a goose. Got the goose from the Alpha Inn Goose Club organised by the Landlord Windigate. Saw Holmes' advertisement in the papers (Globe, Star, Pall Mall, St. James's, Evening News Standard, Echo, ETC.) stating that a goose had been found and the owner could collect. Arrived at Baker street, he explained how he had lost his hat and the goose, but knew nothing about the gem.

Josef Friedrich

F. C. Swayze

Baker's Goose [BLUE] Dead Strictly speaking, there were two geese, the first one is of great importance, because this is the one that carried the Blue Carbuncle in it's crop. It started life in Mrs. Maggie Oakshott's egg and Poultry firm in the Brixton Road, but it's adventure really began shortly before it die, as it was forced to swallow the Gem, by Jem (James Ryder), who promptly released it and then took another bird away by mistake. The goose then went to Breckenridge, the poultry dealer in Covent Garden, who sold it to Windigate, the landlord of the Alpha Inn, near the British Museum, who gave it to Henry Baker, who dropped it while being attacked. It was then picked up the commissioner Peterson, who took it to Sherlock Holmes, who left it on the side table until it started to smell, who returned it to Peterson, whose wife cut it open and found the Gem, phew! The second goose was one Peterson bought on Holmes' behalf, and Holmes gave it to Henry Baker.

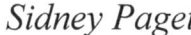

Sidney Paget

Ernest Flammarion

(appropriately, this is a cropped image)

Baker, Mrs [BLUE] Female Alive Wife of Mr. Henry Baker. Mrs. Henry Baker' was printed upon a small card which was tied to the bird's left leg. It was a peace offering to her from her husband.

Baldwin, Brother Teddy (Ted) [VALL] Male dead He was a handsome, dashing young man of about the same age and build as McMurdo himself. Under his broad-brimmed black felt hat, there was a handsome face with fierce, domineering eyes and a curved hawk-bill of a nose. [While in USA] Jacob Shafter said "He is a boss of Scowrers.", was this a translation problem, certainly Baldwin was higher level lodge official, but the title 'Boss' actually belonged to Jack McGinty. Regarded Ettie Shafter as his, but john McMurdo thought otherwise and this lead to a hatred between the two and conflict in the Lodge. Was the leader of the group that attacked the Editor of the Herald newspaper Stanger. Others in the group were Gower, Mansel, Scanlan, the two willabys and John McMurdo, there were two others to guard the door. The instructions from Boss McGinty were that Stanger should receive "A pretty severe warning', however Baldwin got carried away and McMurdo pulled a gun on him during the raid, to make him stop beating the old Editor. Was involved in the killing of William Hales of Stake Royal. Picked to capture Birdy Edwards along with Boss McGinty, Harraway, Tiger Cormac, Carter and the two Willabys. Got ten years in prison. [While in UK] Alias used by Ted Baldwin while he was staying in UK was Hargrave. He was staying at the Eagle Commercial and had taken a room two days before. The bicycle left behind at Birlstone Manor House and a small valise were his only belongings. He had registered his name as coming from London, but had given no address. The valise was London made, and the contents were British; but the man himself was undoubtedly an American. Travelled to Birlstone Manor House by bicycle, which was found after the events. Killed by John Douglas, who acted in self-defence, he receiving both barrels of a sawn-off shotgun.

Frank Wiles

Frank Wiles

Balfour, Arthur James   [MAZA]   Male Alive   (Real Person 1848 – 1930)
Although not implicitly named, The prime minister was said to have visited Holmes along with the Home Secretary, Aretas Akers-Douglas to ask if he could help in the recovery of the Mazarin Stone. Balfour was Prime Minster from 12 July 1902 until 4 December 1905. About the Prime Minster and Home Secretary, Billy the page says "Mr. Holmes was very nice to them. He soon put them at their ease and promised he would do all he could."

Balmoral, Duchess of [NOBL] Female Alive Attended the Wedding of Miss Hatty Doran and Lord Robert St. Simon. Mother of Lord Robert St. Simon (Second son) and Lord Eustace St. Simon)Third Son) and Lady Clara St. Simon.

Balmoral, Duke of [SILV][NOBL] Male Alive Owner of the Horse Iris. Yellow and black stripes taking part in the Wessex Cup. Came in a bad third place. Wessex Plate 50 Sovereigns each h ft. with 1000 Sovereigns added for four and five year olds. Second, £300. Third, £200. New course (one mile and five furlongs). [NOBL] Father of Lord Robert St. Simon (Second son) but did not attend his son's Wedding.

Balmoral, Lord [EMPT] [NOBL] Male Alive [EMPT] Member of the Bagatelle card club and had lost, along with Godfrey Milner some £420 to Ronald Adair and Colonel Moran recently. This might be the first son of Duke and Duchess of Balmoral or Robert (2nd) or Eustace (3rd). I like the idea that it was Robert, because [NOBL] he was marrying Hatty Doran, because she was loaded.

Balzac, Honore De [IDEN] Male dead (Real Person 1799 – 1850) French Playwright and novelist. Magnum opus La Comedie Humaine Holmes points out to Watson that the letters are very commonplace. Absolutely no clue in them to Mr. Hosmer Angel, save that he quotes Balzac once. There is one remarkable point, however, that they are typewritten.

Bannister, (Butler) [3STU] Male Alive He was a little, white-faced, clean-shaven, grizzly-haired fellow of fifty. He was still suffering from this sudden disturbance of the quiet routine of his life. His plump face was twitching with his nervousness, and his fingers could not keep still. Had looked after Mr. Hilton Soames' rooms for ten years. Left his keys in the lock, which allowed one of the students to come in and look at the examination paper. Used to be the Butler of old Sir Jabez Gilchrist. Knew Mr. Gilchrist from his days as Butler. Protected Mr. Gilchrist from being discovered by flopping down on the chair, where Gilchrist had left his gloves.

Frederic Dorr Steele   *Martin Van Maele*

Barclay, Colonel James   [CROO]   Male dead   He was a dashing, jovial old soldier in his usual mood, but there were occasions on which he seemed to show himself capable of considerable violence and vindictiveness. Showed signs of a singular sort of depression which came upon him at times. His smile had often been struck from his mouth, as if by some invisible hand, when he has been joining the gayeties and chaff of the mess-table. Would sink into the deepest gloom for days. Had a superstition that took the form of a dislike to being left alone, especially after dark. Colonel in charge of the Royal Munsters at Aldershot. Leader of the most famous Irish regiments in the British army. A Gallant Veteran, who started as a full private, was raised to commissioned rank for his bravery at the time of the Mutiny, and so lived to command the regiment in which he had once carried a musket. Colonel Barclay's family life appears to have been a uniformly happy one. Barclay's devotion to his wife was greater than his wife's to Barclay. Thirty years previously when he was a sergeant in the Royal Munsters (which is the old 117th). He sent off his rival, Henry Wood, for the affections of Nancy Devoy on a suicide mission and tipped off the rebels. It was the sudden appears of this man Henry Wood (The Crooked Man) that struck him Dead As Wood put it "The bare sight of me was like a bullet through his guilty heart."

Address : Lachine villa in Aldershot

Barclay, Mrs. Nancy [CROO] Female Alive She was a woman of great beauty, and that even now, when she has been married for upwards of thirty years, she is still of a striking and queenly appearance. Daughter of a former colour-sergeant in the same corps. Was as popular with the ladies of the regiment as her husband was with his brother officers. Barclay's devotion to his wife was greater than his wife's to Barclay. Member of the Roman Catholic Church. Helped out in the establishment of the Guild of St. George, which was formed in connection with the Watt Street Chapel for the purpose of supplying the poor with cast-off clothing. A meeting of the Guild had been held that evening at eight, and Mrs. Barclay had hurried over her dinner in order to be present at it. On returning home, she got into an argument with her husband and was heard to hear 'You coward!' she repeated over and over again. 'What can be done now? What can be done now? Give me back my life. I will never so much as breathe the same air with you again! You coward! You Coward!' Then there was a sudden dreadful cry in the man's voice, with a crash, and a piercing scream from the woman. Heard to call her husband 'David' despite his name being 'James'

Address : Lachine villa in Aldershot

Sidney Paget

Bardle, Inspector [LION] Male Alive He was a steady, solid, bovine man with thoughtful eyes. A burly, phlegmatic man. Inspector of the Sussex Constabulary. Admitted to Holmes that he was "fairly up against it in this McPherson case" and wanted to know whether he should arrest Ian Murdoch. "The question is, shall I make an arrest, or shall I not?"

Barelli, Augusto   [REDC]   Male Alive   Father of Emilia Barelli now, Emilia Lucca. Was the chief lawyer and once the deputy of Posilippo near Naples. Employed Gennaro Lucca, he might have known of Gennaro's links to the Red Circle. Forbade Emilia to marry Gennaro, so they eloped.

Address : Posilippo, Italy

Barker, (Detective)   [RETI]   Male Alive   He was a tall, dark, heavily moustached, rather military-looking man. Wore grey-tinted sunglasses and a Masonic tie-pin. Private detective, who had been engaged by Dr. Ray Ernest's family to look into his disappearance. Had been watching Amberley's house and had seen Watson's arrival and departure from the home. As Holmes emerged from the pantry window, having 'burgled' the house to find clues, he clapped him on the collar and asked "Now, you rascal, what are you doing in there?" Decided to work with Holmes in finding out what had happened to both the Doctor and wife. Solved the case together. "He is my hated rival upon the Surrey shore."

Sherlock Holmes Quotes : "He is my hated rival upon the Surrey shore."

"This is my friend Mr. Barker."

Frederic Dorr Steele   *Frank Wiles*

Barker, Cecil James   [VALL]   Male Alive   Tall, loose-jointed figure. Straight, broad-chested fellow with a clean-shaved, prize-fighter face, thick, strong, black eyebrows, and a pair of masterful black eyes which might, even without the aid of his very capable hands, clear a way for him through a hostile crowd. Undoubted Englishman, but had know John Douglas in America and had there lived on intimate terms with him. He appeared to be a man of considerable wealth, and was reputed to be a bachelor. In age he was rather younger than Douglas. He neither rode nor shot, but spent his days in wandering round the old village with his pipe in his mouth, or in driving with his host, or in his absence with his hostess, over the beautiful countryside. Ames the butler, said of him "An easy-going, free-handed gentleman, but, my word! I had rather not be the man that crossed him!" He was cordial and intimate with Douglas, and he was no less friendly with his wife—a friendship which more than once seemed to cause some irritation to the husband, so that even the servants were able to perceive his annoyance. Discovered the body, but faked footprints on the window sill. Conspired with Mrs. Douglas to pass off the dead body as belonging to John Douglas.

Frank Wiles

Barnes, Josiah [SHOS] Male Alive   Landlord of the Green Dragon at Crendall. Acquired Lady Beatrice's spaniel dog, given to him by Sandy Bains, the jockey at Shoscombe Old Place. Help Holmes and Watson, when they posed as Fisherman and let them take Lady Beatrice's dog for a walk.

Address : The Green Dragon, Crendall

Barnicot, Dr. [SIXN] Male Alive   Doctor who had one of the largest practices upon the south side of the Thames. His residence and principal consulting-room was at Kennington Road, but he had a branch surgery and dispensary at Lower Brixton Road, two miles away. He was an enthusiastic admirer of Napoleon, and his house was full of books, pictures, and relics of the French Emperor. He purchased two busts from Morse Hudson, One of these he placed in his hall in the house at Kennington Road, and the other on the mantelpiece of the surgery at Lower Brixton. Both of these busts were stolen and smashed.

Address : Kennington Road & Lower Brixton Road

Barraud, Mr. [STUD]   Male   Family name of the clock makers in London In 1838 John Richard Lund joined Frederick Philip Barraud and the company became known as Barraud & Lund. Made the gold watch, No. 97163 on a gold Albert chain, very heavy and solid, that Enoch J. Drebber had on his person, when he was murdered.

Barrett, Police-constable   [SECO]   Male Alive   Police-constable walking his beat was passing along Godolphin Street at a quarter to twelve. He observed that the door of No. 16 was ajar. He discovered the body of Eduardo Lucas who had been stabbed to the heart and must have died instantly. The knife with which the crime had been committed was a curved Indian dagger, plucked down from a trophy of Oriental arms which adorned one of the walls.

Barrymore, Mr. John   [HOUN]   Male Alive   He was a remarkable-looking man, tall, handsome, with a square black beard and pale, distinguished features. Butler at Baskerville Hall. Discovered Sir Charles Baskerville's body on the 4th May 1888. One fact which has not been explained is the statement of Barrymore that his master's footprints altered their character from the time that he passed the moor-gate, and that he appeared from thence onward to have been walking upon his toes. Was left £500 in Sir Charles Baskerville's will. Lied to Sir Henry Baskerville and Watson when he said that it was not like wife that was crying at night. Was in the habit of making a signal from a window at night to his brother-in-law, Seldon the Convict. Gave Seldon Sir Henry Baskerville's discarded clothes, which were ultimately the convicts downfall. Gave Sir Henry Baskerville and Watson information regarding the individual who Sir Charles Baskerville was meeting the night of his death. (Person with initials L.L. from Coombe Tracey)

Address : Manor of Baskerville

Paul Thiriat   *Sidney Paget*

Barrymore, Mrs. Eliza   [HOUN]   Alive   She is a heavy, solid person, very
limited, intensely respectable, and inclined to be puritanical. Wife of John
Barrymore, housekeeper at the Manor of Baskerville. Sister of the Convict Selden.
Was left £500 in Sir Charles Baskerville's will.

Address : Manor of Baskerville

Paul Thiriat   *Sidney Paget*

Barton, Dr. Hill   [ILLU]   Male Alive   See Dr. John Watson   When Watson visited Baron Gruner in order to keep him busy, while Holmes tried to find the Baron's secret diary, he posed as Dr. Hill Barton, a collector of fine Chinese ceramics with a precious saucer in my hand, but the Baron started to suspect him and said "Might I ask you a few questions to test you? I am obliged to tell you, Doctor—if you are indeed a doctor—that the incident becomes more and more suspicious. I would ask you what do you know of the Emperor Shomu and how do you associate him with the Shoso-in near Nara? Dear me, does that puzzle you? Tell me a little about the Northern Wei dynasty and its place in the history of ceramics." and so the jig was up, but sufficient time had been gained to allow Holmes to find the Baron's hidden secret diary.

Barton, Inspector   [TWIS]   Male Alive   Was in charge of the Neville Saint-Clair disappearance case. Searched the room in the 'Bar of Gold' where Neville Saint-Clair was last seen, but found nothing. Arrested Hugh Boone.

Josef Friedrich

Basil, Captain   [BLAC]   Male dead   See Sherlock Holmes, pseudonym Holmes used when he needed a marine background.

Baskerville, Elizabeth [HOUN] Female Knew nothing about the legend of the hound of the Baskerville. Sister to Rodger, Charles and John Baskerville. Aunt of Sir Henry Baskerville.

Address : Manor of Baskerville

Baskerville, Hound of [HOUN] Male dead [Original Hound] a foul thing, a great, black beast, shaped like a hound, yet larger than any hound that ever mortal eye has rested upon. Killed Hugo Baskerville [Modern Hound] In mere size and strength it was a terrible creature which was lying stretched before Holmes, Watson and Lestrade. It was not a pure bloodhound and it was not a pure mastiff; but it appeared to be a combination of the two—gaunt, savage, and as large as a small lioness. Even in the stillness of death, the huge jaws seemed to be dripping with a bluish flame and the small, deep-set, cruel eyes were ringed with fire. Watson placed his hand upon the glowing muzzle, and as he held them up his own fingers smouldered and gleamed in the darkness. It was phosphorus. The dog Stapleton bought in London from Ross and Mangles, the dealers in Fulham Road. It was the strongest and most savage in their possession. It was brought down by the North Devon line and walked a great distance over the moor so as to get it home without exciting any remarks. Responsible for the deaths of Sir Charles Baskerville and Selden the convict.

Sherlock Holmes Quote : "The beast was savage and half-starved. If its appearance did not frighten its victim to death, at least it would paralyse the resistance which might be offered."

Sidney Paget

George Newnes Ltd

Baskerville, Hugo (modern) [HOUN] Male dead   Writer of the 1742 paper regarding the Legend of the hound of the Baskerville. Father of three brothers, Rodger (youngest and black Sheep of family), Charles (eldest) and john (father of Henry) and Elizabeth. Grandfather of Henry Baskerville.

Address : Manor of Baskerville

Baskerville, Hugo (of the legend) [HOUN] Male dead   He was a most wild, profane, and godless man. Died Michaelmas day 29th September, sometime around 1642-1651 (the Great Rebellion) "Of the origin of the Hound of the Baskervilles there have been many statements, yet as I come in a direct line from Hugo Baskerville, and as I had the story from my father, who also had it from his, I have set it down with all belief that it occurred even as is here set forth. And I would have you believe, my sons, that the same Justice which punishes sin may also most graciously forgive it, and that no ban is so heavy but that by prayer and repentance it may be removed. Learn then from this story not to fear the fruits of the past, but rather to be circumspect in the future, that those foul passions whereby our family has suffered so grievously may not again be loosed to our undoing. "Know then that in the time of the Great Rebellion (the history of which by the learned Lord Clarendon I most earnestly commend to your attention) this Manor of Baskerville was held by Hugo of that name, nor can it be gainsaid that he was a most wild, profane, and godless man. This, in truth, his neighbours might have pardoned, seeing that saints have never flourished in those parts, but there was in him a certain wanton and cruel humour which made his name a byword through the West. It chanced that this Hugo came to love (if, indeed, so dark a passion may be known under so bright a name) the daughter of a yeoman who held lands near the Baskerville estate. But the young maiden, being discreet and of good repute, would ever avoid him, for she feared his evil name. So it came to pass that one Michaelmas this Hugo, with five or six of his idle and wicked companions, stole down upon the farm and carried off the maiden, her father and brothers being from home, as he well knew. When they had brought her to the Hall the maiden was placed in an upper chamber, while Hugo and his friends sat down to a long carouse, as was their nightly custom. Now, the poor lass upstairs was like to have her wits turned at the singing and shouting and terrible oaths which came up to her from below, for they say that the words used by Hugo Baskerville, when he was in wine, were such as might blast the man who said them. At last in the stress of her fear she did that which might have daunted the bravest or most active man, for by the aid of the growth of ivy which covered (and still covers) the south wall she came down from under the eaves, and so homeward across the moor, there being three leagues betwixt the Hall and her father's farm. "It chanced that some little time later Hugo left his guests to carry food and drink—with other worse things, perchance—to his captive, and so found the cage empty and the bird escaped. Then, as it would seem, he became as one that hath a devil, for, rushing down the stairs into the dining-hall, he sprang upon the great table, flagons and trenchers flying before him, and he cried aloud before all the company that he would that very night render his body and soul to the Powers of Evil if he might but overtake the wench. And while the revellers stood aghast at the fury of the man, one more wicked or, it may be, more drunken than the rest, cried out that they should put the hounds upon her. Whereat Hugo ran from the house, crying to his grooms that they should saddle his mare and unkennel the pack, and giving the hounds a kerchief of the maid's, he swung them to the line, and so off full cry in the moonlight over the moor. "Now, for some space the revellers stood agape, unable to understand all that had been done in such haste. But anon their bemused wits awoke to the nature of the deed which was like to be done upon the moorlands. Everything was now in an uproar, some calling for their pistols, some for their horses, and some for another flask of wine. But at length some sense came back to their crazed minds, and the whole of them, thirteen in number, took horse and started in pursuit. The moon shone clear above them, and they rode swiftly abreast, taking that course which the maid must needs have taken if she were to reach her own home. "They had gone a mile or two when they passed one of the night shepherds upon the moorlands, and they cried to him to know if he had seen the hunt. And the man, as the story goes, was so crazed with fear that he could scarce speak, but at last he said that he had indeed seen the unhappy maiden, with the hounds upon her track. 'But I have seen more than that,' said he, 'for Hugo Baskerville passed me upon his black mare, and there ran mute behind him such a hound of hell as God forbid should ever be at my heels.' "So the drunken squires cursed the shepherd and rode onward. But soon their skins turned cold, for there came a galloping across the moor, and the black mare, dabbled with white froth, went past with trailing bridle and empty saddle. Then the revellers rode close together, for a great fear was on them, but they still followed over the moor, though each, had he been alone, would have been right glad to have turned his horse's head. Riding slowly in this fashion they came at last upon the hounds. These, though known for their valour and their breed, were whimpering in a cluster at the head of a deep dip or goyal, as we call it, upon the moor, some slinking away and some, with starting hackles and staring eyes, gazing down the narrow valley before them. "The company had come to a halt, more sober men, as you may guess, than when they started. The most of them would by no means advance, but three of them, the boldest, or it may be the most drunken, rode forward down the goyal. Now, it opened into a broad space in which stood two of those great stones, still to be seen there, which were set by certain forgotten peoples in the days of old. The moon was shining bright upon the clearing, and there in the centre lay the unhappy maid where she had fallen, dead of fear and of fatigue. But it was not the sight of her body, nor yet was it that of the body of Hugo Baskerville lying near her, which raised the hair upon the heads of these three daredevil roysterers, but it was that, standing over Hugo, and plucking at his throat, there stood a foul thing, a great, black beast, shaped like a hound, yet larger than any hound that ever mortal eye has rested upon. "And even as they looked the thing tore the throat out of Hugo Baskerville, on which, as it turned its blazing eyes and dripping jaws upon them, the three shrieked with fear and rode for dear life, still screaming, across the moor. One, it is said, died that very night of what he had seen, and the other twain were but broken men for the rest of their days. "Such is the tale, my sons, of the coming of the hound which is said to have plagued the family so sorely ever since. If I have set it down it is because that which is clearly known hath less terror than that which is but hinted at and guessed. Nor can it be denied that many of the family have been unhappy in their deaths, which have been sudden, bloody, and mysterious. Yet may we shelter ourselves in the infinite goodness of Providence, which would not forever punish the innocent beyond that third or fourth generation which is threatened in Holy Writ. To that Providence, my sons, I hereby commend you, and I counsel you by way of caution to forbear from crossing the moor in those dark hours when the powers of evil are exalted. "[This from Hugo Baskerville to his sons Rodger and John, with instructions that they say nothing thereof to their sister Elizabeth.]"

Address : Manor of Baskerville

Paul Thiriat *Sidney Paget*

Baskerville, John [HOUN] Male dead Son of Hugo Baskerville (1742), who was told about the legend of the hound of the Baskervilles. Brother to Rodger, Charles and Elizabeth Baskerville.

Address : Manor of Baskerville

Baskerville, Rear-Admiral [HOUN] Male dead One of the Portraits in Baskerville Hall was of this gentleman. "Who is the gentleman with the telescope?" Served under Rodney in the West Indies.

Baskerville, Rodger [HOUN] Male dead Son of Hugo Baskerville (1742), who wrote about the legend of the hound of the Baskerville. Brother to Sir Charles, John and Elizabeth Baskerville. Uncle of Henry Baskerville. Father of Jack Stapleton. Was the black sheep of the family. He came of the old masterful Baskerville strain, and was the very image of the family picture of old Hugo. He made England too hot to hold him, fled to Central America, and died there in 1876 of yellow fever.

Address : Manor of Baskerville then Central America

Baskerville, Sir Charles   [HOUN] Male dead He was a strong-minded man, shrewd, practical, and as unimaginative as Dr. Mortimer. Son of the later Sir Hugo Baskerville. Brother to John an Rodger and Elizabeth. Uncle to Sir Henry Baskerville. Gave the 1742 Document to Dr. James Mortimer. Probable Liberal candidate for Mid-Devon at the next election. Resided at Baskerville Hall for a comparatively short period, but his amiability of character and extreme generosity had won the affection and respect of all who had been brought into contact with him. Made his own fortune and brought it back with him to restore the fallen grandeur of his line. Made large sums of money in South African speculation. More wise than those who go on until the wheel turns against them, he realised his gains and returned to England with them. It was only two years since he took up his residence at Baskerville Hall, and it is common talk how large were those schemes of reconstruction and improvement which were been interrupted by his death. Childless. Made generous donations to local and county charities which have been frequently chronicled in the columns of The Devon County Chronicle. "The circumstances connected with the death of Sir Charles could not be said to have been entirely cleared up by the inquest, but at least enough was done to dispose of those rumours to which local superstition have given rise. There was no reason whatever to suspect foul play, or to imagine that his death could be from any but natural causes. Sir Charles was a widower, and a man who may be said to have been in some ways of an eccentric habit of mind. Simple in his personal tastes. His indoor servants at Baskerville Hall consisted of a married couple named Barrymore, the husband acting as butler and the wife as housekeeper. Their evidence, corroborated by that of several friends, tends to show that Sir Charles's health has for some time been impaired, and points especially to some affection of the heart, manifesting itself in changes of colour, breathlessness, and acute attacks of nervous depression. Dr. James Mortimer, the friend and medical attendant of the deceased, gave evidence to the same effect. Sir Charles Baskerville was in the habit every night before going to bed of walking down the famous Yew Alley of Baskerville Hall. The evidence of the Barrymores shows that this had been his custom. On the 4th of May Sir Charles had declared his intention of starting next day for London, and had ordered Barrymore to prepare his luggage. That night he went out as usual for his nocturnal walk, in the course of which he was in the habit of smoking a cigar. He never returned. At twelve o'clock Barrymore, finding the hall door still open, became alarmed, and, lighting a lantern, went in search of his master. The day had been wet, and Sir Charles's footmarks were easily traced down the Alley. Halfway down this walk there was a gate which lead out on to the moor. There were indications that Sir Charles had stood for some little time here. He then proceeded down the Alley, and it was at the far end of it that his body was discovered. The Baskerville inheritance went to his Nephew, Sir Henry Baskerville.

Address : Manor of Baskerville

Sidney Paget   *John Murray*

Baskerville, Sir Henry [HOUN] **Male Alive** Young baronet. A small, alert, dark-eyed man about thirty years of age, very sturdily built, with thick black eyebrows and a strong, pugnacious face. He wore a ruddy-tinted tweed suit and had the weather-beaten appearance of one who has spent most of his time in the open air, and yet there was something in his steady eye and the quiet assurance of his bearing which indicated the gentleman. Son of Sir Charles Baskerville's brother, John Baskerville. Grandson of the modern Hugo Baskerville. Son of Sir Charles Baskerville's brother, John Baskerville. Grandson of the modern Hugo Baskerville. Had travelled back from Canada, where he had been farming on the death of Sir Charles Baskerville. He had inherited the Baskerville estate. Was followed while he was in London and had boots stolen from outside his hotel room. Received an envelope which contained a half-sheet of foolscap paper folded into four. Across the middle of it a single sentence had been formed by the expedient of pasting printed words upon it. It ran: 'as you value your life or your reason keep away from the moor.' The word 'moor' only was printed in ink. He decided to ignore the warnings and went down to Dartmoor, travelling with Dr. Mortimer and Watson, Holmes 'remained' in London. He met up with various people including the Stapletons, Jack and his sister Beryl. He took a fancy to Beryl and started courting her. He had an adventure with Selden the Notting Hill murderer and finally on the return journey from an evening's meal at the Stapletons, he had been attacked by a giant hound and only survived when Holmes, Watson and Lestrade killed the dog.

Address : 1. Northumberland hotel, 2. Manor of Baskerville

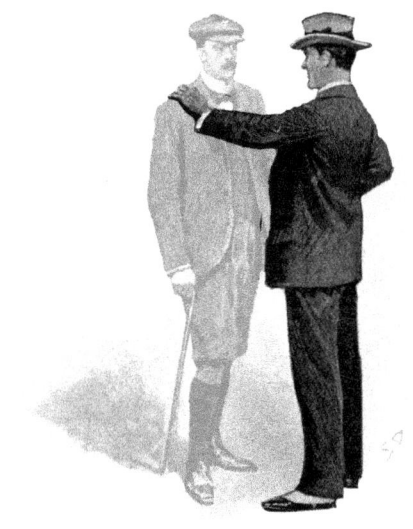

Paul Thiriat   *Sidney Paget*

Baskerville, Sir William   [HOUN]   Male dead   The man with the blue coat and the roll of paper is Sir William Baskerville, who was Chairman of Committees of the House of Commons under Pitt."

Bates, Mr. Marlow   [THOR]   Male Alive   He was a thin, nervous wisp of a man with frightened eyes and a twitching, hesitating manner —a man whom my own professional eye would judge to be on the brink of an absolute nervous breakdown. Manager of Neil Gibson's estate. He arrived at 221b Baker street and warned Holmes about his employer, Neil Gibson, he said "he is a villain—an infernal villain." He told Holmes how Gibson was brutal to his wife, but did not know how she had been killed, nor by whom.

Address : Thor Place, the Hampshire

G. Patrick Nelson

Bathsheba   [CROO] Female dead   Biblical reference   Wife of Uriah the
Hittite, impregnated by King David and made a widow by the same. Became King
David's eighth wife. Nancy Barclay calls her husband 'David', since her husband
had behaved like King David, sending Henry Wood on a suicide mission, so that
he could court Henry's girl to be (then Devoy, now Nancy Barclay) Nancy Devoy
would have been Bathsheba, Henry Wood = Uriah and James Barclay= King
David

Baxter, Edith   [SILV]   Female Alive   Maid at King's Pyland, took meal of Curry mutton to Ted Hunter on the evening of the disappearance of Silver Blaze and the death of John Straker.

Address : King's Pyland, Dartmoor

THE MAID CARRIED HIS SUPPER TO THE STABLES.

William H. Hyde

Martin Van Maele

Baxter, Richard   [BOSC]   Male dead (Real Person 1615 – 1691)   English puritan church leader and poet. Holmes misquotes John Bradford's phrase and attributes it to this man

Sherlock Holmes Quote : "God help us! Why does fate play such tricks with poor, helpless worms? I never hear of such a case as this that I do not think of Baxter's words, and say, 'There, but for the grace of God, goes Sherlock Holmes.'"

Bayard the Horse [SILV] Male Horse Alive   Horse owned by Colonel Ross.
Not as fast as Silver Blaze Bayard could give the other a hundred yards in five
furlongs Bayard did not in fact run in the Wessex Plate.

Address : King's Pyland, Dartmoor

Baynes, Inspector [WIST] Male Alive   Baynes was a stout, puffy, red man,
whose face was only redeemed from grossness by two extraordinarily bright eyes,
almost hidden behind the heavy creases of cheek and brow. Inspector of the
Surrey Constabulary. He was wrongly convinced that don Murillo should be sent
at Guildford Assizes. Inspector Tobias Gregson of Scotland Yard introduced
inspector Baynes to Sherlock Holmes. Found the note thrown into the fire by
Garcia, which escaped the flames because the fire had a log-grate and Garcia over
pitched it. Baynes noted that "The note is written upon ordinary cream-laid paper
without watermark. It is a quarter-sheet. The paper is cut off in two snips with a
short-bladed scissors. It has been folded over three times and sealed with purple
wax, put on hurriedly and pressed down with some flat oval object. It is addressed
to Mr. Garcia, Wisteria Lodge. It says: "Our own colours, green and white. Green
open, white shut. Main stair, first corridor, seventh right, green baize. Godspeed.
D. "It is a woman's writing, done with a sharp-pointed pen, but the address is
either done with another pen or by someone else. It is thicker and bolder, as you
see." Holmes responded "I must compliment you, Mr. Baynes, upon your attention
to detail in your examination of it. A few trifling points might perhaps be added.
The oval seal is undoubtedly a plain sleeve-link—what else is of such a shape?

The scissors were bent nail scissors. Short as the two snips are, you can distinctly see the same slight curve in each."

Sherlock Holmes Quote : "I must congratulate you, Inspector, on handling so distinctive and instructive a case. Your powers, if I may say so without offence, seem superior to your opportunities."

Arthur Twidle

Arthur Twidle

Beatrice's dog   [SHOS]   Male Alive   A most beautiful Spaniel Not a named character, but one worthy of inclusion because of the help he gave Holmes in detecting the counterfeit Lade Beatrice. He was the real Shoscombe breed. There wasn't a better in England. Belonged to Lady Beatrice Falder, but when she died, he started howling outside the old well-house. Sir Robert Norberton gave the dog to Sandy Bains, the jockey and told to take it to Josiah Barnes, the landlord at the Green Dragon pub. He helped Holmes discover that the person being driven around in the carriage, was not Lady Beatrice, but someone dressed up as her.

Address : Shoscombe Old Place then The Green Dragon Pub.

Frederic Dorr Steele   *Frank Wiles*

Becher, Dr. **[ENGR]** **Male Alive** See Mr. Ferguson

Beddington, Mr. **[STOC]** **Male in prison** There were two brothers called Beddington, one was a Forger and cracksmith, the other kept Hall Pycroft busy. We are never told the names of these two brothers and also don't meet the cracksmith brother, the other is active calling himself both Harry and Arthur Pinner. The cracksmith brother was only just out after a five year spell of penal servitude. Caught by Constable Pollack and Sergeant Tuson trying to leave Mawson & Williams with a bag containing a hundred thousand pounds' worth of American railway bonds, with a large amount of scrip in mines and other companies. The other brother was saved/caught in Birmingham by Holmes, who stopped him hanging himself when he found out that his brother would likely hang for the murder of the watchman. See Arthur and Harry Pinner.

Beddoes, Mr. **[GLOR]** **Male Alive** Probably not his real name. prisoner along with James Armitage. One of the five convicts who survived the wreck of the 'Gloria Scott' Friend of Old Trevor and sent him the message that lead to his death. Sent the message read; "The supply of game for London is going steadily up,' it ran. 'Head-keeper Hudson, we believe, has been now told to receive all orders for fly-paper and for preservation of you hen-pheasant's life.' to Old Trevor. (reading every third word gives you) "'The game is up. Hudson has told all. Fly for your life.' Probably killed Hudson and then escaped.

Address : Fordingbridge, Hampshire

Beecher, Henry Ward   [CARD, RESI]   Male dead (Real Person 1813 – 1887)
American Congregationalist clergyman, social reformer, and speaker, known for his support of the abolition of slavery. There is clearly a case of Groundhog day going on at the beginning of the Cardboard Box and The resident patient, Watson was being lazy virtually using the same introduction in both stories. Watson had an unframed portrait of Henry Ward Beecher which stands upon the top of his books.

Bellamy, Miss Maud   [LION]   Female dead   She had a perfect clear-cut face, with all the soft freshness of the downlands in her delicate colouring. Holmes thought that she possessed strong character as well as great beauty. A note from her was found on the dead body of Fitzroy McPherson. Was the daughter of Tom Bellamy and had a brother called William. She was of the opinion that her father and brother might have a hand in the death of McPherson. She was secretly engaged to Fitzroy McPherson. She also had a note from him that read; DEAREST The old place on the beach just after sunset on Tuesday. It is the only time I can get away. F. M.

Address : The Haven, Fulworth

Howard K. Elcock *Frederic Dorr Steele*

Bellamy, Tom   [LION]   Male Alive   A middle-aged man with a flaming red beard. Father of Maud and William Owns all the boats and bathing-cots at Fulworth. He was a fisherman to start with, but was now a man of some substance. He and his son William ran the business. Said that Mr. McPherson's attentions to Maud were insulting. The word 'marriage' was never mentioned, and yet there were letters and meetings, and a great deal more of which neither of us could approve. He objected to his daughter picking up with men outside her own station.

Address : The Haven, Fulworth

Howard K. Elcock

Frederic Dorr Steele

Bellamy, William   [LION]   Male Alive He was a powerful young man, with a heavy, sullen face. Brother of Maud Bellamy and along with his father was against her being involved with Fitzroy McPherson. His sister thought he might have been involved in the death of McPherson, but he wasn't.

Address : The Haven, Fulworth

Howard K. Elcock

Frederic Dorr Steele

Bellinger, Lord   [SECO]   Male Alive   Austere, high-nosed, eagle-eyed, and dominant. He had thin, blue-veined hands were clasped tightly over the ivory head of his umbrella, and his gaunt, ascetic face looked gloomily from Holmes to Watson. Twice Premier of Britain. He and the Right Honourable Trelawney Hope arrived at 221b baker street on the morning of the 12 October 1886. He was there to help explain the situation. Asked Holmes to try and recover a lost letter that had been stolen from the dispatch case of Trelawney Hope.

Sherlock Holmes Quote : "We also have our diplomatic secrets,"

Sidney Paget

Richard Gutschmidt

Belminster, Duke of   [SECO]   Male Alive   Father of Lady Hilda Trelawney Hope.

Bender, Mr   [STUD]   Male dead   In PART II. The Country of the Saints, he was the first to die on the trail in the Great Alkali Plain.

Bennett, Trevor   [CREE]   Male Alive   He was a tall, handsome youth about thirty, well dressed and elegant, but with something in his bearing which suggested the shyness of the student rather than the self-possession of the man of the world. He was the professional assistant to the great scientist, Professor Presbury and lived under his roof, and was engaged to his only daughter, Edith. He thought that the professor had every claim upon his loyalty and devotion and knew the matter was very delicate and needed tact. Was worried about the behaviour of his employer and wondered about the mysterious communications the professor had been receiving. Went to Holmes for help.

Frederic Dorr Steele   *Howard K. Elcock*

Bentley. Mr.   [MISS]   Male   Owner of the hotel that Godfrey Staunton and the other members of the Cambridge Rugby squad stayed at while in London. The Day porter was able to give Holmes much needed help.

Benz, Karl Friedrich   [LAST]   Male Alive (Real Person 1844 – 1929) German engine designer and automotive engineer, who formed the Mercedes-Benz company. Baron Von Herling, the chief secretary of the legation, drove a huge 100-horse-power Benz car. Probably a Mercedes 38/100hp

Beppo **[SIXN]** **Male Alive** An alert, sharp-featured simian man with thick eyebrows, and a very peculiar projection of the lower part of the face like the muzzle of a baboon. Was a kind of Italian piece-work man, who made himself useful in the shop of Gelder and Co. He could carve a bit and gild and frame, and do odd jobs. The fellow left and nothing had been heard of him since. His second name was never known. He had once been a skilful sculptor and had earned an honest living, but he had taken to evil courses and had twice already been in gaol—once for a petty theft and once, for stabbing a fellow-countryman. He could talk English perfectly well Managed to smash five of the six Napoleon busts. Killed Pietro Venucci as he made his escape after taking the fourth bust from Horace Harker. Was captured by Holmes, Watson and Lestrade as he stole the fifth Bust outside the house of Josiah Brown.

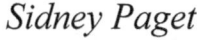

Sidney Paget

Nos Loisirs

Bernstone, Mrs **[SIGN]** **Female Alive** Had thin, work-worn hands. Tall, old Housekeeper at Pondicherry Lodge. Only Woman at the house. Discovered the dead body of Mr. Bartholomew Sholto. Got in a bit of a state and was glad when Thaddeus Sholto arrived. Was arrested by the over-zealous Athelney Jones, but was soon released.

Bertillon, Alphonse   [NAVA,HOUN]   Male Alive (Real Person 1853 – 1914)
French police officer and biometrics researcher who applied the anthropological technique of anthropometry to law enforcement creating an identification system based on physical measurements. Inventor of the Mug Shot. [NAVA] Holmes' conversation, was about the Bertillon system of measurements, and he expressed his enthusiastic admiration of the French savant. [HOUN] Dr. Mortimer upsets Holmes a little when he says "To the man of precisely scientific mind the work of Monsieur Bertillon must always appeal strongly."

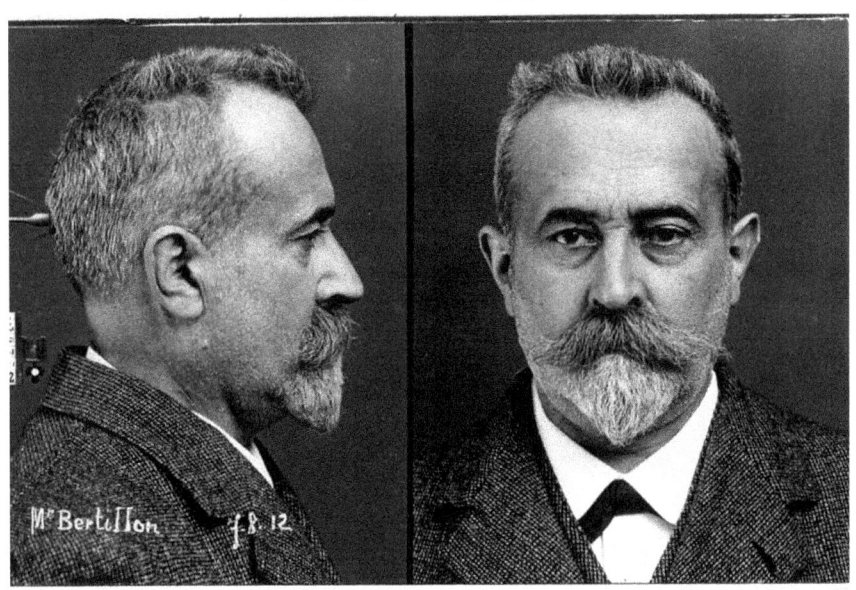

Beverley, Baron   [PRIO]   Male Alive   See Duke of Holdernesse

Bevington, Mr   [LADY]   Male Alive   The owner of a pawn shop in Westminster Road. Dr. Shlessinger had taken in a silver-and-brilliant pendant of old Spanish design, that had belonged to Lady Frances Carfax. Hon. Philip Green spent three days waiting for someone to return and try and pawn additional jewellery belonging to Lady Frances. When Shlessinger's wife visited, Philip Green followed her to an undertakers and then finally to No. 36, Poultney Square, Brixton.

Biddle, Mr.   [RESI]   Male dead   One of five men who robbed the bank and got away with £7,000. Blessington or Sutton, who was the worst of the gang, turned informer. On his evidence Cartwright was hanged and the other three got fifteen years apiece. On an early release from prison, the three gang members Biddle, Hayward and Moffat, located the residence of Blessington, gave him a mock trial and hanged him. Blessington was discovered the following morning by Dr. Percy Trevelyan. It is likely that all three members of the gang, died on the ill-fated steamer 'Norah Creina , which was lost some years ago with all hands upon the Portuguese coast, some leagues to the north of Oporto.

Martin Van Maele

William H. Hyde

Bill, (Breckinridge's helper) [BLUE] Male Alive   Small boy who helped Breckinridge at his stall in Covent Garden.

Sidney Paget

Billy, (Holmes' page) [VALL,MAZA,THOR] Male Alive   [VALL] Holmes was waiting for the second letter, from Porlock, that would specify the book that the cipher used. It was delivered by Billy the page. [MAZA] The young but very wise and tactful page, who had helped a little to fill up the gap of loneliness and isolation which surrounded the saturnine figure of the great detective.

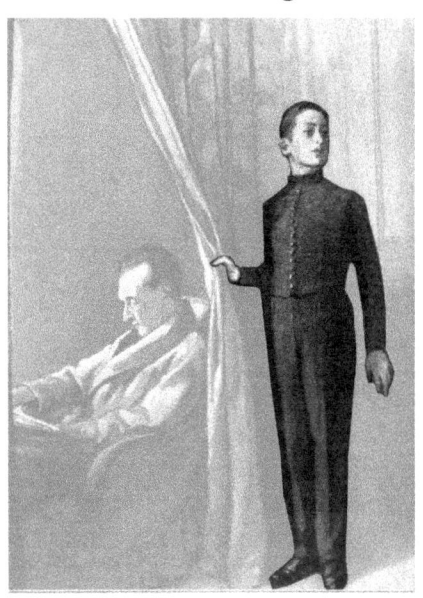

Alfred Gilbert

Bird, Simon   [VALL]   Male dead   One of the victims of Lawlers & Andrews. They were prepared to talk until the cows come home about the killing of Charlie Williams or of Simon Bird

Black Gorgiano   [REDC]   Male dead   See Giuseppe Gorgiano

Black Jack of Ballarat   [BOSC]   Male Alive   See John Turner

Black Peter   [BLAC]   Male dead   See Captain Peter Carey

Black Steve   [3GAB]   Male Alive See Steve Dixie

Blackwater, Earl of   [PRIO]   Male Alive   Entrusted his son to Dr. Thorneycroft Huxtable and the Priory School

Blaker, Foreman   [VALL]   Male Unknown   Foreman of a mine or ironworks who Ted Baldwin said "And time, too! Folk are gettin' out of hand in these parts. It was only last week that three of our men were turned off by Foreman Blaker. It's been owing him a long time, and he'll get it full and proper." Meaning "The business end of a buckshot cartridge!"

Blessington, Mr. [RESI] Male dead Member of the Worthingdon bank gang. Posed as the Resident Patient for Dr. Percy Trevelyan. Had a weak heart. The worst of the gang, but escaped a prison sentence by turning informer. Of the other four members of the gang, Cartwright was hanged and the other three got fifteen years apiece, but were released early and finally catch up with Blessington. Blessington is given a mock trial and hanged by his former gang members.

Address : 403 Brook Street, London

Sidney Paget

William H. Hyde

Blondin, Charles [SIGN] Male Alive (Real Person 1834 – 1897) French Tightrope walker and acrobat Holmes alludes to himself as Blondin when he climbs down the outside of Pondicherry Lodge.

Sherlock Holmes Quote : "Now run downstairs, loose the dog, and look out for Blondin."

Blount, (Student)   [LION]   Male Alive   A student at 'The Gables' coaching
establishment. He and Sudbury found the body of Fitzroy McPherson's dog, dead
on the very edge of the pool within which his master had swam. He may have
been one of the students that joined McPherson in morning swims and had been
saved Ian Murdoch's algebraic demonstration.

Boccaccio, Giovanni   [STUD]   Male dead (Real Person 1313 – 1375) Italian
writer, Poet and correspondent of Petrarch. Boccaccio's Decameron was a
collecion of Novellas and is Structured as a frame story containing 100 tales told
by a group o seven young women and three young men sheltering in a secluded
villa just outside Florence to escape the Black Death. A pocket edition of his work
was found on the body of Enoch Drebber and belonged to Joseph Stangerson.

Bohemia, The King of   [SCAN]   male Alive See Wilhelm Gottsreich
Sigismond von Ormstein

**Bonaparte, Napoleon   [FINA,SIXN,VALL]   Male dead (Real Person 1769 –
1804)** French statesman and military leader who became famous as an artillery
commander during the French Revolution. But this story is about six Napoleon
busts produced by Gelder and Co. in church street, Stepney. The first three busts
were sold to Morse Hudson's shop where

1 Was smashed inside the shop

2 & 3. Dr. Barnicot at Kennington Road and Lower Brixton Road The second set of
three busts were sold to Harding Brothers shop and then onto

4 Mr. Horace Harker of Pitt Street, Kensington.

5 Mr. Josiah Brown of Laburnum Lodge, Laburnum Vale, Chiswick

6 Mr. Sandeford of Lower Grove Road, Reading.

Frederic Dorr Steele

Boots, (at Halliday's Private Hotel)   [STUD]   Male Alive   Worked as a boot-boy at Halliday's Private Hotel, cleaning boots and shoes and helping out around the hotel. Together with Inspector Lestrade, discovered the body of Joseph Stangerson. Nearly fainted when he saw the blood seeping under the door.

George Hutchinson

Borgia, Lucrezia   [SIXN]   Female dead (Real Person 1480 – 1519)   She was described as having heavy blonde hair that fell past her knees, a beautiful complexion, hazel eyes that changed colour, a full, high bosom, and a natural grace that made her appear to "walk on air" George R. Marek from The Bed and the throne: the Life of Isabella d'Este, Harper & Row. This story is really all about the Black pearl of the Borgia, but this is only revealed at the end when Holmes reveals it's hiding place. The House of Borgia was a Spanish-Aragonese noble family, which rose to prominence during the Italian Renaissance. We don't know who the Pearl actually belonged to, but the most famous female Borgia would have been Lucrezia Borgia, so here are her details. Married three times. 1. Giovanni Storza (annulled). 2. Alfonso of Aragon. 3. Alfonso I d'Este.

Lucrezia Borgia

Boswell, James   [SCAN]   Male dead (Real Person 1740 – 1795)   Real biographer of Samuel Johnson. Mentioned by Holmes when he refers to Watson as his Boswell.

James Boswell

Bouguereau, William-Adolphe   [SIGN]   Male Alive (Real Person 1825 –
1905) French Academic painter. Thaddeus Sholto had one of his paintings.

William-Adolphe Bouguereau

Bovington, Mr   [LADY]   Male Alive   See Mr. Bevington

Brackenstall, Lady Mary [ABBE] Female Alive Watson says that Lady Brackenstall was no ordinary person. Seldom have I seen so graceful a figure, so womanly a presence, and so beautiful a face. She was a blonde, golden-haired, blue-eyed, and would, no doubt, have had the perfect complexion which goes with such colouring had not her recent experience left her drawn and haggard. Her sufferings were physical as well as mental, for over one eye rose a hideous, plum-coloured swelling. From Adelaide. She had been married about a year. But it was not a happy marriage. She said that while walking around the house, at eleven o'clock, to make sure everything was secure, she entered the Dining-room and encountered the three burglars. She was knocked out and tied to a chair. while her husband was struck down and killed. Lied to Holmes about the events surrounding the death of her husband, who was actually killed by Captain Jack Croker, but it was self-defence.

Address : Abbey Grange, Marsham, Kent,

Frederic Dorr Steele

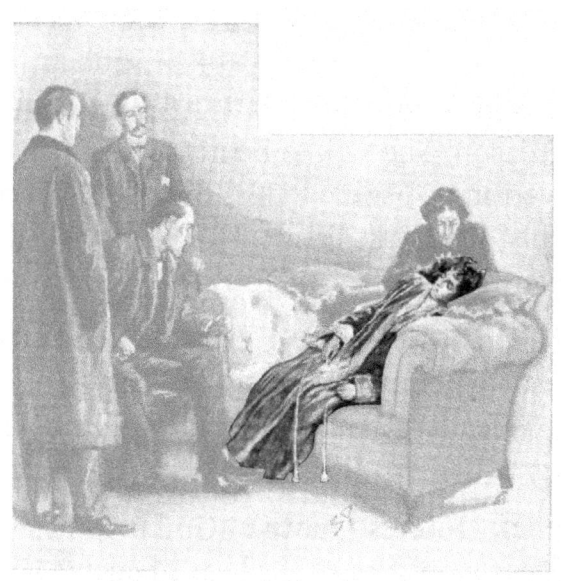

Sidney Paget

Brackenstall, Sir Eustace [ABBE] Male dead He was dressed in his shirt and trousers, with his favourite blackthorn cudgel in his hand One of the richest men in Kent. A confirmed drunkard. Lady Brackenstall said that he was killed by the father and two sons thieves called Randall. Died, in his Dining-room, by having his head knocked in with his own poker. He fell without a groan, and never moved again. Actually killed by Captain Jack Croker in self defence.

Address : Abbey Grange, Marsham, Kent,

Sidney Paget

Brackwell, Lady Eva   [CHAS]   Female Alive   The most beautiful debutante of last season. She was to be married in a fortnight to the Earl of Dovercourt, but Milverton had some letters that would certainly stop the marriage if they had reached the Earl's hands. Holmes is asked to mediate on her behalf with Milverton.

Bradford, John   [BOSC]   Male dead (Real Person 1510 – 1555)   Holmes made a mistake here when he quotes 'Baxter', it isn't Richard Baxter (English Puritan church leader), but John Bradford, English Reformer, Prebedary of St. Paul's and martyr.

Sherlock Holmes Quote : "God help us! Why does fate play such tricks with poor, helpless worms? I never hear of such a case as this that I do not think of Baxter's words, and say, 'There, but for the grace of God, goes Sherlock Holmes.'"

John Bradford

Bradley, (Tobacconist) [HOUN] Male Unknown   Owner of a Tobacco Shop. Holmes ask Watson to get tobacco from this shop. Watson also smoked cigarettes from this tobacconist.

Address : Oxford Street, London

Sherlock Holmes Quotes : "When you pass Bradley's would you ask him to send up a pound of the strongest shag tobacco"
"when I see the stub of a cigarette marked Bradley, Oxford Street, I know that my friend Watson is in the neighbourhood."

Bradshaw, George [VALL] Male dead (Real Person 1800 – 1853) English cartographer, printer and publisher. He developed Bradshaw's Guide, a widely sold series of combined railway guides and timetables. Watson suggested that Bradshaw was a possible source of the words in Porlock's message, this was not the case.

Sherlock Holmes Quote : "There are difficulties, Watson. The vocabulary of Bradshaw is nervous and terse, but limited. The selection of words would hardly lend itself to the sending of general messages. We will eliminate Bradshaw

G_Bradshaw

Bradstreet, Inspector   [TWIS,BLUE, ENGR]   Male Alive A Tall, stout
official in a peaked cap and frogged jacket. [TWIS] Bow street police station. In B
Division [BLUE] He gave evidence as to the arrest of Horner, who struggled
frantically, and protested his innocence in the strongest terms. [ENGR]
Accompanied Holmes, Watson and Hatherley to Eyford to hunt for the coiners
Stark and Ferguson.

Sidney Paget   *Josef Friedrich*

Breckinridge, Mr **[BLUE]** **Male Alive** A horsey-looking man, with a sharp face and trim side-whiskers. Sold Geese in Covent Garden. A bit of a betting man. Had been pestered by James Ryder asking about geese and wasn't going to give Holmes information. In order to get information from him, Holmes has a bet regarding the source of the goose that had had the Blue Carbuncle in its crop.

Josef Friedrich

- Sidney Paget

Brewer, Sam **[SHOS]** **Male Alive** He was a well-known Curzon Street moneylender. Was Horsewhipped on Newmarket Heath by Sir Robert Norberton and nearly killed. Was the chief creditor of Sir Robert and his most bitter enemy. Did hold his hand to allow Shoscombe Prince to run.

Brickfall, Mr. **[RETI]** **Male In a mental ward of a hospital** A He was Senior partner of Brickfall and Amberley, who were manufacturers of artistic materials. You would see their names upon paint-boxes. Probably carried on the business after Amberley retired from business in 1896.

Address : The Haven, Lewisham

Brinvilliers, Marchioness de **[STUD]** **Female dead (Real Person 1630 – 1676)** French aristocrat accused of three murders. Convicted on strength of letter written by her dead lover and confession obtained by torture. referenced in the Daily Telegraph regarding the murder of Enoch Drebber "After alluding airily to the Vehmgericht, aqua tofana, Carbonari, the Marchioness de Brinvilliers, the Darwinian theory, the principles of Malthus, and the Ratcliff Highway murders, the article concluded by admonishing the Government and advocating a closer watch over foreigners in England."

Britannia [LAST] Female In the 2nd century, Roman Britannia came to be
personified as a goddess, armed with a trident and shield and wearing a Corinthian
helmet. Von Bork says of Martha Hudson "She might almost personify Britannia,
with her complete self-absorption and general air of comfortable somnolence.

Broderick, Mr. **[SIGN]** **Male** Senior partner in the company Broderick and Nelson, a Large timber-yard, just past the White Eagle tavern that Toby leads Holmes and Watson to by mistake after the creosote paths cross at the corner of Knight's Place.

Brooks, Mr. **[BRUC]** **Male** The current situation with fog, swirling around the streets of London made Holmes ponder about crime. A villain, who would liked to have ended Holmes' life

Sherlock Holmes Quote : "Suppose that I were Brooks or Woodhouse, or any of the fifty men who have good reason for taking my life, how long could I survive against my own pursuit? A summons, a bogus appointment, and all would be over."

Brown, Lieutenant Bromley **[SIGN]** **Male Alive** Lieutenant under the command of Captain Morstan and Major Sholto, in charge of native troops, there to guard the prisoners in the camp on the Andaman Island.

Brown, Mr. Josiah **[SIXN]** **Male Alive** He was the owner of the Napoleon Bust number 5. He received a note by Holmes warning him to lock every door on the inside and awaited developments. Beppo was captured after he exited his house.

Address : Laburnum Lodge, Laburnum Vale, Chiswick,

Sidney Paget

Brown, Police Constable Sam   [SIGN]   Male Alive   Policeman. Sam Brown and Athelney Jones were on board the boat on the track of the Aurora. He would have got a tenner if the treasure had been recovered, as would the genial inspector that accompanied Watson on his journey to show the Agra treasure to Mary Morstan.

Brown, Silas   [SILV]   Male Alive   Wearer of Square toed boots. His face was ashy pale, beads of perspiration shone upon his brow, and his hands shook until the hunting-crop wagged like a branch in the wind. His bullying, overbearing manner was all gone too, and he cringed along at Holmes' side like a dog with its master. Manager and trainer at Mapleton Stables in charge of the horse Desborough he was always the first stirring in the morning. A fierce-looking elderly man who strode out from the gate with a hunting-crop swinging in his hand. Discovered Silver Blaze and hid him away until Holmes discovered his plans and made him return the horse.

Sherlock Holmes Quote : "Oh, an old horse-fakir like him has many a dodge."

Address : Mapleton training establishment.

Sidney Paget   *Martin Van Maele*

Browner, James (or Jim)   [CARD]   Male in prison   Steward of a steamer called ' S.S. May Day'. Married Mary Cushing and they had a nice life until Sarah came to stay, she made an advance to Jim and he refused and in revenge she drove a wedge between him and his wife. As the break-up of their marriage continued, he started drinking and this made matter worse. Mary started seeing another sailor called Alec Fairbairn. He promised Sarah Cushing that he would send her Alec Fairbairn's ear if he ever caught him around his wife. In fact he caught Fairbairn with Mary together, killed them both and sent one of each of their ears to S. Cushing, but they went to Susan Cushing and not Sarah. Was caught by Lestrade, with lots of help from Holmes.

Address : Somewhere in Liverpool

Sidney Paget *G. Dutriac*

Browner, Mary [CARD] Female dead   Married to Jim Browner, Killed by Jim Browner. Had sisters, Susan and Sarah. James Browner said that Susan was a good woman, Sarah was a Devil and his Mary was an angel. Her sister, Sarah came to stay and made a pass at James, he spurned her, and so Sarah took every opportunity to drive the married couples apart. James took to drink, seeing that Mary was distancing herself from him, this made matters worse. She start a going out with Alec Fairbairn and was caught out in a boat with him, by James and he killed them both and sent her ear to S. Cushing, but instead of going to 'the Devil' (Sarah) it went to the good woman (Susan).

Address : Somewhere in Liverpool

Sidney Paget   *Sidney Paget*

Bruce-Partington [BRUC] Probably Male   It's possible that a single person drew up the plans for the submarine, but it is more likely to be a collaboration of someone called Bruce and another called Partington. The Plans were split up and put on 10 sheets. When they were stolen by Colonel Valentine Walter, three seven were found on Arthur Cadogen West's body, but the others were only recovered when Holmes got involved.

Brunton, Richard [MUSG] Male dead He was a well-grown, handsome man, with a splendid forehead. Butler at Manor House of Hurlstone. He was a bit of a Don Juan. He was a young schoolmaster out of place when he was first taken up by Reginald Musgrave's father, but he was a man of great energy and character, and he soon became quite invaluable in the household. Worked at the Manor for twenty years. Could speak several languages and play nearly every musical instrument The butler of Hurlstone was always a thing that was remembered by all who visit us. Solved the Riddle of the Musgrave Ritual "'Whose was it?' "'His who is gone.' "'Who shall have it?' "'He who will come.' "'Where was the sun?' "'Over the oak.' "'Where was the shadow?' "'Under the elm.' "How was it stepped?' "'North by ten and by ten, east by five and by five, south by two and by two, west by one and by one, and so under.' "'What shall we give for it?' "'All that is ours.' "'Why should we give it?' "'For the sake of the trust.' Accidental or murdered after he discovered the secret treasure of the Musgraves. If he was murdered it had to be Rachel Howell, but in either case the fact that Rachel Howell did not report the incident or go for help was certainly suspicious.

Address : Manor House of Hurlstone

Martin Van Maele   *Sidney Paget*

Buddha   [VEIL]   Male dead   Was a philosopher, mendicant, meditator, spiritual
teacher, and religious leader who lived in Ancient India.   After Mrs. Merrilow
had left Baker street, Holmes was said to have sat Crossed legs, like some strange
Buddha.

Buddha statue near Belum Caves

Bull, John   [LAST]   Male Alive   Personification of the United Kingdom. He first appeared in 1712. Von Bork was talking to Altamont and says that England won't be ready for War "I fancy that in the future we have our own very definite plans about England, and that your information will be very vital to us. It is today or tomorrow with Mr. John Bull. If he prefers today we are perfectly ready. If it is tomorrow we shall be more ready still."

Bunsen, Robert Wilhelm Eberhard   [STUD]   Male   Alive (Real Person 1811-1899) German Chemist who invented the Bunsen burner/ lamp. Sherlock was first seen by Watson as Holmes in the laboratory, lined and littered with countless bottles. Broad, low tables were scattered about, which bristled with retorts, test- tubes, and little Bunsen lamps, with their blue flickering flames.

Robert Bunsen

Burnet, Miss   [WIST]   Female Alive   English governess at High Gable, governess to two girls aged eleven and thirteen. Schemed with Aloysius Garcia to kill Mr. Henderson. While writing a note to Garcia, she was discovered by Mr. Lucas, who used the note to ambush and kill Garcia. Held capture by Messrs Henderson and Lucas, but managed to escape from their clutches and explained the background to the story.

Address : High Gable

Arthur Twidle

Frederic Dorr Steele

Burnwell, Sir George   [BERY]   Male Alive   A man of the world to his fingertips, one who had been everywhere, seen everything, a brilliant talker, and a man of great personal beauty. Cold blooded. Involved in the theft of the Beryl Coronet. Seduced Mary Holder and got her to steal the Coronet from the locked cabinet of her uncle, but she was observed by Arthur Holder, who chased after Burnwell and in the scuffle, the coronet was broken, Sir George got three of the Beryls and Arthur, returning the main part was caught and accused. He sold the three gems he had for three hundred for the lot. Holmes found out who he had sold the gems to and paid three thousand for them.

Josef Friedrich

Sidney Paget

C is for The Cardboard Box

Cadogen West, Arthur   [BRUC]   Male dead   Young man who was found dead on the Underground on Tuesday morning. a clerk who worked at Woolwich Arsenal. Was out on Monday night with his fiancée, Miss Violet Westbury, he left abruptly in the fog about 7:30 that evening. His body was discovered by a plate-layer named Mason, just outside Aldgate Station on the Underground system in London. Metropolitan line. Items found on his body included; His purse contained £2.15s. He had also a chequebook on the Woolwich branch of the Capital and Counties Bank. Two dress-circle tickets for the Woolwich Theatre, dated for that very evening. A small packet of technical papers. But had no train ticket. It seems that Ten papers relating to the Bruce-Partington submarine were taken from Woolwich. There were seven in the pocket of Cadogan West, three of the most essential ones are missing. He had been ten years in the service and had done good work. He had the reputation of being hot-headed and imperious, but a straight, honest man. Second in command under Sidney Johnson in the office. His duties brought him into daily, personal contact with the plans. Saw Colonel Valentine Walter exit the Woolwich Arsenal with the Bruce-Partington plans, he followed the Colonel to the home of Oberstein on Caulfield Gardens, Kensington. He was hit over the head by Oberstein and was killed. His body was placed on a passing Underground carriage roof and fell off at Aldgate.

Arthur Twidle   *P. B. Hickling*

Cadogen West, Mrs. **[BRUC]** **Female Alive** Mother of Arthur Cadogen West
The old lady was too dazed with grief to be of any use to us, but at her side was a
white-faced young Violet Westbury.

P. B. Hickling

Cairns, Patrick **[BLAC]** **Male Alive** A fierce bull-dog face was framed in a
tangle of hair and beard, and two bold dark eyes gleamed behind the cover of
thick, tufted, overhung eyebrows. The third and last applicant for a position on
board ship that Captain Basil (Holmes) advertised for, while he was trying to get
the murderer of Captain Peter Carey. Had been on twenty-six voyages from
Dundee. Was paid Eight pounds a month. Harpooner, who killed Captain Peter
Carey in self-defence while drinking with him in his cabin. Captain Peter Carey
attacked him with a knife and Patrick Cairns ran him through with a steel harpoon
and left him pinned to the wall. "You say I murdered Peter Carey; I say I KILLED
Peter Carey,"

The hoarse voice of the seaman broke in on

Richard Gutschmidt   *Frederic Dorr Steele*

Calhoun, Captain James   [FIVE]   Male dead   Captain of the Barque Lone
Star, Savannah, Georgia Leader of the KKK members who killed John Openshaw,
Joseph Openshaw and Elias Openshaw. Was sent five orange pips by Holmes, but
he never received them because Calhoun and all members of the crew were killed
when the ship was wrecked.

Campbell, Field Marshal Colin   [SIGN]   Male dead (Real Person 1792- 1863)
As Commander-in-Chief of India he relieved and then evacuated Lucknow.
Mentioned in Jonathan Small narrative.   Also known as 1st Baron Clyde

Cantlemere, Lord   [MAZA]   Male Alive   A thin, austere figure with a hatchet face and drooping mid-Victorian whiskers of a glossy blackness which hardly corresponded with the rounded shoulders and feeble gait. Wanted the Gem recovered but didn't think Holmes was up to the task and would rather Holmes failed. Bill the Page said of him "He's a stiff'un, ... I can't stand his Lordship. Neither can Mr. Holmes, sir. You see, he don't believe in Mr. Holmes and he was against employing him. He'd rather he failed." Called on Holmes to see how much progress he had made. Holmes put the gem in his pocket as a joke and although Cantlemere was not very amused and said "We are greatly your debtors, Mr. Holmes. Your sense of humour may, as you admit, be somewhat perverted, and its exhibition remarkably untimely, but at least I withdraw any reflection I have made upon your amazing professional powers."

Sherlock Holmes Quote : "He is an excellent and loyal person, but rather of the old regime."

Carère, Mademoiselle   [HOUN]   Female   Holmes defended the Unfortunate Madame Montpensier from the charge of murder which hung over her in connection with the death of her stepdaughter, Mlle. Carère, the young lady who, as it will be remembered, was found six months later alive and married in New York.

Carey, Captain Peter   [BLAC]   Male dead   He was a most daring and successful seal and whale fisher. In 1883 he commanded the steam sealer Sea Unicorn, of Dundee. He had then had several successful voyages in succession, and in the following year, 1884, he retired. After that he travelled for some years, and finally he bought a small place called Woodman's Lee, near Forest Row, in Sussex. There he has lived for six years, and there he died on 26 June 1895. He was an intermittent drunkard, and when he had the fit on him he was a perfect fiend. He has been known to drive his wife and his daughter out of doors in the middle of the night, and flog them through the park until the whole village outside the gates was aroused by their screams. On the day of his death, he was in one of his blackest moods, flushed with drink and as savage as a dangerous wild beast. At around two o'clock his daughter reported hearing a most fearful yell, but nobody took any notice of it and it wasn't until midday, that his body was found with a steel harpoon which had been driven into his chest so that it had sunk deep into the wood of the wall behind him. He was pinned like a beetle on a card.

Address : Woodman's Lee, near Forest Row, in Sussex

Martin Van Maele   *Sidney Paget*

Carey, Miss. **[BLAC]** **Female Alive** A pale, fair-haired girl, whose eyes blazed defiantly as she said that she was glad that her father was dead, and that she blessed the hand which had struck him down. Daughter of Captain Peter Carey. Her father had been known to drive his wife and her out of doors in the middle of the night, and flog them through the park until the whole village outside the gates was aroused by their screams.

Carey, Mrs. **[BLAC]** **Female Alive** A haggard, grey-haired woman, whose gaunt and deep-lined face, with the furtive look of terror in the depths of her red-rimmed eyes, told of the years of hardship and ill-usage which she had endured. Her Husband had been known to drive her and his daughter out of doors in the middle of the night, and flog them through the park until the whole village outside the gates was aroused by their screams.

Carfax, Lady Frances **[LADY]** **Female Alive** A rather pathetic figure, a beautiful woman, still in fresh middle age, and yet, by a strange change, the last derelict of what only twenty years ago was a goodly fleet. She was still handsome and bore every sign of having in her youth been a very lovely woman. She was the sole survivor of the direct family of the late Earl of Rufton. She did not inherit the estates because these passed down on the male line. She was left with limited means, but with some very remarkable old Spanish jewellery of silver and curiously cut diamonds to which she was fondly attached. She was a lady of precise habits, and for four years it has been her invariable custom to write every second week to Miss Susan Dobney, her old governess, who has long retired and lives in Camberwell. This stopped nearly five weeks ago. She refused to leave her jewellery with her banker and always carried them about with her. Befriended a couple called Dr. & Mrs. Shlessinger, a missionary couple , while she was staying at Baden Spa. Travelled with them back to England, where she was held captive and some of her jewellery sold off. The Dr. Shlessinger arranged for a funeral of an old lady who they claimed was his wife's nurse. Holmes didn't notice that the coffin was far to big for the small frame of this nurse. The following day, the funeral was interrupted by Holmes and Watson and when they opened up the coffin, they found that Lady Frances had been chloroformed and placed within on top of the nurse. Lady Frances was removed from the coffin and Watson managed to revive her motionless form.

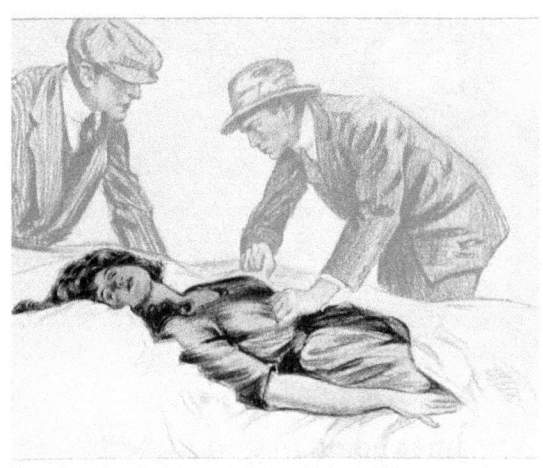

T. V. McCarthy

Alec Ball

Carina   [RETI]   Female Alive   Holmes suggested that he and Watson should go and see Carina sings tonight at the Albert Hall.

Carlo the Mastiff   [COPP]   Male dead   A giant dog, as large as a calf, tawny tinted, with hanging jowl, black muzzle, and huge projecting bones. Feed him once a day, and not too much then, so that he is always as keen as mustard. Toller lets him loose every night. Shot by Holmes.

Josef Friedrich   *Sidney Paget*

Carlo, the Spaniel   [SUSS]   Male Alive   A spaniel belonging to Robert Ferguson. Walked with difficulty, his hind legs moved irregularly and its tail was on the ground. The local vet was puzzled by his condition and put the paralysis down to Spinal meningitis. In actual fact he had been used as a test subject by young master Jack Ferguson, who had discovered curare dipped arrows in a quiver of a bird bow. It seems that there was still some potency in the poison. Was on the mend however as his symptoms were reducing.

Address : Cheeseman's, Lamberley, Sussex, South of Horsham

G. Dutriac

Carlyle, Thomas   [STUD,SIGN]   Male dead (Real Person 1795 – 1881)
British historian, satirical writer, essayist, translator, philosopher, mathematician, and teacher. [STUD] Holmes' ignorance was as remarkable as his knowledge. Of contemporary literature, philosophy and politics he appeared to know next to nothing. Upon Watson quoting Thomas Carlyle, he inquired in the naivest way who he might be and what he had done. [SIGN] Watson was a reader of Thomas Carlyle When Watson quoted him, Holmes asked who he might be.

Carnaway, Brother Jim   [VALL]   Male dead   Vermissa Scowrer who was dead before the start of this story. His Widow was given a pension. He was struck down doing the work of the lodge. "Jim was shot last month when they tried to kill Chester Wilcox of Marley Creek," McMurdo was informed him. Chester Wilcox had killed him while he are walking around outside the house.

Carnaway, Mrs.   [VALL]   Female Alive   Widow of the dead Vermissa Scowrer Jim Carnaway. She was given a pension by the Lodge.

Carriton, Mr.   [SUSS]   Male dead   Builder of a house in Lamberley. As Watson says "I know that country, Holmes. It is full of old houses which are named after the men who built them centuries ago. You get Odley's and Harvey's and Carriton's—the folk are forgotten but their names live in their houses."

Carruthers, Bob   [SOLI]   Male Alive   He was a dark, sallow, clean-shaven, silent person; but he had polite manners and a pleasant smile. Was very kind and very musical. Said that he was a friend of Violet Smith's Uncle, Ralph Smith and offered Violet a job as governess of his daughter. Fell in love with Violet Smith that was not reciprocated. Had a ten year old daughter and Violet Smith was employed to teach her music at Chiltern Grange. Followed Violet Smith on a bicycle as she travelled to and from Chiltern Grange. When Violet Smith was abducted by Jack Woodley and forced into marriage by Mr. Williamson, he shot Woodley injuring him. For his involvement with Jack Woodley and Mr. Williamson, was given a few months gaol time.

Address : Chiltern Grange

Martin Van Maele   *Sidney Paget*

Carruthers, Colonel [WIST] Male Alive   This is not the same Carruthers as Robert Carruthers from the story of the Solitary cyclist.

Sherlock Holmes Quote : My dear Watson, you know how bored I have been since we locked up Colonel Carruthers."

Carston, Earl of   [PRIO] Male Alive   See Duke of Holdernesse

Carter, Mr. [VALL] Male in prison   He was the treasure of Lodge 341, Vermissa. He was one of the members of the Committee that had to decide what to do with the Birdy Edwards problem. Other members were committee were ; Bodymaster McGinty, Ted Baldwin, Harraway the secretary, Tiger Cormac the brutal young assassin, and the brothers Willaby (Arthur and another).

Cartwright, (Master) [HOUN] Male Alive   A bright, keen face, Was employed by Wilson the manager of a district messenger offices Able employee of Wilson. Was asked to go around twenty-three hotels to see if he could find the person who sent the warning note to Sir Henry Baskerville. Holmes employed him to bring supplies while Holmes was camped out on Dartmoor.

Sherlock Holmes Quote : "I have some recollection, Wilson, that you had among your boys a lad named Cartwright, who showed some ability during the investigation."

- Raymond Pallier   *- Raymond Pallier*

Cartwright, Mr. [RESI] Male dead   Member of the Worthingdon bank gang (1875). One of five men who robbed the bank and got away with £7,000. Blessington or Sutton, who was the worst of the gang, turned informer. On his evidence Cartwright was hanged and the other three got fifteen years apiece.

Castalotte, Tito [REDC] Male Alive   Senior partner of the great firm of Castalotte and Zamba, who were the chief fruit importers of New York. Gennaro Lucca saved him from some ruffians in the place called the Bowery. He took Gennaro into his employment, made him head of a department, and showed his goodwill towards him in every way. Signor Castalotte was a bachelor, and Emilia Lucca felt that Gennaro was treated more like the man's son. Refused to be blackmailed by Gorgiano and the Red Circle and faced death by Gennaro's hands, but Gennaro refused and together with his wife escaped to London.

Catullus, Gaius Valerius [EMPT] Male dead (Real Person 84BC 54BC) Roman Poet best known for his Love Poems.

Sherlock Holmes Quote : "you'll find my little bookshop at the corner of Church Street, and very happy to see you, I am sure. Maybe you collect yourself, sir. Here's British Birds, and Catullus, and The Holy War–a bargain, everyone of them. With five volumes you could just fill that gap on that second shelf. It looks untidy, does it not, sir?"

Caunter, Master [PRIO] Male Alive   The elder boy in the inner room of priory school and was a very light sleeper.

Chandos, Sir Charles   [VALL]   Male Unknown   Previous employer of Ames the butler, now at Birlstone Manor House. Ames had worked for him for ten years and was as solid as a rock.

Charles I, King   [MUSG, VALL]   Male dead (Real Person 1600 – 1649)
King of England and Ireland from 27 March 1625 until his execution (beheaded) 30 January 1648. It was the time of the English Civil war with Roundheads and Cavaliers fighting over who should rule England. After his death it would be 11 years before there was another king of England [STUD] While Holmes and Watson were awaiting the arrival of the murderer of Enoch J. Drebber, Holmes mentioned a book he had picked up at a stall the previous day "De Jure inter Gentes - published in Latin at Liège in the Lowlands, in 1642. Charles's head was still firm on his shoulders when this little brown-backed volume was struck off." [MUSG] The crown of England was hidden away after the king was executed and hidden in Musgrave manor, so that a future king would reclaim it, only it never was.   [VALL] John Douglas concealed himself in a room that may have once been used by King Charles.

Van Dyck

Charles II, King   [MUSG]   Male dead (Real Person 1630 – 1685)   Eldest surviving son of King Charles l. Reigned from 29 May 1660 until his death 6 February 1685. Never reclaimed the Stuart crown, which remained hidden until Richard Brunton worked out the clues in the Musgrave Ritual and died for his efforts.

John Michael Wright

Charpentier, Arthur [STUD] Male Alive   Sub-lieutenant in Her Majesty's navy Arrested by inspector Gregson for killing Enoch Drebber. Carried the heavy stick which the mother described him as having with him when he followed Drebber. It was a stout oak cudgel. Innocent of any wrongdoing.

Address : At Sea and Torquay Terrace, Camberwell

The Bristol Observer

Charpentier, Madame   [STUD]   Female Alive   Had two children, Arthur and Alice. Boarding-house keeper who hired out rooms to Enoch Drebber and Joseph Stangerson. They left on 4th March departing for Euston Station in order to catch the Liverpool express. Said that the Two American's had left the boarding house at eight o'clock Stated that "His secretary, Mr. Stangerson, said that there were two trains—one at 9.15 and one at 11. He was to catch the first." In either event they didn't catch either.

Address : Torquay Terrace, Camberwell

The Bristol Observer

Charpentier, Miss Alice   [STUD]   Female Alive   Uncommonly fine girl. looked red behind the eyes and had a trembling lip. Daughter of Madam Charpentier. Was attacked by Enoch Drebber and saved by the arrival of her brother Arthur, who kicked Drebber out of the house.

Address : Torquay Terrace, Camberwell

The Bristol Observer

Charybdis [RESI] Alive   In classical mythology, Scylla was a horrible six-headed monster who lived on a rock on one side of a narrow strait. Charybdis was a whirlpool on the other side. When ships passed close to Scylla's rock in order to avoid Charybdis, she would seize and devour their sailors. Watson says "The small matter which I have chronicled under the heading of "A Study in Scarlet," and that other later one connected with the loss of the Gloria Scott, may serve as examples of this Scylla and Charybdis which are forever threatening the historian." We would now say, "Caught between a rock and a hard place." or "between the devil and the deep blue sea".

Charybdis

Cheeseman, Mr. [SUSS] Male dead   Robert Ferguson lived in the house built by this man. As Watson says "I know that country, Holmes. It is full of old houses which are named after the men who built them centuries ago. You get Odley's and Harvey's and Carriton's—the folk are forgotten but their names live in their houses."

Chopin, Frederic Francois   [STUD]   Male dead (Real Person 1810 – 1849) Polish composer and virtuoso pianist. Holmes and Watson took a little break and went to see one of Chopin's works played by Norman Neruda. Probably the piece Holmes is talking about is the Waltz op.34 n.1

Sherlock Holmes Quote : "And now for lunch, and then for Norman Neruda. Her attack and her bowing are splendid. What's that little thing of Chopin's she plays so magnificently: Tra-la-la-lira-lira-lay."

Frederic Chopin

Chowdar, Lal   [SIGN]   Male dead   Loyal servant of Major John Sholto. Believed that his master had killed Captain Arthur Morstan and helped dispose of the body.

The Bristol Observer

Christie, James   [3GAR]   Male dead (Real Person 1730 – 1803)   Was the
founder of auction house Christie's. Nathan Garrideb said that would drive down
to Sotheby's or Christie's now and again.

Chubb, Charles   [GOLD]   Male dead (Real Person 1779 – 1845)   Started the
Chubb Lock company, maker of high quality locks The bureau belonging to the
Professor has a Chubb lock on it.

Charles Chubb

Clarendon, Lord [HOUN] Male dead   "Know then that in the time of the Great Rebellion (the history of which by the learned Lord Clarendon I most earnestly commend to your attention) The History of the Rebellion by Edward Hyde, 1st Earl of Clarendon is his account of the English Civil War. This work (originally published in 1702–1704 as The History of the Rebellion and Civil Wars in England) was the first full-scale, detailed history of the Civil War and was written by a key player in the events contained within it.

Clay, John   [REDH] Male In Prison   See Vincent, Spaulding

Clayton, John   [HOUN] Male Alive   Cabman is out of Shipley's Yard, near Waterloo Station. Cabman no 2047. Driven his cab for seven years and never a word of complaint. Drove a man around, who followed Sir Henry Baskerville and Mr. James Mortimer around. This man said he was a detective called "Sherlock Holmes" He was hailed at half-past nine in Trafalgar Square. the man said that he was a detective, and he was offered two guineas if he would do exactly what was wanted all day and ask no questions. He was glad enough to agree. First they drove down to the Northumberland Hotel and waited there until two gentlemen came out and took a cab from the rank. They followed their cab until it pulled up somewhere near here. The fare was dropped off at Waterloo Station.

Address : 3, Turpey Street, the Borough

Paul Thiriat   *Sidney Paget*

Clergyman of the Church of St. Monica   [SCAN]   Male Alive   Notes:
Unnamed clergyman. Married Spinster Irene Adler to Bachelor Godfrey Norton
Clergyman at the Church of St. Monica

Sidney Paget

Cobb, John   [BOSC]   Male Alive   Charles McCarthy's groom, who
accompanied him on a visit to Ross

Colonna, Prince of   [SIXN]   Male Alive   Previous Owner of the Black Pearl of
the Borgias. Holmes had the good fortune, by a connected chain of inductive
reasoning, to trace it from the Prince of Colonna's bedroom at the Dacre Hotel, to
one of the six Napoleon busts.

Address : Dacre Hotel

Commissionaire   [STUD]   Male Alive   Stalwart, plainly-dressed individual who
delivered a large blue envelope to Holmes from Tobias Gregson retired sergeant
of Marines Has a great blue anchor tattooed on the back of his hand. He had a
military carriage and regulation side whiskers. Some amount of self-importance
and a certain air of command. His uniform away for repairs and a sergeant in
Royal Marine Light Infantry. So ok he is not a named individual, but it might be
that he is Peterson the Commissionaire in BLUE. And anyway I have an image of
him and he looks quite smart even if his uniform was away for repairs.

Richard Gutschmidt

Conk, Mr. [SIXN] Involved in some way with the Conk-Singleton Forgery case, but in what way is never revealed, but clearly he is linked in some way with Singleton.

Sherlock Holmes Quote : "Put the pearl in the safe, Watson and get out the papers of the Conk-Singleton forgery case."

Cook, Garcia's [WIST] Male Alive Size twelve shoe His face was "a kind of queer shade like clay with a splash of milk in it. Then there was the size of it—it was twice normal. And the look of it—the great staring goggle eyes, and the line of white teeth like a hungry beast" A perfect savage, as strong as a cart-horse and as fierce as the devil. Could speak hardly a word of English, and just grunted. Practised Voodoo Had various items of his religion in the kitchen including a torn bird, a pail of blood, some charred bones, and an extraordinary object which stood at the back of the dresser. It was so wrinkled and shrunken and withered that it was difficult to say what it might have been. One could but say that it was black and leathery and that it bore some resemblance to a dwarfish, human figure. it might have been a mummified Negro baby or a very twisted and ancient monkey. Whatever it was, be it Human or animal, it had a double band of white shells strung round the centre of it. Upon capture, bit off Police-constable Downing's thumb nearly off. 'The true voodoo-worshipper attempts nothing of importance without certain sacrifices which are intended to propitiate his unclean gods. In extreme cases these rites take the form of human sacrifices followed by cannibalism. The more usual victims are a white cock, which is plucked in pieces alive, or a black goat, whose throat is cut and body burned.'

Sherlock Holmes Quote : "He must certainly have been a giant."

Address : Wisteria Lodge.

Arthur Twidle

Arthur Twidle

Cook, Police-Constable [FIVE]   Male Alive   Police Constable of the H Division, on duty near Waterloo Bridge, heard a cry for help and a splash in the water. Then he found the corpse of John Openshaw. The Water-Police eventually recovered the body.

Cook, Thomas   [LADY]   Male dead (Real Person 1808 – 1892)   Thomas Cook businessman who started up the travel company Thomas Cook & sons. Watson visited the manager of Cook's local office to find out the movements of Lady Frances Carfax after she left Hotel National at Lausanne. She went to the Spa town of Baden and stayed at the Englischer Hof.

Thomas Cook

Copernicus, Nicolaus [STUD] Male Dead (Real person 1473 - 1543)
Renaissance era astronomer and mathematician who formulated the heliocentric model of the Solar systems. Watson said that Holmes was ignorant of the Copernican Theory and of the composition of the Solar System.

Nicolaus Kopernicus/Copernicus

Coram, Anna   [GOLD]   Female dead   A woman of good address, attired like a lady. She had a remarkably thick nose, with eyes which are set close upon either side of it. She had a puckered forehead, a peering expression, and probably rounded shoulders. Wore remarkable strength Golden Pince-nez. Wife of Professor Coram. Self-confessed reformer—revolutionist—Nihilist, working in Russia. An incident occurred that resulted in the death of a police officer and many in her group were killed, many were arrested including a very good innocent friend of hers called Alexis. Professor Coram, who was a member, turned informer and betrayed her and her companions. They were all arrested upon his confession. Some of them found their way to the gallows and some to Siberia. Her husband came to England with his ill-gotten gains, and had lived in quiet ever since, knowing well that if the Brotherhood knew where he was, not a week would pass before justice would be done. She broke into her husband's house, took the package of documents that would prove the innocence of her good friend Alexis, killed the secretary and fled into his bedchambers where he hid her in a secret room. Being found by Holmes, she handed over the documents to him so that they could be presented at the Russian Embassy and then committed suicide by poison.

Sherlock Holmes Quote : "Wanted, a woman of good address, attired like a lady. She has a remarkably thick nose, with eyes which are set close upon either side of it. She has a puckered forehead, a peering expression, and probably rounded shoulders. There are indications that she has had recourse to an optician at least twice during the last few months. As her glasses are of remarkable strength and as opticians are not very numerous, there should be no difficulty in tracing her."

Sidney Paget

Sidney Paget

Coram, Professor Sergius   [GOLD]   Male Alive   Watson thought that he had seldom seen a more remarkable-looking person. He had a gaunt, aquiline face with piercing dark eyes, which lurked in deep hollows under overhung and tufted brows. His hair and beard were white, save that the latter was curiously stained with yellow around his mouth. A cigarette glowed amid the tangle of white hair, and the air of the room was foetid with stale tobacco-smoke. As he held out his hand to Holmes Watson perceived that it also was stained yellow with nicotine An elderly man He was an invalid, keeping to his bed half the time, and the other half hobbling round his house with a stick or being pushed about the grounds by the gardener in a bath-chair. Was a chain smoker of fresh Alexandrian cigarettes. He was well liked by the few neighbours who called upon him, and he had the reputation down there of being a very learned man Former reformer—revolutionist—Nihilist in Russia, who turned informer leading to the arrest of his wife and her very good friend Alexis. Had papers that could prove the innocence of Alexis in his bureau, his wife broke into the house, took the package, killed the secretary and fled into his bedchambers where he hid her in a secret room.

Address : Yoxley Old Place

Stanley E. Armstrong

Charles Raymond Macauley

Cormac, Brother Tiger   [VALL]   Male Alive   A thick-set, dark-faced, brutal-looking young man, whose ferocity had earned him the nickname of "Tiger." Involved in the murder of Andrew Rae. Boss McGinty said that "If you handle it as well as you did the last, you won't be wrong." Had been chosen, along with Boss McGinty, Ted Baldwin, Harraway, Carter, brothers Willaby to capture Birdy Edwards. He might have escaped hanging, as some other members of the Scowrers had, but would certainly have ended up in prison.

Cornelius, Mr   [NORW]   Male Alive   See John Oldacre

Corot, Jean-Baptiste-Camille   [SIGN]   Male dead   French Landscape and portrait painter. Thaddeus Sholto had a genuine landscape painting of his.

Jean-Baptiste-Camille Corot

Coventry, Sergeant   [THOR]   Male Alive   He was a tall, thin, cadaverous man, with a secretive and mysterious manner which conveyed the idea that he knew or suspected a very great deal more than he dared say. Local Police officer who was looking into the murder of Mrs. M. Gibson. He had a trick, too, of suddenly sinking his voice to a whisper as if he had come upon something of vital importance, though the information was usually commonplace enough. Behind these tricks of manner he soon showed himself to be a decent, honest fellow who was not too proud to admit that he was out of his depth and would welcome any help. As he said to Holmes "I'd rather have you than Scotland Yard, Mr. Holmes, If the Yard gets called into a case, then the local loses all credit for success and may be blamed for failure. Now, you play straight, so I've heard." He used the little front room of his humble cottage as the local police-station. Was asked to retrieve both Watson's revolver and also the murder weapon using a grappling-hook.

Alfred Gilbert

Alfred Gilbert

Cowper, Mr [STUD] Male Alive Mormon member known to Jeffeson Hope, who informs him that Lucy has been married to Enoch Drebber and that Joseph Stangerson killed John Ferrier.

Cox, Mr [THOR] Male Owner of the Bank Cox & Co. and somewhere in their vaults at Charing Cross, there is a travel-worn and battered tin dispatch-box with the name, John H. Watson, M.D., Late Indian Army, painted upon the lid. It is crammed with papers, nearly all of which are records of cases to illustrate the curious problems which Mr. Sherlock Holmes had at various times to examine.

Coxon, Mr [STOC]Male Alive Senior partner in Coxon & Woodhouse's, of Draper's Gardens. The Venezuelan loan had caused a crash and the company a nasty cropper. This resulted in twenty-seven clerks being laid off. Gave Hall Pycroft a ripping good testimonial.

Address : Draper's Gardens

Crabbe, Mr [VALL] Male dead Old man living in Stylestown, who was killed by either Lander or Egan. Both claimed the head money given by the lodge.

Crockford, John   [RETI]   Male dead (Real Person 1823 – 1863)   He was an English book publisher who produced Crockford's Clerical Directory. Holmes used this directory to look up the details of Rev J.C. Elman, in the parish of Little Purlington in Essex.

Croker, Capt. Jack   [ABBE]   Male Alive   He was a very tall young man, golden-moustached, blue-eyed, with a skin which had been burned by tropical suns, and a springy step which showed that the huge frame was as active as it was strong. The first officer on board the Rock Of Gibraltar, he had been made a captain and was to take charge of their new ship, the Bass Rock, sailing in two days' time from Southampton. He lived at Sydenham. Met Mary Fraser onboard the Rock of Gibraltar while she travelled from Australia to England. Fell in love with her, but she married Sir Eustace Brackenstall when she arrived in England. Later he discovered that her husband was a brute and when he visited her on the night of the tragedy to find out the truth, he was attacked by her husband and killed him in self-defence. Together with the maid Theresa Wright, they fabricated the scene, but Holmes saw through their ruse. When he was interviewed by Holmes, he proved himself a gentleman and when given the option, by Holmes to run away and save himself but at the expense of Lady Brackenstall, he said "What sort of proposal is that to make a man? I know enough of law to understand that Mary would be had as accomplice. Do you think I would leave her alone to face the music while I slunk away? No, sir; let them do their worst upon me, but for Heaven's sake, Mr. Holmes, find some way of keeping my poor Mary out of the courts." Holmes decides to hold his own court, making Watson the jury and they declared that he was not guilty and allow Croker to go free, to come back to the lady in a year.

Sherlock Holmes Quote : "Vox populi, vox Dei. You are acquitted, Captain Croker"

Richard Gutschmidt *Sidney Paget*

Crosby the banker [GOLD] Male dead As Watson looks at all the cases in 1894, that Holmes had taken, he mentioned the repulsive story of the red leech and the terrible death of Crosby the banker. Unfortunately this was never published and instead he told us the story of The Golden Pince-nez.

Crowder William [BOSC] Male Alive Game-keeper in the employ of Mr. Turner. Witnessed Charles McCarthy around 3pm going town to Boscombe Pool and then saw Mr. James McCarthy, with a gun under his arm, a few minutes later heading in the same direction. He believed that the father was actually in sight at the time and the son was following him.

Paul Thiriat

Cubitt, Elsie [DANC] Female Alive Young American Lady. On the day before her wedding to Hilton Cubitt, dropped a bombshell 'I have had some very disagreeable associations in my life, I wish to forget all about them. I would rather never allude to the past, for it is very painful to me. If you take me, Hilton, you will take a woman who has nothing that she need be personally ashamed of; but you will have to be content with my word for it, and to allow me to be silent as to all that passed up to the time when I became yours. If these conditions are too hard, then go back to Norfolk and leave me to the lonely life in which you found me.' Received a letter from America in June 1898 which turned her deadly white, she read the letter, and threw it into the fire. She was the daughter of the crime boss 'Old Patrick' who had a gang of seven. Her father invented the Dancing Men Cipher. She fled America because she didn't want to get involved in crime and had money of her own, but was followed by a one-time suitor Abe Slaney. Elsie Cubitt tried to buy Abe Slaney off, because she was happily Married, but in an encounter between the three of them, her husband was shot dead and she attempted suicide. Made a full recovery and she remained a widow, devoting her whole life to the care of the poor and to the administration of her husband's estate.

Address : Riding Thorpe Manor, Norfolk

Sidney Paget   *Frederic Dorr Steele*

Cubitt, Hilton   [DANC]   Male dead   A tall, ruddy, clean-shaven gentleman,
whose clear eyes and florid cheeks told of a life led far from the fogs of Baker
Street. He seemed to bring a whiff of his strong, fresh, bracing, east-coast air with
him as he entered. Said of himself that "he was only a simple Norfolk squire."
Visited Holmes because of Dancing men figures had started appearing in letters to
his wife and later on Window Sill etc. Copied down the 'dancing men' and sent
them along to Holmes so that they could be deciphered. As more and more
messages appeared, Holmes was able to read the messages. Holmes and Watson
travelled up to Norfolk, but arrived to late to save him from being killed, they
were able to solve the case and give Inspector Martin the murder.

Address : Riding Thorpe Manor, Norfolk

Frederic Dorr Steele   *Sidney Paget*

Cummings, Mr. Joyce [THOR] Male   The rising barrister who was entrusted with the defence of Miss Grace Dunbar from the charge of murder of Mrs. Gibson.

Frederic Auer

Cunard, Sir Samuel 1st Baronet   [ILLU]   Male dead (Real Person 1787 – 1865)   British-Canadian shipping magnate and founder of the Cunard Line in 1840. In this story, the evening papers reported that Baron Gruner was among the passengers on the Cunard boat, Ruritania, starting from Liverpool on Friday and setting sail for America. He had some important financial business to settle before his impending wedding to Miss Violet de Merville.

Samuel Cunard

Cunningham, Alec   [REIG]   Male in prison   A dashing young fellow, whose bright, smiling expression and showy dress were in strange contract with the business which had brought him there. He said that he saw the Murdered man William Kirwan from dressing room window. Along with his father, attacked Holmes, but was arrested and taken away. Just like his father wrote his 'E' in a Greek fashion. When questioned by the police was a perfect demon, ready to blow out his own or anybody else's brains if he could have got to his revolver.

Sidney Paget   *William H. Hyde*

Cunningham, Old   [REIG]   Male in prison   An elderly man, with a strong, deep-lined, heavy-eyed face, Colonel Hayter said that he was a leading man in the area and a very decent fellow too. Was in legal action with Mr. Acton, who had some claim on half Cunningham's estate. He said that he saw the Murdered man William Kirwan from his bedroom window. Offered a reward of Five hundred pounds for the finding of the murderer. Along with his son, Alec, attacked Holmes, but was arrested and taken away. Just like his Son wrote his 'E' in a Greek fashion. Explained why the murder took place after arrest.

Sidney Paget   *William H. Hyde*

Cusack, Catherine   [BLUE]   Female Alive   Maid to the Countess of Morcar, who together with James Ryder stole the Blue Carbuncle from her employer.

Cushing, Mary   [CARD]   Female dead   See Mary Browner

Cushing, Miss Sarah   [CARD]   Female Alive   She was a fine tall woman, black and quick and fierce, with a proud way of carrying her head, and a glint from her eye like a spark from a flint Had two sisters, Susan and Mary. Didn't get on well with her other sisters. Stayed first with Mary after she married James Browner and got spurned when she made advances to him. Decided to get her own back, but telling Mary that she didn't want to be left alone with James, giving the impression that James had made a pass at her. Really started stirring things up and was asked to leave, so she moved next door and took in lodgers, including Alec Fairbairn, who Mary liked. As Mary and James grew further and further apart, Mary spent more time with Alec. James Browner warned Sarah that if he caught Alec in his house again, he would send her one of his ears. Sarah moved down to London to stay with Susan, but that didn't work out so she moved. James was meant to ship out, but there was a delay and he went back home, only to see Mary and Alec together. One thing lead to another and James killed Mary and Alec and cut off their ears and sent them to the only address in London that he knew, but the parcel ended up being opened by Susan Cushing, who didn't know another about James Browner's promise to Sarah. Sarah is devastated when she learns about the ears and needs to be treated by a Doctor.

Address : New Street Wallington

Cushing, Miss Susan   [CARD]   Female Alive   She was a placid-faced woman, with large, gentle eyes, and grizzled hair curving down over her temples on each side. A worked antimacassar lay upon her lap and a basket of coloured silks stood upon a stool beside her. Received a small packet containing two human ears, apparently quite freshly severed. The box was sent from Belfast and she at thought that it might have been sent by three young medical students, who she was obliged to get rid of on account of their noisy and irregular habits, when she rented rooms. Had two sisters, Sarah and Mary

Address : Cross Street, Croydon

Sidney Paget

J. Baste

Cuvier, Frederic   [FIVE]   Male dead (Real Person 1773 – 1838) French zoologist and palaeontologist. referred to by Holmes. French zoologist and palaeontologist. referred to by Holmes.

Sherlock Holmes Quote : "As Cuvier could correctly describe a whole animal by the contemplation of a single bone, so the observer who has thoroughly understood one link in a series of incidents should be able to accurately state all the other ones, both before and after

Frederic Cuvier

D is for The Dancing Men

d'Albert, Countess [CHAS] Female Alive   The mysterious Lady said that she worked for this lady and had five letters which would compromise her. No such letters existed and it was just a ruse for the mysterious Lady to meet up with Milverton in order to kill him.

d'Aubray, Marie-Madeleine-Marguerite [STUD] Female dead   See Marchioness de Brinvilliers

Dalai Lama [EMPT] Male Alive (Real Person 1876 – 1933) Of course it is Lama with single 'L' not two. Thubten Gyatso was Dalai Lama from 31 July 1878 until his death on the 17 December 1933 also called Ngawang Lobsang Thupten Gyatso Jigdral Chokley Namgyal He would have been around 17 years of age when Holmes visited him in Tibet. He was just over three years of age when he became the 13th Dalai Lama. Thubten Gyatso was an intellectual reformer who proved himself a skilful politician. He was responsible for countering the British expedition to Tibet, restoring discipline in monastic life, and increasing the number of lay officials to avoid excessive power being placed in the hands of the monks.

Dalai Lama

Damery, Colonel Sir James [ILLU] Male Alive It is hardly necessary to describe him, for many will remember that large, bluff, honest personality, that broad, clean-shaven face, and, above all, that pleasant, mellow voice. Frankness shone from his grey Irish eyes, and good humour played round his mobile, smiling lips. His lucent top-hat, his dark frock-coat, indeed, every detail, from the pearl pin in the black satin cravat to the lavender spats over the varnished shoes, spoke of the meticulous care in dress for which he was famous. The big, masterful aristocrat dominated the little room. Sent a note to Holmes that read; "Sir James Damery presents his compliments to Mr. Sherlock Holmes and will call upon him at 4:30 tomorrow. Sir James begs to say that the matter upon which he desires to consult Mr. Holmes is very delicate and also very important. He trusts, therefore, that." Mr. Holmes will make every effort to grant this interview, and that he will confirm it over the telephone to the Carlton Club." Holmes confirmed the interview. Damery told the tale of Miss Violet De Merville and how she had come under the influence of Baron Gruner, the Austrian Murderer, how she loved him and intended to marry the Baron, despite being warned about his unsavoury background. It was not however Miss Violet's father that had requested that Holmes get involved, but an Illustrious Client, who Damery would not name.

Sherlock Holmes Quote : "He has rather a reputation for arranging delicate matters which are to be kept out of the papers. You may remember his negotiations with Sir George Lewis over the Hammerford Will case. He is a man of the world with a natural turn for diplomacy. I am bound, therefore, to hope that it is not a false scent and that he has some real need for our assistance."

Address : Carlton Club

Howard K. Elcock

Danton, George, Jacques   [VALL]   Male dead (Real Person 1759 – 1794)
Leading figure in the early stages of the French revolution. He was initially friends
with Maximillen Robespierre, but towards the end, they became enemies and
Danton was Guillotined. Robespierre was blamed for the execution of Danton. In
this story Evans Potts, the county delegate is likened to Robespierre and Boss
McGinty is Danton. Evans Potts being small framed like Robespierre and
McGinty being of a larger frame like Danton. "Only once did McMurdo see him,
a sly, little grey-haired rat of a man, with a slinking gait and a sidelong glance
which was charged with malice. Evans Pott was his name, and even the great Boss
of Vermissa felt towards him something of the repulsion and fear which the huge
Danton may have felt for the puny but dangerous Robespierre."

George Danton

Darbyshire, Madame   [SILV]   Female Alive   'Wife' of Mr. Darbyshire who had costumes and hats lavished upon her. The milliner's account for £37.15s. made out by Madame Lesurier, of Bond Street, to William Darbyshire. Actually Mr Darbyshire was the married horse trainer John Straker, living a double life.

Sherlock Holmes Quote : Madam Darbyshire had somewhat expensive tastes," remarked Holmes, glancing down the account. "Twenty-two guineas is rather heavy for a single costume."

Darbyshire, William   [SILV]   Male dead   See John Straker

Darwin, Charles   [STUD]   Male Alive (Real Person 1809 – 1882)   English Naturalist, geologist and biologist, who proposed the theory of Evolution. Holmes quotes from Darwin's The Descent of Man.

Sherlock Holmes Quote : "Do you remember what Darwin says about music? He claims that the power of producing and appreciating it existed among the human race long before the power of speech was arrived at. Perhaps that is why we are so subtly influenced by it. There are vague memories in our souls of those misty centuries when the world was in its childhood."

Charles Darwin

Davenport, J. [GREE]   Male Alive   A middle-aged man with a weak
  constitution. Sent a letter written with a J pen on royal cream paper. His letter
  said, 'Sir, in answer to your advertisement of today's date, I beg to inform you that
  know the young lady in question very well. If you should care to call upon me I
  could give you some particulars as to her painful history. She is living at present at
  The Myrtles, Beckenham. Yours faithfully, J. Davenport.' It might be that J.
  Davenport was the coachman that worked at The Myrtles, Beckenham, but there is
  no proof of this.

  Address : Lower Brixton

David, King CROO]   Male dead   Bible Reference   Nancy Barclay calls her
  husband 'David', since her husband had behaved like King David, sending Henry
  Wood on a suicide mission, so that he could court Henry's girl to be (then Devoy,
  now Nancy Barclay) Nancy Devoy would have been Bathsheba, Henry Wood =
  Uriah and James Barclay= King David

King David

Dawson, Groom [SILV] Male Alive   Groom at Mapleton stables. Greeted Holmes and Watson when they arrived at Mapleton stables. Said to Holmes and Watson "We don't want any loiterers about here," He wouldn't accept money from Holmes within the Site of Mr. Silas Brown. (afterwards perhaps)

Address : Mapleton training establishment.

Sidney Paget

Dawson, Mr. [SIGN] Male dead   He and his wife used to do the book-work on the Indigo plantation belonging to Abel White. Jonathan Small found his body lying on his face, quite dead, with an empty revolver in his hand and four Sepoys lying across each other in front of him.

Dawson, Mrs [SIGN] Female dead   Wife, who helped her husband to do the book-work on the Indigo plantation belonging to Abel White. Jonathan Small found her body all cut into ribbons, and half eaten by jackals and native dogs.

Day Porter (at Bentley's [MISS] Male Alive   Day Porter at Bentley's private hotel. Told of a visitor to Godfrey Staunton's rooms, a rough-looking man with a beard who called with a note for Godfrey. He continued that he was not a gentleman, neither was he a working man. He was simply what he described as a "medium-looking chap"

Sidney Paget

De Capus, Hugo [VALL] Male   This might be Hugo Comes, the name of a nephew and companion of William the Conqueror, whose descent from Hugh Capet, King of France, could account for the "de Capus" "Hugo's father, the half-brother of William." In the story part of the Manor House of Birlstone dated back to the time of the first crusade, when Hugo de Capus built a fortalice in the centre of the estate, which had been granted to him by the Red King(William Rufus).

De Croy, Philippe   [STUD] (Real Person) Male dead   Publisher of 'De Jure inter Gentes'—published in Latin at Liege in the Lowlands, in 1642. English translation being 'Of the law between men' Holmes was talking about a book he was reading, while he awaited the murderer of Enoch Drebber.

Sherlock Holmes Quotes : "This is a queer old book I picked up at a stall yesterday–De Jure inter Gentes–published in Latin at Liege in the Lowlands, in 1642. Charles's head was still firm on his shoulders when this little brown-backed volume was struck off."
"Who is the printer?"
"Philippe de Croy, whoever he may have been. On the flyleaf, in very faded ink, is written 'Ex libris Guliolmi Whyte.' I wonder who William Whyte was. Some pragmatical seventeenth-century lawyer, I suppose. His writing has a legal twist about it.

Philippe de Croy

De Lassus, Orlande   [BRUC]   Male dead (Real Person 1532 – 1593)
Composer of the Renaissance, considered to be one of the three most famous musicians of the 16th century. Also called Roland de Lassus, Orlando di Lasso, Orlandus Lassus, Orlande de Lattre or Roland de Lattre. Holmes was writing a monograph upon the Polyphonic Motets of Lassus

Orlande de Lassus

De Merville, General [ILLU] Male Alive Father of Miss Violet de Merville. Totally unable to persuade his daughter of the dangers in marrying Baron Gruner. Colonel Sir James Damery said of him "De Merville is a broken man. The strong soldier has been utterly demoralised by this incident. He has lost the nerve which never failed him on the battlefield and has become a weak, doddering old man, utterly incapable of contending with a brilliant, forceful rascal like this Austrian."

Sherlock Holmes Quote : "De Merville of Khyber fame? Yes, I have heard of him."

De Merville, Violet [ILLU] Female Alive Described as young, rich, beautiful, accomplished, a wonder-woman in every way. Daughter of General de Merville. Under Baron Gruner's spell, she wanted to marry him despite the warnings that he was a murderer. Nobody was able to change her mind. Holmes visited her with Miss Kitty Winters, but they were unable to make her change her mind. At the end of the story, her engagement was broken off, when she was shown the Baron's secret lust diary, written in his own hand.

John R. Flanagan

Frederic Dorr Steele

De Quincey, Thomas [TWIS] Male dead   English essayist, best known for his
Confessions of an English Opium-Eater (1821)   Watson mentions him in the story
as he tells us about Isa Whitney, who was much addicted to opium. The habit
grew upon him from some foolish freak when he was at college; for having read
De Quincey's description of his dreams and sensations, he had drenched his
tobacco with laudanum in an attempt to produce the same effects.

Thomas De Quincey

De Reszke, Edouard   [HOUN]   Male Alive (Real Person 1853 – 1919)   Polish Bass and Opera star. Brother of Jean De Reszke '

Sherlock Holmes Quote : "I have a box for 'Les Huguenots'. Have you heard the De Reszkes?"

Edouard de Reszke

De Reszke, Jean   [HOUN]   Male Alive (Real Person 1850 – 1925)   Polish Tenor and Opera star. Brother of Edouard De Reszke

Sherlock Holmes Quote : "I have a box for 'Les Huguenots'. Have you heard the De Reszkes?"

Jean De Reszke

Dennis, Sally   [STUD]   Female Alive   Fictitious Wife of the fictitious Tom Dennis. Daughter of Mrs. Sawyer, who lost her wedding ring while on a trip to the circus.

Address : 3, Mayfield Place, Peckham.

Dennis, Tom   [STUD]   Male Alive   Mrs Sawyer says that he is a smart, clean lad, as long as he's at sea, and no steward in the company more thought of; but when on shore, what with the women and what with liquor shops Husband of Sally Dennis.

Address : 3, Mayfield Place, Peckham.

Derbyshire, Madame   [SILV]   Female Alive   See Madame Darbyshire USA version of Madame Darbyshire

Derbyshire, William   [SILV]   Male dead   See John Straker USA version of William Darbyshire

Desborough the Horse   [SILV]   Male Horse Alive   Horse belonging to Lord Backwater. Second favourite in the Wessex Plate. Wessex Plate 50 Sovereigns each h ft. with 1000 Sovereigns added for four and five year olds. Second, £300. Third, £200. New course (one mile and five furlongs). Yellow cap and sleeves. taking part in the Wessex Cup. Came in second place. Five to fifteen against Desborough! Five to four on the field!

Address : Mapleton training establishment.

Desmond, Mr. James   [HOUN]   Male Alive   An elderly gentleman of a very amiable disposition. He was a man of venerable appearance and of saintly life Next in line to inherit the Baskerville fortune. Elderly Clergyman. He refused to accept any settlement from Sir Charles, though he pressed it upon him.

Address : Westmoreland

Devine, Miss Marie   [LADY]   Female Alive   Miss Marie Devine had been the maid of Lady Frances Carfax. But left service to get married. She was engaged to Jules Vibart, one of the head waiters at the Hotel National at Lausanne. The last cheque drawn on Lady Frances Carfax's bank account was for the sum of £50 in the name of Miss Marie Devine. Lady Frances had given her the money as a wedding-present. It had been cashed three weeks previously at Credit Lyonnais at Montpellier.

Address : 11 Rue de Trajan, Montpellier

Frederic Dorr Steele

Devive, Artist   [SIXN]   Male   French sculptor who designed the Napoleon Bust involved in the story.

Devonshire, Duchess of   [IDEN]   Female dead (Real Person 1757 – 1806)
English Socialite renowned for her Beauty, Charisma love affairs and Style, including large hats.

Duchess of Devonshire

Devoy, Colour-Sergeant [CROO] Male Father of Miss Nancy Devoy, who later became Mrs. Nancy Barclay. Former Colour-Sergeant in the Royal Munsters.

Devoy, Miss Nancy [CROO] Female Alive See Mrs. Nancy Barclay

Dixie, Steve [3GAB] Male Alive he was dressed in a very loud grey-check suit with a flowing salmon-coloured tie. His broad face and flattened nose were thrust forward. He had sullen dark eyes, with a smouldering gleam of malice in them. Burst in on Holmes at Baker street and started threatening him. Thrust a fist into Holmes face, but Holmes' icy coolness started to unsettle Dixie and as soon as the killing of young Perkins outside the Holborn was mentioned, Holmes was in command, as Dixie backed away. He claimed that he was "trainin' at the Bull Ring in Birmingham when this boy done gone get into trouble." Dixie admitted that Barney Stockwell had sent him around to Holmes to warn him off the case, but he didn't know who asked Stockwell. Broke into the Three Gables house belonging to Mrs. Mary Maberley with Barney Stockdale and took the only remaining copy of Douglas Maberley's tell-all book.

Frederic Dorr Ste   *Howard K. Elcock*

Dixon, Jeremy   [MISS]   Male Alive   Keeper of the dog Pompey, who lived somewhere in Trinity College.

Dixon, Mrs. [SOLI]   Female   She was a very respectable, elderly person, The lady-housekeeper for Mr Bob Carruthers.

Address : Hiltern Grange, about six miles from Farnham

Dobney, Miss Susan [LADY]   Female Alive   Lady Frances' old governess, who had long retired and lived in Camberwell. It was Miss Dobney who had consulted Holmes regarding the Disappearance of Lady Frances Carfax. For four years, Lady Frances had always written every second week to Her. Nearly five weeks had passed without a word. The last letter she had received was from the Hotel National at Lausanne. Lady Frances seemed to have left there and given no address.

Address : Camberwell

Dodd, James (Jimmie) M.   [BLAN]   Male Alive   A big, fresh, sunburned, upstanding Briton. Visited Holmes in January, 1903, just after the conclusion of the Boer War (11 October 1899 - 31 May 1902), Holmes deduced that he was from South Africa, in the Imperial Yeomanry, with the Middlesex Corps and was a stockbroker from Throgmorton Street. He had recently been staying at Tuxbury Old Park, the country home of his good army friend Godfrey Emsworth. He had been looking for details as to the disappearance of this friend. They had joined up together, in 1901 and were in the same squadron and became best friends. Godfrey had been hit with a bullet from an elephant gun in action near Diamond Hill outside-Pretoria, he was sent to a hospital at Cape Town and then been shipped off back to England. Dodd had received two letters from Godfrey, one from the Hospital and another from Southampton, but that had been over six months previous, and he had not heard anything since from his closest Pal. He wrote letters to Godfrey at Tuxbury Old Park, and Godfrey's father Colonel Emsworth (Emsworth the Crimean V.C.) had written back saying that his son was on a voyage round the world, and it was not likely that he would be back for a year. This didn't satisfy Dodd, so he wrote to Godfrey's mother, who invited him to stay, much to the annoyance of the Colonel. He and the Colonel didn't hit it off, right from the start Old Ralph the butler came into his room to make up the fire and they started talking about Godfrey, the butler said "He was a fine boy—and oh, sir, he was a fine man.", which Dodd seized on. Then old Ralph really put his foot in it, when Dodd asked if Godfrey was dead, he cried "'I wish to God he was!" Dodd began to speculate about what all this meant, but as he looked out his window, he saw Godfrey's pale white face staring in at him, When Godfrey saw that Dodd had seen him, he sprang back and ran away and Dodd tried to follow, but couldn't get the window open and so lost him in the grounds. The following day, he began searching for Godfrey in the grounds and was finally discovered by the Colonel, who ordered him out and that is when he approached Holmes. Holmes arranged to go down with him and another to Tuxbury Old Park and then Godfrey's story and plight were finally revealed.

Sherlock Holmes Quote : "When a gentleman of virile appearance enters my room with such tan upon his face as an English sun could never give, and with his handkerchief in his sleeve instead of in his pocket, it is not difficult to place him. You wear a short beard, which shows that you were not a regular. You have the cut of a riding-man. As to Middlesex, your card has already shown me that you are a stockbroker from Throgmorton Street. What other regiment would you join?"

Howard K. Elcock　　　　　　　　*Frederic Dorr Steele*

Dodd, Mr **[SUSS]** **Male** Junior Partner in a firm of solicitors. Part of the Firm Morrison, Morrison & Dodd They sent a letter to Holmes that read 46, OLD JEWRY, Nov. 19th. Re Vampires SIR: Our client, Mr. Robert Ferguson, of Ferguson and Muirhead, tea brokers, of Mincing Lane, has made some inquiry from us in a communication of even date concerning vampires. As our firm specialises entirely upon the assessment of machinery the matter hardly comes within our purview, and we have therefore recommended Mr. Ferguson to call upon you and lay the matter before you. We have not forgotten your successful action in the case of Matilda Briggs. We are, sir, Faithfully yours, MORRISON, MORRISON, AND DODD. per E.J.C.

Dolores, Ms **[SUSS]** **Female Alive** A tall, slim, brown-faced girl. She was the maid and friend rather than a servant of Mrs Ferguson. Had known Mrs Ferguson for many years, even before her marriage to Robert Ferguson.

Address : Cheeseman's, Lamberley, Sussex, South of Horsham

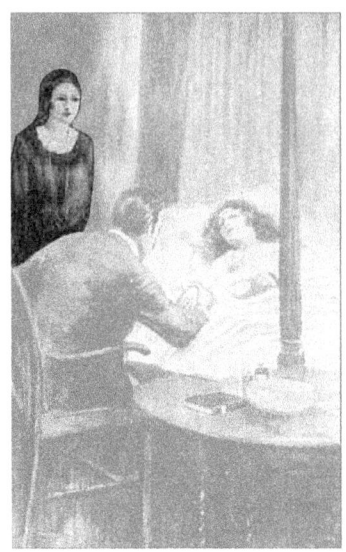

Howard K. Elcock

Dolsky in Odessa [STUD] dead One of the cases Holmes mentions, that was clearly one where the victim was forcible poisoned.

Dorak. A [CREE] Male Alive A Suave Bohemian, elderly man. Owner of a Large General Store. Supplied Professor Presbury with the 'Elixir of life' he was taking to remain young. It was derived from the Langur, the great black-faced monkey of the Himalayan slopes, biggest and most human of climbing monkeys.

Sherlock Holmes Quote : "Dorak—a curious name. Slavonic, I imagine"

Address : Commercial Road

Doran, Aloysius [NOBL] Male From San Francisco, Cal., U.S.A Millionaire from mining in McQuire's camp, near the Rockies. Father of the Bride, Miss Hatty Doran. Flora Millar made a disturbance at his house on the morning of the Wedding.

Address : Furnished house at Lancaster Gate

Doran, Miss Hatty [NOBL] Female Alive Lustrous black hair, the large dark eyes, and the exquisite mouth Only daughter of Aloysius Doran. Esq., of San Francisco, Cal., U.S.A Dowry would have run to considerably over the six figures. Wedding took place at St. George's, Hanover Square. Honeymoon would be passed at Lord Backwater's place, near Petersfield. Vanished after the wedding. She had met and married Frank Moulton back sometime in 1884-5. Thought Frank had been killed and was thus able to remarry, but Frank wasn't dead and turned up at the Wedding. They reunited and met with Lord St. Simon to resolved the situation.

Address : Furnished house at Lancaster Gate

Sidney Paget

Josef Friedrich

Dorking, Colonel [CHAS] Male Alive Was to have been married to Honourable Miss Miles. but the engagement was suddenly ended two days before their wedding. Milverton wanted £1200 from one of this party, but was not paid and so the wedding got called off.

Douglas, John [VALL] Male dead [His life in England] In age he may have been about fifty, with a strong-jawed, rugged face, a grizzling moustache, peculiarly keen grey eyes, and a wiry, vigorous figure which had lost nothing of the strength and activity of youth. He was cheery and genial to all, but somewhat offhand in his manners, giving the impression that he had seen life in social strata on some far lower horizon than the county society of Sussex. He had a remarkable face, bold grey eyes, a strong, short-clipped, grizzled moustache, a square, projecting chin, and a humorous mouth. [His life in America] He was a fresh-complexioned, middle-sized young man, not far, one would guess, from his thirtieth year. He has large, shrewd, humorous grey eyes which twinkle inquiringly from time to time as he looks round [His life in England] His body was found with horrible injuries to his head as a result of shotgun discharge. The shotgun had had it's triggers wired together so that both barrels went off simultaneously. He soon acquired a great popularity among the villagers, subscribing handsomely to all local objects, and attending their smoking concerts and other functions, where, having a remarkably rich tenor voice, he was always ready to oblige with an excellent song. He appeared to have plenty of money, which was said to have been gained in the California gold fields, and it was clear from his own talk and that of his wife that he had spent a part of his life in America. The good impression which had been produced by his generosity and by his democratic manners was increased by a reputation gained for utter indifference to danger. Though a wretched rider, he turned out at every meet, and took the most amazing falls in his determination to hold his own with the best. When the vicarage caught fire he distinguished himself also by the fearlessness with which he re-entered the building to save property, after the local fire brigade had given it up as impossible. Had owned Birlstone Manor House for five years. Was attacked by Ted Baldwin with a double barrelled sawn-off shotgun, but it was Baldwin who was killed. John Douglas' cloths were put on the now disfigured body of Ted Baldwin, but Douglas couldn't remove his wedding finger, so they just put on the rough nugget ring which made Holmes question the situation i.e. it now looked as if someone had removed the nugget ring, then the wedding ring and then put the nugget ring back on. Had concealed himself in a hiding place that may have once been used by King Charles within Birlstone Manor House. [His life in America] Was the Pinkerton man known as Birdy Edwards. Went undercover and joined the Scowrers of Vermissa Lodge 341 as John McMurdo, Lodge 29, Chicago. Bodymaster J.H. Scott. His back story was that he was a murderer and coiner in Chicago. Upon joining the Lodge was branded on his left forearm which was a circle with a triangle within it. Rose through the ranks, gaining power and influence. Rumours of a Pinkerton agent being in the valley surfaced and he arranged for the arrest of all of the leaders of the lodge when they gathered to trap the Pinkerton. His evidence was crucial in the conviction of members of the lodge, many being hanged, but Ted Baldwin escaped the death penalty but ended up in prison for around fifteen years.

Address : Birlstone Manor House

Frank Wiles   *Arthur I. Keller*

Douglas, Mrs. Ivy [VALL] Female Alive She was a beautiful woman, tall, dark, and slender, some twenty years younger than her husband she was an English lady who had met Mr. Douglas in London, he being at that time a widower. there were signs sometimes of some nerve-strain upon the part of Mrs. Douglas, and that she would display acute uneasiness if her absent husband should ever be particularly late in his return. Was involved in the conspiracy to pass off the dead body as being her husband. Escaped with her husband and set sail with him for South Africa, but he was murdered on the ship at the orders of Professor James Moriarty.

Address : Birlstone Manor House

Arthur I. Keller

Frank Wiles

Dovercourt, Earl of   [CHAS]   Male Alive   Was to have been married to Lady Eva Blackwell in a fortnight. His fiancée contacts Holmes to get some incriminating letters from Milverton.

Downing, Police-Constable   [WIST]   Male Alive   Police-constable involved in the capture of Aloysius Garcia's giant cook. He had his thumb nearly bitten off.

Arthur Twidle

Dowson, Old Baron [MAZA] Male dead Old Baron Dowson said the night before he was hanged that in Holmes' case what the law had gained the stage had lost.

Drebber, Elder [STUD] Male In PART II. The Country of the Saints section of the book. John Ferrier was provided with as large and as fertile a tract of land as any of the settlers, with the exception of Young himself, and of Stangerson, Kemball, Johnston, and Drebber, who were the four principal Elders. Elder Drebber is the father of Enoch J. Drebber.

Drebber, Enoch J. [STUD] Male dead Forty-three or forty-four years of age Middle-sized, broad shouldered, with crisp curling black hair, and a short stubbly beard. Dressed in a heavy broadcloth frock coat and waistcoat, with light-coloured trousers, and immaculate collar and cuffs. A top hat, well brushed and trim, was placed upon the floor beside him. His hands were clenched and his arms thrown abroad, while his lower limbs were interlocked as though his death struggle had been a grievous one. On his rigid face there stood an expression of horror. This malignant and terrible contortion, combined with the low forehead, blunt nose, and prognathous jaw gave the dead man a singularly simious and ape-like appearance, which was increased by his writhing, unnatural posture. distorted baboon-like countenance of the murdered man Drebber. Murdered in an empty house at 3, Lauriston Gardens, off the Brixton Road by Jefferson Hope. A wedding ring was found when his body was moved. In his pockets Drebber had ; A gold watch, No. 97163, by Barraud, of London. Gold Albert chain, very heavy and solid. Gold ring, with Masonic device. Gold pin—bull-dog's head, with rubies as eyes. Russian leather card-case, with cards of Enoch J. Drebber of Cleveland, corresponding with the E. J. D. upon the linen. No purse, but loose money to the extent of seven pounds thirteen. Pocket edition of Boccaccio's 'Decameron,' with name of Joseph Stangerson upon the fly-leaf. Two letters— one addressed to E. J. Drebber and one to Joseph Stangerson." While in America he had seven wives. Was once a member of the Mormon church, was responsible for the death of Lucy Ferrier, who he married in order to get her land. She was his wife for less than a month before she died of a broken heart.

Address : Cleveland, Ohio, U.S.A, Torquay Terrace, Camberwell

George Hutchinson   *Arthur Twidle*

Dubugue, Monsieur [NAVA] Male Holmes demonstrated the true facts of a case to Monsieur Dubugue of the Paris Police, who had wasted their energies upon what proved to be side-issues.

Dubuque, Monsieur [NAVA] Male See Dubugue, Monsieur

Dudevant, Baroness [REDH] Female dead See George Sand

Dunbar, Miss Grace [THOR] Female Alive The whole world has proclaimed that she also is a very beautiful woman. She was a brunette, tall, with a noble figure and commanding presence. She was Neil Gibson's Governess for his two children. Was accused of murdering Gibson's wife, Maria Gibson, who was found on Thor Bridge with a bullet in her head. It was true that she was the last person to see Maria Gibson, who actually held a note from Dunbar still in her hand, asking for the meeting, but there was no pistol next to her body. A revolver was found in Miss Dunbar's wardrobe, with one discharged chamber. She was arrested and sent to Winchester Prison, where she remained under guard until Holmes cleared her of the crime of murder.

Address : Thor Place, the Hampshire

G. Patrick Nelson   *G. Dutriac*

Dundas, Mr [IDEN] Male Alive   Teetotaller Details of the case appeared in the newspaper with the title 'A husband's cruelty to his wife' The conduct complained of was that he had drifted into the habit of winding up every meal by taking out his false teeth and hurling them at his wife

Dunlop, John Boyd [PRIO] Male (Real Person 1840 – 1921)   Scottish inventor and veterinary surgeon. reinvented the pneumatic tyres for his child's tricycle. Heidegger's bicycle tyre were not Dunlop, but Palmer.

Sherlock Holmes Quote : "I am familiar with forty-two different impressions left by tyres. This, as you perceive, is a Dunlop, with a patch upon the outer cover. Heidegger's tyres were Palmer's, leaving longitudinal stripes. Aveling, the mathematical master, was sure upon the point. Therefore, it is not Heidegger's track."

John Boyd Dunlop

Dunn, Josiah H   [VALL]   Male dead   New England Manager of a mine at
Crow Hill. Two assassins Lawlers and Andrews were sent over by the County
Delegate. Lawlers and Andrews arriving at the mine, Andrews walked up to
Josiah H. Dunn and shot him in the stomach, as he turned to run, Lawlers shot him
in the back and he went down sidewise, kicking and clawing among a heap of
clinkers. In the confusion the assassins escaped.

Frank Wiles

Dupin, Amantine Lucile Aurore [REDH] Female dead   See George Sand.

Dupin, C. Auguste [STUD]   Was a fictional character created by Edgar Allan Poe. Dupin made his first appearance in Poe's 1841 short story "The Murders in the Rue Morgue", widely considered the first detective fiction story.

Sherlock Holmes Quote : "No doubt you think that you are complimenting me in comparing me to Dupin," he observed. "Now, in my opinion, Dupin was a very inferior fellow. That trick of his of breaking in on his friends' thoughts with an apropos remark after a quarter of an hour's silence is really very showy and superficial. He had some analytical genius, no doubt; but he was by no means such a phenomenon as Poe appeared to imagine."

Address : 33 Rue Donat, Faubourg St. Germln. Paris.

Frederic Theodore Lix

Durando, Signora Victor [WIST] Female Alive See Miss Burnet

Durando, Victor [WIST] Male dead   Husband to Miss Burnet. The San Pedro minister in London. Met and married Miss Burnet there. A nobler man never lived upon earth. Unhappily, Murillo heard of his excellence, recalled him on some pretext, and had him shot. With a premonition of his fate he had refused to take his wife with him.

E is for Empty House

E.J.C. **[SUSS]** **Alive** A clerk or a secretary working in the firm of solicitors called Morrison, Morrison & Dodd, who sent out this letter to Holmes which read:

46, OLD JEWRY,

Nov. 19th.

Re Vampires

SIR:

Our client, Mr. Robert Ferguson, of Ferguson and Muirhead, tea brokers, of Mincing Lane, has made some inquiry from us in a communication of even date concerning vampires. As our firm specialises entirely upon the assessment of machinery the matter hardly comes within our purview, and we have therefore recommended Mr. Ferguson to call upon you and lay the matter before you. We have not forgotten your successful action in the case of Matilda Briggs.

We are, sir,

Faithfully yours,

MORRISON, MORRISON, AND DODD. per E.J.C.

Eccles, Mr. John Scott **[WIST]** **Male Alive** A stout, tall, grey-whiskered and solemnly respectable person. Had heavy features and a pompous manner. wore spats and gold-rimmed spectacles He was a Conservative, a churchman, a good citizen, orthodox and conventional to the last degree. Very sociable. Cultivate a large number of friends. It was at the retired brewer Melville, that he was introduced to Aloysius Garcia, of Spanish descent who had some connection with the embassy. Was invited down to stay with Garcia at Wisteria Lodge, near Esher. The following morning, he discovered that the lodge was empty, sent a telegram to Holmes who read the telegram aloud.

"HAVE JUST HAD MOST INCREDIBLE AND GROTESQUE EXPERIENCE. MAY I CONSULT YOU?—SCOTT ECCLES, POST OFFICE, CHARING CROSS." Visited 221b baker street and was joined by police inspectors, Gregson and Baynes. and so the story started.

Address : Popham House, Lee

Frederic Dorr Steele   *Arthur Twidle*

Eckermann, Johann Peter   [WIST]   Male dead (Real Person 1792 – 1854)
Eckermann's Voodooism and the Negroid Religions: was a fictitious book. But Johann Peter Eckermann did exist and was a German poet and author.

Sherlock Holmes Quote : "I spent a morning in the British Museum reading up on that and other points. Here is a quotation from Eckermann's Voodooism and the Negroid Religions:"

Johann Peter Eckermann

Edison, Thomas Alva   [HOUN]   Male Alive (Real Person 1847 – 1931)
American Inventor who co-invented the Electric Lamp (see Joseph Swan). The
British Company of Edison and Swan United Electric Light Company or Ediswan
produced Electric lamps from 1883 onwards. Sir Henry Baskerville said "I'll have
a row of electric lamps up here inside of six months, and you won't know it again,
with a thousand candlepower Swan and Edison right here in front of the hall
door."

Thomas Edison

Edmunds, Detective   [VEIL]   Male Alive A smart lad. A thin, yellow-haired
man. County detective of the Berkshire Constabulary. He said, in so many words,
that when Mr. Ronder was drunk, he was horrible. Was worried about the death of
Mr. Ronder, as Holmes said "It was so deucedly difficult to reconstruct the affair.
Look at it from the lion's point of view. He is liberated. What does he do? He
takes half a dozen bounds forward, which brings him to Ronder. Ronder turns to
fly—the claw-marks were on the back of his head —but the lion strikes him down.
Then, instead of bounding on and escaping, he returns to the woman, who was
close to the cage, and he knocks her over and chews her face up. Then, again,
those cries of hers would seem to imply that her husband had in some way failed
her. What could the poor devil have done to help her? You see the difficulty?"

Edward Hyde, 1st Earl of Clarendon   [HOUN]   Male dead   Dr. Mortimer related the history of the Baskervilles saying "Know then that in the time of the Great Rebellion (the history of which by the learned Lord Clarendon I most earnestly commend to your attention)..." The History of the Rebellion by Edward Hyde, 1st Earl of Clarendon is his account of the English Civil War. This work (originally published in 1702–1704 as The History of the Rebellion and Civil Wars in England) was the first full-scale, detailed history of the Civil War and was written by a key player in the events contained within it.

Edwards, Birdy   [VALL]   Male dead   See John Douglas

Egan, Brother   [VALL]   Male in prison   Scowrer. Tried to claim the head money given by the lodge for the shooting of old man Crabbe over at Stylestown. This money was also claimed by Lander.

Eley, Charles   [SPEC]   Male dead (Real Person 1797 – 1875)   The brothers Charles and William gained public attention through an advertisement in the London Morning Chronicle on 10th July 1828 and from then on manufactured and sold cartridges. The Eley No.2 Webley revolver chambered for an Eley cartridge. Indeed, some of the discussion touches on the fact that an ammunition label might read something like "Eley's Cartridges for Webley's No. 2 Revolver" .... At any rate, the revolver would likely be either a .440 rimfire Webley "Revolver No. 2" - i.e. "The British Bull Dog" or a Webley R.I.C. No. 2 revolver.

Eley, William   [SPEC]   Male dead (Real Person 1794 – 1841)   Brother of Charles, started the Eley cartridge company in London on 10th July 1828. The brothers gained public attention through an advertisement in the London Morning Chronicle on 10th July 1828 and from then on manufactured and sold cartridges. The Eley No.2 Webley revolver chambered for an Eley cartridge. Indeed, some of the discussion touches on the fact that an ammunition label might read something like "Eley's Cartridges for Webley's No. 2 Revolver" .... At any rate, the revolver would likely be either a .440 rimfire Webley "Revolver No. 2" - i.e. "The British Bull Dog" or a Webley R.I.C. No. 2 revolver

Elise, (friend of Lysander Stark [ENGR] Female Alive Eager and beautiful face. Spoke in Broken English. It is possible that she was the wife or sister of Lysander Stark. Called Lysander Stark 'Fritz' Tried to stop Lysander Stark killing Victor Hatherley.

Josef Friedrich

Gaston Simoes da Fonseca

Elman, Rev J.C. [RETI] Male Alive He was a big, solemn, rather pompous clergyman. Holmes faked a telegram from this clergyman and sent Watson and Amberley on a wild goose chase, so that he could have a good look around the inside of Amberley's home. Holmes' Telegram read;

"COME AT ONCE WITHOUT FAIL. CAN GIVE YOU INFORMATION AS TO YOUR RECENT LOSS. ELMAN. THE VICARAGE."

Holmes got his vicar's details by looking in Crockford's Clerical Directory. When Watson and Amberley interviewed him, they found that he had not sent this message and was very upset and would be contacting the police to investigate this scandalous forgery.

Frank Wiles

Elrige, Mr [DANC] Male Alive Owner of the farm Elrige's Farmer who lived some miles off in the direction of East Ruston. Lived on a very lonely farm and supported his income by renting out rooms. Rented out to Mr. Abe Slaney from America.

Address : Elrige's Farm, East Ruston

Emsworth, Colonel [BLAN] Male Alive A huge, bow-backed man with a smoky skin and a straggling grey beard, He had a red-veined nose jutted out like a vulture's beak, and two fierce grey eyes under tufted brows. Was a hard nail. His only son was Godfrey. Won the V.C. for his actions in the Crimean war (16 October 1853 - 30 March 1856) Was called 'Emsworth the Crimean V.C.' He was the greatest martinet in the Army in his day, and it was a day of rough language, too. When his son returned from the Boer War, he tried to keep everyone away, but a really good friend of Godfrey wouldn't let matters lie and proved to be troublesome. Eventually Holmes and Sir James Saunders were able to bring about a happy ending.

Address : Tuxbury Old Park

Howard K. Elcock

Frederic Dorr Steele

Emsworth, Godfrey [BLAN] Male Alive His appearance was certainly extraordinary. One could see that he had indeed been a handsome man with clear-cut features sunburned by an African sun, but mottled in patches over this darker surface were curious whitish patches which had bleached his skin. Volunteered for Imperial Yeomanry, with the Middlesex Corps in January 1901 and became best mates with James M. Dodd. Lance-Corporal of B Squadron. He was involved in a morning fights at Buffelsspruit (Buffelspruit), outside Pretoria and was hit with an elephant bullet thought his shoulder. His two countrymen Baldy Simpson and Anderson were both killed, but Godfrey managed to get away on horse, but loss of blood , caused him to fall off his horse and it was not until night-time that he woke up. Seeing a fairly large house in the close by, he staggered to it, went in and collapsed on a bed. In the morning when he awoke, he discovered that he had entered a Leper colony and had slept in one of the resident's bed. He was put into a private room, treated kindly, and within a week or so was removed to the general hospital at Pretoria and thence to Tuxbury Old Park and kept in secret under the care of the Surgeon Mr. Kent. He developed every symptom of Leprosy. When his best friend James Dodd arrived, he wanted to at least see his friend, who he had not seen in some time, so he left the remote estate lodge where he was living and peered in through Dodd's bedroom window, but he got to close and was spotted and only just managed to elude his chasing friend. Was eventually examined by specialist Sir James Saunders, who found that he was suffering from pseudo-leprosy or ichthyosis, a scale-like affection of the skin, unsightly, obstinate, but possibly curable, and certainly non-infective.

Address : Tuxbury Old Park

Howard K. Elcock   Paul Thiriat

Emsworth, Mrs [BLAN] Female Alive A gentle little white mouse of a
woman. She really wanted to hear about her son's adventure and invited James M.
Dodd to come and stay and talk about them, much to her husband's annoyance.
She fainted at the end of the story on hearing the good news and had to be treated
by Mr. Kent.

Ernest, Dr. Ray   [RETI] Male dead   Young Doctor friend of Josiah
Amberley. Liked to play chess. His family had employed the private detective Mr.
Barker to look into his disappearance. Called a Lothario by Josiah Amberley. Was
said to have run away with Amberley's wife and seven thousand pounds in cash
and securities. Was actually gassed and buried, along with Mrs. Amberley, in a
disused well, cleverly concealed by a dog-kennel.

Escott, Mr. **[CHAS]** **Male Alive** See Sherlock Holmes. Holmes said he was a plumber with a rising business, Escott used to walk out with Agatha, Milverton's Maid, each evening, in order find out information about Milverton and his house. She would lock up the dog, so that he could call.

Frederic Dorr Steele

Etherege, Mrs. **[IDEN]** **Female Alive** Mrs. Etherege recommended Sherlock Holmes to Mary Sutherland. The detective found her husband so easily when the police and everyone had given him up for dead.

Euclid of Alexandria **[STUD,SIGN]** **Male dead (Real Person 4th century BC – 3rd century BC)** Referred to by Watson "His conclusions were as infallible as so many propositions of Euclid" [STUD] The Fifth Proposition is if a straight line falling on two straight lines make the interior angles on the same side less than two right angles, the two straight lines, if produced indefinitely, meet on that side on which are the angles less than the two right angles. Founder of Geometry and Greek mathematician. [STUD] Referred to by Watson "His conclusions were as infallible as so many propositions of Euclid" The Fifth Proposition is if a straight line falling on two straight lines make the interior angles on the same side less than two right angles, the two straight lines, if produced indefinitely, meet on that side on which are the angles less than the two right angles.

Sherlock Holmes Quote : [SIGN] "Honestly, I cannot congratulate you upon it. Detection is, or ought to be, an exact science, and should be treated in the same cold and unemotional manner. You have attempted to tinge it with romanticism, which produces much the same effect as if you worked a love-story or an elopement into the fifth proposition of Euclid."

Euclid

Evans, (Convict [GLOR] Male Alive See Mr. Beddoes

Evans, Carrie [SHOS] Female Alive A florid young woman. Had been a maid for Lady Beatrice Falder for five years. Married to Mr. Norlett But devoted to Sir Robert Norberton (gossip from Mr. Mason)

Address : Shoscombe Old Place

Frank Wiles

Evans, Killer **[3GAR]** **Male Alive** See John Garrideb

Evans, Policemen **[VALL]** **Male dead** One of two Policeman shot dead because they had ventured to arrest two members of the society. The other Policeman shot was called Hunt.

F is for the Final Problem

Faber, Johann Eberhard [3STU] Male dead (Real Person 1822 – 1879) Pencil Manufacturer. Pieces of pencil, where the miscreant had sharpened it were found by Holmes and they include a chip with the letters 'NN' on them.

Sherlock Holmes Quote : "You are aware that Johann Faber is the most common maker's name. Is it not clear that there is just as much of the pencil left as usually follows the Johann?"

Johann Eberhard Faber

Fairbairn, Alec [CARD] Male dead In James Browner's confession at the end of the story he says of Alec Fairbairn "He was a man with winning ways, and he made friends wherever he went. He was a dashing, swaggering chap, smart and curled, who had seen half the world and could talk of what he had seen. He was good company, I won't deny it, and he had wonderful polite ways with him for a sailor man, so that I think there must have been a time when he knew more of the poop than the forecastle. For a month he was in and out of my house, and never once did it cross my mind that harm might come of his soft, tricky ways. And then at last something made me suspect, and from that day my peace was gone forever." Friend of Sarah Cushing, Lover of Mary Cushing and murder victim of James Browner.

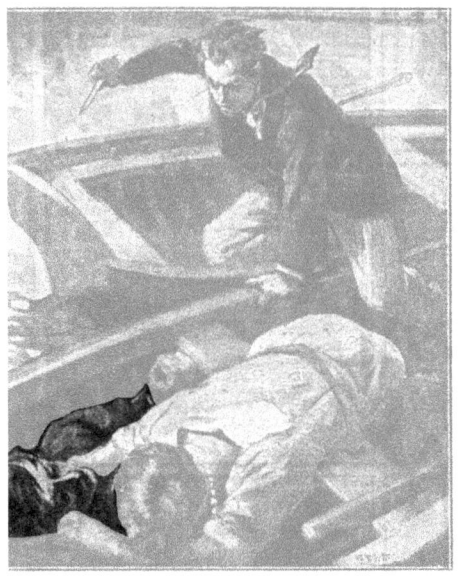

G. Dutriac

Sidney Paget

Falder, Hugo [SHOS] Male dead   Ancestor of Sir James Falder, his grave was found Holmes as he made a very careful examination of the crypt.

Address : Shoscombe Old Place

Falder, Lady Beatrice [SHOS] Female dead   The widowed sister of Sir Robert Norberton. Shoscombe Old Place belonged to her late husband, Sir James. Norberton had no claim on it at all. It was only a life interest and reverted to her husband's brother. Meantime, she drew the rents every year and Norberton spent it. She had a weak heart and dropsy. Carrie Evans was her maid and had been with her five years. She died at the end of April 1902 of Dropsy. Since that time Mr. Norlett had been masquerading as Lady Beatrice, riding in her carriage, etc. Her Body was hidden in the crypt and her dog given to Barnes, Josiah, the Landlord of the Green Dragon. Her body was moved to the crypt by Mr. Norlett and Sir Robert. Holmes discovered her body in the crypt and then Sir Robert Norberton was force to tell the story.

Address : Shoscombe Old Place

Frederic Dorr Steele

Falder, Norman   [SHOS]   Male dead   Ancestor of Sir James Falder, his grave was found Holmes as he made a very careful examination of the crypt.

Address : Shoscombe Old Place

Falder, Odo   [SHOS]   Male dead   Ancestor of Sir James Falder, his grave was found Holmes as he made a very careful examination of the crypt.

Address : Shoscombe Old Place

Falder, Sir Denis   [SHOS]   Male dead   Ancestor of Sir James Falder, his grave was found Holmes as he made a very careful examination of the crypt. He died in the eighteenth century.

Address : Shoscombe Old Place

Falder, Sir James   [SHOS]   Male dead   Deceased husband of Lady Beatrice Falder, the sister of Sir Robert Norberton. He would have been buried in the Crypt on the Estate. His wife only had a life interest in the estate and after her death the estate would pass to his brother.

Address : Shoscombe Old Place

Falder, Sir William **[SHOS]** **Male dead** Ancestor of Sir James Falder, his grave was found by Holmes as he made a very careful examination of the crypt. He died in the eighteenth century.

Address : Shoscombe Old Place

Farintosh, Mrs. **[SPEC]** **Female Alive** Holmes helped in the hour of her sore need. She gave Helen Stoner Holmes' address. The Farintosh case was concerned with an opal tiara, which took place before Holmes met Watson.

Farquhar, Mr. **[STOC]** **Male Unknown** He had St. Vitus's dance. Old doctor from whom Watson purchased his practice. Based in the Paddington district.

Ferguson, Baby **[SUSS]** **Male Alive** A very beautiful child, dark-eyed, golden-haired, a wonderful mixture of the Saxon and the Latin. He had a small, angry red pucker upon his cherub throat. Unnamed baby of the unnamed wife of Robert Ferguson. The potential murder victim of this story. Had only been saved by the swift actions of his mother. Was cared for by the Nurse Mrs. Mason.

Address : Cheeseman's, Lamberley, Sussex, South of Horsham

G. Dutriac   *Howard K. Elcock*

Ferguson, Captain   [3GAB]   Male Unknown   A retired sea captain who owned the house before Mrs. Maberley. Holmes asked if there was anything remarkable about him, and if he had buried something. Mrs. Maberley answered in the negative.

Address : old address was The Three Gables, Harrow Weald

Ferguson, Jack   [SUSS]   Male Alive   Walked with a curious, shambling gait which showed that he was suffering from a weak spine. Child from first marriage of Robert Ferguson. Mr. Robert Ferguson had a rather rose-tinted view of his son Jack "he is a poor little inoffensive cripple.... The dearest, most loving heart within." He had been experimenting with the poison curare tipped arrows from the quiver of a small bird bow that had been on display in the house. Had tested the effectiveness of the poison on the dog, first and found that it paralysed the dog's back legs, then tried to poison the baby, but was discovered by Mrs. Ferguson, who sucked the poison from the wound and was discovered with blood on her lips. Was beaten with a stick and once, very savagely, with Mrs. Ferguson's hand. After his actions were revealed by Holmes, he suggested that sending jack away for a year at sea would be the best course of action.

Address : Cheeseman's, Lamberley, Sussex, South of Horsham

Howard K. Elcock

Ferguson, Mr [ENGR] Male Alive A short thick man with a chinchilla beard growing out of the creases of his double chin. Colonel Lysander Stark's secretary and manager. Appeared to be a morose and silent man, There wasn't a man in the parish who has a better-lined waistcoat. He was a Coiner.

Ferguson, Mr. [THOR] Male Alive Secretary to Neil Gibson, the Gold King. He told Gibson's Estate manager, Mr. Bates that Gibson would be visiting Holmes, which caused Mr. Bates to see Holmes first and warn him of Gibson's true nature.

Ferguson, Mrs. [SUSS] Female Alive The lady was very beautiful First name not revealed in this story. Had been married to Robert Ferguson for five years. Daughter of a Peruvian merchant, with whom Ferguson had met in connection with the importation of nitrates. Probably Roman Catholic. Was accused of drinking the blood of her new born baby boy, but was actually sucking out the poison from a bird-bow arrow wound. Had a maid and friend called Dolores, who had known her for many years.

Address : Cheeseman's, Lamberley, Sussex, South of Horsham

G. Dutriac

Wladyslaw Teodor Benda

Ferguson, Robert [SUSS] Male Alive Big Bob Ferguson, the finest three-quarter Richmond ever had. He was always a good-natured chap. Had been A long, slab-sided man with loose limbs and a fine turn of speed which had carried him round many an opposing back. Was now His great frame had fallen in, his flaxen hair was scanty, and his shoulders were bowed. Tea merchant on Mincing Lane. Acquaintance of Watson, he had been a three-quarter for Richmond in a Rugby game, years ago, when Watson played for Blackheath. He send the following letter to Holmes at the start of the story.

DEAR MR HOLMES: I have been recommended to you by my lawyers, but indeed the matter is so extraordinarily delicate that it is most difficult to discuss. It concerns a friend for whom I am acting. This gentleman married some five years ago a Peruvian lady, the daughter of a Peruvian merchant, whom he had met in connection with the importation of nitrates. The lady was very beautiful, but the fact of her foreign birth and of her alien religion always caused a separation of interests and of feelings between husband and wife, so that after a time his love may have cooled towards her and he may have come to regard their union as a mistake. He felt there were sides of her character which he could never explore or understand. This was the more painful as she was as loving a wife as a man could have—to all appearance absolutely devoted. Now for the point which I will make more plain when we meet. Indeed, this note is merely to give you a general idea of the situation and to ascertain whether you would care to interest yourself in the matter. The lady began to show some curious traits quite alien to her ordinarily sweet and gentle disposition. The gentleman had been married twice and he had one son by the first wife. This boy was now fifteen, a very charming and affectionate youth, though unhappily injured through an accident in childhood. Twice the wife was caught in the act of assaulting this poor lad in the most unprovoked way. Once she struck him with a stick and left a great weal on his arm. This was a small matter, however, compared with her conduct to her own child, a dear boy just under one year of age. On one occasion about a month ago this child had been left by its nurse for a few minutes. A loud cry from the baby, as of pain, called the nurse back. As she ran into the room she saw her employer, the lady, leaning over the baby and apparently biting his neck. There was a small wound in the neck from which a stream of blood had escaped. The nurse was so horrified that she wished to call the husband, but the lady implored her not to do so and actually gave her £5 as a price for her silence. No explanation was ever given, and for the moment the matter was passed over. It left, however, a terrible impression upon the nurse's mind, and from that time she began to watch her mistress closely and to keep a closer guard upon the baby, whom she tenderly loved. It seemed to her that even as she watched the mother, so the mother watched her, and that every time she was compelled to leave the baby alone the mother was waiting to get at it. Day and night the nurse covered the child, and day and night the silent, watchful mother seemed to be lying in wait as a wolf waits for a lamb. It must read most incredible to you, and yet I beg you to take it seriously, for a child's life and a man's sanity may depend upon it. At last there came one dreadful day when the facts could no longer be concealed from the husband. The nurse's nerve had given way; she could stand the strain no longer, and she made a clean breast of it all to the man. To him it seemed as wild a tale as it may now seem to you. He knew his wife to be a loving wife, and, save for the assaults upon her stepson, a loving mother. Why, then, should she wound her own dear little baby? He told the nurse that she was dreaming, that her suspicions were those of a lunatic, and that such libels upon her mistress were not to be tolerated. While they were talking a sudden cry of pain was heard. Nurse and master rushed together to the nursery. Imagine his feelings, Mr. Holmes, as he saw his wife rise from a kneeling position beside the cot and saw blood upon the child's exposed neck and upon the sheet. With a cry of horror, he turned his wife's face to the light and saw blood all round her lips. It was she—she beyond all question—who had drunk the poor baby's blood. So the matter stands. She is now confined to her room. There has been no explanation. The husband is half demented. He knows, and I know, little of vampirism beyond the name. We had thought it was some wild tale of foreign parts. And yet here in the very heart of the English Sussex—well, all this can be discussed with you in the morning. Will you see me? Will you use your great powers in aiding a distracted man? If so, kindly wire to Ferguson, Cheeseman's, Lamberley, and I will be at your rooms by ten o'clock.

Yours faithfully,

ROBERT FERGUSON.

P.S. I believe your friend Watson played Rugby for Blackheath when I was three-quarter for Richmond. It is the only personal introduction which I can give. He tried to pretend that his was happening to a friend of his, but Holmes was not fooled for one second. Was worried that his wife was drinking the blood from his baby son.

Address : Cheeseman's, Lamberley, Sussex, South of Horsham

Howard K. Elcock   *Wladyslaw Teodor Benda*

Ferrers, Mr [PRIO] Holmes mentioned the Ferrers Documents as one excuse for not being able to help Thorneycroft Huxtable. He changed his mind.

Sherlock Holmes Quote : "My colleague, Dr. Watson, could tell you that we are very busy at present. I am retained in this case of the Ferrers Documents, and the Abergavenny murder is coming up for trial. Only a very important issue could call me from London at present."

Ferrier, Bob [STUD] Male dead Brother of Lucy Ferrier. If he had survived, he would have been adopted by John Ferrier, like his sister, but he died on the trail.

Ferrier, Dr. [NAVA] Male Alive Doctor who lived close to Percy Phelps, who was travelling on the same train and took charge of him because he had a fit in the station, and before they reached home, Phelps was practically a raving maniac. Explained what had happened to Annie Harrison, who decided that Percy Phelps should stay in Joseph Harrison's bedroom.

Ferrier, John [STUD] Male dead All members of the wagon train had died on the trip except for himself and Lucy Ferrier. Father of Lucy Ferrier, who he brought up from the age of five. Rescued by passing Mormons trying to find the promised land. Had to become a Mormon in order to be rescued. Worked hard and became rich, but as soon as Lucy Ferrier became of marrying age, tried to escape with her, but was killed by Joseph Stangerson.

George Hutchinson   *D. H. Friston*

Ferrier, Lucy [STUD] Female dead Born sometime in 1842 Mother died
when she was five years old. All members of the wagon train she was in, died on
the trip except for her and John Ferrier. They were rescued by Mormons and taken
to Salt Lake City, but had to convert to Mormonism. Ferrier is not her real name,
but the last name of her 'adopted' father John Ferrier. As year succeeded to year
she grew taller and stronger, her cheek more ruddy, and her step more elastic. Fell
in love with Jefferson Hope, but was forced to Marry Enoch Drebber. Died from a
broken heart within the month.

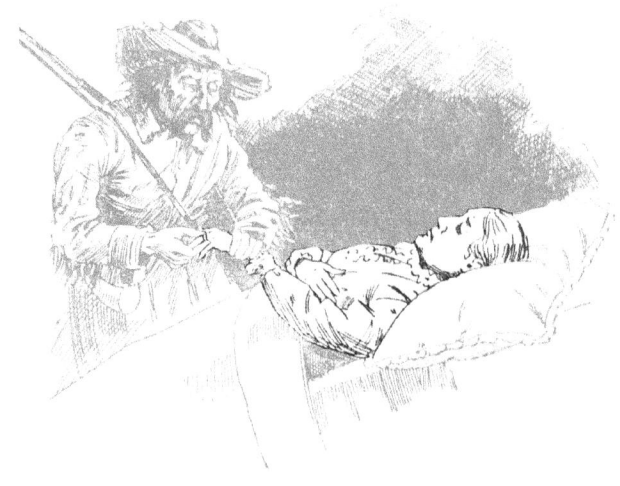

Richard Gutschmidt   *George Hutchinson*

Ffolliott, Sir George   [WIST]   Male Alive   Owner of a large house in the Esher area. His details were sent to Holmes by the Allan brothers, chief land agents in the village of Esher.

Address : Oxshott Towers, Esher

Fisher, Dr. Penrose   [DYIN]   Male Alive   When Holmes refused to let Watson examine him to see what illness he had, Watson suggested other Doctors that Holmes might find more acceptable, one of them was Penrose Fisher Watson regarded him as one of the best Doctors in London.

Flaccus, Quintus Horatius   [IDEN]   Male dead   See Horace

Flaubert, Gustave   [REDH]   Male dead (Real Person 1821 - 1880   Referenced at the end of the story along with George Sands Regarded as the prime mover of the realist novelist school of French Literature. Best known for his masterpiece, Madame Bovary (1857) Corresponded with George Sands from 1863-1876. Had a Parrot called Loulou

Sherlock Holmes Quote : "Well, perhaps, after all, it is of some little use, 'L'homme c'est rien–l'oeuvre c'est tout,' as Gustave Flaubert wrote to George Sand."

Gustave Flaubert

Flowers, Lord   [SECO]   Male Alive   A note from this gentleman was still in the Right Honourable Trelawney Hope's despatch box.

Forbes, Inspector   [NAVA]   Male Alive   Inspector of Scotland Yard. He was decidedly frigid in his manner to Holmes and Watson, especially when he heard the errand upon which they had come. He says "I've heard of your methods before now, Mr. Holmes. You are ready enough to use all the information that the police can lay at your disposal, and then you try to finish the case yourself and bring discredit on them." Holmes responds "On the contrary, out of my last fifty-three cases my name has only appeared in four, and the police have had all the credit in forty-nine. I don't blame you for not knowing this, for you are young and inexperienced, but if you wish to get on in your new duties you will work with me and not against me." Only appeared in this one Story.

Sidney Paget

Sidney Paget

Ford, Henry   [LAST]   Male   American industrialist and car builder. Watson drove Altamont (Holmes) to his rendezvous with Von Bork in a little Ford car.

Fordham, Dr.   [GLOR]   Male Alive   Doctor who tried to save the life of Old Trevor, but to no avail.

Fordham, Mr.   [FIVE]   Male Alive   Mr. Fordham was a Horsham lawyer. Elias Openshaw asked his servant Mary to send down Mr. Fordham, the Horsham lawyer. Drew up Elias Openshaw's will leaving everything to his brother Joseph.

Forrester, Inspector   [REIG]   Male Alive   He was a smart, keen-faced young fellow. Police official from Surrey. He was in charge of the Reigate squire case. He knew Holmes by reputation and asked him to help. Was worried that Holmes was not quite himself. Almost tipped off the culprits to an important piece of evidence and Holmes had to fake a faint in order to distract him.

Sidney Paget

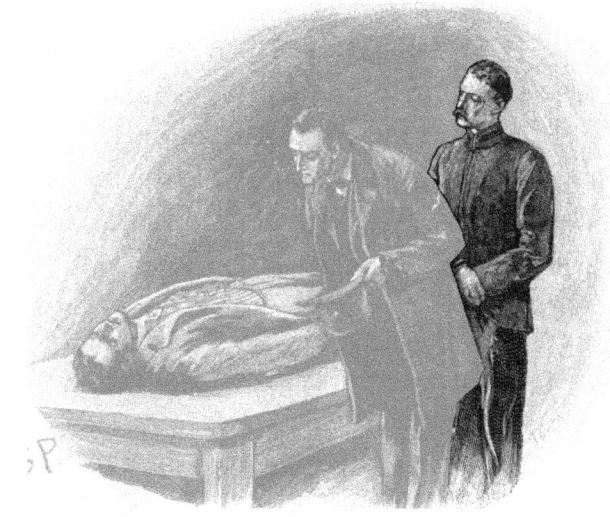

Sidney Paget

Forrester, Mrs. Cecil   [SIGN]   Female Alive   Employer of Mary Morstan. Holmes was Involved in her case to unravel a little domestic complication A middle-aged, graceful woman.

Sherlock Holmes Quote : "I believe that I was of some slight service to her. The case, however, as I remember it, was a very simple one."

Address : Lower Camberwell

Fortescue, Mr   [3STU]   Male   Person who established the Fortescue Scholarship. The Three students, Gilchrist, Daulat Ras and Miles McLaren were working towards this Scholarship, but one of them cheated.

Fournaye, Mme. Henri   [SECO]   Female In a mental ward of a hospital Wife of man posing as Mr. Eduardo Lucas, but whose real name was Henri Fournaye. Returned to Paris from a trip to London, insane after killing her husband, who had been leading a double life. Of Creole origin and was of an extremely excitable nature. She had suffered in the past from attacks of jealousy which had amounted to frenzy. It was conjectured that it was in one of these that she committed the terrible crime which had caused such a sensation in London. It was probable, that the crime was either committed while she was insane, or that it's immediate effect was to drive the unhappy woman out of her mind. At present she was unable to give any coherent account of the past, and the doctors hold out no hopes of the re-establishment of her reason.

Address : Small villa in the Rue Austerlitz

Fowler, Mr [COPP] Male Alive A small bearded man in a grey suit. "Mr. Fowler was a very kind-spoken, free-handed gentleman," said Mrs. Toller serenely. Later married Miss Rucastle, by special license, in Southampton the day after their flight, and he is now the holder of a government appointment in the island of Mauritius. Was a good seaman. Paid Mrs. Toller to help him in affecting an escape of Alice Rucastle.

Ernest Flammarion

Frankland, Mr. [HOUN] Male Alive He was an elderly man, red-faced, white-haired, and choleric. His passion was for the British law, and he had spent a large fortune in litigation. He fought for the mere pleasure of fighting and was equally ready to take up either side of a question, so that it is no wonder that he had found it a costly amusement. Sometimes he would shut up a right of way and defy the parish to make him open it. At others he would with his own hands tear down some other man's gate and declare that a path had existed there from time immemorial, defying the owner to prosecute him for trespass. He was learned in old manorial and communal rights, and he applied his knowledge sometimes in favour of the villagers of Fernworthy and sometimes against them, so that he was periodically either carried in triumph down the village street or else burned in effigy, according to his latest exploit. He was said to have about seven lawsuits upon his hands at present, which would probably swallow up the remainder of his fortune and so draw his sting and leave him harmless for the future. Apart from the law he seems a kindly, good-natured person He thought he knew who was helping the convict Selden, out on the moors, but he had actually discovered the means that Holmes was employing to keep up to date with Watson's letters and acquire food and drink. Had a daughter Laura Lyons, with whom he was estranged.

Address : Lafter Hall, Dartmoor

Sidney Paget

Raymond Pallier

Fraser, Miss Mary   [ABBE]   Female Alive   See Lady Mary Brackenstall.

Fraser, the tutor   [HOUN]   Male dead   Mr. Vandeleur (Later Jack Stapleton) had struck up an acquaintance with a consumptive tutor upon his voyage home from America, Vandeleur used this man's ability to make the running of the school (St. Oliver's) a success. Fraser, the tutor, died however, and the school which had begun well sank from disrepute into infamy.

Address : St. Oliver's Private School, Yorkshire

Freebody, Major   [FIVE]   Male Alive   Old friend of Joseph Openshaw. Major Freebody was in command of one of the forts upon Portsdown Hill. Joseph Openshaw went to visit him on 7th January 1885

G is for Gloria Scott

Gaboriau, Emile [STUD] Male dead (Real Person 1832 – 1873) French Writer and pioneer of Detective fiction. Invented the detective Monsieur Lecoq

Sherlock Holmes Quote : "Lecoq was a miserable bungler, he had only one thing to recommend him, and that was his energy. That book made me positively ill. The question was how to identify an unknown prisoner. I could have done it in twenty-four hours. Lecoq took six months or so. It might be made a textbook for detectives to teach them what to avoid."

Emile Gaboriau

Gabriel, Archangel [VEIL] Male Alive   Gabriel means 'God is my strength' He certainly was a busy angel visiting lots of religious leaders. Other Archangels include, Michael and Raphael. Mrs. Ronder likened Leonardo the strongman to the angel Gabriel(thereby demoting Gabriel from his normal title of Archangel). "Then Leonardo came more and more into my life. You see what he was like. I know now the poor spirit that was hidden in that splendid body, but compared to my husband he seemed like the angel Gabriel."

Archangel Gabriel

Garcia, Beryl   [HOUN]   Female Alive   See Mrs. Beryl Stapleton

Garcia, Mr.   [WIST]   Male The former highest dignitary in San Pedro. His son was Aloysius Garcia.

Garcia, Mr. Aloysius   [WIST]   Male dead   Met with John Scott Eccles at a meal hosted by a retired brewer called Melville. Was of Spanish descent. Said that he was connected in some way with the embassy. Was actually the son of the former highest dignitary in San Pedro. Rented Wisteria Lodge from the Allan Brothers. Invited Eccles to stay for a few days. His dead body was discovered on Oxshott Common, nearly a mile from his home. His head had been smashed to pulp by heavy blows of a sandbag or some such instrument, which had crushed rather than wounded. I He had apparently been struck down first from behind, but his assailant had gone on beating him long after he was dead. It was a most furious assault. He attempted to kill Don Murillo, once call the Tiger of San Pedro, but was ambushed when his plot was discovered.

Address : Wisteria Lodge, near Esher

G. Dutriac

Garrideb, Alexander Hamilton   [3GAR]   Male dead   Rich American
Deceased Landowner who made his money in real estate, and afterwards in the
wheat pit at Chicago, then he spent it in buying up as much land as would make
one of an English county, lying along the Arkansas River, west of Fort Dodge He
was supposed to have left money to three Garridebs if they could be found. 5
million dollars each was promised.

Garrideb, Howard   [3GAR]   Male Alive   See John Garrideb Alias used by the
person claiming to be John Garrideb. He put an advertisement into a local
Birmingham paper saying

HOWARD GARRIDEB CONSTRUCTOR OF AGRICULTURAL
MACHINERY Binders, reapers, steam-and hand-plows, drills, harrows, farmer's
carts, buckboards, and all other appliances. Estimates for Artesian Wells. Apply
Grosvenor Buildings, Aston He intended that the advertisement would make
Nathan Garrideb leave his house, so that he could get to at the printing press
hidden in a secret room. Holmes saw through this ruse, with all the Americanisms
in the advert, Plow instead of Plough and also Artesian Wells and Buckboards.

Garrideb, John   [3GAR]   Male Alive   A short, powerful man with the round,
fresh, clean-shaven face characteristic of so many American men of affairs The
general effect was chubby and rather childlike, so one received the impression of
quite a young man with a broad set smile upon his face. His eyes, however, were
arresting. Seldom in any human head have I seen a pair which bespoke a more

intense inward life, so bright were they, so alert, so responsive to every change of thought. His accent was American, but was not accompanied by any eccentricity of speech. Native of Chicago. Was a native of Chicago. Known to have shot three men in the States. Escaped from penitentiary through political influence. Came to London in 1893. Shot Rodger Prescott over cards in a nightclub in the Waterloo Road in January, 1895. Prescott died, but he was shown to have been the aggressor in the row. released from Prison 1901. Very dangerous man, usually armed and was prepared to use them. shot Dr. Watson in thigh when he was caught by Holmes and Watson as he tried to remove the counterfeit equipment from the home of Nathan Garrideb.

Address : Counsellor at Law, Moorville, Kansas, U. S. A and also Topeka

Howard K. Elcock

G. Dutriac

Garrideb, Nathan   [3GAR]   Male In a mental ward of a hospital   Had a thin, quavering voice Very tall, loose-jointed, round-backed person, gaunt and bald, some sixty-odd years of age. He had a cadaverous face, with the dull dead skin of a man to whom exercise was unknown. Large round spectacles and a small projecting goat's beard combined with his stooping attitude to give him an expression of peering curiosity. The general effect, however, was amiable, though eccentric. A collecting hermit, who seldom left his house. What he didn't know was that there was a secret room under his floor that had been used by the previous owner to print counterfeit money. An American claiming to be John Garrideb, spun him a yarn about a fortune in money if they could find a third Garrideb. Nathan Garrideb contacted Holmes to help them find the third one, much to the annoyance of John Garrideb. As if by magic, John Garrideb finds an advertisement in a Birmingham newspaper from a Howard Garrideb and asks Nathan to go up and see him. This ruse is to get Nathan out of the house, so that John can remove the printing presses and other illegal things, with a view to carrying on. After Nathan leaves, John breaks in and finds the press, only to discover that Holmes and Watson were waiting to arrest him. The disappointment for Nathan is to great and he returns from his trip a broken man.

Address : 156 Little Ryder Street, W.

John R. Flanagan

Howard K. Elcock

Gelder, Mr. [SIXN] Male Alive Gelder and Co., in Church Street, Stepney. The Company of Gelder and Co. were a well-known house in the trade, and had been in business some twenty years. They employed Beppo as a kind of Italian piece-work man, who made himself useful in the shop. He would carve a bit and gild and frame, and do odd jobs.

Address : Church Street, Stepney.

Sidney Paget

George l, King   [3GAR]   Male dead (Real Person 1660 – 1727)   King of England from 1 August 1714 until 20 October 1727 Predecessor was Anne Successor George ll Start of the Georgian Period Architectural style developed around the time of the first four Georges, 1714 - 1830, and sometimes William lV. Holmes asked Nathan Garrideb about his home, whether it was Queen Anne or Georgian period.

Sherlock Holmes Quote : "I am a bit of an archaeologist myself when it comes to houses, I was wondering if this was Queen Anne or Georgian."

King George l

George ll, King   [VALL, 3GAR]   Male dead (Real Person 1683 – 1760)
[VALL] King of England from 11 June 1727 until 25 October 1760 Predecessor was George l Successor George lll [3GAR] Start of the Georgian Period Architectural style developed around the time of the first four Georges, 1714 - 1830, and sometimes William lV. Holmes asked Nathan Garrideb about his home, whether it was Queen Anne or Georgian period.

Sherlock Holmes Quote : [VALL] "Tut, tut, Mr. Mac!—the first sign of temper I have detected in you. Well, I won't read it verbatim, since you feel so strongly upon the subject. But when I tell you that there is some account of the taking of the place by a parliamentary colonel in 1644, of the concealment of Charles for several days in the course of the Civil War, and finally of a visit there by the second George, you will admit that there are various associations of interest connected with this ancient house."
[3GAR] "I am a bit of an archaeologist myself when it comes to houses, I was wondering if this was Queen Anne or Georgian."

King George ll

George lll, King   [3GAR]   Male dead (Real Person 1738 – 1820)   King of England from 25 October 1760 until 29 January 1820 Predecessor was George ll Successor George lV Start of the Georgian Period Architectural style developed around the time of the first four Georges, 1714 - 1830, and sometimes William lV. Holmes asked Nathan Garrideb about his home, whether it was Queen Anne or

Georgian period.

Sherlock Holmes Quote : "I am a bit of an archaeologist myself when it comes to houses, I was wondering if this was Queen Anne or Georgian."

King George lll

George lV, King   [3GAR]   Male dead (Real Person 1762 – 1830)   King of England from 29 January 1820 until 26 June 1830 Predecessor was George lll Successor William lV The Georgian Period Architectural style developed around the time of the first four Georges, 1714 - 1830, and sometimes William lV. Holmes asked Nathan Garrideb about his home, whether it was Queen Anne or Georgian period.

Sherlock Holmes Quote : "I am a bit of an archaeologist myself when it comes to houses, I was wondering if this was Queen Anne or Georgian."

George lV

Gibson, Mrs. Maria   [THOR]   Female dead   Mr Bates, the estate manager waxed lyrically regarding his employer's late wife "She was a creature of the tropics, a Brazilian by birth. Tropical by birth and tropical by nature. A child of the sun and of passion. She had loved him as such women can love, but when her own physical charms had faded—I am told that they once were great—there was nothing to hold him. We all liked her and felt for her and hated him for the way that he treated her." Neil Gibson explained "I met my wife when I was gold-hunting in Brazil. Maria Pinto was the daughter of a government official at Manaos, and she was very beautiful. I was young and ardent in those days, but even now, as I look back with colder blood and a more critical eye, I can see that she was rare and wonderful in her beauty. It was a deep rich nature, too, passionate, wholehearted, tropical, ill-balanced, very different from the American women whom I had known. Well, to make a long story short, I loved her and I married her. It was only when the romance had passed—and it lingered for years—that I realised that we had nothing—absolutely nothing—in common. My love faded. If hers had faded also it might have been easier. But you know the wonderful way of women! Do what I might, nothing could turn her from me. If I have been harsh to her, even brutal as some have said, it has been because I knew that if I could kill her love, or if it turned to hate, it would be easier for both of us. But nothing changed her. She adored me in those English woods as she had adored me twenty years ago on the banks of the Amazon. Do what I might, she was as devoted as ever." Killed herself on Thor Bridge and arranged to have the

Governess Miss Grace Dunbar blamed. Placed on revolver with a discharged chamber in the Governess' wardrobe. Had a note in her dead hand that read "I will be at Thor Bridge at nine o'clock. G. DUNBAR.", which Miss Dunbar admitted she had written. There was no gun anywhere near her body. Holmes eventually found that the case was a suicide and that the pistol had been tied to a suspended rock over the river and when it had been released by the dead hand of Mrs. Gibson, it had flown through the air, hit the side of the bridge and was lying at the bottom of the river.

Address : Thor Place, the Hampshire

G. Patrick Nelson

Frederic Auer

Gibson, Neil J. [THOR] Male Alive Senator Gibson was an attractive person. His tall, gaunt, craggy figure had a suggestion of hunger and rapacity. An Abraham Lincoln keyed to base uses instead of high ones would give some idea of the man. His face might have been chiselled in granite, hard-set, craggy, remorseless, with deep lines upon it, the scars of many a crisis. Cold grey eyes, looking shrewdly out from under bristling brows. he was better known as the greatest gold-mining magnate in the world and thus got the name 'The Gold King' Was an American Senator for some Western State. He had lived in England for some time. Sent a letter to Holmes that ran as follows: CLARIDGE'S HOTEL, October 3rd.
DEAR MR. SHERLOCK HOLMES:
I can't see the best woman God ever made go to her death without doing all that is possible to save her. I can't explain things—I can't even try to explain them, but I

know beyond all doubt that Miss Dunbar is innocent. You know the facts—who doesn't? It has been the gossip of the country. And never a voice raised for her! It's the damned injustice of it all that makes me crazy. That woman has a heart that wouldn't let her kill a fly. Well, I'll come at eleven tomorrow and see if you can get some ray of light in the dark. Maybe I have a clue and don't know it. Anyhow, all I know and all I have and all I am are for your use if only you can save her. If ever in your life you showed your powers, put them now into this case.
Yours faithfully,
J. NEIL GIBSON.

His Estate manager Mr. Bates said "he is a villain—an infernal villain." Gibson called upon Holmes and Watson to ask them to prove the innocence of Miss Grace Dunbar. He got on the wrong side of Holmes by offering him lots of money and when that didn't work, Fame, which Holmes said was of no interest to him. When Holmes asked about his relationship with Miss Dunbar, Gibson denied any involvement and when Holmes called his bluff, Gibson had stormed out only to return some minutes later, a chastened man. It seems that he had fallen out of love with his wife and wanted to marry his governess Miss Dunbar. Then his wife had been killed and the blame was put on Miss Dunbar. Gibson wanted Holmes to prove she was not guilty.

Address : Thor Place, the Hampshire

G. Patrick Nelson

Frederic Auer

Gilchrist, Mr. **[3STU]** **Male Alive** A tall, flaxen-haired, slim young fellow. A fine figure of a man, tall, lithe, and agile, with a springy step and a pleasant, open face. Gilchrist, a fine scholar and athlete; plays in the Rugby team and the cricket team for the college, and got his Blue for the hurdles and the long jump. He is a fine, manly fellow. His father was the notorious Sir Jabez Gilchrist, who ruined himself on the turf. My scholar has been left very poor, but he is hardworking and industrious. He will do well. Entered the Tutor's room and looked at the examination papers. But decided that this was not an honourable thing to do. Said that he was determined not to go in for the examination. Had have been offered a commission in the Rhodesian Police, and was going out to South Africa at once."'

Frederic Dorr Steele   *Sidney Paget*

Gilchrist, Sir Jabez **[3STU]** **Male dead** Notorious gambler, who ruined himself on the turf. Left his son very poor, Father of the unnamed Gilchrist student at St. Luke's college, who was going to cheat in an examination.

Gladstone, William Ewart **[TWIS]** **Male Alive (Real Person 1809 – 1898)** There is no reference to Gladstone per se, but a Gladstone Bag is mentioned, which is named after the British Statesman and Politician.

William Gladstone

Gold King, The [THOR] Male Alive See Neil J. Gibson

Goldini, Restaurant [BRUC] Male Alive Restaurant where Holmes and Watson met prior to breaking into Mr. Hugo Oberstein's house, of 13 Caulfield Gardens.

Sherlock Holmes Quote : Goldini's Restaurant, Gloucester Road, Kensington. Please come at once and join me there. Bring with you a jemmy, a dark lantern, a chisel, and a revolver—S.H."
"Have you had something to eat? Then join me in a coffee and curacao. Try one of the proprietor's cigars. They are less poisonous than one would expect. Have you the tools?"

Address : Gloucester Road, Kensington

Gordon, Major-General Charles George [CARD,RESI] Male dead (Real Person 1833 – 1885) British Army officer. Saw action in the Crimean War as an officer in the British Army. Gordon and his men were instrumental in putting down the Taiping Rebellion. Given the name Chinese Gordon because of his accomplishments in China. [CARD] & [RESI]. Watson had a newly framed picture of General Gordon. Watson used the same opening section in both stories.

General Gordon

Gorgiano, Giuseppe   [REDC]   Male dead   An enormous man. Clean-shaven, swarthy face. Had the body of a giant but everything about him was grotesque, gigantic, and terrifying. His voice was like thunder. Waved his great arms around when he talked. His thoughts, his emotions, his passions, all were exaggerated and monstrous. He talked, or rather roared, with such energy that others could but sit and listen, cowed with the mighty stream of words. His eyes blazed at you and held you at his mercy. He was a terrible and wonderful man. Known by a number of names including Gorgiano of the Red Circle, Black Gorgiano and had earned the name of 'Death' in the south of Italy, for he was red to the elbow in murder! Came from Posilippo. Took a fancy to Gennaro Lucca's wife, Emilia. Had to leave Italy to escape the law and found Gennaro, a former Red Circle member, in New York. Tried to enlist Gennaro back into a life of crime, that he had left years ago. When Gennaro and Emilia Lucca fled to London, Gorgiano, followed. The final encounter between Gorgiano and Lucca, did not go the former's way and he ended up lying in a pool of blood with a knife protruding from his throat.

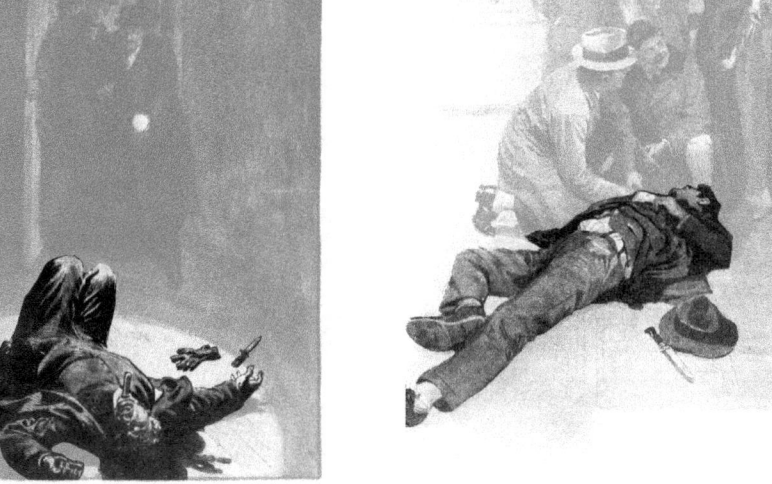

H. M. Brock   *Richard W. Wallace*

Gorot, Charles   [NAVA]   Male Alive   Fellow clerk who worked in the same office as Percy Phelps. Of Huguenot extraction, but as English in sympathy and tradition as anyone. Suspected of taking the Naval Treaty. Was shadowed by police for nine weeks, without result.

Gower, Brother   [VALL]   Male in prison   Was involved in the attack on the Editor of the Herald newspaper Stanger. The group was lead by Ted Baldwin and others in the group were Mansel, Scanlan, the two willabys and John McMurdo, there were two others to guard the door.

Graham, Mr.   [NORW]   Male Alive   Senior partner of Graham and McFarlane London solicitors

Address : based at 426, Gresham Buildings, E.C.

Gravelet, Jean Francois   [SIGN]   Male Alive   See Charles Blondin

Greathed, General Sir Edward Harris   [SIGN]   Male dead (Real Person 1812 – 1881)   Rose through the ranks to become commanding officer of the 8th Regiment of Foot and helped defeated and dispersed rebels at the Battle of Agra during the Indian Rebellion. Mentioned by Jonathan Small in his story "After Wilson took Delhi and Sir Colin relieved Lucknow the back of the business was broken. Fresh troops came pouring in, and Nana Sahib made himself scarce over the frontier. A flying column under Colonel Greathed came round to Agra and cleared the Pandies away from it. Peace seemed to be settling upon the country, and we four were beginning to hope that the time was at hand when we might safely go off with our shares of the plunder. In a moment, however, our hopes were shattered by our being arrested as the murderers of Achmet."

General Greathed

Green, Admiral peter [LADY] Male Famous Admiral who commanded the Sea of Azof fleet in the Crimean War. Had a son of the same name.

Green, Hon. Philip   [LADY] Male Alive He was a bulky, bearded, sunburned fellow, who looks as if he would be more at home in a farmers' inn than in a fashionable hotel. A hard, fierce man. A huge, swarthy man with a bristling black beard. "Un sauvage—un veritable sauvage!" He had a grip of iron and the fury of a fiend. He was a wild youngster Had spent some time in South Africa. He was the son of the famous admiral of that name who commanded the Sea of Azof fleet in the Crimean War.

Address : Langham Hotel

Knott   *Alec Ball*

Gregory, Inspector [SILV] Male Alive He is a tall fair man with lion-like hair and beard, and curiously penetrating light blue eyes. Involved in the Greek interpreter case. Only appeared in this one story. Invited Holmes to help in this case. A man who was rapidly making his name in the English detective service. Holmes said that he lacked imagination, it was one quality he missed.

Sherlock Holmes Quote : "Inspector Gregory, to whom the case has been committed, is an extremely competent officer. Were he but gifted with imagination he might rise to great heights in his profession."

Sidney Paget   *Sidney Paget*

Gregson, Inspector Tobias   [STUD,GREE,WIST,REDC]   Male Alive   [SIGN]
Tall, white-faced, flaxen-haired man   [STUD] He worked with Lestrade on this case and arrested, the innocent, Arthur Charpentier for the murder of Enoch J. Drebber. The Echo newspaper concluded an article about the Drebber and Stangerson murders by saying "It is an open secret that the credit of this smart capture belongs entirely to the well-known Scotland Yard officials, Messrs. Lestrade and Gregson. The man was apprehended, it appears, in the rooms of a certain Mr. Sherlock Holmes, who has himself, as an amateur, shown some talent in the detective line and who, with such instructors, may hope in time to attain to some degree of their skill. It is expected that a testimonial of some sort will be presented to the two officers as a fitting recognition of their services." [GREE] Holmes and Watson on reaching Scotland Yard, have to wait more than an hour before we could get Inspector Gregson and comply with the legal formalities which would enable them to enter the house 'The Myrtles' holding Mr. Melas and Paul Kratides. Mr Melas and Paul Kratides we placed in a room and gassed and the later died as a result. [WIST] An energetic, gallant, and, within his limitations, a capable officer. Worked with Inspector Baynes on this case. Appears in Four of Holmes' stories [STUD,GREE,WIST & REDC] and is mentioned in [SIGN, [REDC] Gregson certainly warmed to Holmes' help in later stories. "Wait a bit!" cried Gregson eagerly. "I'll do you this justice, Mr. Holmes, that I was never in a case yet that I didn't feel stronger for having you on my side."

Sherlock Holmes Quotes : [STUD] "Gregson is the smartest of the Scotland Yarders, he and Lestrade are the pick of a bad lot. They are both quick and energetic, but conventional—shockingly so. They have their knives into one another, too. They are as jealous as a pair of professional beauties. There will be some fun over this case if they are both put upon the scent."
[SIGN] "I am the last and highest court of appeal in detection. When Gregson or Lestrade or Athelney Jones are out of their depths—which, by the way, is their normal state—the matter is laid before me."

D. H. Friston   *Arthur Twidle*

Greuze, Jean Baptiste   [VALL]   Male Alive (Real Person 1725 – 1805)
French painter of portraits and history painting. "All knowledge comes useful to the detective," remarked Holmes. "Even the trivial fact that in the year 1865 a picture by Greuze entitled La Jeune Fille à l'Agneau fetched one million two hundred thousand francs —more than £40,000—at the Portalis sale may start a train of reflection in your mind." "That painting was by Jean Baptiste Greuze."
Sherlock Holmes Quote : "Jean Baptiste Greuze, was a French artist who flourished between the years 1750 and 1800. I allude, of course to his working career. Modern criticism has more than endorsed the high opinion formed of him by his contemporaries."

Jean Baptiste Greuze

Greyminster, Duke of **[BLAN]** **Male Alive** At the start of this story, Holmes was working on a case that Watson had described as that of the Abbey School, in which the Duke of Greyminster was so deeply involved.

Griggs, Jimmy **[VEIL]** **Male Alive** Described by Mrs. Ronder as little Jimmy Griggs, the clown. Poor devil, he had not much to be funny about, but he did what he could to hold things together in the circus. Helped in rescuing Mrs. Ronder from the Lion.

Frederic Dorr Steele

Grimm, Jacob Ludwig Karl [SUSS] Male dead (Real Person 1785 – 1863)
At the start of the story, as they talk about the letter they have received from Morrison, Morrison & Dodd, they consider what they know about Vampires and wonder if they are entering a Grimms' fairy tale The eldest of the two brothers who are now chiefly known for their collection of Fairy tales. At the start of the story, as they talk about the letter they have received from Morrison, Morrison & Dodd, they consider what they know about Vampires and wonder if they are entering a Grimms' fairy tale

Sherlock Holmes Quote : "Matilda Briggs was not the name of a young woman, Watson," said Holmes in a reminiscent voice. "It was a ship which is associated with the giant rat of Sumatra, a story for which the world is not yet prepared. But what do we know about vampires? Does it come within our purview either? Anything is better than stagnation, but really we seem to have been switched on to a Grimms' fairy tale. Make a long arm, Watson, and see what V has to say."

Jacob Grimm

Grimm, Wilhelm [SUSS] Male dead (Real Person 1786 – 1859)   At the start of the story, as they talk about the letter they have received from Morrison, Morrison & Dodd, they consider what they know about Vampires and wonder if they are entering a Grimms' fairy tale The youngest of the two brothers who are now chiefly known for their collection of Fairy tales. At the start of the story, as they talk about the letter they have received from Morrison, Morrison & Dodd, they consider what they know about Vampires and wonder if they are entering a Grimms' fairy tale

Sherlock Holmes Quote : "Matilda Briggs was not the name of a young woman, Watson," said Holmes in a reminiscent voice. "It was a ship which is associated with the giant rat of Sumatra, a story for which the world is not yet prepared. But what do we know about vampires? Does it come within our purview either? Anything is better than stagnation, but really we seem to have been switched on to a Grimms' fairy tale. Make a long arm, Watson, and see what V has to say."

Wilhelm Grimm

Gruner, Baron Adelbert [ILLU] Male Alive   Murderer of his wife in Austria, it was purely a technical legal point and the suspicious death of a witness that saved him! Currently residing in London. About to marry Miss Violet de Merville. Collector and expert on fine Chinese ceramic. Kept a secret love/lust diary when he detailed his passions, written in his own hand. Was a very dangerous man, he arranged to have Le Brun crippled, when this French agent made inquiries into his affair. Also arrange for a murderous attack on Holmes. Disfigured for life, when Miss Kitty Winters throw Vitriol into his face. One Eye was certainly lost. His engagement to Miss de Merville was ended when she read his Diary.

Sherlock Holmes Quote : "You mean the Austrian murderer?"
"I am as sure that he killed his wife when the so-called 'accident' happened in the

Splugen Pass as if I had seen him do it."

Address : Vernon Lodge, near Kingston

John R. Flanagan   *Howard K. Elcock*

Gyatso, Thubten   **[EMPT]**   **Male Alive**   See Dalai Lama of course it is Lama with one 'L' not two.

H is for Hound of the Baskerville)

Hafiz [IDEN] Male dead (Real Person 1317 – 1390) He was a Persian poet whose collected works (The Divan) are regarded as a pinnacle of Persian literature and are to be found in the homes of most people in Iran, who learn his poems by heart and still use them as proverbs and sayings. He states that there is as much sense in Hafiz as in Horace, and as much knowledge of the world.

Sherlock Holmes Quotes : "There is danger for him who taketh the tiger cub, and danger also for whoso snatches a delusion from a woman "
He states that there is as much sense in Hafiz as in Horace, and as much knowledge of the world.

Hafiz or Hafez

Haines, Mr. [3GAB] Male Alive Senior partner in the House agent company of Haines-Johnson, Auctioneer and Valuer Holmes was of the opinion that he didn't consider them as Honest business men, because they concealed their place of business.

Hales, William [VALL] Male dead The county Delegate had sent over five good men to strike a blow in Vermissa, he had now demanded that in return three Vermissa men should be secretly selected and sent across to kill William Hales of Stake Royal, one of the best known and most popular mine owners in the Gilmerton district, a man who was believed not to have an enemy in the world; for he was in all ways a model employer. He had insisted, however, upon efficiency in the work, and had, therefore, paid off certain drunken and idle employees who were members of the all-powerful society. Coffin notices hung outside his door had not weakened his resolution, and so in a free, civilised country he found himself condemned to death. Ted Baldwin had been the leader of the party. Baldwin has said how They had waited for their man as he drove home at nightfall, taking their station at the top of a steep hill, where his horse must be at a walk. He was so furred to keep out the cold that he could not lay his hand on his pistol. They had pulled him out and shot him again and again. He had screamed for mercy.

Hallamshire, Lord Lieutenant of   [PRIO]   Male Alive   See Duke of Holdernesse

Halle, Charles   [STUD]   Alive (Real Person 1819 – 1895)   Anglo-German pianist and conductor and founder of the Halle orchestra in 1858.

Sherlock Holmes Quote : "We must hurry up, for I want to go to Halle's concert to hear Norman Neruda this afternoon."

Charles Halle

Halliday, Mr.   [STUD]   Male Alive   Owner of the Private Hotel , where Enoch J. Drebber and Joseph Stangerson agreed to meet up, after Drebber when back to see Alice Charpentier in Camberwell. Drebber never arrived at this hotel and the dead body of Stangerson was found my Lestrade and the Boots.

Address : Little George street

Harden, John Vincent [SOLI] Male Holmes was immersed in a very abstruse and complicated problem concerning the peculiar persecution to which John Vincent Harden, the well-known tobacco millionaire, had been subjected.

Harding, Mr. [SIXN] Male Alive A brisk, crisp little person, very dapper and quick, with a clear head and a ready tongue. Together with his brother, they owned a pottery shop, called Harding Brothers, When Holmes called, he was told by the assistant that Mr. Harding would be absent until afternoon, and that he was himself a newcomer who could give us no information. Holmes' face showed his disappointment and annoyance. They had three Napoleon Busts, they sold one to Horace Harker, another to Josiah Brown and the final one to Mr. Sandeford.

Address : two doors down from Kensington High Street Station

Hardy, Mr. [IDEN] Male Alive Was the foreman in the plumbing business of Mr. Sutherland, whose business was in Tottenham Court Road.

Hardy, Sir Charles [SECO] Male Alive A report from this gentleman was still in the Right Honourable Trelawney Hope's despatch box.

Hardy, Sir John [EMPT] Male Alive Played Whist with Ronald Adair on the day of his death with Mr. Murray and Colonel Moran.

Hare, John [SCAN] Male Alive Mr John Hare (later Sire John Hare, 1907) was an English actor and theatre Holmes dressed up as a character of an amiable and simple-minded Nonconformist clergyman. His broad black hat, his baggy trousers, his white tie, his sympathetic smile, and general look of peering and benevolent curiosity were such as Mr. John Hare alone could have equalled manager Hare was admired for his carefully observed characterisations, and his 'Men of the World' roles

John Hare

Hargrave, Mr   [VALL]   Male dead   See Alias used by Brother Ted Baldwin while he was staying in UK.

Hargreave, Wilson   [DANC]   Male Alive   Friend of Holmes, who worked for the New York Police Bureau. Holmes had helped him on a number of occasions regarding London Crime , but this time Holmes wanted Wilson to give him information regarding Abe Slaney. He sent back his reply: 'The most dangerous crook in Chicago.'

Harker, Horace   [SIXN]   Male Alive   An exceedingly unkempt and agitated elderly man, clad in a flannel dressing-gown, was pacing up and down Horace Harker worked for the Central Press Syndicate. Owner of the house on Pitt street that saw the fatal meeting of Pietro Venucci and Beppo. Pietro Venucci's dead body was found by Horace Harker. Beppo had come to rob the house and escaped with Harker's Napoleon bust, which he took off the Mantelpiece. This bust was found smashed a few hundred feet away in the front garden of an empty house in Campden House Road, under a street lamp.

Address : 131, Pitt Street, Kensington

Nos Loisirs   *Sidney Paget*

Harold, Mrs. **[MAZA]** **Female dead** A lady Count Sylvius got involved with and Holmes knew the real facts as to the death of old Mrs. Harold. She had left the Count the Blymer estate, but he had rapidly gambled it away.

Harraway, Brother **[VALL]** **Male in prison** He was the secretary of Lodge 341, Vermissa. He was one of the members of the Committee that had to decide what to do with the Birdy Edwards problem. Other members were committee were ; Bodymaster McGinty, Ted Baldwin, Tiger Cormac the brutal young assassin, Carter, the treasurer, and the brothers Willaby (Arthur and another).

Harringby, Lord **[WIST]** **Male Alive** An owner of a large house in the Esher area. His details were sent to Holmes by the Allan brothers, chief land agents in the village of Esher.

Address : The Dingle, Esher

Harris, Mr **[STOC]** **Male Alive** See Holmes Alias Holmes used when introduced to Harry Pinner in Birmingham Holmes said he was an accountant.

Address : of Bermondsey

Harrison, Joseph **[NAVA]** **Male Alive** Rather stout man who received Holmes and Watson with much hospitality. His age may have been nearer forty than thirty, but his cheeks were so ruddy and his eyes so merry that he still conveyed the impression of a plump and mischievous boy. Stole the Naval treaty from the desk of Percy Phelps, while the latter was downstairs with the commissionaire.

Hid the treaty under his bedroom floorboards, but was moved out of the room so that Percy Phelps could recover from the brain-fever. Finally when Percy Phelps was in London with Watson, recovered the treaty only to be caught by Holmes, who had been waiting for him to make his move. Escaped to parts unknown.

Address : Briarbrae, Woking

- Sidney Paget   *- Sidney Paget*

Harrison, Miss Annie **[NAVA]** Female Alive She was a striking-looking woman, a little short and thick for symmetry, but with a beautiful olive complexion, large, dark, Italian eyes, and a wealth of deep black hair. She had rich tints. Fiancée of Percy Phelps. Sister of Joseph Harrison. Helped Percy Phelps recover from brain-fever after the Naval Treaty was stolen. Was asked by Holmes to remain in Percy Phelps' bedroom all day and lock it up at night so that the Naval Treaty Holmes thought was hidden there couldn't be stolen during the day.

Address : Briarbrae, Woking

Sidney Paget   *William H. Hyde*

Harvey, Master [SHOS] Male Alive One of the Lads working at Shoscombe Old Place. In charge of the furnace at the house and found strange bones in the cinders and reported his findings to Mr. Mason.

Address : Shoscombe Old Place

Harvey, Mr. [SUSS] Male dead Builder of a house in Lamberley. As Watson says "I know that country, Holmes. It is full of old houses which are named after the men who built them centuries ago. You get Odley's and Harvey's and Carriton's—the folk are forgotten but their names live in their houses."

Hatherley, Victor [ENGR] Male Alive Hydraulic Engineer. He was quietly dressed in a suit of heather tweed with a soft cloth cap Round one of his hands he had a handkerchief wrapped, which was mottled all over with bloodstains. He was young, not more than five-and-twenty. A strong, masculine face; but he was exceedingly pale and was suffering from some strong agitation, which it took all his strength of mind to control. Missing his thumb from the root. Orphan and a bachelor, residing alone in lodgings in London. Hydraulic Engineer. Victor Hatherley was apprenticed with Venner & Matheson for seven years. Left them in 1887, using the inheritance from his poor father's death. Started own business in 1887, but had only three consultations and one small job, amounting to £27 10s. Lysander Stark called and ask him to look at a steam engine he had in his house. The Hydraulic press was large enough to easily fit inside and after Hatherley had found the problem, he had a second look in the piston and the door was locked trapping him inside. The steam engine then started and as the top of the chamber gradually lowered, a small side door opened and it was Elise, who helped him escape. He was chased thought out the house and just as he was going to jump out an upstairs window, Stark appeared with a butcher's cleaver, cutting off his thumb. Hatherley eventually found his was to Watson and then Watson took him to Holmes to tell his story.

Address : business chambers - 16A, Victoria Street (3rd Floor)

Sidney Paget

Josef Friedrich

Hayes, Mr. Reuben   [PRIO]   Male in prison   Squat, dark, elderly man was smoking a black clay pipe when Holmes first met him. Landlord of the the Fighting Cock Inn. Arranged to kidnap Lord Arthur Saltire with James Wilder. Borrowed special horse shoes, shaped like cow feet from Holdernesse Hall. Collected Arthur at night, but was followed by the purser, Heidegger, who was killed when he was struck with a stick and left for dead. Kept Arthur in rooms at his inn. Holmes arranged for his capture after he attempted to escape. Will probably Hang for the killing of Heidegger.

Address : The Fighting Cock Inn,

Sidney Paget

Hayes, Mrs.   [PRIO]   Male Alive A kindly woman, but entirely under the control of her brutal husband. Wife of Rueben Hayes Lord Arthur Satire was there for three days under the charge of Mrs. Hayes.

Hayling, Jeremiah   [ENGR]   Male dead   Advertisement about his disappearance appeared in the new paper. Went missing in 1888 and killed by Lysander Stark. A hydraulic engineer, who left his lodgings at ten o'clock at night, and had not been heard of since.

Hayter, Colonel   [REIG]   Male Alive   Watson's old friend, Colonel Hayter, who had come under Watson's professional care in Afghanistan, had now taken a house near Reigate in Surrey, and had frequently asked Watson to come down to him upon a visit. Hayter was a fine old soldier who had seen much of the world, and he soon found, as Watson had expected, that Holmes and he had much in common.

Martin Van Maele   *Sidney Paget*

Hayward, Mr. [RESI] Male Alive   One of five men who robbed the bank and got away with £7,000. Blessington or Sutton, who was the worst of the gang, turned informer. On his evidence Cartwright was hanged and the other three got fifteen years apiece. On an early release from prison, the three gang members Biddle, Hayward and Moffat, located the residence of Blessington, gave him a mock trial and hanged him. Blessington was discovered the following morning by Dr. Percy Trevelyan. It is likely that all three members of the gang, died on the ill-fated steamer 'Norah Creina , which was lost some years ago with all hands upon the Portuguese coast, some leagues to the north of Oporto.

Martin Van Maele   *William H. Hyde*

Hebron, Effie **[YELL]** **Female Alive** See Effie Munro

Hebron, John **[YELL]** **Male dead** A man strikingly handsome and intelligent-looking man, but bearing unmistakable signs upon his features of his African descent. Lawyer with a good practice. Had one child with Effie Hebron called Lucy Die of Yellow Fever.

Address : Atlanta, Georgia, USA

Hebron, Lucy **[YELL]** **Female Alive** She was far darker than her father was in complexion. She was dressed in a red frock, and long white gloves. She wore the strangest livid tinted mask. Daughter of John and Effie Hebron. Her mother left her in America, while she went to England because of Lucy's weak health. When she recovered, her mother sent for her and moved her into a neighbouring cottage. Lucy's mother was caught making frequent visits to the cottage, by her husband and so he sought council with Holmes, who completely got it wrong. It was all resolved in the end and a happy family life completed the story.

Sidney Paget

Sidney Paget

Heidegger, the German master **[PRIO]** **Male dead** Heidegger, the German master German Master at School. He had been at the school for two years, and came with the best references He was a silent, morose man, not very popular either with masters or boys. Bicycle rider. His Bicycle had Palmer tyres leaving longitudinal stripes. Saw Lord Saltire leaving the school at night and followed but was killed by a blow to the head by Reuben Hayes, Landlord of the Fighting Cock Inn.

Sidney Paget

Richard Gutschmidt

Henderson, Mr. [WIST,NORW] Male dead Dark, deep-set, brooding eyes He is a man of fifty, strong, active, with iron-grey hair, great bunched black eyebrows. The step of a deer and the air of an emperor A fierce, masterful man, with a red-hot spirit behind his parchment face. His skin is yellow and sapless, but tough as whipcord. [WIST] Living at High Gable, Esher. Was actually Don Murillo, or the Tiger of San Pedro. Had two daughters aged eleven and thirteen. Tyrant. He had made his name as the most lewd and bloodthirsty tyrant that had ever governed any country with a pretence to civilisation. Strong, fearless, and energetic, he had sufficient virtue to enable him to impose his odious vices upon a cowering people for ten or twelve years. His name was a terror through all Central America. At the end of that time there was a universal rising against him. But he was as cunning as he was cruel, and at the first whisper of coming trouble he had secretly conveyed his treasures aboard a ship which was manned by devoted adherents. His policy was to murder, on one pretext or another, every man who showed such promise that he might in time come to be a dangerous rival. Discovered a plot to assassinate him by Miss Burnett and Aloysius Garcia, but turned the tables on them and killed Garcia and tried to flee with Miss Burnett. posing as Marquess of Montalva, he was murdered in his rooms at the Hotel Escurial at Madrid [NORW] Watson was looking over his old notes and mentions the case of the papers of ex-President Murillo

Address : High Gable, Esher

Arthur Twidle   *Frederic Dorr Steele*

Hercules   [RESI, SCAN]   Male Alive   Roman hero and God, equivalent to the
Greek Heracles. Noted for being very strong and the son of Jupiter (Zeus)
[SCAN] Watson said "A man entered who could hardly have been less than six
feet six inches in height, with the chest and limbs of a Hercules." [RESI] Dr.
Trevelyan said "He was an elderly man, thin, demure, and commonplace –by no
means the conception one forms of a Russian nobleman. I was much more struck
by the appearance of his companion. This was a tall young man, surprisingly
handsome, with a dark, fierce face, and the limbs and chest of a Hercules."

Hercules

Higgins, Treasurer [VALL] Male Alive Treasurer of Merton County Lodge 249. He was put in charge of two good men, who were to deal with Andrew Rae of Rae & Sturmash. Tiger Cormac and Wilson volunteered.

Hill, Inspector [SIXN] Male Alive Inspector of Scotland Yard. He made a speciality of Saffron Hill and the Italian quarter. Was able to identify the dead body found on Pitt street, as Pietro Venucci from Naples.

Hobbs, Mr. Fairdale   [REDC] Male The name of a former lodger of Mrs. Warner. "Mrs. Warner reminded Holmes had helped him "You arranged an affair for a lodger of mine last year,—Mr. Fairdale Hobbs." Fairdale Hobbs was very impressed with Holmes work, according to Mrs. Warner "He would never cease talking of it—your kindness, sir, and the way in which you brought light into the darkness. I remembered his words when I was in doubt and darkness myself. I know you could if you only would."

Hoffman, Ernst Theodor Amadeus [MAZA] Male   German Romantic author of fantasy and Gothic horror His Tales were turned into an Opera by Jacques Offenbach call The tales of Hoffmann. When Holmes says he is going to play Hoffmann 'Barcarole', he is probably referring to Offenbach's "Belle nuit, o nuit d'amour'. Now since this piece is under three minutes in length, his five minute return must be taken with a pinch of salt.

Sherlock Holmes Quote : "I shall try over the Hoffman 'Barcarole' upon my violin.

In five minutes I shall return for your final answer."

E. T. A. Hoffmann

Holder Alexander [BERY] Male Alive He was a man of about fifty, tall, portly, and imposing, with a massive, strongly marked face and a commanding figure. He was dressed in a sombre yet rich style, in black frock-coat, shining hat, neat brown gaiters, and well-cut pearl-grey trousers. Had grief and despair in his eyes Watson refers to him as madman as he looks out on him from the window. Uncle to Miss Mary Holder and father to Arthur Holder. He is the Holder of Holder & Stevenson, of Threadneedle Street, the banking firm. Senior partner in the second largest private banking concern in the City of London Agreed to make a loan of £50,000 to a noble man, suing the Beryl Coronet as security. Took said Coronet home and put it in an insecure cabinet. His niece took the Coronet and gave it to her lover, Sir George Burnwell. Found his son trying to return the coronet to the cabinet after he had managed to retrieve most of it from Burnwell, but three gems are missing. Accuses Arthur of stealing coronet and has him taken away by police. Asks Holmes to try and recover the missing three beryls from the coronet. Out of pocket to the tune of £4,000 in this venture. This bank is going under with this sort of investments.

Address : Fairbank, Streatham

Sidney Paget   *Josef Friedrich*

Holder Arthur [BERY] Male Alive   Son of Alexander Holder. Had been a disappointment to his father. When he was young he became a member of an aristocratic club, and there, having charming manners, he was soon the intimate of a number of men with long purses and expensive habits. He learned to play heavily at cards and to squander money on the turf, until he had again and again to go to his father and implore him to give him an advance upon his allowance, that he might settle his debts of honour. He tried more than once to break away from the dangerous company which he was keeping, but each time the influence of his friend, Sir George Burnwell, was enough to draw him back again. Was called a blackguard by his father, who thought that he had tried to steel the beryl coronet, but it was the niece Mary, that had tried to do that. He had actually behaved very well, he had seen Mary taking the coronet out to her lover, Sir George Burnwell, had tackled him and managed to get most of the coronet back, save three gems, when he was surprised by his father. Holmes found the real culprits in this story and cleared his name with the police and his father.

Address : Fairbank, Streatham

Sidney Paget   *Josef Friedrich*

Holder Mary [BERY] Female Alive Rather above the middle height, slim, with dark hair and eyes (black), which seemed the darker against the absolute pallor of her skin. Watson thought that "He did not think that he had ever seen such deadly paleness in a woman's face. Her lips, too, were bloodless, but her eyes were flushed with crying." she was evidently a woman of strong character, with immense capacity for self-restraint. Niece of Alexander Holder. Daughter of Alexander Holder's deceased brother. Had been living in Mr. Holder's home for five years. She was said to be Mr Holder's "sunbeam in my house—sweet, loving, beautiful, a wonderful manager and housekeeper, yet as tender and quiet and gentle as a woman could be." She was his right hand. I do not know what I could do without her. Twice she refused to marry Arthur Holder, who loved her. Involved in the theft of the Beryl Coronet, afterwards, left to Join Sir George Burnwell. Never to be heard off again.

Address : Fairbank, Streatham

Sidney Paget   *Josef Friedrich*

Holder, Sergeant John   [SIGN]   Male Company sergeant in the 3rd Buffs. (Royal East Kent Regiment) Saved Jonathan Small's life after he was attacked by a crocodile while swimming in the Ganges. One of the finest swimmers in the service. (john-holden.gif - Thomas J. Nicholl)

Holdernesse, Duchess Edith of   [PRIO]   Male Alive   Separation by mutual consent from her husband, the Duke, she had taken up her residence in the South of France. The separation was because of the Duke's illegitimate son, who he called James Wilder, and was working with him. With the removal of James Wilder, Holmes was of the opinion that a reconciliation was possible.

Sherlock Holmes Quote : "Holdernesse, 6th Duke, K.G., P.C.'—half the alphabet! 'Baron Beverley, Earl of Carston'—dear me, what a list! 'Lord Lieutenant of Hallamshire since 1900. Married Edith, daughter of Sir Charles Appledore, 1888. Heir and only child, Lord Saltire. Owns about two hundred and fifty thousand acres. Minerals in Lancashire and Wales. Address: Carlton House Terrace; Holdernesse Hall, Hallamshire; Carston Castle, Bangor, Wales. Lord of the Admiralty, 1872; Chief Secretary of State for—' Well, well, this man is certainly one of the greatest subjects of the Crown!"

Holdernesse, Duke of   [PRIO]   Male Alive   He was a tall and stately person, scrupulously dressed, with a drawn, thin face, and a nose which was grotesquely curved and long. His complexion was of a dead pallor, which was more startling by contrast with a long, dwindling beard of vivid red, which flowed down over his white waistcoat, with his watch-chain gleaming through its fringe The late Cabinet Minister He employed his illegitimate son, James Wilder, as a secretary. Was separated from his wife, who had moved to the South of France. His son Lord Saltire, was kidnapped by Wilder and Reuben Hayes. Gave Holmes a cheque for six thousand pounds for finding his son and finding the murder of the German Master Heidegger.

Sherlock Holmes Quote : "Holdernesse, 6th Duke, K.G., P.C.'—half the alphabet! 'Baron Beverley, Earl of Carston'—dear me, what a list! 'Lord Lieutenant of Hallamshire since 1900. Married Edith, daughter of Sir Charles Appledore, 1888. Heir and only child, Lord Saltire. Owns about two hundred and fifty thousand acres. Minerals in Lancashire and Wales. Address: Carlton House Terrace; Holdernesse Hall, Hallamshire; Carston Castle, Bangor, Wales. Lord of the Admiralty, 1872; Chief Secretary of State for—' Well, well, this man is certainly one of the greatest subjects of the Crown!"

Frederic Dorr Steele   *Sidney Paget*

Holdhurst, Lord   [NAVA]   Male Alive Slight, tall figure, his sharp features, thoughtful face, and curling hair prematurely tinged with grey, he seemed to represent that not to common type, a nobleman who is in truth noble. The great conservative politician Uncle of Percy Phelps, being Phelps' mother's Brother. foreign minister in the Foreign Office. Used his influence to help his nephew. He gave him several missions of trust which always ended in a successful conclusion. On the 23rd May 1889, asked Phelps to copy out a Naval Treaty, but it was stolen. The Treaty remained stolen until recovered by Holmes on 1 August 1889. Had chambers in Downing Street. Received Holmes and Watson with that old-fashioned courtesy for which he is remarkable.

Sherlock Holmes Quote : "He's a fine fellow. But he has a struggle to keep up his position. He is far from rich and has many calls. You noticed, of course, that his boots had been re-soled."

Sidney Paget

William H. Hyde

Hollis, Mr. [LAST] Male Alive A spy working for Von Bork. Von Bork called him Mad. Holmes arranged to have him captured by the British authorities.

Holloway, Mr [3GAR] Male Alive Senior partner in Holloway and Steele, who were the House agents for the Georgian house at 156 Little Ryder Street currently owned by Nathan Garridebs Told Holmes that Mr. Garrideb had been at the address for five years previously it had been empty for a year and before that a Mr. Waldron (Prescott) had lived there.

Address : Edgeware road

Holly, Sir Edward [GLOR] Male Alive House owner who was attacked by members of a poaching gang after it had been broken up by Justice of the Peace Trevor. Might have been knifed.

Holmes, Mycroft [GREE, FINA, BRUC] Male Alive A much larger and stouter man than Sherlock. His body was absolutely corpulent, but his face, though massive, had preserved something of the sharpness of expression which was so remarkable in that of his brother. His eyes, which were of a peculiarly light, watery grey, seemed to always retain that far-away, introspective look which I had only observed in Sherlock when he was exerting his full powers. Had a broad, fat hand like the flipper of a seal Had a tortoise-shell snuff box and a large, red silk handkerchief. [GREE] Seven years older that his brother Sherlock. Spent much time in the Diogenes club (the queerest club in London,) Is always there from quarter to five to twenty to eight. (4:45pm to 7:40pm) He is to be found in Whitehall, Diogenes club or Pall Mall lodgings only. He has an extraordinary faculty for figures, and audits the books in some of the government departments. He takes no other exercise. He was one of the founders of the Diogenes club, that caters for some of the most unsociable and unlovable men in town. Here No member is permitted to take the least notice of any other one. Save in the Stranger's Room, no talking is, under any circumstances, allowed, and three offences, if brought to the notice of the committee, render the talker liable to expulsion. Outdid Sherlock with his observational skills as the two of them looked at a Billard-marker outside the window of the Diogenes Club. Introduced Mr Melas, The Greek interpreter, to Sherlock and started the story. [FINA] A brougham was waiting with a very massive driver wrapped in a dark cloak, this was Mycroft. [BRUC] A moment later the tall and portly form of Mycroft Holmes was ushered into the room. Heavily built and massive, there was a suggestion of uncouth physical inertia in the figure, but above this unwieldy frame there was perched a head so masterful in its brow, so alert in its steel- grey, deep-set eyes, so firm in its lips, and so subtle in its play of expression, that after the first glance one forgot the gross body and remembered only the dominant mind.

Sherlock Holmes Quotes : [GREE] "When I say, therefore, that Mycroft has better powers of observation than I, you may take it that I am speaking the exact and literal truth."
"I said that he was my superior in observation and deduction. If the art of the detective began and ended in reasoning from an armchair, my brother would be the greatest criminal agent that ever lived. But he has no ambition and no energy. He will not even go out of his way to verify his own solution, and would rather be considered wrong than take the trouble to prove himself right. Again and again I have taken a problem to him, and have received an explanation which has afterwards proved to be the correct one. And yet he was absolutely incapable of working out the practical points which must be gone into before a case could be laid before a judge or jury."
[BRUC] "Draws £450 a year, remains a subordinate, has no ambitions of any kind, will receive neither honour nor title, but remains the most indispensable man in the country."

"Well, his position is unique. He has made it for himself. There has never been anything like it before, nor will be again. He has the tidiest and most orderly brain, with the greatest capacity for storing facts, of any man living. The same great powers which I have turned to the detection of crime he has used for this particular business. The conclusions of every department are passed to him, and he is the central exchange, the clearinghouse, which makes out the balance. All other men are specialists, but his specialism is omniscience. We will suppose that a minister needs information as to a point which involves the Navy, India, Canada and the bimetallic question; he could get his separate advices from various departments upon each, but only Mycroft can focus them all, and say offhand how each factor would affect the other. They began by using him as a short-cut, a convenience; now he has made himself an essential. In that great brain of his everything is pigeonholed and can be handed out in an instant. Again and again his word has decided the national policy. He lives in it. He thinks of nothing else save when, as an intellectual exercise, he unbends if I call upon him and ask him to advise me on one of my little problems."

Address : Lives in Pall Mall lodgings and Diogenes Club

Sidney Paget   *Arthur Twidle*

Sherlock Holmes

Holmes, Sherlock [ALL] Male Alive Born in 1854 if he was Sixty in 1914 [LAST]. Ancestors were country squires and he had a grandmother who was the sister of the Artist Vernet (see Vernet). Had a brother 7 years older called Mycroft. When he was twenty and still an undergraduate, he solved his first case, [GLOR], this may have been when he was living in Montague Street, just around the corner from the British Museum., he was certainly living there in 1879 when he solved the Musgrave Mystery and was likely there still in 1881, when he first encountered Watson. They took rooms at 221b Baker street on 4th March , Watson says that "Holmes was quiet in his ways, and his habits were regular". His first words to Watson were "How are you? You have been in Afghanistan, I perceive."

Watson's famous summary SHERLOCK HOLMES—his limits.

1.   Knowledge of Literature.—Nil.
2.   Philosophy.—Nil.
3.   Astronomy.—Nil.
4.   Politics.—Feeble.
5.   Botany.—Variable. Well up in belladonna, opium, and poisons generally. Knows nothing of practical gardening.
6.   Geology.—Practical, but limited. Tells at a glance different soils from each other. After walks has shown me splashes upon his trousers, and told me by their colour and consistence in what part of London he had received them.
7.   Chemistry.—Profound.
8.   Anatomy.—Accurate, but unsystematic.
9.   Sensational Literature.—Immense. He appears to know every detail of every horror perpetrated in the century.
10.   Plays the violin well.
11.   Is an expert single stick player, boxer, and swordsman.
12.   Has a good practical knowledge of British law.

Holmes and Watson lived together until around 1888/9, when Watson moved out after his marriage to Mary Morstan. Holmes continued to live there until 1891, when he travelled to Switzerland with Watson and 'Died' falling into the Reichenbach Falls. The rooms remained empty until Holmes returned in 1894 and continued to live there with Watson again until 1904. But enough talk, let's see some illustrations.

From Alpha to Omega, or should that be from Beta to Omega?

Strictly speaking this first image is not the illustration showing the youngest Holmes, but it is his first image to appear and to complicate matter even more the second image is not the last Holmes image, but it is the one showing him at his oldest.

The first illustration of Sherlock Holmes in Beeton's Christmas Annual 1887 by *D. H. Friston*. Holmes would have been around Thirty-Three during this story.	Then twenty-seven years later at the age of Sixty, the 1914 story His Last Bow, shows a ...contemplative Holmes on the cover of Collier's by *Frederic Dorr Steele*.

Holmes in Disguise

Of course Sherlock Holmes is well known for his different disguises. So in chronological order here are a list of them.

SIGN

SIGN

Clad in a rude sailor dress with a pea-jacket and a coarse red scarf round his neck, Sherlock Holmes disguised himself in the Sign of Four.

Richard Gutschmidt.

In the same story, he disguised himself as a painfully asthmatic mariner and fooled Athelney Jones, who tried to stop him leaving.

F. H. Townsend

SCAN

SCAN

Holmes as a groom.

Sidney Paget

As a simple-minded Nonconformist clergyman.

Sidney Paget

Sherlock Holmes in the Bar of Gold Opium
den, trying to find out what had happened to
Neville St. Clair.

Sidney Paget

And again Holmes in the Bar of Gold in
an illustration by

Josef Friedrich

BERY

BERY

Sherlock Holmes as a common loafer
as represented by

Sidney Paget

And the Same loafer as shown by

Josef Friedrich

In the Final Problem, Sherlock Holmes has to don the clothes of a venerable Italian priest to escape Moriarty.

Sidney Paget

Holmes and Watson only just manage to escape Moriarty, but he follows and there is a terrible price to pay.

Harry C. Edwards

EMPT   **EMPT**

When Sherlock Holmes returns in the story 'The Empty House' he poses as an old Book seller.

Stanley E. Armstrong

These four illustrations of the old book seller are quite similar

Frederic Dorr Steele

EMPT

EMPT

Once again, Watson fails to recognise
Holmes in his disguise, Clearly he didn't
look at the Ears.

Sidney Paget

The world had to wait ten years for
Holmes' return after his reported death at
the Reichenbach falls. (not including
Hound)

Charles-Raymond-Macauley

Sherlock Holmes did probably wear a disguise when he posed as Captain Basil in
the story Black Peter, but there are no illustrations of him and so we have to wait
until Charles Augustus Milverton.

Sherlock Holmes plays the part of a plumber called Escott to woe Agatha, Milverton's maid in order to get information about the house.

Frederic Dorr Steele

Sherlock Holmes and John Watson wearing masks in case they should be seen as they attempt to burgle Charles Augustus Milverton's home and recover blackmail letters

Sidney Paget

Unfortunately there are no illustrations of Sherlock Holmes in disguise from the story of the Mazarine Stone, despite him dressed up as

1. A workman looking for a job
2. An old sporting man
3. An elderly woman with the parasol.

LADY

Sherlock Holmes disguised as an unshaven French Ouvier leaps forward to save Watson from the Grip of Philip Green

Alec Ball

LAST

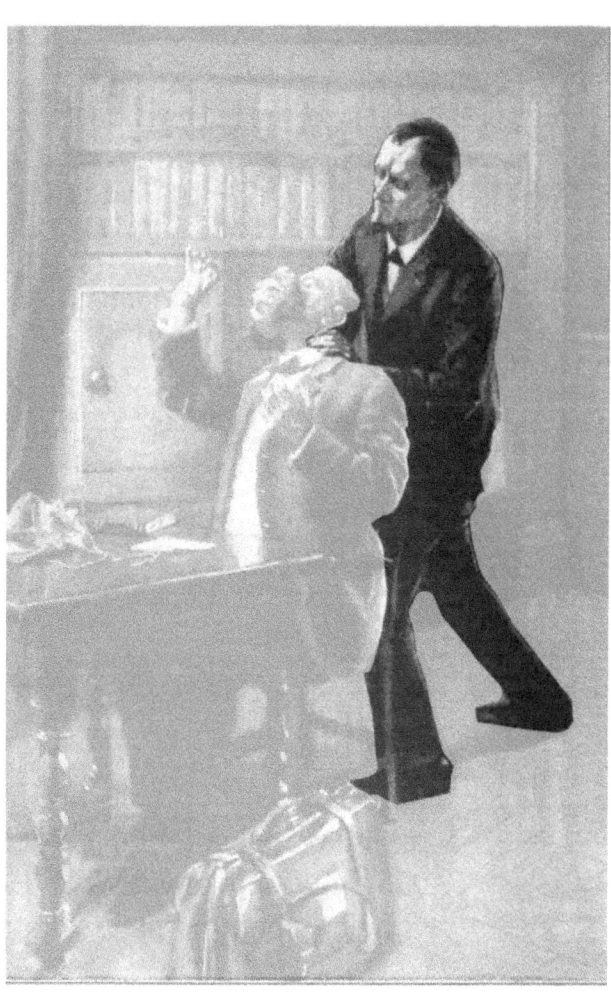

Sherlock, now Sixty, disguised as Altamont, turns the tables on Von Bork. He's looking good for his age in this illustration by

Alfred Gilbert

The last story (chronically) story is His Last Bow, set in 1914, we see Holmes disguised as Altamont, I prefer FDS's version of Holmes, who looks much younger and less bald than RWW's version.

LAST

More relaxed, but looking older, we see Sherlock Holmes, again as Altamont, enjoying a smoke with Von Bork, the German spy. He shows his age more with Grey hair in this illustration by the long-time illustrator

Frederic Dorr Steele

*Nouvelles aventures.
de Sherlock Holmes
I. — Service de Guerre*

In the final image we see an almost balding Sherlock Holmes. But I would argue that Holmes looks older as the asthmatic mariner in Sign of the Four, than he does in this story

R. W. Wallace

A section called Sherlock Holmes Lonely or Solitary?

Look at these four illustrations and decide.

The man with the twisted lip gave us this illustration of Holmes staring off into the distance, while Watson slept.

Sidney Paget

The Famous three-pipe problem quote comes from the Red-headed league story

Sidney Paget

Sherlock Holmes could have been named Pipe-Smoker of the year, but he also smoked cigarettes and cigars.

He had a collection of pipes, three of which were identified

- An old and oily black clay pipe
- An old brier-root pipe
- A cherrywood pipe

He kept his tobacco in a Persian slipper.

"What a lovely thing a rose is!" quote perfectly illustrated in The Naval treaty Story by

Sidney Paget

Front row seats for Sherlock Holmes while he listens in Violin-land from The Red-Headed League Story.

Sidney Paget

He was described as thin, in fact the fact that he was thin is mentioned in so many stories.

He also had thin knees, fingers, sinewy arms, a thin and eager face with a long thin nose and narrow face.

He is also said to be tall six feet and with his thinness, he appeared to look taller.

He had a dolichocephalic skull with a well-marked supra-orbital development.

He had grey eyes and black hair.

Practiced Baritsu, Boxing, Fencing and singlestick, which helped him in the next section.

The Courier Journal

Harry C. Edwards

These two images are so similar, they are almost carbon-copies of each other, but the one on the left came out in November 1893 and the one on the right December 1893

The most famous version is of course this one, which appeared in the Strand in 1893.

Sidney Paget

This version comes from a comic strip by

Leo O'Mealia

Home Secretary, The   [MAZA]   Male Alive   See Akers-Douglas, Aretas

Homer   [REIG]   Male dead   odd volume of Pope's 'Homer,' semi-legendary author of the Iliad and the Odyssey, two epic poems that are the central works When Holmes asked if the items stolen from Old Acton's house were of interest, he was told "I fancy not. The thieves ransacked the library and got very little for their pains. The whole place was turned upside down, drawers burst open, and presses ransacked, with the result that an odd volume of Pope's Homer, two plated candlesticks, an ivory letter-weight, a small oak barometer, and a ball of twine are all that have vanished." A copy of Pope's 'Homer' was stolen from Mr. Acton's house, but really, the thieves wanted certain documents.

Homer

Hones, Johnny   [STUD]   Male dead   In PART II. The Country of the Saints, he was the fourth to die on the trail in the Great Alkali Plain. The order was Mr. Bender, Indian Pete, Mrs. McGregor, then Johnny Hones.

Hood, John Bell   [FIVE]   Male dead (Real Person   Confederate General who had a reputation for bravery and aggressiveness that sometimes bordered on recklessness. Mentioned by John Openshaw, who said that his uncle Elias had fought in Jackson's army and then afterwards with Hood.

John Bell Hood

Hope, Jefferson [STUD]   Male Alive Wore a brown overcoat. Had a florid face, and the fingernails of his right hand were remarkably long. Red Faced. originally from St. Louis. Was employed driving a herd of cow to raise money so that he could continue his silver mining prospecting. His family knew Lucy's father John Ferrier. First met Lucy Ferrier, when he rescued her as her horse started panicking on being surrounded by a herd of cows. Fell in love with her, but had to go off to sort out business for a couple of months. Returned to find Lucy soon to be engaged. Escaped with Lucy and her father, but while he was out hunting for food, John Ferrier was murdered and Lucy was brought back home. Wasn't in a position to help, Lucy was married and died within a month and so he sought out revenge. Revenge was a long time coming to Enoch J. Drebber and Joseph Stangerson, around 20 years in fact. Worked as a hansom cab driver, following the two men around. He found out where they would be staying, they separated and he even managed to take a drunk Drebber as a fare to a disused house, where he forced him to choose a pill from a box, one pill was safe, but the other one was poison. Drebber chose the poison and died. Then Jefferson hope when to see Stangerson in his rooms and when attacked, stabbed him. Walked into a trap at baker street and was arrested by Lestrade and Gregson, who claimed the credit. Died before his case came to court from an aortic aneurism.

Sherlock Holmes Quote : "He was more than six feet high, was in the prime of life, had small feet for his height, wore coarse, square-toed boots and smoked a Trichinopoly cigar."

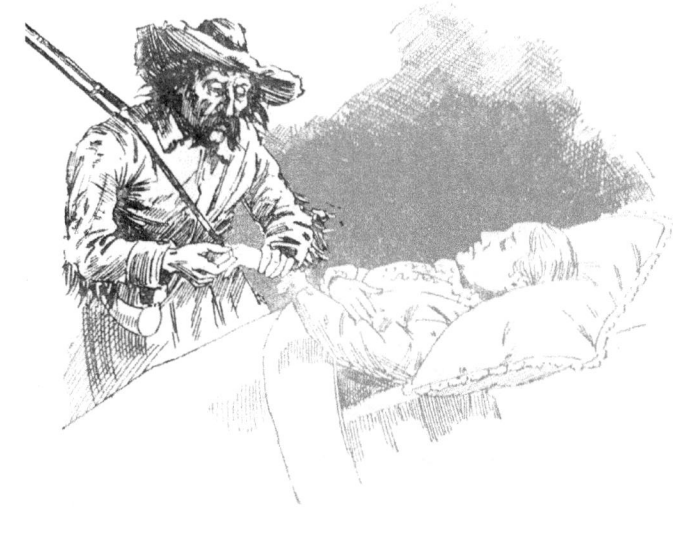

Richard Gutschmidt   *George Hutchinson*

Hope, Lady Hilda Trelawney   [SECO]   Male Alive   The most lovely woman in London. Tall, graceful, and intensely womanly, wearing white gloves. Youngest daughter of the Duke of Belminster. Entered 221b baker street and she manoeuvred herself so that she had the light at her back. She did not wish Holmes and Watson to read her expression. She asked about the lose of the letter and how it would affect her Husband. He had in fact stolen the important letter from the despatch box and exchanged it for an indiscreet letter she had written before her marriage that Eduardo Lucas had in his possession. While making the exchange, a frantic woman and burst into the room, Lady Hilda had escaped. It was only later that she discovered that the woman had in fact killed Eduardo Lucas. She affected a recovery of the important letter, disturbing the carpet in the process. She gave the letter to Holmes and he was able to return it, back into the despatch box and everyone was happy.

Address : Whitehall Terrace

Sidney Paget   *Richard Gutschmidt*

Hope, Right Honourable Trelawney   [SECO]   Male Alive   Dark, clear-cut, and elegant, hardly yet of middle age, and endowed with every beauty of body and of mind. Secretary for European Affairs, and the most rising statesman in the country. The European Secretary pulled nervously at his moustache and fidgeted with the seals of his watch-chain. He and Lord Bellinger arrived at 221b baker street on the morning of the 12 October. They asked for help from Holmes in finding a very important letter that had gone missing from Trelawney Hope's locked despatch box. It had been there the previous night, but on checking the box in the morning, was found to be gone. This letter's recovery was of such importance, that failure would probably result in War. Remained in ignorance of how the letter disappeared and how it was rediscovered in his box.

Address : Whitehall Terrace

Sidney Paget   *Richard Gutschmidt*

Hopkins, Ezekiah   [REDH]   Male dead   American Millionaire Had started from London as a young man Who was very peculiar in his ways. Was Red-headed Said to have formed the Red-Headed League. which advertised in the Morning Chronicle on Sunday 27th April 1890. TO THE RED-HEADED LEAGUE: On account of the bequest of the late Ezekiah Hopkins, of Lebanon, Pennsylvania, U. S. A., there is now another vacancy open which entitles a member of the League to a salary of £4 a week for purely nominal services. All red-headed men who are sound in body and mind, and above the age of twenty-one years, are eligible. Apply in person on Monday, at eleven o'clock, to Duncan Ross, at the offices of the League, 7 Pope's Court, Fleet Street.

Address : Lebanon, Pennsylvania, U.S.A.

Hopkins, Stanley   [BLAC, GOLD, ABBE,MISS]   Male Alive   [BLAC] An exceedingly alert man, thirty years of age, dressed in a quiet tweed suit, but retaining the erect bearing of one who was accustomed to official uniform. He was a young police inspector for whose future Holmes had high hopes, while he in turn professed the admiration and respect of a pupil for the scientific methods of the famous amateur.   [GOLD] Inspector of Scotland Yard. A young promising detective from Scotland Yard in whose career Sherlock Holmes had several times shown a very practical interest. He was in charge of the following murder cases: [ABBE] The Killing of Sir Eustace Brackenstall [BLAC] The Killing of Peter Carey [GOLD] The Killing of Willoughby Smith He asked help from Holmes about the murder of Willoughby Smith, secretary to Professor Coram. [MISS] He advised Cyril Overton to consult Sherlock Holmes. [BLAC] Report that this case was a failure, absolute failure, with no progressing having been made. [ABBE] Sent a note to Holmes Abbey Grange, Marsham, Kent, 3.30 a.m. MY DEAR MR. HOLMES,—I should be very glad of your immediate assistance in what promises to be a most remarkable case. It is something quite in your line. Except for releasing the lady I will see that everything is kept exactly as I have found it, but I beg you not to lose an instant, as it is difficult to leave Sir Eustace there. Yours faithfully, Stanley Hopkins Holmes said that Hopkins had called him in Seven times and on each occasion his summons have been entirely justified.

Address : 46, Lord Street, Brixton

Frederic Dorr Steele   *Sidney Paget*

Horace   [IDEN]   Male dead (Real Person 65 BC – 8 BC)   Holmes compares Hafiz with Horace at the end of the story He states that there is as much sense in Hafiz as in Horace, and as much knowledge of the world. Leading Roman Lyric Poet during the reign of Emperor Augustus (Octavian). Holmes compares Hafiz with Horace at the end of the story He states that there is as much sense in Hafiz as in Horace, and as much knowledge of the world.

Horace

Horner, John [BLUE] Male Alive   Plumber accused of abstracting the Gem from the Lady's jewel-case on the 22nd December 1887. Was working in the Dressing room of the Countess of Morcar at the Hotel Cosmopolitan, soldering the second bar of the grate, which was loose . Had a previous conviction for robbery, but protested his innocence. He had shown signs of intense emotion during the proceedings and fainted away at the conclusion and was carried out of court. Innocent man.

Ernest Flammarion

Horsom, Dr. **[LADY]** **Male Alive** Doctor who wrote out the death certificate for Rose Spender. He visited the deceased and stated that she had died from Senile Decay.

Address : 13 Firbank Villas

Howells, Rachel **[MUSG]** **Female Alive** Second housemaid at Hurlstone. A very good girl, but of an excitable Welsh temperament. Was engaged to Richard Brunton until he broke it off. Might have killed Brunton as she helped him to find the Musgrave treasure. Brunton was in the hole in the ground and the piece of wood holding the heavy stone slipped, closing the top and he suffocated. Did she move the wood or had she just been guilty of silence, in not getting help, only one person knows and she didn't stay to answer questions.

Address : Manor House of Hurlstone

William H. Hyde

Hudson, Head-keeper **[GLOR]** **Male dead** A little wizened fellow with a cringing manner and a shambling style of walking. He wore an open jacket, with a splotch of tar on the sleeve, a red-and-black check shirt, dungaree trousers, and heavy boots badly worn. His face was thin and brown and crafty, with a perpetual smile upon it, which showed an irregular line of yellow teeth, and his crinkled hands were half closed in a way that is distinctive of sailors. Young seaman on board the 'Gloria Scott' who was rescued by James Armitage after the boat exploded. Years later visited Old Trevor, Armitage's new Alias, with the view of blackmail. Was first made gardener and then, as that did not satisfy him, he was promoted to be butler. He wandered about the house and did what he chose in it. The maids complained of his drunken habits and his vile language. Would take the boat and Old Trevor's best gun and treat himself to little shooting trips. All this with such a sneering, leering, insolent face. Had a falling out with Victor Trevor and left with ill-spirits to see if he could do better blackmailing Mr. Beddoes. Believed by police to have killed Beddoes and run off, but it is more likely that it is the other way around.

Sidney Paget

Martin Van Maele

Hudson, Morse [SIXN] Male Alive Was the owner of a shop that sold pictures and statues in the Kennington Road. Sold three of the Napoleon Busts, two to Dr. Barnicot's and one smashed in broad daylight on own counter. The assistant had left the front shop for an instant when he heard a crash, and hurrying in he found a plaster bust of Napoleon, which stood with several other works of art upon the counter, lying shivered into fragments. He rushed out into the road, but, although several passers-by declared that they had noticed a man run out of the shop, he could neither see anyone nor could he find any means of identifying the rascal. It seemed to be one of those senseless acts of Hooliganism which occur from time to time, and it was reported to the constable on the beat as such. The plaster cast was not worth more than a few shillings, and the whole affair appeared to be too childish for any particular investigation. They employed Beppo as a kind of Italian piece-work man, who made himself useful in the shop. He would carve a bit and gild and frame, and do odd jobs.

Address : Kennington Road.

Hudson, Mr. [FIVE] Male Mentioned in the remaining ledger page belonging to the KKK dated March 1869 4th. Hudson came. Same old platform

Hudson, Mrs. Martha [SPEC, NAVA, EMPT, DYIN, LAST,MAZA, 3GAR, BLAC] Female Alive [LAST] A dear old ruddy-faced woman in a country cap A pleasant old lady Mrs. Hudson was the landlady of Sherlock Holmes. [NAVA] She was Scottish. She served tea and coffee to Holmes and Watson, and then curried chicken to Holmes and ham and eggs for Watson. She was involved in creating a surprise effect to Mr. Phelps by hiding the stolen documents under the cover of the plate her served. [DYIN] Mrs. Hudson, the landlady of Sherlock Holmes, was a long-suffering woman. She called on Watson, because she feared that Holmes was dying. She waited outside, while Watson went to talk to Holmes, trembling and weeping in the passage. [SCAN] She was temporarily replaced by Mrs. Turner. [EMPT] The chambers of Holmes and Watson had been left unchanged, through the immediate care of Mrs. Hudson. She went into violent hysterics when Holmes returned after his Hiatus. She was involved in moving the bust of Holmes once every quarter of an hour so that observers would think it was truly Holmes. [LAST] She was a knitter and a cat lover, since she sat knitting and stopped occasionally to stroke a large black cat upon a stool beside her. [LADY] Holmes sent a cable to Mrs Hudson asking her to make one of her best efforts for two hungry travellers at seven-thirty tomorrow. [BLAC] Sharp at the hour named Inspector Stanley Hopkins appeared, and Holmes and Watson sat down together to the excellent breakfast which Mrs Hudson had prepared. Climbed the stairs and informed Holmes that there were three men inquiring for Captain Basil.

Sherlock Holmes Quote : [SPEC] "Mrs. Hudson has had the good sense to light the fire"
[NAVA] "Her cuisine is a little limited, but she has as good an idea of breakfast as a Scotch-woman."
[LAST] "She might almost personify Britannia, with her complete self-absorption and general air of comfortable somnolence."

Frederic Dorr Steele   *Frederic Dorr Steele*

Hudson's (Mrs.) Cat LAST Alive Unnamed large black cat that was keeping
Mrs. Hudson company as she bend over her knitting and who received the
occasional stroke. We don't know if the cat belonged to Mrs. Hudson or maybe
Von Bork.

Frederic Door Steele

Hudson's (Mrs.) Dog   [STUD]   Dead   A poor little devil of a terrier that might have belonged to Mrs. Hudson. Watson said that it's snow-white muzzle proclaimed that it had already exceeded the usual term of canine and it was brought up from downstairs and was put out of its pain, when Holmes give it a drink containing the second pill found at the scene of the murder of Joseph Stangerson. '

Richard Gutschmidt

George W. Hutchinson

Hung-wu   [ILLU]   Male dead (real Person 1328 – 1398)   The founding emperor of the Ming dynasty(1368-1644), reigning from 1368 to 1398.

Predecessor Ukhaghatu Khan Toghon Temür

Successor Jianwen Emperor

Holmes asked Watson to learn as much as he could about Chinese ceramics, so in the process, Watson he learned of the hallmarks of the great artist-decorators, of the mystery of cyclical dates, the marks of the Hung-wu and the beauties of the Yung-lo, the writings of Tang-ying, and the glories of the primitive period of the Sung and the Yuan dynasties. So Watson was learning about early Ming items

Hung Wu

Hunt, Policemen   [VALL]   Male dead   One of two Policeman shot dead because they had attempted to arrest two members of the Scowlers' society. The other Policeman shot was called Evans.

Hunter, Ned   [SILV]   Male Alive   One of three Stable-boys who worked at King's Pyland. Was on guard the night of the murder of John Straker and the disappearance of Silver Blaze. Was brought out a dish of curried mutton by Edith Baxter at nine o'clock. Drank only water, which was the rule of the stables. Chased after Fitzroy Simpson His supper contained an appreciable quantity of powdered opium.

Address : King's Pyland, Dartmoor

Stanley E. Armstrong   *Leo O'Mealia*

Hunter, Violet **[COPP]** **Female Alive** She was plainly but neatly dressed, with a bright, quick face, freckled like a plover's egg, and with the brisk manner of a woman who has had her own way to make in the world. Her hair was somewhat luxuriant, and of a rather peculiar tint of chestnut. It had been considered artistic. Was a governess for five years in the family of Colonel Spence Munro, but two months ago the colonel received an appointment at Halifax, in Nova Scotia, and took his children over to America with him, so that I found myself without a situation. I advertised, and I answered advertisements, but without success. At last the little money which I had saved began to run short, and I was at my wit's end as to what I should do. Was paid £4 a month with Colonel Spence Munro. Her accomplishments included a little French, a little German, music, and drawing— Was offered the sum of £100 a year by Jephro Rucastle and when she turned it down, he wrote to her offering £120 a year. She was asked to cut off her hair. she was now the head of a private school at Walsall, where Watson believes she has met with considerable success.

Sidney Paget   *Josef Friedrich*

Huret the Boulevard Assassin   [GOLD]   Probably Male While considering which story to tell, mentioned The tracking and arrest of Huret, the Boulevard assassin—an exploit which won for Holmes an autograph letter of thanks from the French President and the Order of the Legion of Honour.

Huxtable,Thorneycroft M.A., Ph.D.,   [PRIO]   Male Alive so large, so pompous, and so dignified that he was the very embodiment of self-possession and solidity, The heavy white face was seamed with lines of trouble, the hanging pouches under the closed eyes were leaden in colour, the loose mouth drooped dolorously at the corners, the rolling chins were unshaven. Collar and shirt bore the grime of a long journey, and the hair bristled unkempt from the well-shaped head. It was a sorely-stricken man who lay before us. His card seemed too small to carry the weight of his academic distinctions. Thorneycroft Huxtable, M.A., Ph.D., etc. Was the founder and principal of the Priory preparatory school. Wrote 'Huxtable's Sidelights on Horace'. Collapsed as soon as he entered Holmes' rooms. Told Holmes how one of his students had disappeared in the night, the son of the duke of Holdernesse, Lord Saltine (Arthur). The German master Heidegger was also missing along with his bicycle. The duke of Holdernesse had offered a reward of five thousand pounds.

Address : Priory School, near Mackleton

Frederic Dorr Steele   *Sidney Paget*

Hyam, Mr. [VALL] Male dead   Possible Mine or Ironworks owner killed by the Scowrers.

Hyams, Mr   [NORW] Male Hyams were John Oldacre's tailor. John Oldacre's trouser buttons were found in the fire that was meant to have consumed John Oldacre's body after he had been killed by John Hector McFarlane. At least one of the buttons was marked with the name of 'Hyams'.

Hyde, Edward 1st Earl of Clarendon (Lord Clarendon I) [HOUN] Male dead (Real Person 1609 – 1674)   "Know then that in the time of the Great Rebellion (the history of which by the learned Lord Clarendon I most earnestly commend to your attention) The History of the Rebellion by Edward Hyde, 1st Earl of Clarendon is his account of the English Civil War. This work (originally published in 1702–1704 as The History of the Rebellion and Civil Wars in England) was the first full-scale, detailed history of the Civil War and was written by a key player in the events contained within it.

Edward Hyde

Hynes, Hynes (J.P.) [WIST] Male Alive   An owner of a large house in the Esher area. His details were sent to Holmes by the Allan brothers, chief land agents in the village of Esher. Justice of the Peace. This does seem a strange name and perhaps the Allan Brothers made a error and it should have been something like Hyam Haynes, but we shall never know.

Address : Purdley Place, Esher

I is for the Case of Identity

Indian Pete **[STUD]** **Male dead**   In PART II. The Country of the Saints, he was the second to die on the trail in the Great Alkali Plain. The order of deaths was Mr. Bender, Indian Pete, Mrs. McGregor and Johnny Hones.

Ionides of Alexandria **[GOLD]** **Male dead**   Producer of Egyptian cigarettes that Professor Coram smoked. The professor was sent a thousand at a time and needed to re-order every fortnight, (that's over 71 a day) Holmes smoked a few of the cigarettes, dropping the ash on the floor and was able later to find the hiding place of the killer of Willoughby Smith.

Sherlock Holmes Quote : "I am a connoisseur," said he, taking another cigarette from the box."

Iris the Horse **[SILV]** **Male Horse Alive**   Horse belonging to Lord of Balmoral. Yellow and black stripes. ran in the Wessex plate, not placed. Wessex Plate 50 Sovereigns each h ft. with 1000 Sovereigns added for four and five year olds. Second, £300. Third, £200. New course (one mile and five furlongs).

J is for Jefferson Hope

Jackson, Dr. [CROO] Male Alive   A Doctor who would take Watson's practice while he went off to Aldershot.

Jackson, Mr. [HOUN] Male   Benefactor of a medical prize, that James Mortimer won around 1883. He instituted the Jackson Prize for Comparative Pathology

Jackson, Thomas Jonathan.   [FIVE]   Male dead (Real Person 1824 – 1863)   Confederate General from 1861-1863) Mentioned by John Openshaw, who said that his uncle Elias had fought in Jackson's army and then afterwards with Hood.

Thomas Jackson

Jacobs, Mr [SECO] Male Alive   Right Honourable Trelawney Hope's Valet. Was allowed to enter Trelawney Hope's Bedroom. Was a trusted servants who have been with them for some time.

Address : Whitehall Terrace

Jacobson, Mr. [SIGN] Male Alive Owner of Jacobson's Yard. Used as a place to store the steam launch 'Aurora' so that it was difficult to locate. It was taken in for Rudder repair.

Sherlock Holmes Quote : "I learned that the Aurora had been handed over to them two days ago by a wooden-legged man, with some trivial directions as to her rudder"

James l, King [VALL,WIST] Male dead (Real Person 1566 – 1625) Was the 6th King James in Scotland and the 1st in England. He reigned from 24th March 1603 until 27th March 1625 His 22 year of reign is called the Jacobean period. [VALL] Holmes said Birlstone house was built during this period. [WIST] The house High Gables was a famous old grange and where Mr. Henderson was living.

Sherlock Holmes Quote :[VALL] "Erected in the fifth year of the reign of James I, and standing upon the site of a much older building, the Manor House of Birlstone presents one of the finest surviving examples of the moated Jacobean residence-'"

King
James l

James, Billy [VALL] Male dead Youth killed by the Scowrers for some reason.

James, Jack [LAST] Male in prison Jack James was an American citizen and spy working for Von Bork. he was said to be doing time in Portland. Von Bork said it was James' own fault that he got arrested, he was a bonehead, but it was probably Holmes that informed on him.

James, Master (Telegraph boy) [HOUN] Male Alive Delivered the telegraph to Mr Barrymore sent by Holmes, or rather delivered it to Mrs Barrymore, since Mr Barrymore was in the loft. Son of the Postmaster in Grimpton.

Jenkins, (Brother of elder) [VALL] Male dead Unknown members of the Vermissa lodge for some reason killed both the elder Jenkins and shortly afterwards his brother (him).

Jenkins, (elder) [VALL] Male dead Unknown members of the Vermissa lodge for some reason killed both the elder Jenkins(him) and shortly afterwards his brother.

Jimmy, (heartbreaker) [REDC] Male Alive A message was addressed to him in The Daily Gazette agony column 'Surely Jimmy will not break his mother's heart'

John, (Dr. Armstrong's butler) [MISS] Male Alive A pompous butler who ushered Holmes and Watson severely to the door on the instructions of Dr. Leslie Armstrong.

John, (Holmes' Driver) [TWIS] Male Alive Driver of a tall dog-cart, who was waiting for Holmes to come out of the Bar of Gold Opium Den.

Sherlock Holmes Quote : "All right, John; we shall not need you. Here's half a crown. Look out for me tomorrow, about eleven."

John, (the Coachman) [SCAN] Male alive Irene Adler's coachman. Landau driver for Irene Adler. The coachman with his coat only half-buttoned, and his tie under his ear, while all the tags of his harness were sticking out of the buckles He drove Irene Adler to St. Monica church where she was married. Fast Driver. Was sent by Irene Adler to watch Holmes and Watson, while she ran upstairs to change into walking clothes.

John, Spencer [3GAB] Male Alive Steve Dixie and Barney Stockdale were member of this person's gang. Holmes was in the process of gathering information so that they could be arrested.

Johnson, Mr. [MISS] Male Alive Johnson was one of the two Oxford fliers, opponents to the Cambridge Rugby squad, skippered by Clive Overton.

Johnson, Shinwell   [ILLU]   Male Alive   A huge, coarse, red-faced, scorbutic man, with a pair of vivid black eyes which were the only external sign of the very cunning mind within. During the first years of the century he became a valuable assistant to Holmes. He started making his name first as a very dangerous villain and served two terms at Parkhurst. He finally repented and allied himself to Holmes, acting as his agent in the huge criminal underworld of London and obtaining information which often proved to be of vital importance. Had Johnson been a "nark" of the police he would soon have been exposed, but as he dealt with cases which never came directly into the courts, his activities were never realised by his companions. With the glamour of his two convictions upon him, he had the entree of every night-club, doss house, and gambling-den in the town, and his quick observation and active brain made him an ideal agent for gaining information. Helped Holmes in this story by finding Miss Kitty Winters, who told Holmes about the Baron Gruner's secret diary.

John R. Flanagan

Johnson, Sidney   [BRUC]   Male Alive   The senior clerk at the Woolwich Arsenal. One of two people who had a key to the safe, the other being Sir James Walter. Married with five children. He was a silent, morose man. Had an excellent record in the public service. He was unpopular with his colleagues, but a hard worker. Kept his key on a watch-chain.

Arthur Twidle

Johnson, Theophilus   [HOUN]   Male Alive   A very active gentleman, the same age as Holmes. Holmes wanted to see if the people who were following Sir Henry Baskerville had booked into the hotel after he had registered. Holmes found this person's name in the hotel register. He had been with his family, he arrived at the Northumberland Hotel after Sir Henry Baskerville's arrival. Coal-owner. Had stayed at the Northumberland Hotel a number of times for many years and was well-known to the staff.

Sherlock Holmes Quote : "We know now that the people who are so interested in our friend have not settled down in his own hotel. That means that while they are, as we have seen, very anxious to watch him, they are equally anxious that he should not see them. Now, this is a most suggestive fact."

Address : Newcastle

Johnston, Elder   [STUD]   In PART II. The Country of the Saints section of the book. John Ferrier was provided with as large and as fertile a tract of land as any of the settlers, with the exception of Young himself, and of Stangerson, Kemball, Johnston, and Drebber, who were the four principal Elders. Johnston seems to have been a fictional character, unlike Kemball

Jones, Inspector Athelney   [SIGN]   Male Alive   He called Holmes 'the theorist.' He continued "I'll never forget how you lectured us all on causes and inferences and effects in the Bishopgate jewel case. It's true you set us on the right track; but you'll own now that it was more by good luck than good guidance." Arrested

Thaddeus with the words "Mr. Sholto, it is my duty to inform you that anything which you may say will be used against you. I arrest you in the Queen's name as being concerned in the death of your brother." Arrested Thaddeus Sholto, McMurdo, the gatekeeper, the housekeeper, and the Indian servant Lal Rao. only appeared in one of Holmes' stories.

Sherlock Holmes Quote : "I am the last and highest court of appeal in detection. When Gregson or Lestrade or Athelney Jones are out of their depths—which, by the way, is their normal state—the matter is laid before me.

Richard Gutschmidt   *The Bristol Observer*

Jones, Inspector Peter [REDH] Male Alive Bulky frame. Official police agent for Scotland Yard. Holmes said he was not a bad fellow, though an absolute imbecile in his profession. He had one positive virtue. He was as brave as a bulldog, and as tenacious as a lobster if he got his claws upon anyone. He was in charge in the City and Suburban Bank robbery.

Paul Carrey   *Sidney Paget*

Jose, (Henderson's Servant)   [WIST]   Male Alive   Servant of Mr. Henderson/ Don Morilla Delivered the note that was written by Miss Burnet and addressed by Lopez to Aloysius Garcia.

Address : High Gables

Josef, Franz   [LAST]   Male (Real Person 1830 – 1916)   More properly named Emperor Franz Joseph l of Austria, King of Hungary, Bohemia, Dalmatia and Croatia... Reigned from 2nd December 1848 - 21st November 1916. The Tokay that Holmes and Watson tried was said, by Von Bork to have come from the Franz Josef's special cellar at the Schönbrunn Palace.

Emperor Francis Joseph

Jove **[STUD, IDEN, BLUE, STOC, MUSG, REIG, PRIO, CHAS, SIXN, 3STU, SHOS, MISS, HOUN, WIST, REDC, BRUC, LION]** **Male Alive** by Jove! (an exclamation used to emphasise an accompanying remark or to express surprise): Jove is the older name the Romans had for the god Jupiter Equivalent to the Greek God Zeus. The word is used 22 times in 17 different stories.

Sherlock Holmes Quote : [BLUE] "By Jove, Peterson!" said he, "this is treasure trove indeed. I suppose you know what you have got?"

Juan, Don   [MUSG]   Male dead   Legendary fictional libertine. 'Don Juan' has become a common expression for a womaniser. Mentioned in the story when Reginald Musgrave said that Richard Brunton was one, because he liked the ladies and was involved firstly with Rachel Howell, but had dropped her and was now with Janet Tregellis.

Don Juan

K is for Kratides

Kemball, Elder Heber Chase   [STUD]   Male dead   This person actually existed. In PART II. The Country of the Saints section of the book. John Ferrier was provided with as large and as fertile a tract of land as any of the settlers, with the exception of Young himself, and of Stangerson, Kemball, Johnston, and Drebber, who were the four principal Elders.   Served as one of the original twelve apostles in the early church of the Latter Day Saints.

Kemp, Wilson   [GREE]   Male dead   A small, mean-looking, middle-aged man with rounded shoulders. he wore glasses. He spoke in a nervous, jerky fashion, and with little giggling laughs in between. Somewhat older than Harold Latimer. His features were peaky and sallow, and his little pointed beard was thready and ill-nourished. When he spoke, his lips and eyelids were continually twitching like a man with St. Vitus's dance. Mr Melas could not help thinking that his strange, catchy little laugh was also a symptom of some nervous malady. The terror of his face lay in his eyes, however, steel grey, and glistening coldly with a malignant, inexorable cruelty in their depths. Together with Harold Latimer, held Paul Kratides against his will and starved him until he was ready to sign over some papers related to his sister Sophy Kratides money. Employed the services of Mr. Melas, the Greek interpreter to translate during 'interviews/interrogations' of Paul Kratides.

Address : The Myrtles, Beckenham

Sidney Paget

Kennedy, Mr [SOLI] Male Alive   The Junior partner of Morton & Kennedy, the famous Westminster electricians. The Morton in the company is Cyril Morton, who married Miss Violet Smith. Violet probably gave her husband money to form the company after an inheritance from her uncle.

Kent, Mr. [BLAN] Male Alive   A small bearded man. Doctor who was looking after Godfrey Emsworth. Got a bit miffed by Holmes asking of him "Mr. Kent has seen the patient. May I ask, sir, if you are an authority on such complaints, which are, I understand, tropical or semi-tropical in their nature?" Declared that he had the ordinary knowledge of the educated medical man in a stiff way as a response. But when Holmes offered to introduce the doctor to the specialist Sir James Saunders, he became very excited. Had to attend to Mrs. Emsworth who fainted from joy at the end of the story.

Address : Tuxbury Old Park

Howard K. Elcock

Keswick, Mr. [STUD] Male Alive   Respectable paperhanger who lived at 13, Duncan Street, Houndsditch He had not heard of anyone named Dennis nor Sawyer. His address was given to the cabman by Mrs Sawyer as she entered the cab.

Khalifa, Abdullah Ibn-Mohammed Al [EMPT] Male Alive   After the death of Mahdi in June 1885, Abdullah succeeded as leader of the Mahdists, Called The Khalifa. He attempted to create a kingdom, which led to widespread discontent, and his eventual defeat and death at the hands of the British. Holmes visited him in Khartoum.

Sherlock Holmes Quote : "I looked in at Mecca, and paid a short but interesting visit to the Khalifa at Khartoum, the results of which I have communicated to the Foreign Office."

Khalifa

Khan, Abdullah   [SIGN]   Male in prison   Tall, fierce-looking chap, was an old fighting-man who had borne arms against the British at Chilian-wallah Could talk English pretty well Slightly taller and fiercer of the pair of Sikhs (Mahomet Singh and Abdullah Khan) One of the Four. An old fighting-man, who was guarding the gate at the red fort with Mahomet Singh, commanded by Jonathan Small Was charged with murder of Achmet the Merchant, was found guilty and given penal servitude for life.

Richard Gutschmidt   *F. H. Townsend*

khitmutgar **[SIGN]** **Male Alive** Hindu servant clad in a yellow turban, white loose-fitting clothes, and a yellow sash. Worked for Thaddeus Sholto. Showed Mary Morstan, Holmes and Watson into Thaddeus Sholto's London Home. Hindi word for a Table-servant or under-butler. So not really his name, but Thaddeus does call him by this "Show them in to me, khitmutgar."

Thomas J. Nicholl

Khwāja Shams-ud-Dīn Muḥammad Ḥāfeẓ-e Shīrāzī [IDEN] Male dead See Hafiz

King, Mrs [DANC] Female Alive Cook at Riding Thorpe Manor, Norfolk. Together with the housemaid, Saunders raised the alarm after discovering the bodies in the study. She and Saunders had adjoining rooms and were awoken by the sound of an explosion, which had been followed a minute later by a second one. They descended the stairs together and found that the door of the study was open and a candle was burning upon the table. They found their master face down in the centre of the room. He was quite dead. Near the window his wife was crouching, her head leaning against the wall. She was horribly wounded, and the side of her face was red with blood. Answered questions asked of her by Holmes and inspector Martin. Holmes was able to work out that the first bang was actually produced by two pistols going off at almost the same time.

Address : Thorpe Manor, Norfolk.

Sidney Paget

Kirwan, William [REIG] Male dead Was a coachman for the Cunninghams. Shot through the heart. Received a letter in the afternoon post from his killer. Shot by a 'Burglar' who fled across the garden and over the hedge Lives at the lodge with his mother. His mother was very old and deaf, and no information was obtained from her. She was never very bright. Had the reputation of being an honest man, but was actually a blackmailer.

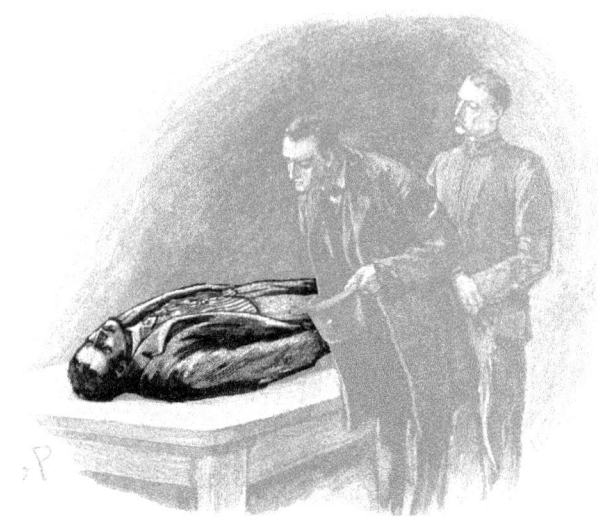

Martin Van Maele   *Sidney Paget*

Klein, Isadora   [3GAB]   Female Alive   tall, queenly, a perfect figure, a lovely
mask-like face, with two wonderful Spanish eyes. She was pure Spanish, the real
blood of the masterful Conquistadors, and her people had been leaders in
Pernambuco for generations. She had married the aged German sugar king, Klein,
and presently found herself the richest as well as the most lovely widow upon
earth. She had had several lovers, and Douglas Maberley, one of the most striking
men in London, was one of them. She was said to be the 'belle dame sans merci'
of fiction. Douglas Maberley wanted marriage but this was not in Isadora Klein's
plans, since he was just a penniless commoner. When he wouldn't take no for an
answer, she sent hiring ruffians to beat him under her own window. Incensed
Maberley wrote a book in which he described his own story. Isadora, was the
wolf; he the lamb. It was all there, under different names, of course; but who in all
London would have failed to recognise it? He sent one copy to her and kept
another for his publisher and then he suddenly died and his belongings, including
the draft, were sent to his mother. Isadora attempted to purchase the house and all
items within, in an attempt to get her hands on the incriminating novel, and when
this fell through, she sent Steve Dixie and Barney Stockdale to steal it. She then
burned it and when Holmes called to recover the document, it was too late, but a
cheque for £5,000 made out to Mrs. Mary Maberley, so that she could go on a
round the world trip was considered a fair price. Holmes did warn her that her
actions were reprehensible.

Sherlock Holmes Quote : "have a care! Have a care! You can't play with edged tools forever without cutting those dainty hands."

Address : Grosvenor Square

Frederic Dorr Steele   *Howard K. Elcock*

Klopman, Nihilist   [LAST]   Male   Anarchist who tried to kill Count Von und Zu Grafenstein, but was stopped by Holmes.

Kneller, Sir Godfrey   [HOUN]   Male dead (Real Person 1646 – 1723) Leading portrait artist in England. Holmes, Sir Henry Baskerville and Watson were looking at all the paintings hanging in Baskerville Hall and Holmes was fascinated by the one of the original Sir Hugo Baskerville.

Sherlock Holmes Quote : "I know what is good when I see it, and I see it now. That's a Kneller, I'll swear, that lady in the blue silk over yonder, and the stout gentleman with the wig ought to be a Reynolds. They are all family portraits, I presume?"

Sir Godfrey_Kneller

Knox, Jack **[VALL]** **Male Alive** Possible mine or ironwork owner who was not on the list, this time, to be murdered by the assassins Lawlers and Andrews. Was based in Ironhill.

Kratides, Paul **[GREE]** **Male dead** Deadly pale and terribly emaciated, with the protruding, brilliant eyes of a man whose spirit was greater than his strength. His face was grotesquely criss-crossed with sticking-plaster, and that one large pad of it was fastened over his mouth. Was held captive by Harold Latimer and J. Davenport until he signed papers for them. Said he would not unless Sophy Kratides was married in his presence by a Greek priest whom he knew. Could speak no English and so the interpreter Mr. Melas was summoned to translate for him. Brother of Sophy Kratides Member of a Wealthy Grecian Family. Had been held three weeks by the kidnappers being starved. Was from Athens. asphyxiated by a burning Charcoal tripod in the middle of a room in which he was tied up.

Address : The Myrtles, Beckenham

Sidney Paget   *William H. Hyde*

Kratides, Sophy [GREE] Female Alive She was tall and graceful, with black hair, and clad in some sort of loose white gown. Spoke English with a broken accent. Member of a Wealthy Grecian Family. Sister of Paul Kradites. Fell in love with Harold Latimer and ran away with him. Went to live at The Myrtles in Beckenham, and kept as a prisoner. Later was forced to flee with the two Englishmen, when Mr. Melas started talking. Believed, by Holmes, to have stabbed Harold Latimer and Wilson Kemp in Buda-Pesth, Hungary.

Address : The Myrtles, Beckenham

Sidney Paget   *William H. Hyde*

L is for the Lion's Mane

La Rothière, Louis [SECO] Male Alive   One of the three people who might have had a hand in taking the letter from the despatch case belonging to the Rt. Hon. Trelawney Hope. This letter from a certain foreign potentate could lead to war if it fell into the wrong hands. He was innocent in this case

Sherlock Holmes Quote : "There are only those three capable of playing so bold a game; there are Oberstein, La Rothière, and Eduardo Lucas. I will see each of them."

Address : Campden Mansions, Notting Hill

Lancaster, James   [BLAC] Male Alive A little ribston-pippin of a man, with ruddy cheeks and fluffy white side-whiskers.   Holmes, using his Captain Basil alias, advertised positions on a ship in order to catch the murderer of Captain Peter Carey. James Lancaster was the first applicant and quickly dismissed as the man Holmes wanted and was given half a sovereign for his troubles.

Lander, Brother [VALL] Male in prison   Scowrer who tried to claim the head money given by the lodge for the shooting of old man Crabbe over at Stylestown. This money was also claimed by Egan.

Lanner, Inspector [RESI] Male Alive A smart-looking police-inspector Inspector of Scotland Yard, who was investigating the suicide of Mr. Blessington until Holmes pointed out it was murder.

Sidney Paget

Larbey, Mrs. **[VALL]** **Female dead** Unknown members of the Vermissa lodge shoot Mrs. Larbey when she was nursing her husband, who had been beaten almost to death by orders of Boss McGinty.

Lascar, **[TWIS]** **Male Alive** Ran the Opium den called the 'Bar of Gold' in Upper Swandam Lane. Stopped Mrs Saint-Clair from going upstairs and finding the her husband Neville, who was dressed as the beggar Hugh Boone. Would have killed Holmes if he had recognised the later while Holmes was in disguise trying to find out information about Neville Saint-Claire's disappearance. Rented out his upper room to Neville Saint-Clair, who used it for changing into Hugh Boone.

Sherlock Holmes Quote : A man of the vilest antecedents.

Sidney Paget

Latimer, Harold **[GREE]** **Male Alive** A very fashionably dressed young man. Had a most formidable-looking bludgeon loaded with lead in his pocket. A powerful, broad-shouldered young fellow Visited Mr. Melas one Monday night and asked him to translate. He said that a Greek friend had come to see him upon business, and as he could speak nothing but his own tongue, the services of an interpreter were indispensable. Said that his house was some little distance off, in Kensington, and hurried Mr. Melas into the cab. Held captive Paul Kratides and was torturing him until he signed over Sophy Kratides money to him. Since Paul could speak no English, Latimer needed an interpreter. Killed Paul Kratides and attempted to kill Mr. Melas. Left 'the Myrtles' just before Holmes and party arrived. Was killed months later in Buda-Pesth (Budapest) and Holmes thought probably by Sophy Kratides.

Address : The Myrtles, Beckenham

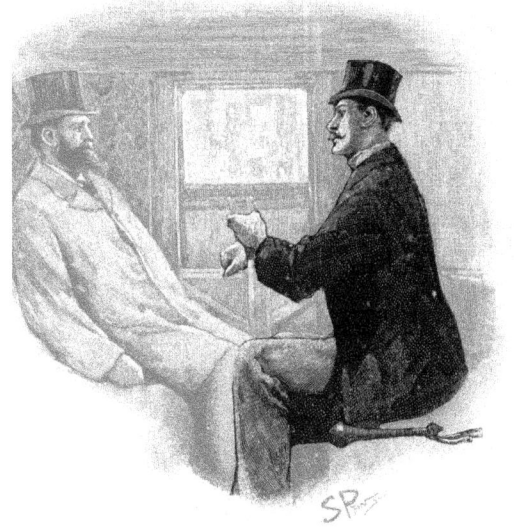

Sidney Paget

William H. Hyde

Lawler, Brother. [VALL] Male Alive Lawler was an elderly man, shrewd, silent, and self-contained, clad in an old black frock coat, which with his soft felt hat and ragged, grizzled beard gave him a general resemblance to an itinerant preacher. One of the two Assassins sent over to kill Josiah H. Dunn at Crow Hill by the County Delegate. He had carried out fourteen previous missions of murder. He had often proved themselves to be most capable instruments for this association of murder. Arriving at the mine, had shot Josiah H. Dunn in the back who went down sidewise, kicking and clawing among a heap of clinkers. Then Shot Menzies, the Scotchman, in the face. As some of the miners surged forward, he had emptied his six-shooters over the heads of the crowd, and they broke and scattered, some of them rushing wildly back to their homes in Vermissa. He escaped.

Le Brun, Monsieur [ILLU] Male Alive Discussed in an interview between Holmes and Baron Bruner. "'By the way, Mr. Holmes,' said the Baron, 'did you know Le Brun, the French agent?' "'Yes,' said Holmes "'Do you know what befell him?' "'I heard that he was beaten by some Apaches in the Montmartre district and crippled for life.' '"Quite true, Mr. Holmes. By a curious coincidence he had been inquiring into my affairs only a week before. Don't do it, Mr. Holmes; it's not a lucky thing to do. Several have found that out. My last word to you is, go your own way and let me go mine. Good-bye!'

lecoq, Monsieur [STUD] Male Fictional detective employed by the Surete. from Emile Gaboriau. French First appears in L'Affaire Lerouge, published in 1866.

Sherlock Holmes Quote : Holmes sniffed sardonically. "Lecoq was a miserable bungler," he said, in an angry voice; "he had only one thing to recommend him, and that was his energy. That book made me positively ill. The question was how to identify an unknown prisoner. I could have done it in twenty-four hours. Lecoq took six months or so. It might be made a text-book for detectives to teach them what to avoid."

Monsieur Lecoq

Lee, Mr [VALL] Male Alive Mine owner, who was forced to sell his mine to the State & Merton County Railroad Company and moved out of the area.

Lee, Robert E. [FIVE] Male dead (Real Person 1807 – 1870) Commander of the Confederate States Army Mentioned by John Openshaw, who said that his uncle Elias returned to his plantation when Lee laid down his arms.

Robert E. Lee

Lefevre of Montpellier   [STUD]   Male Alive   Holmes says that this person escaped hanging in Montpellier because Holmes' blood test wasn't around.

Leo XIII, Pope   [HOUN,BLAC]   Male Alive (Real Person 1810 – 1903)
Roman Catholic Pope from 20 February 1878 to 20 July 1903 [HOUN] Holmes was exceedingly preoccupied by that little affair of the Vatican cameos and in his anxiety to oblige the Pope, who would have been Leo XIII. [BLAC] In 1895 Holmes investigated the sudden death of Cardinal Tosca for this Pope. [HOUN]
Sherlock Holmes Quote : "I must thank you, for calling my attention to a case which certainly presents some features of interest. I had observed some newspaper comment at the time, but I was exceedingly preoccupied by that little affair of the Vatican cameos, and in my anxiety to oblige the Pope I lost touch with several interesting English cases. This article, you say, contains all the public facts?"

Pope Leo XIII

Leonardo [VEIL] Male dead He was clearly a professional acrobat, a man of magnificent physique, taken with his huge arms folded across his swollen chest and a smile breaking from under his heavy moustache—the self-satisfied smile of the man of many conquests. Leonardo the strong man at Ronder's Circus. It was only Leonardo, Mrs. Ronder and little Jimmy Griggs, the clown, who kept the circus going. He pitied Mrs. Ronder and this pity, turned to a deep, deep passionate love. Mr Ronder suspected this, but he was scared of Leonardo, so he took out his revenge on his wife. They decided that Mr. Ronder had to die and Leonardo used his clever, scheming brain to work out a plan. He fashioned a fake lion's paw from a weighted club with five long steel nails, with points outwards, to deliver a death-blow. He waited one evening by the side of the big van, for Mr. Ronder and his wife to pass by and as Mrs. Ronder got to the lion's cage, struck down her husband from behind with his club, he fell down dead instantly. But things started to go wrong as soon as the cage door was opened, instead of running away, the lion attacked Mrs. Ronder tearing at her face with his teeth, in a panic Leonardo ran away rather than save Mrs. Ronder, but he later returned with Jimmy Griggs and together with others dragged her from under the creature's paws. He had a wonderful body, but a poor spirit. He probably threw the lion club into the deep green pool at the bottom of the local chalk-pit. He drowned in September 1896, while bathing near Margate

Frederic Door Steele

Lestrade G.   [STUD,SIGN, NOBL,BOSC,CARD, HOUN, EMPT,CHAS, SIXN, SECO,BRUC,LADY, 3GAR]   Male Alive [BOSC] Described as a Lean, ferret-like man, furtive and sly-looking. Wore a light brown dust coat and leather leggings which he wore in deference to his rustic surrounds. His left foot has an inward twist. [NOBL] The Detective was attired in a pea-jacket and cravat, which gave him a decidedly nautical appearance, and he carried a black canvas bag in his hand. [SECO] bulldog features [BRUC] thin and austere Inspector at Scotland Yard. First name unknown. He is mentioned in Thirteen of Holmes' stories STUD, SIGN, NOBL, BOSC, CARD, HOUN, EMPT, CHAS, SIXN, SECO,BRUC, LADY, 3GAR [SIGN] Just referenced [STUD] Used to visit Holmes three or four times in a single week. Discovered the word 'RACHE' written on the wall at 3, Lauriston Gardens. Thought that Stangerson might have killed Enoch J. Drebber, but changed his mind when he found his dead body at Halliday's private Hotel. Along with Gregson, he was given the credit for finding the murderer Jefferson Hope, which of course should have been given to Holmes. [BOSC] He was retained by Miss Turner to help prove the innocence of James McCarthy, he in turn refers the case to Holmes [SIXN] Lestrade had got into the habit of visiting Holmes in the Evening and on one such occasion mentions some puzzling events, the smashing of Busts of Napoleon. At the end of the Story, he makes a profound statement "Well, I've seen you handle a good many cases, Mr Holmes, but I don't know that I ever knew a more workmanlike one than that. We're not jealous of you at Scotland Yard. No, sir, we are damned proud of you, and if you come down tomorrow there's not a man, from the oldest inspector to the youngest constable, who wouldn't be glad to shake you by the hand." [CHAS] Was given the task of finding the murderer of Charles Augustus Milverton and asks Holmes to help out, but help is not forthcoming. [SECO] Discovered the second stain, the stain on the carpet, did not match the location of the stain on the floor at 16, Godolphin Street. He was trying to track down the murderer of Eduardo Lucas and knew nothing about the important missing document. [NOBL] Lord Robert St. Simon says that Lestrade is acting already in the matter. He had been dragging the Serpentine in order to find the body of Lady St. Simon. Lestrade finds a note in the pocket of the dress he finds and this leads Holmes on the path of locating the Hatty Moulton [CARD] He visited Miss Susan Cushing along with Holmes and Watson to look at a cardboard box the lady had received containing two ears. Was asked by Holmes to arrest James Browner for murder. [HOUN] He was called up from London to help in the arrest of Jack Stapleton. He brought up an unsigned arrest warrant. When asked, by Holmes, if he was armed, he replied The little detective smiled. "As long as I have my trousers I have a hip-pocket, and as long as I have my hip-pocket I have something in it." [EMPT] Meets up with Watson and Holmes to arrest Colonel Moran at the end of the story, not for the attempted murder of Holmes with an air-gun, but the murder of Ronald Adair. [BRUC] Followed Holmes and Watson around as they investigated the case. [LADY] Helped Holmes and Watson in this case, but might have been a little late in arresting Holy Peters and assistant. [3GAR] Lestrade didn't do much in this case, Holmes visited him

Sherlock Holmes Quotes : [STUD] "Lestrade is a well-known detective. He got himself into a fog recently over a forgery case, and that was what brought him here."

[STUD] "Gregson is the smartest of the Scotland Yarders, he and Lestrade are the pick of a bad lot. They are both quick and energetic, but conventional—shockingly so. They have their knives into one another, too. They are as jealous as a pair of professional beauties. There will be some fun over this case if they are both put upon the scent."

[SIGN] "I am the last and highest court of appeal in detection. When Gregson or Lestrade or Athelney Jones are out of their depths—which, by the way, is their normal state—the matter is laid before me.

George Hutchinson   *D. H. Friston*   *Sidney Paget*

Lesurier, Madame   **[SILV]**   **Female** Owner of a milliners shop. William Darbyshire purchase a hat for thirty-seven pounds fifteen made out by this lady.

Address : Bond Street, London

Leturier in Montpellier   **[STUD]**   **dead**   Clearly a victim of forcible poisoning.

Sherlock Holmes Quote : "The forcible administration of poison is by no means a new thing in criminal annals. The cases of Dolsky in Odessa, and of Leturier in Montpellier, will occur at once to any toxicologist."

Leverstoke, Lord   **[PRIO]**   **Male Alive**   He entrusted his son to Dr. Thorneycroft Huxtable and the Priory School

Address : Priory School, near Mackleton

Leverton, Mr.   **[REDC]**   **Male Alive**   A quiet, business like young man, with a clean-shaven, hatchet face. An American who worked for the Pinkerton's American Agency, who met up with Holmes and Watson as they went to the room, from which light signals were sent out. His name and fame was known to Holmes.

Sherlock Holmes Quote : "The hero of the Long Island cave mystery? Sir, I am pleased to meet you."

Richard W. Wallace

Lewis, Sir George [ILLU] Male Alive Was involved in the Hammerford Will case. Colonel Sir James Damery was involved in the negotiations of this case.

Sherlock Holmes Quote : "Well, I can tell you a little more than that. He has rather a reputation for arranging delicate matters which are to be kept out of the papers. You may remember his negotiations with Sir George Lewis over the Hammerford Will case. He is a man of the world with a natural turn for diplomacy. I am bound, therefore, to hope that it is not a false scent and that he has some real need for our assistance."

Lexington, Mrs. [NORW] Female Alive A little, dark, silent person, with suspicious and sidelong eyes. Jonas Oldacre's housekeeper. she had let Mr McFarlane into the house at half-past nine. She wished her hand had withered before she had done so. She had gone to bed at half-past ten. Her room was at the other end of the house, and she heard nothing o She had been awakened by the alarm of fire. Her poor, dear master had certainly been murdered. She discovered the thumb print in blood belonging to Mr. McFarlane, on the white wall in the hall. She conspired with Oldacre to get McFarlane convicted for his murder.

Address : Deep Dene House, at the Sydenham end of the road, Lower Norwood.

Frederic Dorr Steele   *R. Thomson*

Lincoln, Abraham   [THOR]   Male dead (Real Person 1809 – 1865)
America's 16th President, who was in power during the American Civil War
Watson commented that Neil J. Gibson had much in common with Abraham
Lincoln, but the former was keyed to base uses instead of high ones like the later.

Abraham Lincoln

Linder, Max **[VALL]** **Male Alive** Owner of the company Max Linder & Co. They paid five hundred to the Scowrer lodge to be left alone.

Lomax, Mr. **[ILLU]** **Male** Worked as sub-librarian at the London Library in St. James's Square. Friend of Watson. Helped Watson select volumes to help him learn about Chinese ceramics.

Lomond, Duke of **[3GAB]** **Male Alive** Isadora Klein was about to marry this young Duke, who was so young, that he might almost be her son. It was said that his Grace's ma might overlook the age, but a big scandal would be a different matter.

Lopez, Mr. **[WIST]** **Male Alive** See Mr. Lucas

Lothario **[RETI]** **Male Alive** Commonly a male name given to someone who unscrupulously seduces women. The name was based upon a character that appears within the story 'The Impertinent Curious Man' that was itself within Don Quixote. Anselmo, in order to test his wife, asks a close friend of his, called Lothario to try and seduce her. It doesn't end well, at least for Anselmo. Dr. Ernest was said to be the gay Lothario in this story

Lowenstein, H. **[CREE]** **Male Alive** Was an obscure scientist who was striving in some unknown way for the secret of rejuvenation and the elixir of life. Lowenstein of Prague! Lowenstein with the wondrous strength-giving serum, tabooed by the profession because he refused to reveal its source. Sent the following in a letter to professor Presbury. HONOURED COLLEAGUE [it ran]: Since your esteemed visit I have thought much of your case, and though in your circumstances there are some special reasons for the treatment, I would none the less enjoin caution, as my results have shown that it is not without danger of a kind. It is possible that the serum of anthropoid would have been better. I have, as I explained to you, used black-faced langur because a specimen was accessible. Langur is, of course, a crawler and climber, while anthropoid walks erect and is in all ways nearer. I beg you to take every possible precaution that there be no premature revelation of the process. I have one other client in England, and Dorak is my agent for both. Weekly reports will oblige.
Yours with high esteem,
H. LOWENSTEIN.

Lucas, Eduardo **[SECO]** **Male dead** Well known in society circles both on account of his charming personality and because he had the well-deserved reputation of being one of the best amateur tenors in the country. Posed as an unmarried man M. Henri Fournaye and Eduardo Lucas were really one and the same person. Was a blackmailer and possible spy, who made Lady Hilda

Trelawney take an important letter from her husbands dispatch case and bring it to him. He hid the letter in a secret compartment under the carpet. While Lady Trelawney was there, Lucas' wife appeared and in a frenzied attack stabbed him, killing him.

Address : 16, Godolphin Street and small villa in the Rue Austerlitz, Paris.

Lucas, Mr. [WIST] Male Alive A foreigner, chocolate brown, wily, suave, and catlike, with a poisonous gentleness of speech. Posed as Mr. Lucas, when he was Secretary to Mr Henderson. Caught Miss Burnett trying to send a message to Aloysius Garcia, and helped in Garcia's murder at the hands of Henderson. Was also called Lopez when he was assistant to Juan Don Murillo. Finally he was Signor Rulli, when he was secretary to Marquess of Montalva. Murdered in rooms at the Hotel Escurial at Madrid

Arthur Twidle

Lucca, Emilia [REDC] Female Alive A tall and beautiful woman. She was born in Posilippo, near Naples, Daughter of Augusto Barelli, who was the chief lawyer and once the deputy of that part. Eloped with Gennaro and married in 1898 at Bari. Sold her jewels and used the money to get them to New York, America. Gennaro got involved with a Murderer called Giuseppe Gorgiano, a murderer and member of the secret crime organisation called 'The Red Circle'. Additionally, Emilia had awakened 'love' in Gordiano heart and he broke into her home and attacked her. She and Gennaro were forced to flee and travelled to London, but Gordiano followed them. She was hidden in Mrs. Warren's house, while her husband Gennaro tried to work with Italian and American police. She received messages from him in the agony columns of the Daily Gazette and eventually light signals from a window of an adjacent Flat. She related her story to Holmes, Watson, Gregson and Mr. Leverton, of the Pinkerton's American Agency. (

Richard W. Wallace   *H. M. Brock*

Lucca, Gennaro   [REDC] Male Alive Middle size, dark, and bearded. Spoke good English, sir, and was a foreigner by his accent. Very smartly dressed, quite the gentleman. Dark clothes —nothing you would note. He had one big brown bag with him—nothing else. Gennaro worked for Augusto Barelli, who was the chief lawyer and once the deputy of that part. Didn't have much money, nor position. Married Emilia Barelli against her father wishes at Bari in 1898. She sold her jewels and they both went to America Had been living and working in New York for four years. Worked for Castalotte and Zamba, the chief fruit importers of New York. When he had been young in his wild and fiery days, he had joined a Neapolitan society, the Red Circle, which was allied to the old Carbonari. The giant Gorgiano, a man who had earned the name of 'Death' in the south of Italy, discovered him in New York and was forming a branch of the Red Circle there and tried to force Gennaro to Kill his friend and employer Tito Castalotte. Gorgiano also had designs on Gennaro's Wife, Emilia, so they fled to London, but where followed by Gorgiano. Gennaro hid his wife in Mrs. Warren's house, while he was communicating with the Italian and American Police. Communicated with his wife by putting the following messages into the agony columns of the Daily Gazette 'Be patient. Will find some sure means of communications. Meanwhile, this column. G.' then three days later 'Am making successful arrangements. Patience and prudence. The clouds will pass. G.' then a week later 'The path is clearing. If I find chance signal message remember code agreed—One A, two B, and so on. You will hear soon. G' and finally "'High red house with white stone facings. Third floor. Second window left. After dusk. G.' Ultimately there was an encounter between Gennaro and Gorgiano at a Howe Street flat and the latter is killed. He put the following messages into the agony columns of the Daily Gazette 'Be patient. Will find some sure means of communications. Meanwhile, this column. G.' then three days later 'Am making successful arrangements. Patience and prudence. The clouds will pass. G.' then a week later 'The path is clearing. If I find chance signal message remember code agreed—One A, two B, and so on. You will hear soon. G' and finally "'High red house with white stone facings. Third floor. Second window left. After dusk. G.'

Lund, John Richard   [STUD]   Male   Strictly speaking this person is not named in the Canon, he formed part of the company of Barraud & Lund, clock makers in London. Prior to 1838 the company was called Barraud, which was the name on Enoch J. Drebber's watch. In 1838 John Richard Lund joined Frederick Philip Barraud and from then company became known as Barraud & Lund. They Made the gold watch, No. 97163 on a gold Albert chain, very heavy and solid, that Enoch J. Drebber had on his person, when he was murdered.

Lynch, Judge   [VALL]   Male Alive   A Judge that Brother Morris suggested might try the case if the Lodge killed James Stanger, the editor of the Herald newspaper.

Lynch, Victor   [SUSS]   Male   As Holmes read through the 'V' section of his notebook looking for information about Vampires, he mentioned Victor Lynch the Forger. Now why this was catalogued under 'V' rather than 'L' will remain a mystery.

Sherlock Holmes Quote : "Voyage of the Gloria Scott, that was a bad business. I have some recollection that you made a record of it, Watson, though I was unable to congratulate you upon the result. Victor Lynch, the forger. Venomous lizard or gila. Remarkable case, that! Vittoria, the circus belle. Vanderbilt and the Yeggman. Vipers. Vigor, the Hammersmith wonder. Hullo! Hullo! Good old index. You can't beat it. Listen to this, Watson. Vampirism in Hungary. And again, Vampires in Transylvania."

Lyons, Artist   [HOUN]   Female Alive   Husband of Laura Lyons He proved to be a blackguard and deserted her. The fault from what I hear may not have been entirely on one side.

Lyons, Laura [HOUN] Female Alive The first impression left by Mrs. Lyons was one of extreme beauty. Her eyes and hair were of the same rich hazel colour, and her cheeks, though considerably freckled, were flushed with the exquisite bloom of the brunette, the dainty pink which lurks at the heart of the sulphur rose. There was something subtly wrong with the face, some coarseness of expression, some hardness, perhaps, of eye, some looseness of lip which marred its perfect beauty. Daughter of Mr. Frankland. Married the Artist Mr. Lyons against her father's wishes and now divorced from her husband, was in desperate need of money. She did typing to earn a living. Wrote a letter to Sir Charles Baskerville to meet with him on the night of his death, but did not attend. This letter was found by Mr. Barrymore and given to Watson, who failed to get any information from Laura Lyons, Holmes did much better later on.

Sidney Paget   *B. Widman*

M is for the Musgrave Ritual

M

Maberley, Douglas   [3GAB]   Male dead   Son of Mortimer and Mary Maberley. Famous in London. Attaché in Rome. At the end of his life he changed from being debonair and splendid to a moody, morose, brooding creature. His heart was broken. In a single month he turned into a worn-out cynical man. Had fallen in love with Isadora Klein and when he was discarded by her and beaten up by ruffians in her employ, he had resolved to get his own back by writing his story and how she treated him. He died from a broken heart as much as from pneumonia in April. The only part of his manuscript that survived was the last page, numbered 245 and it went; "...face bled considerably from the cuts and blows, but it was nothing to the bleeding of his heart as he saw that lovely face, the face for which he had been prepared to sacrifice his very life, looking out at his agony and humiliation. She smiled—yes, by Heaven! she smiled, like the heartless fiend she was, as he looked up at her. It was at that moment that love died and hate was born. Man must live for something. If it is not for your embrace, my lady, then it shall surely be for your undoing and my complete revenge."

Sherlock Holmes Quote : "I have never known anyone so vitally alive. He lived intensely—every fibre of him!"

Maberley, Mary   [3GAB]   Female Alive   Sent a letter to Holmes asking for help, which read;

DEAR MR. SHERLOCK HOLMES :

I have had a succession of strange incidents occur to me in connection with this house, and I should much value your advice. You would find me at home any time tomorrow. The house is within a short walk of the Weald Station. I believe that my late husband, Mortimer Maberley, was one of your early clients. Yours faithfully,

MARY MABERLEY.

She was the mother of the famous Douglas Maberley. After the death of her son, his belongings were sent to her, including a manuscript that exposed the actions of Isadora Klein, something she was loathed to have revealed to the world. She wanted to go around the world, and was offered a very large amount of money for her house, with the proviso that ALL the contents came with the house. She refused and her house was broken into by Steve Dixie and Barney Stockdale, she was attacked and Douglas' manuscript was taken. Holmes managed to get a cheque from Isadora Klein for £5,000, so that she could travel around the world.

Address : The Three Gables, Harrow Weald

Frederic Dorr Steele

Frederic Dorr Steele

Maberley, Mortimer   [3GAB]   Male dead   Deceased husband of Mary Maberley. He had once been an early client of Holmes.

MacDonald, Inspector Alec   [VALL]   Male Alive   Was a tall, bony figure which gave promise of exceptional physical strength, while his great cranium and deep-set, lustrous eyes spoke no less clearly of the keen intelligence which twinkled out from behind his bushy eyebrows. He was a silent, precise man with a dour nature and a hard Aberdonian accent. Inspector of Scotland Yard Was far from having attained the national fame which he has now achieved. He was a young but trusted member of the detective force, who had distinguished himself in several cases which had been entrusted to him. Holmes had twice helped him to attain success in his career. Because Holmes' sole reward was in the intellectual joy of the problem, the affection and respect of the Scotchman for his amateur colleague were profound, and he showed them by the frankness with which he consulted Holmes in every difficulty. Holmes was not prone to friendship, but he was tolerant of the big Scotchman, and smiled at the sight of him.

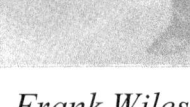

Frank Wiles   *Frank Wiles*

Machiavelli, Niccolò di Bernardo dei   [VALL]   Male dead (Real Person 1469 – 1527) Italian Renaissance Philosopher and writer, his most famous work is 'The Prince' Said that politics had always been played with deception, treachery and crime and the ends justifies the means Considering the book Porlock had used for his cipher, Holmes makes a snide remark to Watson.

Sherlock Holmes Quote : "Perhaps there are points which have escaped your Machiavellian intellect. Let us consider the problem in the light of pure reason. This man's reference is to a book. That is our point of departure."

Niccolo Machiavelli

MacKinnon, Inspector   [RETI]   Male Alive   a smart young police inspector. Inspector Holmes called in at the end of this case. Remarked on the strong smell of paint about the house. Holmes explained what he had found and MacKinnon asked that Holmes step right out of the case and turn over all results over to the police force, a request to which Holmes agreed to do. The Papers attributed the solving of the crime to Brilliant Police investigation, saying "The remarkable acumen by which Inspector MacKinnon deduced from the smell of paint that some other smell, that of gas, for example, might be concealed; the bold deduction that the strong-room might also be the death-chamber, and the subsequent inquiry which led to the discovery of the bodies in a disused well, cleverly concealed by a dog-kennel, should live in the history of crime as a standing example of the intelligence of our professional detectives."

Sherlock Holmes Quote : "Well, well, MacKinnon is a good fellow,"

MacNamara, Widow   [VALL]   Female Alive   She was as true as steel and as deaf as a post. Rented lodgings on the edge of town. She was an easy-going old Irishwoman who left her boarders to themselves John McMurdo took up a room here after he was asked to leave Jacob Shafter's boarding house. McMurdo was later joined by Mike Scanlan at the lodgings. She had no other boarders. The house was selected because of its remoteness to be the place where they would trap the Pinkerton agent Birdy Edwards.

Address : extreme outskirts of the town of Vermissa.

Macphail, Mr. **[CREE]** **Male Alive** Able bodied Professor Presbury's coachman. Slept in the stables. Stayed with the professor after his last attack by Roy, while Holmes, Watson and Mr. Bennett looked over the professor's room trying to find out what was going on.

MacPherson, Constable **[SECO]** **Male Alive** A big constable Was put on guard at 16, Godolphin Street. Was meant to keep people out, but was tricked into letting Lady Hilda Trelawney Hope retrieve her Husband's important letter from a secret compartment underneath the carpet. unfortunately/fortunately she didn't replace the carpet in the correct position which lead to Holmes being called and the Adventure of the Second Stain.

Malthus, Reverend Thomas Robert **[STUD]** **Male dead (Real Person 1766 – 1834)** English Cleric, Scholar and economist in the fields of political economy and demography. Wrote an Essay on the Principles of Population in 1798. referenced in the Daily Telegraph regarding the murder of Enoch Drebber "After alluding airily to the Vehmgericht, aqua tofana, Carbonari, the Marchioness de Brinvilliers, the Darwinian theory, the principles of Malthus, and the Ratcliff Highway murders, the article concluded by admonishing the Government and advocating a closer watch over foreigners in England."

Thomas Malthus

Manders, Brother **[VALL]** **Male Alive** Lodge member who helped John McMurdo to blow up the house of Chester Wilcox.

Mangles, Mr. **[HOUN]** **Male** Ross and Mangles, the Pet shop dealers in Fulham Road "Having conceived the idea he proceeded to carry it out with considerable finesse. An ordinary schemer would have been content to work with a savage hound. The use of artificial means to make the creature diabolical was a flash of genius upon his part. The dog he bought in London from Ross and Mangles, the dealers in Fulham Road. It was the strongest and most savage in their possession. He brought it down by the North Devon line and walked a great distance over the moor so as to get it home without exciting any remarks. He had already on his insect hunts learned to penetrate the Grimpen Mire, and so had found a safe hiding-place for the creature. Here he kennelled it and waited his chance.

Mansel, Brother **[VALL]** **Male Alive** was a reckless youngster. Was involved in the attack on the Editor of the Herald newspaper Stanger. The group was lead by Ted Baldwin and others in the group were Gower, Scanlan, the two willabys and John McMurdo, there were two others to guard the door.

Manson, Mr **[VALL]** **Male Alive** Owner of an Ironworks in Vermissa Valley, who was forced to sell his business because of threats from the Scowrers. He sold his ironworks to West Gilmerton General Mining Company.

Marbank, Mr. **[IDEN]** **Male** Junior partner in the company Westhouse & Marbank, the great claret importers of Fenchurch Street. The wine company has an office in Bordeaux, France.

Marcini, restaurant owner **[HOUS]** **Male** and we can stop at Marcini's for a little dinner on the way?"

Marconi, Guglielmo Giovanni Maria **[LAST]** **Male Alive (Real Person 1874 – 1937)** Italian inventor and electrical engineer, famous for his work on Radio transmissions.

Sherlock Holmes Quote : "Same as I said in my cable. Every last one of them, semaphore, lamp code, Marconi—a copy, mind you, not the original. That was too dangerous. But it's the real goods, and you can lay to that."

Guglielmo Marconi

Marker, Mrs [GOLD] Female Alive   A sad-faced, elderly woman. Worked as
a housekeeper for professor Coram at Yoxley Old Place Had worked there for
some years. A woman of excellent character She was prepared to swear that the
Professor was still in his night-clothes and that it was impossible for him to dress
without the help of Mortimer the gardener. Had cleaned the Bureau on the
morning of the killing. Did not see the scratch on the Bureau lock. Noticed that the
professor had not lost his appetite after the killing of Willoughby Smith, in fact, he
seemed to be eating more.

Address : Yoxley Old Place

Sidney Paget

Martha, (Von Bork's Housekeeper)   [LAST]   Female Alive See Mrs. Hudson

Martin, Inspector   [DANC]   Male Alive He was a dapper little man, with a quick, alert manner and a waxed moustache. He was trim. He was in charge of the murder of Hilton Cubitt. He was considerably astonished when he heard the name of Sherlock Holmes. Inspector of the Norfolk Constabulary based in Norwich. Said "I should be proud to feel that we were acting together, Mr. Holmes." Had the good sense to allow Holmes to do things in his own fashion, and contented himself with carefully noting the results. At first he had shown some disposition to assert his own position; but now he was overcome with admiration and ready to follow without question wherever Holmes led. Slipped the handcuffs over Abe Slaney's wrists.

Sidney Paget   *Richard Gutschmidt*

Martin, Lieutenant [GLOR] Male dead   Officer aboard the 'Gloria Scott' vessel when it set sail for Australia. Onboard were twenty-six members of the crew, eighteen soldiers, a captain, three mates, a doctor, a chaplain, and four warder There were thirty-eight prisoners aboard. Killed aboard the 'Gloria Scott' in the battle with the rioting prisoners.

Martini, Friedrich von   [SIGN]   Male Alive (Real Person 1833 – 1897) Swiss designer who worked with a number of people to improve both rifles and bullets from the 1871 to 1918. Holmes would rather face a bullet than one of the poison darts fired by Tonga.

Sherlock Holmes Quote : "They are hellish things," said he. "Look out that you don't prick yourself. I'm delighted to have them, for the chances are that they are all he has. There is the less fear of you or me finding one in our skin before long. I would sooner face a Martini bullet, myself. Are you game for a six- mile trudge, Watson?"

Friedrich von martini

Marvin, Captain Teddy [VALL] Male Alive Wore a quiet blue uniform and peaked cap of the mine police. Member of a special body raised by the railways and colliery owners to supplement the efforts of the ordinary civil police, who were perfectly helpless in the face of the organised ruffianism which terrorised the district. Captain of Police. Recognised Jack McMurdo as a person of interest in the killing of Jonas Pinto, when he entered McGinty's Saloon. He and his men surrounded the rooms of Widow MacNamara lodgings on the evening of the capture of the Scowrers' leaders

Frank Wiles

Marx , Mr [WIST] Male Alive   Owner of the company Marx and Co., High Holborn. Were the supplies of a good deal of clothing that was left behind in Wisteria Lodge after it was abandoned.   Marx knew nothing of Aloysius Garcia save that he was a good payer.

Mary (Openshaw's servant) [FIVE] Female Alive   Elias Openshaw's servant. Elias Openshaw asked his servant Mary to set a fire in his room and send down to Fordham, the Horsham lawyer

Mary Jane Watson's maid [SCAN] Female alive   Former maid of the Watsons. A most clumsy and careless servant girl A particularly malignant boot-slitting specimen of the London slavey Mrs. Watson had just given her notice as she was incorrigible.

Mary, Maberley's maid [3GAB] Female Alive   Worked for Mrs. Maberley, along with Susan the Maid at the Three Gables. When the house was burgled, her screams summoned the Police, but not before the rascals had got away.

Address : The Three Gables, Harrow Weald

Mason, John   [SHOS] Male Alive   A tall, clean-shaven man with the firm, austere expression which is only seen upon those who have to control horses or boys. Mr. John Mason had many of both under his sway, and he looked equal to the task. Head trainer at Shoscombe Old Place and it was he who approached Holmes concerning the antics of his employer, Sir Robert Norberton. Said he thought his employer had gone mad. Used the trick of running Shoscombe Prince's Half-brother in spins so that the touts didn't know the true speed of the favourite. Showed Holmes the location of the crypt.

Address : Shoscombe Old Place

Mason, Mr. [BRUC] Male Alive   Plate-layer who worked for the Underground railway system, who discovered John Cadogen West's body just outside Aldgate Station on the Underground system in London.

Mason, Mrs. [SUSS] Female Alive   A tall, gaunt woman. The baby's nurse in the Ferguson household. Had sworn that she would not leave the baby night or day. Robert Ferguson said that he can absolutely trust her.

Address : Cheeseman's, Lamberley, Sussex, South of Horsham

G. Dutriac   *Wladyslaw Teodor Benda*

Mason, of Bradford   [STUD]   Male Alive   Holmes says that this person escaped hanging in Bradford because Holmes' Blood test wasn't around.

Mason, White   [VALL]   Male Alive   He was a quiet, comfortable-looking person in a loose tweed suit, with a clean-shaved, ruddy face, a stoutish body, and powerful bandy legs adorned with gaiters, looking like a small farmer, a retired gamekeeper, or anything upon earth except a very favourable specimen of the provincial criminal officer. White Mason, the local officer, was a personal friend of inspector Alec MacDonald At the start of the story, sent a message to MacDonald saying "DEAR INSPECTOR MACDONALD: Official requisition for your services is in separate envelope. This is for your private eye. Wire me what train in the morning you can get for Birlstone, and I will meet it—or have it met if I am too occupied. This case is a snorter. Don't waste a moment in getting started. If you can bring Mr. Holmes, please do so; for he will find something after his own heart. We would think the whole thing had been fixed up for theatrical effect if there wasn't a dead man in the middle of it. My word! it is a snorter." MacDonald said of him "White Mason is a very live man, if I am any judge." Sergeant Wilson of the Sussex Constabulary said of him "White Mason is a smart man. No local job has ever been too much for White Mason."

Sherlock Holmes Quote : "Your friend seems to be no fool,"

Frank Wiles *Frank Wiles*

Matheson, Mr. [ENGR] Male Partner in the Company Venner & Matheson. The well-known firm, of Greenwich. Victor Hatherley was apprenticed with them for seven years. Left them in 1887, using the inheritance from his poor father's death.

Mathews, Mr. [EMPT] Probably Male In Sherlock Holmes' index of biographies from the shelf. Knocked out Holmes' left canine in the waiting-room at Charing Cross. That's all we know

Sherlock Holmes Quote : "My collection of M's is a fine one," said he. "Moriarty himself is enough to make any letter illustrious, and here is Morgan the poisoner, and Merridew of abominable memory, and Mathews, who knocked out my left canine in the waiting-room at Charing Cross, and, finally, here is our friend of tonight."

Maudsley, Mr [BLUE] Male Alive Friend of James Ryder who went to the bad and was going to fence the Blue Carbuncle for James Ryder.

Address : Kilburn

Maupertuis, Baron   [REIG]   Male It was some time before the health of my friend Mr. Sherlock Holmes recovered from the strain caused by his immense exertions in the spring of '87. The whole question of the Netherland-Sumatra Company and of the colossal schemes of Baron Maupertuis are too recent in the minds of the public, and are too intimately concerned with politics and finance to be fitting subjects for this series of sketches.

Mawson, Mr.   [STOC]   Male Alive   Senior partner in the company, Mawson & Williams', the great stockbroking firm in Lombard Street. They were about the richest house in London. Guardians of securities which amount in the aggregate to a sum of considerably over a million sterling. They advertised for a position and offered it to Hall Pycroft, sight unseen. But they almost lost a fortune when the person pretending to be Hall Pycroft, Nearly a hundred thousand pounds' worth of American railway bonds, with a large amount of scrip in mines and other companies, were discovered in the bag of the thief.

Maynooth, Earl of   [EMPT]   Male Alive   Governor of one of the Australian Colonies. His wife had returned from Australia to undergo the operation for cataract, while he stayed in Australia. Father to Hilda and Ronald Adair.

Maynooth, Lady   [EMPT]   Female Alive   Mother of Ronald and Hilda Adair. Had returned from Australia to undergo the operation for cataract. Discovered Ronald's body in his locked second floor room.

Address : 427, Park Lane, London

McCarthy, Charles   [BOSC]   Male dead   Ex-Australian. Worked Hatherley Farm Father of James McCarthy "Friend" of Mr. John Turner. Fond of Sport and spent time at race meetings. Kept 2 servants - a man and a woman. died 3rd June 1889. Killed by repeated blows to the head by some heavy and blunt weapon. The injuries were such as might very well have been inflicted by the butt-end of his son's gun. Verdict of 'wilful murder' was been returned at the inquest on Tuesday 4th June 1889. The surgeon's deposition stated that the posterior third of the left parietal bone and the left half of the occipital bone had been shattered by a heavy blow from a blunt weapon. Such a blow must have been struck from behind

Josef Friedrich *Sidney Paget*

McCarthy, James **[BOSC]** **Male Alive** Son of Charles McCarthy. Charged with killing his father on Wednesday 5th June 1889 by magistrates at Ross. Thought he was married to a barmaid in Bristol, which is why he did press his suit with Miss Turner. This unnamed barmaid actually had a husband in the Bermuda Dockyard.

Paul Thiriat *Sidney Paget*

McCauley, Mr. [FIVE] Male Alive   Mentioned in the remaining ledger page belonging to the KKK dated March 1869 7th. Set the pips on McCauley, Mr., Paramore, and John Swain of St. Augustine. 9th. McCauley, Mr. cleared. not killed by KKK

McFarlane, John Hector   [NORW] Male Alive   A wild-eyed and frantic young man, pale, dishevelled, He was flaxen-haired and handsome in a washed-out negative fashion, with frightened blue eyes and a clean-shaven face, with a weak, sensitive mouth. His age may have been about twenty-seven; his dress and bearing that of a gentleman. From the pocket of his light summer overcoat protruded the bundle of endorsed papers which proclaimed his profession. Junior partner of Graham and McFarlane London solicitors based at 426, Gresham Buildings, E.C. Solicitor who burst in on Holmes and had been followed by the police and was arrested by Lestrade, who allowed him to continue his story for Holmes. He related how Mr. Jonas Oldacre had asked him to cast his rough will into proper legal shape and then visit him that evening to discuss various matters relating to the will. It seems that Oldacre had left all his money to McFarlane, because in the past he had know His mother. McFarlane arrived at Deep Dene House at 9pm and was shown into the house by Housekeeper Mrs Lexington. He left at between 11pm and 12pm and the first thing he knew about the death of Oldacre until the morning. Holmes visited McFarlane's parents and Deep Dene House. The following day, Holmes got a telegram from Lestrade that read "Important fresh evidence to hand. McFarlane's guilt definitely established. Advise you to abandon case." Lestrade has found a thumb print in blood in the hall, but the problem is that that print had not existed the previous day when Holmes had examined the house. Holmes was able to prove that Oldacre was not dead and that McFarlane had been framed.

Sherlock Holmes Quote : "You mentioned your name as if I should recognise it, but I assure you that, beyond the obvious facts that you are a bachelor, a solicitor, a Freemason, and an asthmatic, I know nothing whatever about you."

Address : Torrington Lodge, Blackheath

Frederic Dorr Steele   *Sidney Paget*

McFarlane, Mr. **[REDH]** **Male Alive** While Holmes and Watson were looking around Saxe-Coburg Square, Holmes listed the shops.

Sherlock Holmes Quote : "Let me see, I should like just to remember the order of the houses here. It is a hobby of mine to have an exact knowledge of London. There is Mortimer's, the tobacconist, the little newspaper shop, the Coburg branch of the City and Suburban Bank, the Vegetarian Restaurant, and McFarlane's carriage-building depot."

McFarlane, Mrs. **[NORW]** **Female Alive** A little, fluffy, blue-eyed person, in a tremor of fear and indignation. Mother of John Hector McFarlane. John Oldacre was her old suitor and she was engaged to him, until she heard a shocking story of how he had turned a cat loose in an aviary, and she was so horrified at his brutal cruelty that she would have nothing more to do with him. she produced a photograph of a woman, shamefully defaced and mutilated with a knife. 'That is my own photograph,' she said. 'He sent it to me in that state, with his curse, upon my wedding morning.'

Address : Union House, Vermissa, McGinty's saloon, Vermissa

McGinty, Bodymaster Jack **[VALL]** **Male dead** A tall, strong, heavily built man. He was a black-maned giant, bearded to the cheekbones, and with a shock of raven hair which fell to his collar. His complexion was as swarthy as that of an Italian, and his eyes were of a strange dead black, which, combined with a slight squint, gave them a particularly sinister appearance. his noble proportions, his fine features, and his frank bearing—fitted in with that jovial, man-to-man manner which he affected. One would say, that he was a bluff, honest fellow, whose heart would be sound however rude his outspoken words might seem. It was only when those dead, dark eyes, deep and remorseless, were turned upon a man that he shrank within himself, feeling that he was face to face with an infinite possibility of latent evil, with a strength and courage and cunning behind it which made it a thousand times more deadly. Bodymaster of Lodge 341, Vermissa . Councillor John McGinty. Leader of the Scowrers in Vermissa Valley (V.V. 341). Worked with other Lodges in the area to truly make it the Valley of Fear. Used terror tactics to extort money out of local companies. Was involved in the murder numerous Men, women and children. Was finally captured by Pinkerton man Birdy Edwards. McGinty met his fate upon the scaffold, cringing and whining when the last hour came.

Address : Union House, Vermissa, McGinty's saloon, Vermissa

Arthur I. Keller   *Frank Wiles*

McGregor, Mrs. **[STUD]** **Female dead** In PART II. The Country of the Saints, she was the third to die on the trail in the Great Alkali Plain.

McLaren, Miles **[3STU]** **Male Alive** He is taller than the Indian, not so tall as Gilchrist. I suppose five foot six would be about it. Had rooms on The top floor, He was a brilliant fellow when he chooses to work—one of the brightest intellects of the University, but he is wayward, dissipated, and unprincipled. He was nearly expelled over a card scandal in his first year. He has been idling all this term, and he must look forward with dread to the examination."

·deric Dorr Steele

McMurdo, John   [VALL]   Male dead   See John Douglas

McMurdo, Mr.   [SIGN]   Male Alive   Had a gruff voice. Short, deep-chested man Prize-fighter who helped protect Major John Sholto. Holmes fought three rounds with him at Alison's rooms on the night of his benefit four years back Porter at Pondicherry Lodge Was arrested in second round by Athelney Jones as an accessory.

Address : Pondicherry Lodge in Upper-Norwood

Richard Gutschmidt

McPherson, Fitzroy [LION] Male dead Was last seen alive wearing a Burberry overcoat(thrown over his shoulders), trousers and unlaced canvas shoes. Fitzroy McPherson was the science master at 'The Gables' coaching establishment. a fine upstanding young fellow whose life had been crippled by heart trouble following rheumatic fever. He was a natural athlete and excelled in every game which did not throw too great a strain upon him. In Summer and winter he went for his swim and on the morning of his death was found by Stackhurst and Holmes at the top of the cliff almost dead. He managed to say the words 'the Lion's Mane' before dying. When his body was examined by Holmes, it was found that he his back was covered with dark red lines as though he had been terribly flogged by a thin wire scourge. The instrument with which this punishment had been inflicted was clearly flexible, for the long, angry weals curved round his shoulders and ribs. There was blood dripping down his chin, for he had bitten through his lower lip in the paroxysm of his agony. His drawn and distorted face told how terrible that agony had been. Owner of an Airdale terrier, who had died in the same place as his master. Had been dating Maud Bellamy, but her family had no love for him, considering his attentions insulting. Had actually been engages to Maud, but kept this secret because Fitzroy's uncle, who was very old and said to be dying, might have disinherited him if he had married against the old man's wishes.

Frederic Dorr Steele

Howard K. Elcock

McPherson's Dog   [LION]   Male dead   Despite not being given a name, this dog had survived being thrown through a plate-glass window. He was an Airedale Terrier. Died in the same way as his master.

Frederic Dorr Steele

Meek, Sir Jasper   [DYIN]   Male Alive   When Holmes refused to let Watson examine him to see what illness he had, Watson suggested other Doctors that Holmes might find more acceptable, one of them was Sir Jasper Meek. Watson regarded him as one of the best Doctors in London.

Melas, Mr.   [GREE]   Male Alive   A short, stout man whose olive face and coal-black hair which proclaimed his Southern origin, though his speech was that of an educated Englishman. Had dark eyes which sparkled with pleasure when he understood that the specialist was anxious to hear his story. Slightly acquaintance with Mycroft Holmes, at least to the extent that he asked for Mycroft's help. Greek by birth. A remarkable linguist. Earns his living partly as interpreter in the law courts and partly by acting as guide to any wealthy Orientals who may visit the Northumberland Avenue hotels. For many years he has been the chief Greek interpreter in London, and his name is very well known in the hotels. Did the translation for Harold Latimer and J. Davenport when they 'interviewed' Paul Kratides. Was told to say nothing to anyone about the meeting, 'if you speak to a human soul about this—one human soul, mind—well, may God have mercy upon your soul!" Was paid five sovereigns for this translation work for Harold Latimer. Returned to Wandsworth Common. Told his tale to both of the Holmes, and was kidnapped by Harold Latimer and taken back to The Myrtles, Beckenham. Here he was tied up and only just avoided the same fate as Paul Kratides, being asphyxiated by a burning Charcoal tripod in the middle of a room. Rescued by the

Sherlock Holmes.

Address : On floor one (or above) in Pall Mall Lodgings.

- Sidney Paget

William H. Hyde

Melville, Mr. [WIST] Male Alive   A retired brewer who was instrumental in the meeting of John Scott Eccles and Aloysius Garcia, when he invited them both to a meal.

Address : Abermarle Mansion, Kensington.

Mendelssohn, Felix [STUD] Male dead (Real Person 1809 – 1847)   German composer, pianist, organist and conductor. Holmes played Mendelssohn's Lieder. aka Jakob Ludwig Felix Mendelssohn Bartholdy

Felix Mendelssohn

Menzies, Mr. [VALL] Male dead   Mine Engineer of a mine at Crow Hill. Two assassins Lawlers and Andrews were sent over by the County Delegate. Lawlers and Andrews arriving at the mine and after killing Josiah H. Dunn, Menzies, the Scotchman, gave a roar of rage at the sight and rushed with an iron spanner at the murderers; but was met by two balls in the face which dropped him dead at their very feet.

Mercer, Mr. [CREE] Male Alive   Agent working for Holmes. Sent Holmes a telegram in answer to questions posed to him by Holmes HAVE VISITED THE COMMERCIAL ROAD AND SEEN DORAK. SUAVE PERSON, BOHEMIAN, ELDERLY. KEEPS LARGE GENERAL STORE. MERCER.

Sherlock Holmes Quote : "Mercer is since your time, He is my general utility man who looks up routine business. "

Meredith, George [BOSC] Male Alive   English Novelist and Poet of Victoria Era. Holmes did a lot of reading in this story.

George Meredith

Mereer, Second mate   [GLOR]   Male dead   Second mate of the 'Gloria Scott' who was the right-hand man of Jack Prendergast. Killed in the explosion of the Vessel.

Merivale, inspector   [SHOS]   Male Alive   Inspector of Scotland Yard. He asked Holmes to look at the St. Pancras' case, where a cap was found lying next to a dead policeman. Holmes had been looking under a microscope at the cap and had found blobs of glue, the accused man was a picture-frame maker and habitually handles glue. The police department were beginning to see how useful the use of the microscope would be in future cases.

Merona, Angel   [STUD]   See Angel Moroni

Merridew of abominable memory   [EMPT]   In Sherlock Holmes' index of biographies from the shelf.

Sherlock Holmes Quote : "My collection of M's is a fine one," said he. "Moriarty himself is enough to make any letter illustrious, and here is Morgan the poisoner, and Merridew of abominable memory, and Mathews, who knocked out my left canine in the waiting-room at Charing Cross, and, finally, here is our friend of tonight."

Merrilow, Mrs.   [VEIL]   Female Alive   A plump lady Was said to waddle. Landlady who had the single lodger, Mrs. Eugenia Ronder who had been staying with her for seven years. She had only ever seen her face once in that time. Told

Holmes that her lodger, Mrs. Ronder want to see him. Mrs. Merrilow admitted that she did not know the background of the lodger and had not been given references, but she did pay in hard cash and plenty of it. Mrs. Ronder chose this lodgings because it stood well back from the road, was more private than most and it was privacy she was after and was ready to pay for it. Mrs. Merrilow did not object to tobacco, Watson, if you wish to indulge your filthy habits. Mrs. Merrilow has an interesting story to tell which may well lead to further developments in which your presence may be useful." Mrs Merrilow was worried about her lodger's health and related to Holmes a conversation she had with her. "Her health, Mr. Holmes. She seems to be wasting away. And there's something terrible on her mind. 'Murder!' she cries. 'Murder!' And once I heard her: 'You cruel beast! You monster!' she cried. It was in the night, and it fair rang through the house and sent the shivers through me. So I went to her in the morning. 'Mrs. Ronder,' I says, 'if you have anything that is troubling your soul, there's the clergy,' I says, 'and there's the police. Between them you should get some help.' 'For God's sake, not the police!' says she, 'and the clergy can't change what is past. And yet,' she says, 'it would ease my mind if someone knew the truth before I died.' 'Well,' says I, 'if you won't have the regulars, there is this detective man what we read about'—beggin' your pardon, Mr. Holmes. And she, she fair jumped at it. 'That's the man,' says she. 'I wonder I never thought of it before. Bring him here, Mrs. Merrilow, and if he won't come, tell him I am the wife of Ronder's wild beast show. Say that, and give him the name Abbas Parva. Here it is as she wrote it, Abbas Parva. 'That will bring him if he's the man I think he is.'" This was indeed true because he and Watson went to interview Mrs. Ronder.

Address : South Brixton

Merrow, Lord   [SECO]   Male Alive   A letter from this gentleman was still in the Right Honourable Trelawney Hope's despatch box.

Merryweather, Mr.   [REDH]   Male Alive   Long, thin, sad-faced man, with a very shiny hat and oppressively respectable frock-coat. Played Whist every first Saturday night for seven-and-twenty years. Chairman of bank director of Coburg branch of the City and Suburban Bank. Accompanied Holmes, Watson and Inspector Jones on a vigil inside the bank vault of City and Suburban Bank, just before it was robbed by Vincent Spalding.

Paul Carrey *Josef Friedrich*

Merton, Sam   [MAZA]   Male in prison   Watson says he is a rough fellow. A prize-fighter, a heavily built young man with a stupid, obstinate, slab-sided face. Had a short-cropped pate. Associate of Count Sylvius, who together stole the Mazarin Stone. It was his insistence on seeing the gem, that allowed Holmes posing as a dummy to snatch the stone from the Count's hand.

Sherlock Holmes Quote : "Sam Merton the boxer. Not a bad fellow, Sam, but the Count has used him. Sam's not a shark. He is a great big silly bull-headed gudgeon. But he is flopping about in my net all the same."

Frederic Dorr Steele *Alfred Gilbert*

Meunier, Monsieur Oscar   [EMPT]   Male Alive   Created the Wax bust of Sherlock Holmes that was used to trap Colonel Sebastian Moran. He spent some days in doing the moulding.

Address : of Grenoble

Sherlock Holmes Quote : "The credit of the execution is due to Monsieur Oscar Meunier, of Grenoble, who spent some days in doing the moulding. It is a bust in wax. The rest I arranged myself during my visit to Baker Street this afternoon."

Meyer, Adolph   [BRUC]   Male Alive   One of the International agent that might have been involved in the missing Bruce-Partington Plans. Was Innocent.

Address : 13 Great George Street, Westminster

Meyers, Mr   [HOUN]   Male Boot makers and retailer based in Toronto. Makers of the boot that belonged to Sir Henry Baskerville

Michael, Mr.   [SUSS]   Male Alive   Stable-hand, working for Robert Ferguson, who slept in the house, at Cheeseman's Lamberley, Sussex.

Middleton, Mr.   [HOUN]   Male Alive   Old Franklin told Watson that it was a great day for him, one of the red-letter days of his life, he had established a right of way through the centre of old Middleton's park, slap across it, within a hundred yards of his own front door.

Miles, Honourable Miss   [CHAS]   Female Alive   Was to have been married to Colonel Dorking but the engagement was suddenly ended two days before their wedding. Milverton wanted £1200 from one of this party, but was not paid and so the wedding got called off.

Millar, Miss Flora   [NOBL]   Female Alive   Caused a disturbance at Mr. Doran's house in the morning, and was actually arrested. It appears that she was formerly a danseuse at the Allegro. She had known the bridegroom for some years. Exceedingly hot-headed and devotedly attached to Lord St. Simon. She wrote dreadful letters to lord St. Simon, when she heard that he was about to be married.

Josef Friedrich   *Sidney Paget*

Milman, Mr. **[VALL]** **Male dead**   Possible Mine or Ironworks owner killed by the Scowrers.

Milner, Godfrey **[EMPT]** **Male Alive**   Member of the Bagatelle card club and had lost, along with Lord Balmoral, some £420 to Ronald Adair and Colonel Moran recently.

Milverton, Charles Augustus **[CHAS]** **Male dead**   A small, stout man in a shaggy astrakhan overcoat. A man of fifty, with a large, intellectual head, a round, plump, hairless face, a perpetual frozen smile, and two keen grey eyes, which gleamed brightly from behind broad, golden-rimmed glasses. There was something of Mr. Pickwick's benevolence in his appearance, marred only by the insincerity of the fixed smile and by the hard glitter of those restless and penetrating eyes. His voice was as smooth and suave as his countenance, as he advanced with a plump little hand extended, murmuring his regret for having missed us at his first visit. He is the king of all the blackmailers. Holmes got involved because Milverton was blackmailing Lady Eva Blackwell and Holmes was asked to mediate. Milverton wanted £7,000 to hand over letters or they would be sent to the Earl of Dovercourt. Rather than pay over the money, Holmes and Watson decide to break in and remove the letters from Milverton's safe while he sleeps. Normally Milverton retires at ten-thirty and although he slept in an adjacent room, was a sound sleeper. On the Night of 13th January 1899, Holmes and Watson break into Appledore Towers at around midnight and everything is going to plan, Holmes manages to open the safe in Milverton's study, and just as he is opening it, hears someone approaching. It is Milverton himself, who enters the study shortly after Holmes and Watson have hidden themselves behind the curtain. Milverton sits at his desk and continues to smoke a cigar. After some minutes a tapping sound is heard on the outside door and Milverton gets up and opens the door to a mysterious Lady. It turns out that this lady is not in the employ of the Countess d'Albert, but a previous victim of one of Milverton's blackmails. She draws out a gun and shoots him again and again. As he lies dying his final words are "You've done me," The lady exits by the same door she entered and Holmes and Watson jump out from behind the curtain and empty the contents of the safe throwing everything in the fire before making their escape.

Sherlock Holmes Quotes : "The worst man in London," "Do you feel a creeping, shrinking sensation, Watson, when you stand before the serpents in the Zoo and see the slithery, gliding, venomous creatures, with their deadly eyes and wicked, flattened faces? Well, that's how Milverton impresses me. I've had to do with fifty murderers in my career, but the worst of them never gave me the repulsion which I have for this fellow. And yet I can't get out of doing business with him—indeed, he is here at my invitation."

Address : Appledore Towers

Frederic Dorr Steele   *Sidney Paget*

Milverton's killer   [CHAS]   Female Alive   See Mysterious Lady

Mitton, John   [SECO]   Male Alive   Valet of Mr. Eduardo Lucas. Was out for the evening, visiting a friend at Hammersmith, when Eduardo Lucas was killed.

Address : 16, Godolphin Street

Moffat, Mr.   [RESI]   Male Alive   One of five men who robbed the bank and got away with £7,000. Blessington or Sutton, who was the worst of the gang, turned informer. On his evidence Cartwright was hanged and the other three got fifteen years apiece. On an early release from prison, the three gang members Biddle, Hayward and Moffat, located the residence of Blessington, gave him a mock trial and hanged him. Blessington was discovered the following morning by Dr. Percy Trevelyan. It is likely that all three members of the gang, died on the ill-fated steamer 'Norah Creina , which was lost some years ago with all hands upon the Portuguese coast, some leagues to the north of Oporto.

Sidney Paget

William H. Hyde

Montalva, Marquess of   [WIST]   Male dead   See Mr. Henderson

Montgomery, Inspector [CARD] Male Alive Inspector of Scotland Yard at the Shadwell Police Station. He took the statement from Jim Browner,, confessing to the murder of his wife, Mary and Alec Fairbairn.

Richard Gutschmidt

Montpensier, Mme. [HOUN] Female Unfortunate Mme. Montpensier from the charge of murder which hung over her in connection with the death of her stepdaughter, Mlle. Carère, the young lady who, as it will be remembered, was found six months later alive and married in New York

Moorhouse, Mr. [MISS] Male Alive Clive Overton said that Moorhouse was "First reserve, but he was trained as a half, and he always edged right in on to the scrum instead of keeping out on the touchline. He was a fine place-kick, it's true, but, then, he had no judgement, and he couldn't sprint for nuts. Why, Morton or Johnson, the Oxford fliers, could romp round him."

Moran, Colonel Sebastian [EMPT, VALL] Male Alive He was an elderly man, with a thin, projecting nose, a high, bald forehead, and a huge grizzled moustache. An opera-hat was pushed to the back of his head, and an evening dress shirtfront gleamed out through his open overcoat. His face was gaunt and swarthy, scored with deep, savage lines. In his hand he carried what appeared to be a stick, but as he laid it down upon the floor it gave a metallic clang.   His father was Sir Augustus Moran, once British Minister to Persia. Played Whist with

Ronald Adair on the day of his death with Mr. Murray and Sir John Hardy . Tried to drop rocks onto Holmes while he lay on a ledge of the Reichenbach Falls after Professor Moriarty fell to his death. Holmes remained in hiding until Colonel Moran killed Ronald Adair with an air rifle. Captured by Holmes as he made an attempt to shot a wax effigy of Holmes in the Window of 221b Baker street. [VALL] Holmes said that he is paid six thousand a year, which is more than the Prime Minster gets.

Sherlock Holmes Quotes : "I have not introduced you yet," said Holmes. "This, gentlemen, is Colonel Sebastian Moran, once of Her Majesty's Indian Army, and the best heavy game shot that our Eastern Empire has ever produced. I believe I am correct, Colonel, in saying that your bag of tigers still remains unrivalled?"
"MORAN, SEBASTIAN, COLONEL. Unemployed. Formerly 1st Bengalore Pioneers. Born London, 1840. Son of Sir Augustus Moran, C.B., once British Minister to Persia. Educated Eton and Oxford. Served in Jowaki Campaign, Afghan Campaign, Charasiab (despatches), Sherpur, and Cabul. Author of 'Heavy Game of the Western Himalayas,' 1881; 'Three Months in the Jungle,' 1884. Address: Conduit Street. Clubs: The Anglo-Indian, the Tankerville, the Bagatelle Card Club."
"The second most dangerous man in London."

Sidney Paget

Frederic Dorr Steele

Moran, Patience [BOSC] Female Alive   Daughter of the lodge-keeper of the Boscombe Valley estate. While out picking flowers witnessed Mr. McCarthy and son using strong words and the son even raised up his hand as if to strike his father. She was so frightened by their violence that she ran away and told her mother when she reached home that she had left the two McCarthys quarrelling near Boscombe Pool, and that she was afraid that they were going to fight. Speculation says that she was the niece of Colonel Sebastian Moran.

Josef Friedrich

Moran, Sir Augustus   [EMPT] Male Alive   Father than Colonel Sebastian Moran. once British Minister to Persia. Award C.B. (Knight Companion)

Morcar, Countess of [BLUE] Female Alive   Owner of the Blue Carbuncle, which was stolen 'allegedly', by John Horner from her rooms at The Hotel Cosmopolitan. She offered a reward of £1,000 for it's safe return, Holmes thought the gem was worth at least twenty times that amount.

Ernest Flammarion

Morecroft, Mr. **[3GAR]** **Male** See John Garrideb

Morgan the poisoner **[EMPT]** In Sherlock Holmes' index of biographies from the shelf.

Sherlock Holmes Quote : "My collection of M's is a fine one," said he. "Moriarty himself is enough to make any letter illustrious, and here is Morgan the poisoner, and Merridew of abominable memory, and Mathews, who knocked out my left canine in the waiting-room at Charing Cross, and, finally, here is our friend of tonight."

Moriarty, Colonel James **[FINA]** **Male Alive** Confusingly He had the same first name of James as his brother, now what type of parent names their two sons with the same name? Watson's hand had been forced, by the recent letters in which Colonel James Moriarty had defended the memory of his brother, and Watson have no choice but to lay the facts before the public exactly as they occurred. He alone knew the absolute truth of the matter, and was satisfied that the time had come when on good purpose was to be served by its suppression.

Moriarty, Professor James   [FINA, EMPT,VALL]   Male dead   He was extremely tall and thin, his forehead domes out in a white curve, and his two eyes were deeply sunken in this head. He was clean-shaven, pale, and ascetic-looking, retaining something of the professor in his features. His shoulders were rounded from much study, and his face protrudes forward, and is forever slowly oscillating from side to side in a curiously reptilian fashion. He peered at Holmes with great curiosity in his puckered eyes. [EMPT]His name was James Moriarty. [FINA] He had a brother with the same first name, colonel James Moriarty. [FINA] He was extremely tall and thin, his forehead domed out in a white curve, and his two eyes were deeply sunken in his head. He was clean-shaven, pale, and ascetic-looking, retaining something of the professor in his features. His shoulders were rounded from much study, and his face protrudes forward, and was for ever slowly oscillating from side to side in a curiously reptilian fashion. [VALL] He'd have made a grand minister, with his thin face and grey hair and solemn-like way of talking. He had one of the first brains of Europe and all the powers of darkness at his back. He had a younger brother who was a stationmaster in the West of England. [FINA] Sherlock Holmes said Moriarty thought he was an antagonist who was his intellectual equal. The Napoleon of crime. A spider in the centre of its web. [VALL] Arch-criminal. He was unmarried. He was a professor, his chair was worth seven hundred a year. He was a very wealthy man. He owned a painting by Jean-Baptiste Greuze (La jeune fille à l'agneau). His career has been an extraordinary one. [FINA] He was a man of good birth and excellent education, endowed by Nature with a phenomenal mathematical faculty. At the age of twenty-one he wrote a treatise upon the Binomial Theorem, which has had a European vogue. On the strength of it, he won the Mathematical Chair at one of the smaller Universities, and had, to all appearance, a most brilliant career before him. But the man had hereditary tendencies of the most diabolical kind. A criminal strain ran in his blood, which, instead of being modified, was increased and rendered infinitely more dangerous by his extraordinary mental powers. Dark rumours gathered round him in the University town, and eventually he was compelled to resign his Chair and to come down to London, where he set up as an army coach. [VALL] He was the greatest schemer of all time, the organiser of every devilry, the controlling brain of the underworld - a brain which might have made or marred the destiny of nations. He was so aloof from general suspicion - so immune from criticism - so admirable in his management and self-effacement. He was the celebrated author of The Dynamics of an Asteroid - a book which ascends to such rarefied heights of pure mathematics that it is said that there was no man in the scientific press capable of criticising it. His cheques were drawn on six different banks. Holmes had no doubt that he had twenty banking accounts with the bulk of his fortune abroad in the Deutsche Bank or the Crédit Lyonnais. He ruled with a rod of iron over his people. His discipline was tremendous. There was only one punishment in his code. It was death. [FINA] He pervaded London, and no one had heard of him. He was put on a pinnacle in the records of crime by Sherlock Holmes. He was the organiser of half that was evil and of nearly all that was undetected in London. He was a genius, a philosopher, an abstract thinker. He has a brain of the first order. He sat motionless, like a spider in the centre of its web, but that web has a thousand radiations, and he knew well every quiver of each of them. He did little himself. He only planed. But his agents are numerous and splendidly organised. He was the cleverest rogue of the most powerful syndicate of criminals in Europe. [VALL] His chief of the staff was Colonel Sebastian Moran which he paid him six thousand a year He fought Sherlock Holmes at the top of Reichenbach Falls, in Switzerland, but fell in the falls and died. Professor Moriarty is mentioned in the following stories: FINA, EMPT, VALL, ILLU, MISS, NORW, LAST He is the Napoleon of crime. He is the organiser of half that is evil and of nearly all that is undetected in this great city. He is a genius, a philosopher, an abstract thinker. He has a brain of the first order. He sits motionless, like a spider in the centre of its web, but that web has a thousand radiations, and he knows well every quiver of each of them. Active in only two stories The Final problem and The Valley of Fear. but mentioned in many more. [FINA] Had at least six different banks. Involved in the location of Birdy Edwards/John Douglas and when the assassin failed, was instrumental in his death while on a boat to South Africa.

Sherlock Holmes Quotes : "The man pervades London, and no one has heard of him. That's what puts him on a pinnacle in the records of crime. I tell you, Watson, in all seriousness, that if I could beat that man, if I could free society of him, I should feel that my own career had reached its summit, and I should be prepared to turn to some more placid line in life. Between ourselves, the recent cases in which I have been of assistance to the royal family of Scandinavia, and to the French republic, have left me in such a position that I could continue to live in the quiet fashion which is most congenial to me, and to concentrate my attention upon my chemical researches. But I could not rest, Watson, I could not sit quiet in my chair, if I thought that such a man as Professor Moriarty were walking the streets of London unchallenged."

"His career has been an extraordinary one. He is a man of good birth and excellent education, endowed by nature with a phenomenal mathematical faculty. At the age of twenty-one he wrote a treatise upon the Binomial Theorem, which has had a European vogue. On the strength of it he won the Mathematical Chair at one of our smaller universities, and had, to all appearance, a most brilliant career before him. But the man had hereditary tendencies of the most diabolical kind. A criminal strain ran in his blood, which, instead of being modified, was increased and rendered infinitely more dangerous by his extraordinary mental powers. Dark rumours gathered round him in the university town, and eventually he was compelled to resign his chair and to come down to London, where he set up as an army coach. So much is known to the world, but what I am telling you now is what I have myself discovered.

"As you are aware, Watson, there is no one who knows the higher criminal world of London so well as I do. For years past I have continually been conscious of some power behind the malefactor, some deep organising power which forever stands in the way of the law, and throws it shield over the wrongdoer. Again and again in cases of the most varying sorts—forgery cases, robberies, murders—I have felt the presence of this force, and I have deduced its action in many of those undiscovered crimes in which I have not been personally consulted. For years I have endeavoured to break through the veil which shrouded it, and at last the time came when I seized my thread and followed it, until it led me, after a thousand cunning windings, to ex-Professor Moriarty of mathematical celebrity.

He is the Napoleon of crime, Watson. He is the organiser of half that is evil and of nearly all that is undetected in this great city. He is a genius, a philosopher, an abstract thinker. He has a brain of the first order. He sits motionless, like a spider in the centre of its web, but that web has a thousand radiations, and he knows well every quiver of each of them. He does little himself. He only plans. But his agents are numerous and splendidly organised. Is there a crime to be done, a paper to be abstracted, we will say, a house to be rifled, a man to be removed—the word is passed to the Professor, the matter is organised and carried out. The agent may be caught. In that case money is found for his bail or his defence. But the central power which uses the agent is never caught—never so much as suspected. This was the organisation which I deduced, Watson, and which I devoted my whole energy to exposing and breaking up.

"But the Professor was fenced round with safeguards so cunningly devised that, do what I would, it seemed impossible to get evidence which would convict in a court of law. You know my powers, my dear Watson, and yet at the end of three months I was forced to confess that I had at last met an antagonist who was my intellectual equal. My horror at his crimes was lost in my admiration at his skill. But at last he made a trip—only a little, little trip—but it was more than he could afford when I was so close upon him. I had my chance, and, starting from that point, I have woven my net round him until now it is all ready to close. In three days—that is to say, on Monday next—matters will be ripe, and the Professor, with all the principal members of his gang, will be in the hands of the police. Then will come the greatest criminal trial of the century, the clearing up of over forty mysteries, and the rope for all of them; but if we move at all prematurely, you understand, they may slip out of our hands even at the last moment.

[VALL] "...But in calling Moriarty a criminal you are uttering libel in the eyes of the law—and there lie the glory and the wonder of it! The greatest schemer of all time, the organiser of every deviltry, the controlling brain of the underworld, a brain which might have made or marred the destiny of nations—that's the man! But so aloof is he from general suspicion, so immune from criticism, so admirable in his management and self-effacement, that for those very words that you have uttered he could hail you to a court and emerge with your year's pension as a solatium for his wounded character. Is he not the celebrated author of The Dynamics of an Asteroid, a book which ascends to such rarefied heights of pure mathematics that it is said that there was no man in the scientific press capable of criticising it? Is this a man to traduce? Foul-mouthed doctor and slandered professor—such would be your respective roles! That's genius, Watson. But if I am spared by lesser men, our day will surely come."

[VALL] "When talking to Inspector MacDonald "I have no doubt that he has twenty banking accounts; the bulk of his fortune abroad in the Deutsche Bank or the Credit Lyonnais as likely as not. Sometime when you have a year or two to spare I commend to you the study of Professor Moriarty."

Sidney Paget

The Courier Journal

Harry C. Edwards   *Martin Van Maele*

Morland, Sir John   [HOUN]   Male Alive   Involved in a court case - Frankland v. Morland, Court of Queens Frankland had Sir John Morland prosecuted for trespass, because he shot in his own warren." It cost Frankland £200, but he did get the verdict.

Moroni, Angel   [STUD]   The angel who Joseph Smith said had visited him and who was the guardian of the golden plates that were the source material for the Book of Mormon. In the story one of the Mormon men said "'we are the persecuted children of God - the chosen of the Angel Merona." But that should have been Moroni rather than Merona.

Morphy, Alice   [CREE]   Female Alive   Was a very perfect girl both in mind and body Daughter of Professor Morphy, who was in the chair of comparative anatomy. Was engaged to Professor Presbury. She seemed to like the professor in spite of his eccentricities, there was only the question of their age difference.

Frederic Dorr Steele *Frederic Dorr Steele*

Morphy, Professor **[CREE]** **Male Alive** Professor in the chair of comparative anatomy. Had a Daughter called Alice, who was engaged to Professor Presbury.

Morris, Brother **[VALL]** **Male Alive** An elderly, clean-shaved man with a kindly face and a good brow. Called a croaker by Bodymaster McGinty. Kept asking questions of McGinty, McGinty responded "I have my eye on you, and have had for some time! You've no heart yourself, and you try to take the heart out of others. It will be an ill day for you, Brother Morris, when your own name comes on our agenda paper, and I'm thinking that it's just there that I ought to place it." Thought of as a disloyal member of the lodge, a scabby sheep. Informed McMurdo of the presence of a Pinkerton agent in the valley.

Frank Wiles

Morris, William   [REDH]   Male in prison   See Duncan Ross

Morrison, Annie   [REIG]   Female Alive   Was involved in the case in some unknown way. Was mentioned in the letter that William Kirwan received that lead to his death. The letter read 'If you will only come around at quarter to twelve to the east gate you will learn what will very much surprise you and maybe be of the greatest service to you and also to Annie Morrison. But say nothing to anyone upon the matter'

Morrison, Miss   [CROO]   Female Alive   A young lady who lives in the next villa to Nancy Barclay. Together with Nancy Barclay worked at the establishment of the Guild of St. George, which was formed in connection with the Watt Street Chapel for the purpose of supplying the poor with cast-off clothing. Was with Nancy Barclay when she encountered Henry Wood, who she had thought had been dead for thirty years. She did lie to the Police regarding the incident at the Chapel.

Sherlock Holmes Quote : "Miss Morrison is a little ethereal slip of a girl, with timid eyes and blond hair, but I found her by no means wanting in shrewdness and common-sense."

Sidney Paget

Morrison, Mr. [SUSS] Male Partner in a firm of solicitors. There were two Morrisons, maybe brothers or possibly Father and Son. Part of the Firm Morrison, Morrison & Dodd They sent a letter to Holmes which read 46, OLD JEWRY, Nov. 19th. Re Vampires SIR: Our client, Mr. Robert Ferguson, of Ferguson and Muirhead, tea brokers, of Mincing Lane, has made some inquiry from us in a communication of even date concerning vampires. As our firm specialises entirely upon the assessment of machinery the matter hardly comes within our purview, and we have therefore recommended Mr. Ferguson to call upon you and lay the matter before you. We have not forgotten your successful action in the case of Matilda Briggs. We are, sir, Faithfully yours, MORRISON, MORRISON, AND DODD. per E.J.C. At the end of the story, Holmes writes back to them to tell them that the matter had been brought to a satisfactory conclusion and to thank them for their recommendation.

Address : 46 Old Jewry

Morstan, Captain Arthur [SIGN] Male dead Senior Captain in the 34th Bombay Infantry Indian regiment. One of the officers in charge of the convict-guard on the Andaman Islands. Obtained twelve months' leave to come home in 1878 to visit his daughter. disappeared 3rd December 1878. Deceased wife. One Child Mary Morstan, who was later to become the first Mrs. Watson. Friend of Major Sholto. He had suffered for years from a weak heart, but he concealed it from every one. Died from heart attack during an argument with Major John Sholto.

Address : Langham Hotel while in London. Andaman Islands

The Bristol Observer

Morstan, Mary [SIGN] Female Alive She was a blonde young lady, small, dainty, well gloved, and dressed in the most perfect taste. Limited means. Her dress was a sombre greyish beige, untrimmed and unbraided, and she wore a small turban of the same dull hue. Her face had neither regularity of feature nor beauty of complexion, but her expression was sweet and amiable, and her large blue eyes were singularly spiritual and sympathetic. Later muffled in a dark cloak, and her sensitive face was composed, but pale. Raised abroad, probably in India. Returned home as a child. Placed in a comfortable boarding establishment at Edinburgh until seventeen years of age. Daughter of Captain Arthur Morstan. Received one very large and lustrous pearl every year for six years. Received a letter to be at the third pillar from the left outside the lyceum theatre at seven o'clock. Watson says my wife has given the maid Mary Jane her notice. [SCAN] Was at breakfast with Watson at start of story.[BOSC] Watson says 'Folk who were in grief came to my wife like birds to a lighthouse.' [TWIS] Was doing needlework when there was a ring of the doorbell. She call Watson 'James' which has lead people to suggest that Watson's middle initial 'H' stands for Hamish, the Gaelic for James.

Sherlock Holmes Quote : "You are certainly a model client. You have the correct intuition." upon presenting Holmes with previous addressed envelopes.

Address : Lower Camberwell

Thomas J. Nicholl

The Bristol Observer

Mortan, Cyril [SOLI] Male Alive   An electrical engineer and fiancee of Violet Smith. He hoped to marry her at the end of the summer. Worked for the Midland Electrical Company, at Coventry. Cyril Morton became the senior partner of Morton & Kennedy, the famous Westminster electricians, perhaps using the inheritance of his wife.

Mortimer (smith-Mortimer case) [GOLD]   At the start of this case, Watson was going over the three manuscript volumes that covered 1894 and mentioned the famous Smith-Mortimer succession case, but there are no further details.

Mortimer, (the gardener) [GOLD] Male Alive   An old Army pensioner from the Crimean war. A man of excellent character. Gardener at Yoxley Old Place. Helped the professor get dressed and would wheel him around in a bath-chair. Went to the Police to report the death of Willoughby Smith.

Address : three-roomed cottage at Yoxley Old Place

Mortimer, Mr [REDH] Male   Owner of an Shop in Saxe-Coburg square that sold Tobacco.

Sherlock Holmes Quote : "Let me see, I should like just to remember the order of the houses here. It is a hobby of mine to have an exact knowledge of London.

There is Mortimer's, the tobacconist, the little newspaper shop, the Coburg branch of the City and Suburban Bank, the Vegetarian Restaurant, and McFarlane's carriage-building depot."

Mortimer, Mr. James, M.R.C.S. [HOUN] Male Alive He was a very tall, thin man, with a long nose like a beak, which jutted out between two keen, grey eyes, set closely together and sparkling brightly from behind a pair of gold-rimmed glasses. He was clad in a professional but rather slovenly fashion, for his frock-coat was dingy and his trousers frayed. Though young, his long back was already bowed, and he walked with a forward thrust of his head and a general air of peering benevolence. Owner of a fine, thick piece of wood, bulbous-headed, of the sort which is known as a "Penang lawyer." Just under the head was a broad silver band nearly an inch across. "To James Mortimer, M.R.C.S., from his friends of the C.C.H.," was engraved upon it, with the date "1884." Medical Directory entry read as follows; "Mortimer, James, M.R.C.S., 1882, Grimpen, Dartmoor, Devon. House-surgeon, from 1882 to 1884, at Charing Cross Hospital. Winner of the Jackson Prize for Comparative Pathology, with essay entitled 'Is Disease a Reversion?' Corresponding member of the Swedish Pathological Society. Author of 'Some Freaks of Atavism' (Lancet 1882). 'Do We Progress?' (Journal of Psychology, March, 1883). Medical Officer for the parishes of Grimpen, Thorsley, and High Barrow." Came to visit Holmes and left, as Holmes was away, leaving his walking stick. Returned and told Holmes of the legend of the Hound of the Baskervilles and tell him of the footprints near the body of Sir Charles Baskerville. Introduced Holmes and Watson to Sir Henry Baskerville. Accompanied Watson and Sir Henry down to Baskerville Hall, Dartmoor. Owner of a small dog, eaten by the Hound.

Address : Grimpen, Dartmoor, Devon

Sidney Paget　　　　　　　　　*Paul Thiriat*

Morton, Inspector   [DYIN]   Male Alive   He was dressed in unofficial tweeds. He was an old acquaintance of Sherlock Holmes. Inspector of Scotland Yard. He was an old acquaintance of Sherlock Holmes. Was working with Holmes in trying to arrest the murdered of Victor Savage. He was waiting outside for a signal from Holmes during his meeting of Culverton Smith. The signal was Turning up the gas and Culverton Smith actually sent the signal for his own arrest.

Walter Paget

Morton, Mr. **[MISS]** **Male Alive** Morton was one of the two Oxford fliers, opponents to the Cambridge Rugby squad, skippered by Clive Overton.

Moser, Mr. M. **[LADY]** **Male Alive** The well-known manager at the Hotel National at Lausanne. Was very Courteous to Watson.

Moulton, Francis (Frank) Hay **[NOBL]** **Male Alive** Met Miss Hatty Doran in 1884, in McQuire's camp, near the Rockies. Then Aloysius Doran struck it rich and wouldn't hear of an engagement. Was engaged to Miss Hatty Doran. Then Married her, but they kept this a secret. Travelled to Montana to try strike it rich, then onto Arizona and then New Mexico. Miss Hatty Doran read in a newspaper about how a miners' camp had been attacked by Apache Indians, and Francis Moulton is report as having been killed. Frank had been a prisoner among the Apaches, had escaped, came on to 'Frisco, found that Miss Hatty Doran had given him up for dead and had gone to England, followed her there, and had come upon her at last on the very morning of my second wedding.

Address : Northumberland Avenue, lodgings at 226 Gordon Square

Sidney Paget   *Josef Friedrich*

Moulton, Mrs. Hatty **[NOBL]** **Female Alive** See Miss Hatty Doran

Mount-James, Lord **[MISS]** **Male Alive** A queer little old man, jerking and twitching in the doorway. He was dressed in rusty black, with a very broad brimmed top-hat and a loose white necktie—the whole effect being that of a very rustic parson or of an undertaker's mute. Yet, in spite of his shabby and even absurd appearance, his voice had a sharp crackle, and his manner a quick intensity which commanded attention. Godfrey Staunton was Lord Mount-James Nephew. Lord Mount-James was one of the richest men in England. He was a miser. Would have disinherited his nephew if he had known of Godfrey's marriage to his old landlady's daughter.

Frederic Dorr Steele

Richard Gutschmidt

Muirhead, Mr. **[SUSS]** **Male Alive**   Junior partner in the Tea brokering company of Ferguson and Muirhead.

Address : Mincing Lane

Muller **[STUD]** **Male Alive**   Holmes says that this Notorious person escaped hanging because Holmes' Blood test wasn't around.

Munro, Colonel Spence **[COPP]** **Male Alive**   Violet Hunter was a governess for five years with him. He received an appointed at Halifax in Nova Scotia two months previously and had gone over with his children, leaving Violet without a position.

Munro, Effie **[YELL]** **Female Alive**   Lived in Atlanta with her first husband and had a child called Lucy with him. When her husband died, she left America and her child and travelled to Pinner. Her husband had left her comfortably off, and she had a capital of about £4,500, which had been so well invested by him that it returned an average of seven per cent. Remarried Grant Munro, but did not tell him that her daughter was still alive. Arranged to have her daughter moved into a neighbouring cottage, but kept being caught as she tried to visit. Eventually mother, daughter were united and her new husband welcomed them both with open arms.

Address : Villa in Norbury

William H. Hyde   *Sidney Paget*

Munro, Grant Jack [YELL] Male Alive A muscular man, left-handed, with an excellent set of teeth, careless in his habits, and with no need to practise economy. A tall young man who was quietly dressed in a dark-grey suit, and carried a brown wide-awake in his hand. Looked around thirty, though he was really some years older. Owner of a nice old brier with a good long stem of what the tobacconists call amber, which he evidently valued highly. The original cost of the pipe was seven and sixpence and had twice been mended, once in the wooden stem and once in the amber. Each of these mends, done, with silver bands, which must have cost more than the pipe did originally. Smokes Grosvenor mixture at eight pence an ounce. Wrote his name on the lining of his hat (brown wide-awake). Hop merchant with an income of seven or eight hundred. Was worried that his wife had a secret and would not tell him, he was correct, her 'dead' daughter was in fact still alive and had been moved in to a neighbouring cottage. To be honest, Holmes isn't really of much help in this case, but it has a happy ending.

Address : Villa in Norbury

William H. Hyde   *Sidney Paget*

Murcher, Policeman Harry [STUD] Male Alive Friend and fellow policeman of John Rance. Covered the Holland Grove beat. Probably worked the beat from 10pm till 6am. Heard Policeman Rance's whistle and ran to 3, Lauriston Gardens, where the body of Enoch J. Drebber had been found inside.

Murdoch, Ian   [LION] Male Alive A tall, dark, thin man, so taciturn and aloof that none could be said to have been his friend. He had coal-black eyes and swarthy face. He was the mathematical coach at the Gables establishment. He seemed to live in some high abstract region of surds and conic sections, with little to connect him with ordinary life. Was prone to occasional outbreaks of temper, which could only be described as ferocious. On one occasion, being plagued by a little dog belonging to McPherson, he had caught the creature up and hurled it through the plate-glass window, an action for which Stackhurst would certainly have given him his dismissal had he not been a very valuable teacher. He seemed to be honestly shocked by Fitzroy's death, despite, in the past, having thrown Fitzroy's dog through a plate glass window. Was sent to fetch the police at Fulworth and brought back the village Constable Anderson. By good fortune, he probably saved the lives of several students who had been planning on going swimming that morning, by giving them an algebraic demonstration before breakfast. Got on quite well with Fitzroy and even acted as go-between for him and his fiancée Maud Bellamy. Any thoughts that he might be implicated in the death of Fitzroy McPherson vanished when he was attacked in the same way. He managed to staggered into Holmes' room, pallid, dishevelled, his clothes in wild disorder, clawing with his bony hands at the furniture to hold himself erect. "Brandy! Brandy!" he gasped, and fell groaning upon the sofa. He had been helped by Harold Stackhurst to get to Holmes' place and on his back there criss-crossed upon the man's naked shoulder, was the same strange reticulated pattern of red, inflamed lines which had been the death-mark of Fitzroy McPherson. His pain was evidently terrible and was more than local, for the sufferer's breathing would stop for a time, his face would turn black, and then with loud gasps he would clap his hand to his heart, while his brow dropped beads of sweat. Holmes thought that at any moment he might die. More and more brandy was poured down his throat, each fresh dose bringing him back to life. Pads of cotton-wool soaked in salad-oil seemed to take the agony from the strange wounds. At last his head fell heavily upon the cushion. Exhausted Nature had taken refuge in its last storehouse of vitality. It was half a sleep and half a faint, but at least it was ease from pain. He was in no condition to be questioned.

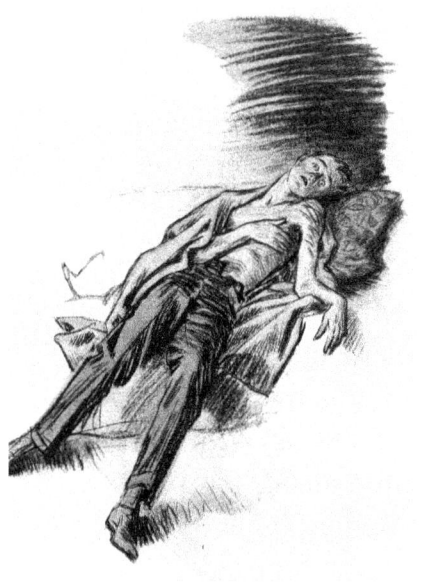

Frederic Dorr Steele

Howard K. Elcock

Murdoch, James   **[VALL]**   **Male** Unknown Members of the Vermissa lodge had mutilated James Murdoch for some reason.

Murger, Henri   [STUD]   Male dead (Real Person 1821 – 1861) French novelist and poet. Author of "Scènes de la vie de bohème" or as mentioned in this story "Vie de Bohème" French novelist and poet. Author of "Scènes de la vie de bohème" or as mentioned in this story "Vie de Bohème" After Holmes' left baker street, to followed Mrs. Sawyer and hopefully to find the murdered of Enoch J. Drebber, Watson sat stolidly puffing at his pipe and skipping over the pages of Henri Murger's Vie de Boheme.

Henry Murger

Murillo, Ex-President Juan Don   [WIST,NORW]   Male dead   See Mr. Henderson

Murphy, Major   [CROO]   Male Alive   Officer under Colonel James Barclay and prime mover in bringing Holmes and Watson into this mystery. Told Holmes that he had never heard of any misunderstanding between Barclay and his wife. On the whole, he thought that Barclay's devotion to his wife was greater than his wife's to Barclay. Barclay was acutely uneasy if he were absent from her for a day. She, on the other hand, though devoted and faithful, was less obtrusively affectionate.

Sidney Paget

Murphy, Mr. **[HOUN]** **Male Alive** One Murphy, a gypsy horse-dealer, was on the moor at no great distance at the time when Sir Charles Baskerville died, but he appeared by his own confession to have been the worse for drink. He declared that he heard cries, but was unable to state from what direction they came.

Murphy, Mr. (of Chicago) **[VALL]** **Male Alive** A friend of John McMurdo, who had recommended Jacob Shafter's boarding house in Vermissa Valley to him. He had got the recommendation from someone else.

Murray, Mr. **[STUD]** **Male Alive** Orderly who saved Dr. John H. Watson from falling into the hands of the murderous Ghazis. He put Watson on the back of a packhorse, and succeeded in bringing him safely to the British lines.

Richard Gutschmidt

Murray, Mr. **[EMPT]** **Male Alive** Played Whist with Ronald Adair on the day of his death with Sir John Hardy, and Colonel Moran.

Musgrave, Reginald **[MUSG]** **Male Alive** In appearance he was a man of exceedingly aristocratic type, thin, high-nosed, and large-eyed, with languid and yet courtly manners. Always a bit of a dandy While supposedly tidying the rooms for Watson, Holmes goes into his bedroom and returned with a large tin box full of papers that he is going to tidy. Watson's plans for a tidy place ruined as Holmes pulls out a crumpled piece of paper, an old-fashioned brass key, a peg of wood with a ball of string attached to it, and three rusty old discs of metal. So unfolds the adventure of the Musgrave Ritual. Holmes and Reginald Musgrave had been at the same college, years ago, and were acquainted but had not bothered to keep in touch with one another, until four years after college, Musgrave calls into Holmes' lodgings , then in Montague street. Musgrave explains that his Butler, Brunton, of twenty years has disappeared without a trace or removing any of his possessions. It turns out that Brunton had been trying to solve the mystery of the Musgrave Ritual, which reads;

- 'Whose was it?'
- 'His who is gone.'
- 'Who shall have it?'"
- 'He who will come.'
- 'Where was the sun?'
- 'Over the oak.'
- 'Where was the shadow?'
- 'Under the elm.'
- 'How was it stepped?'
- 'North by ten and by ten, east by five and by five, south by two and by two, west by one and by one, and so under.'
- 'What shall we give for it?'
- 'All that is ours.'
- 'Why should we give it?'
- 'For the sake of the trust.'

Holmes joins Musgrave at Hurlstone and works out the meaning of the ritual and finds Brunton's dead body.

Address : Manor House of Hurlstone

Sidney Paget

Sidney Paget

Musgrave, Sir Ralph [MUSG] Male dead Ancestor of Reginald Musgrave and a prominent Cavalier and the right-hand man of Charles the Second in his wanderings. Involved in the hiding of the Crown and writing the Musgrave Ritual.

Mysterious Lady (Milverton's killer) [CHAS] Female Alive there stood a tall, slim, dark woman, a veil over her face, a mantle drawn round her chin. Her breath came quick and fast, and every inch of the lithe figure was quivering with strong emotion. She had a dark, handsome, clear-cut face with a curved nose, strong, dark eyebrows shading hard, glittering eyes, and a straight, thin-lipped mouth set in a dangerous smile. This Ladies name will forever be a mystery, Holmes and Watson knew who she was, but Watson never named her, but she is important enough to be included here for killing Milverton. Her life was ruined by Milverton, who tried to blackmail her with some incriminating letters. She had begged and prayed for mercy from Milverton, who had just laughed in her face. The Letters were received by her husband and he had died from a broken heart. Say had said that she had five letters which compromise the Countess d'Albert in order to get the late night interview with Milverton. She Shot him at least four times and as he lay dead on the carpet, ground her heel into his upturned face and then left through the same door she had entered by.

Frederic Dorr Steele

Sidney Paget

N is for the Noble Bachelor

Napoleon, Emperor   [FINA,SIXN,VALL]   Male dead   See Napoleon Bonaparte

Neal, Mr.   [VALL]   Male Alive   Owner of an Outfitters based in Vermissa, U.S.A, where Ted Baldwin purchased his overcoat, an overcoat, which was full of suggestive touches like the inner pocket prolonged into the lining in such fashion as to give ample space for the truncated fowling piece. There was the tailor's tab is on the neck.

Negro, The Horse   [SILV]   Male Horse Alive   Horse belonging to Mr. Heath Newton, Red cap, Cinnamon jacket. ran in the Wessex plate, not placed. Wessex Plate 50 Sovereigns each h ft. with 1000 Sovereigns added for four and five year olds. Second, £300. Third, £200. New course (one mile and five furlongs).

Neill, Brigadier-General James George Smith   [CROO]   Male dead (Real Person 1810 – 1857)   Scottish military officer of the East India Company, who served during the Indian rebellion of 1857. He was infamous for the indiscriminate killing of native Indians in revenge for the murder of British women and children during the Bibighar massacre. Corporal Henry Wood volunteered to find General Neill's column so that everyone at Bhurtee could be saved.

Brigadier-General James George Smith Neill

Neligan, John Hopley **[BLAC]** **Male Alive** He was a young man, frail and thin, with a black moustache, which intensified the deadly pallor of his face. Watson had never seen any human being who appeared to be in such a pitiable fright, for his teeth were visibly chattering, and he was shaking in every limb. He was dressed like a gentleman, in Norfolk jacket and knickerbockers, with a cloth cap upon his head. Son of the disgraced Banker, Old Neligan, who's company failure had ruined half the county families of Cornwall in August 1883. He was trying to track down some securities his father had taken when he attempted to sail to Norway He had thought these securities had been lost at sea together with his father, but they had recently reappeared on the London market and the seller was Captain Peer Carey, which was by he was caught searching the Captain's cabin. Holmes could see that he did not possess the strength to have killed the Captain, pinning him to the wall with a Harpoon, but Inspector Hopkins took him away to charge him for murder. Holmes was left to find the true killer and get Neligan released.

Frederic Dorr Steele

Sidney Paget

Neligan, old **[BLAC]** **Male dead** Father to John Hopley Neligan. West-country bankers, who's company failure had ruined half the county families of Cornwall in August 1883. Escaped with valuable securities that he hoped given enough time would realise more that was owing and clear his name, but he was murdered by Captain Peter Carey, who found list little boat at sea. The Captain, had kept the securities and he was kiled by being tipped overboard.

Sherlock Holmes Quote : "You mean the West-country bankers," said he. "They failed for a million, ruined half the county families of Cornwall, and Neligan disappeared."

Nelson, Mr. **[SIGN]** **Male** Junior partner in the company Broderick and Nelson, a Large timber-yard, just past the White Eagle tavern that Toby leads Holmes and Watson to by mistake after the creosote paths cross at the corner of Knight's Place.

Neruda, Wilhelmine Maria Franziska **[STUD]** **Female Alive (Real Person 1838 – 1911)** Moravia virtuoso Violinist, chamber musician and teacher Chopin Piece is likely the Waltz op.34 n.1

Sherlock Holmes Quotes :"We must hurry up, for I want to go to Halle's concert to hear Norman Neruda this afternoon.""
"And now for lunch, and then for Norman Neruda. Her attack and her bowing are splendid. What's that little thing of Chopin's she plays so magnificently: Tra-la-la-lira-lira-lay."

Wilhelmine Maria Franziska Neruda

Newton, Heath **[SILV]** **Male Alive** Owner of the Horse The Negro. Red cap. Cinnamon jacket, which ran in the Wessex plate, not placed. Wessex Plate 50 Sovereigns each h ft. with 1000 Sovereigns added for four and five year olds. Second, £300. Third, £200. New course (one mile and five furlongs).

Nicholson, Family [VALL] dead Unknown Members of the Vermissa lodge had killed this Family for some reason.

Norberton, Sir Robert [SHOS] Male Alive He was a terrible figure, huge in stature and fierce in manner. He had a strong, heavily moustached face and angry eyes. Watson said of him "Well, he has the name of being a dangerous man. He is about the most daredevil rider in England—second in the Grand National a few years back. He is one of those men who have overshot their true generation. He should have been a buck in the days of the Regency—a boxer, an athlete, a plunger on the turf, a lover of fair ladies, and, by all account, so far down Queer Street that he may never find his way back again. he horsewhipped Sam Brewer, the well-known Curzon Street moneylender, on Newmarket Heath. He nearly killed the man." Needed his horse Shoscombe Prince to win in the Derby, so that he could pay off his creditors. He was too clever for the touts and had got good odds on his horse, by taking the Prince's half-brother out for spins. He was terrible jealous of touts. His Sister died of dropsy and since the horse was part of her estate, he had to keep her death secret, arranging for Norlett to drive around pretending to be the sister. Holmes uncovered the truth, the creditors held their hand and Shoscombe Prince won the Derby, netting Sir Robert £80,000.

Address : Shoscombe Old Place

Frank Wiles

Frederic Dorr Steele

Norlett, Mr.   [SHOS]   Male Alive   A small rat-faced man with a disagreeably furtive manner. Chief worker at Shoscombe Old Place. Helped Sir Robert Norberton move the body of his sister, Lady Beatrice Falder from where she died, down to one of the coffins in the crypt., then dressed up as Lady Beatrice and was driven around in a carriage to give the impression that she was still alive. He tried to distance himself from the actions of Sir Robert saying "As to me, I entirely disclaim all responsibility."

Address : Shoscombe Old Place

Frank Wiles

Norton, Godfrey   [SCAN]   Male Alive   Godfrey Norton is a lawyer, engaged and married with Irene Adler in St. Monica church Holmes (disguised as a groom) acted as a last-minute best-man.   He worked at the Inner Temple. He went to Gross & Hankey's, Regent Street before going to St. Monica church. He marry Irene Adler at the St. Monica church, Edgware Road.

Norton, Irene   [SCAN]   Female alive   See Irene Adler

O is for Orange, as in Five Orange Pips

Oakshott, Maggie [BLUE] Female Alive Breeder of Geese. Sold 24 geese at 7s. 6d each to Mr Breckinridge. Sister of James Ryder, who stole the Blue Carbuncle. Breeder of Geese. Ryder hid the gem in the crop of one of the geese with a with a barred tail, but it struggled and got away. Unfortunately for him, there were two such geese and he took the wrong one away and when he discovered his error and returned to Brixton road, Maggie had already sold them. Sold 24 geese at 7s. 6d each to Mr Breckinridge.

Address : 117, Brixton Road

Oakshott, Mr. [BLUE] Male Husband of Maggie Oakshott. Doesn't appear in story.

Oakshott, Sir Leslie [ILLU] Male Alive After the murderous attack on Sherlock Holmes, Watson hurried to Baker street and as he arrived, he found Sir Leslie Oakshott, the famous surgeon, in the hall and his brougham waiting at the curb. "No immediate danger," was his report. "Two lacerated scalp wounds and some considerable bruises. Several stitches have been necessary. Morphine has been injected and quiet is essential, but an interview of a few minutes would not be absolutely forbidden." Holmes said that he would be able to malinger well enough to fool the Doctor

Oberstein, Hugo [BRUC,SECO] Male Alive [BRUC] International agent involved in the missing Bruce-Partington papers. Holmes visited the front of his home and satisfied himself that the bird was indeed flown. He lived in a considerable house, unfurnished in the upper rooms. Oberstein lived there with a single valet, who was probably a confederate entirely in his confidence. Oberstein had gone to the Continent to dispose of his booty, but not with any idea of flight; for he had no reason to fear a warrant, and the idea of an amateur domiciliary visit would certainly never occur to him. Yet that is precisely what Holmes and Watson were about to make. (i.e., breaking and entering) The backstairs' windows of Caulfield Gardens opened onto the Underground line but the even more essential fact that, owing to the intersection of one of the larger railways, the Underground trains were frequently held motionless for some minutes at that very spot. Holmes found blood marks around the back window, where Cadogen West's body was rested before being lowered onto the top of a stationary train carriage roof. Offered Colonel Valentine Walter five thousand pounds for the Bruce-Partington plans. Communicated with Walter though the advertisement columns of The

Daily Telegraph using the pseudonym Pierot. On the evening of Cadogen West's death, he had been waiting for the arrival of Walter and the plans, when Cadogen West had rushed up and demanded to know what they were about to do with the papers. He always carried a short life-preserver and as Cadogen West forced his way into the house, Oberstein struck him on the head. The blow was a fatal one and Cadogen West was dead within five minutes. He kept three of the most essential parts of the plans and placed the other seven parts on Cadogen West's body as they lowered it on the underground carriage roof from his back window. He then went off to Europe to sell the plans staying at the Hotel du Louvre, Paris. Was contacted by Colonel Valentine Walter and met him in the the smoking-room of the Charing Cross Hotel, but it was a trap and he was arrested, the missing three papers, recovered and he was sentenced to fifteen years in prison.

Sherlock Holmes Quote : [SECO]

"There are only those three capable of playing so bold a game; there are Oberstein, La Rothière, and Eduardo Lucas. I will see each of them."

Address : 13 Caulfield Gardens, Kensington

P. B. Hickling   *Arthur Twidle*

Odley, Mr. [SUSS] Male dead   Builder of a house in Lamberley. As Watson says "I know that country, Holmes. It is full of old houses which are named after the men who built them centuries ago. You get Odley's and Harvey's and Carriton's—the folk are forgotten but their names live in their houses."

Oldacre, Mr. Jonas   [NORW]   Male in prison   Mr. Jonas Oldacre, of Lower Norwood, aka the Norwood Builder. The events relating to Oldacre and John Hector McFarlane appeared in the stop-press of the paper; "Late last night, or early this morning, an incident occurred at Lower Norwood which points, it is feared, to a serious crime. Mr. Jonas Oldacre is a well-known resident of that suburb, where he has carried on his business as a builder for many years. Mr. Oldacre is a bachelor, fifty-two years of age, and lives in Deep Dene House, at the Sydenham end of the road of that name. He has had the reputation of being a man of eccentric habits, secretive and retiring. For some years he has practically withdrawn from the business, in which he is said to have amassed considerable wealth. A small timber-yard still exists, however, at the back of the house, and last night, about twelve o'clock, an alarm was given that one of the stacks was on fire. The engines were soon upon the spot, but the dry wood burned with great fury, and it was impossible to arrest the conflagration until the stack had been entirely consumed. Up to this point the incident bore the appearance of an ordinary accident, but fresh indications seem to point to serious crime. Surprise was expressed at the absence of the master of the establishment from the scene of the fire, and an inquiry followed, which showed that he had disappeared from the house. An examination of his room revealed that the bed had not been slept in, that a safe which stood in it was open, that a number of important papers were scattered about the room, and, finally, that there were signs of a murderous struggle, slight traces of blood being found within the room, and an oaken walking-stick, which also showed stains of blood upon the handle. It is known that Mr. Jonas Oldacre had received a late visitor in his bedroom upon that night, and the stick found has been identified as the property of this person, who is a young London solicitor named John Hector McFarlane, junior partner of Graham and McFarlane, of 426, Gresham Buildings, E.C. The police believe that they have evidence in their possession which supplies a very convincing motive for the crime, and altogether it cannot be doubted that sensational developments will follow. LATER.—It is rumoured as we go to press that Mr. John Hector McFarlane has actually been arrested on the charge of the murder of Mr. Jonas Oldacre. It is at least certain that a warrant has been issued. There have been further and sinister developments in the investigation at Norwood. Besides the signs of a struggle in the room of the unfortunate builder it is now known that the French windows of his bedroom (which is on the ground floor) were found to be open, that there were marks as if some bulky object had been dragged across to the woodpile, and, finally, it is asserted that charred remains have been found among the charcoal ashes of the fire. The police theory is that a most sensational crime has been committed, that the victim was clubbed to death in his own bedroom, his papers rifled, and his dead body dragged across to the wood-stack, which was then ignited so as to hide all traces of the crime. The conduct of the criminal investigation has been left in the experienced hands of Inspector Lestrade, of Scotland Yard, who is following up the clues with his accustomed energy and sagacity." He had known McFarlane's mother in his past, but she had found out about his true nature when she discovered that he had released a cat into an aviary. He tried to frame John Hector McFarlane for murder. He had been skimming off profits from his company and paying them into an account using an assumed name of Mr. Cornelius. Under the pretence of discussing his new will and other business, he invited McFarlane over in the evening and then, set light to a stack of wood in his small timber yard. He smeared blood around and put some on McFarlane's walking stick. He then hid in a concealed room within the house. His fatal mistake was in trying to add further evidence against McFarlane. He had a copy of McFarlane's thumb print on sealing wax and using this and a little blood, added a print onto the wall in the hall. The problem was that Holmes had already searched the hall and knew that the print had not been their originally. His hiding place was discovered after he panicked when he thought that a fire had broken out in the house, but it was just a ruse by Holmes.

Address : Deep Dene House, at the Sydenham end of the road, Lower Norwood.

Frederic Dorr Steele   *R. Thomson*

Oldmore, Mr.   **[HOUN]**   **Male** He was once Mayor of Gloucester. His wife or widow stayed at the Northumberland Hotel and might have been involved in the Baskerville case. She was innocent.

Oldmore, Mrs.   [HOUN]   Female Alive   She was an invalid lady. Holmes wanted to see if the people who were following Sir Henry Baskerville had booked into the hotel after he had registered. Holmes found this person's name in the hotel register. Together with her maid, she arrived at the Northumberland Hotel after Sir Henry Baskerville's arrival. Her husband was once Mayor of Gloucester. She always stayed at the Northumberland Hotel when she was in town."

Sherlock Holmes Quote : "We know now that the people who are so interested in our friend have not settled down in his own hotel. That means that while they are, as we have seen, very anxious to watch him, they are equally anxious that he should not see them. Now, this is a most suggestive fact."

Openshaw, Colonel Elias   [FIVE]   Male dead   Elias Openshaw emigrated to America when he was a young man and became a planter in Florida,. At the time of the American Civil war he fought in Jackson's army, and afterwards under Hood, where he rose to be a colonel. When Lee laid down his arms he returned to his plantation, where he remained for three or four years. About 1869 or 1870 he came back to Europe and took a small estate in Sussex, near Horsham. He had made a very considerable fortune in the States, and his reason for leaving them was his aversion to the Negroes, and his dislike of the Republican policy in extending the franchise to them. He was a singular man, fierce and quick-tempered, very foul-mouthed when he was angry, and of a most retiring disposition. During all the years that he lived at Horsham, he probably never set foot in the town. He had a garden and two or three fields round his house, and there he would take his exercise, though very often for weeks on end he would never leave his room. He drank a great deal of brandy and smoked very heavily, but he would see no society and did not want any friends, not even his own brother. Received five orange pips in letter postmarked Pondicherry, 10th March 1883. Red ink upon the inner flap of envelope, just above the gum, the letter K three times repeated. Left his estate and £14,000 which lay to his credit at the bank to his brother Joseph Openshaw. Died May 2, 1883 (seven weeks after receiving letter)

Sidney Paget   *Josef Friedrich*

Openshaw, John   [FIVE]   Male dead   Young. Some two-and-twenty at the outside. Well-groomed and trimly clad, with something of refinement and delicacy in his bearing. Long shining waterproof told of the fierce weather through which he had come. His face was pale and his eyes heavy, like those of a man who is weighed down with some great anxiety. Golden pince-nez. Holmes was recommend to him by Major Prendergast (Tankerville Club scandal). Father was Joseph Openshaw and uncle was Elias Openshaw. Son of Joseph Opershaw and nephew of Elias Opershaw. His uncle and father were murdered after receiving orange pips in the post. He visited Holmes on a stormy September night after he had received five orange pips in the post. He had been living with his uncle until his death and had learnt something about his shady past and his membership of the Ku Klux Klan. Members of this organisation wanted documents his uncle had taken with him when he returned to England having lived for some time in America. His uncle burned them and when he did not hand them over, was killed. They next asked Joseph Opershaw to hand over the documents and he laughed it off and was also killed. Letter containing five orange pips arrived 28th September 1887, asking for the destroyed papers. The letter was Postmarked London. He was killed after leaving Holmes on his way home. Holmes discovered who the murderers were and sent them orange pips, but they died when their boat wrecked.

Address : Horsham

Josef Friedrich   *Sidney Paget*

Openshaw, Joseph [FIVE] Male dead Father of John Openshaw. Owned a
Bicycling factory in Coventry He was a patentee of the Openshaw unbreakable
tire, and his business met with such success that he was able to sell it and to retire
upon a handsome competence. Owned a Bicycling factory in Coventry Had a
brother called Elias and a son called John. He was a patentee of the Openshaw
unbreakable tire, and his business met with such success that he was able to sell it
and to retire upon a handsome competence. Took possession of his late brother's
estate in the beginning of 1884. Received a letter with five orange pips 4th
January 1885. The letter was postmarked Dundee. Died on 9th January 1885 by
falling into a deep chalk-pit and shattering his skull.

Sidney Paget

Josef Friedrich

Overton, Mr. Cyril [MISS] Male Alive An enormous young man, sixteen stone of solid bone and muscle, who spanned the doorway with his broad shoulders. Attending Trinity College, Cambridge. He was first reserve for England against Wales, and has skippered the 'Varsity all this year. Had skippered the Rugger team of Cambridge 'Varsity. Called upon Holmes to see if he could find his missing Three-quarter Godfrey Staunton

Frederic Dorr Steele

Richard Gutschmidt

P is for Priory School

Paganini, Niccolo   [CARD]   Male dead (Real Person 1782 – 1840)   Italian violinist, violist, guitarist, and composer Holmes spoke about Paganini, while he and Watson talked for an hour over a bottle of claret while he told Watson anecdote after anecdote of that extraordinary man.

Niccolo Paganini

Palladio, Andrea   [ABBE]   Male dead (Real Person 1508 – 1580)   Andrea Palladio was an Italian Renaissance architect active in the Venetian Republic. The house at Abbey Grange, Marsham, Kent Abbey Grange, Marsham, Kent where The avenue ran through a noble park, between lines of ancient elms, and ended in a low, widespread house, were pillared in front after the fashion of Palladio.

Andrea Palladio

Palmer, John F. [PRIO] Male   American born cord tyre maker who patented them for bicycles in America in 1892 and then moved to England where his tires were so much faster in Bicycle races that the officials handicapped the riders who used them.

Sherlock Holmes Quote : "I am familiar with forty-two different impressions left by tyres. This, as you perceive, is a Dunlop, with a patch upon the outer cover. Heidegger's tyres were Palmer's, leaving longitudinal stripes. Aveling, the mathematical master, was sure upon the point. Therefore, it is not Heidegger's track."

Palmer, William   [SPEC]   Male dead   English doctor who was convicted of murder in one of the most notorious cases of the 19th century.

On 18 January, 1849, Killed his mother-in-law Ann Mary Thornton

On 10 May, 1850, Leonard Bladen died.

On 6 January 1851, Elizabeth Palmer.(two and a half months old.)

On 6 January 1852, Henry Palmer. (about a month old.)

On 19 December 1852, Frank Palmer. (only 7 hours old.)

On 29 September 1854,wife Ann Palmer (maybe cholera)

On 16 August 1855, his brother Walter Palmer died [SEP]

On 21 November 1855, Friend John Cook was poisoned.[SEP]

John Palmer. Died on 27 January 1854. He was three or four days old. At hanging Palmer is said to have looked at the trapdoor and exclaimed, "Are you sure it's safe?"

Sherlock Holmes Quote : "Subtle enough and horrible enough. When a doctor does go wrong he is the first of criminals. He has nerve and he has knowledge. Palmer and Pritchard were among the heads of their profession. This man strikes even deeper, but I think, Watson, that we shall be able to strike deeper still. But we shall have horrors enough before the night is over; for goodness' sake let us have a quiet pipe and turn our minds for a few hours to something more cheerful."

William palmer

Paramore, Mr.   [FIVE]   Male dead   Mentioned in the remaining ledger page belonging to the KKK dated March 1869 7th. Set the pips on McCauley, Mr., Paramore, and John Swain of St. Augustine. 12th. Visited Paramore. All well. probably killed by the KKK

Parker, Mr   [STOC]   Male Alive   Coxon & Woodhouse's, of Draper's Gardens Coxon's manager. Arthur Pinner said of Mr. Parker "The fact is that I have heard some really extraordinary stories about your (Hall Pycroft) financial ability."

Parker, Mr.   [EMPT]   Male Alive   Described as a harmless fellow, despite being a garrotter by trade. A remarkable performer upon the Jew's harp (Jaw Harp) Was acting as a lookout in Baker street for Sebastian Moran.

Sherlock Holmes Quote : "I recognised their sentinel when I glanced out of my window. He is a harmless enough fellow, Parker by name, a garrotter by trade, and a remarkable performer upon the Jew's harp. I cared nothing for him.

Parker, Rev. [DANC] Male Alive Vicar of the parish in which Hilton Cubitt lived. While the vicar was staying at a boarding-house in Russell Square, Hilton Cubitt visited him and met with an American young lady called Elsie Patrick.

Address : North Walsham Parish

Parr, Lucy [BERY] Female Alive She is a very pretty girl and has attracted admirers who have occasionally hung about the place. Believed to be a thoroughly good girl in every way. The second waiting-maid, had only been in Alexander Holder's service a few months. She came with an excellent character. Sweetheart is Francis Prosper, the one legged greengrocer.

Address : Fairbank

Partington, Mr. [BRUC] Probably Male See Bruce-Partington

Paterson, inspector [FINA] Male Alive Inspector of Scotland Yard. Inspector of Scotland Yard who is briefly mentioned only in this story.

Sherlock Holmes Quote : "Tell Inspector Patterson that the papers which he needs to convict the gang are in pigeonhole M., done up in a blue envelope and inscribed 'Moriarty.'"

Patersons, Grice [FIVE] Male While Watson was looking at cases for the year 1887, he mentions the adventure of the Paradol Chamber, of the Amateur Mendicant Society, the loss of the British bark Sophy Anderson, of the singular adventures of the Grice Patersons in the island of Uffa, and finally of the Camberwell poisoning case.

Patrick, Crime Boss [DANC] Male dead Crime boss of a gang of seven people in Chicago. Very clever man. Invented the form of writing using stick figure to represent letters (The Dancing Men). Father of Elsie Patrick.

Patrick, Elsie [DANC] Female Alive See Elsie Cubitt

Pattins, Hugh [BLAC] Male Alive Long, dried-up creature, with lank hair and sallow cheeks. The second applicant for a position on board ship that Captain Basil (Holmes) advertised for, while he was trying to get the murderer of Captain Peter Carey. Was given half a sovereign for his troubles.

Paul, Jean [SIGN] Male dead (Real Person 1763 – 1825)   See Jean-Paul Friedrich Richter.

Peace, Charlie   [ILLU]   Male dead (Real Person 1832 – 1879)   He was an English burglar and murderer, who embarked on a life of crime. He taught himself to play tunes on a violin with one string, and at entertainments which he attended was described as "the modern Paganini." Holmes mentioned him when talking about Criminals and artists.

Sherlock Holmes Quote : "A complex mind, All great criminals have that. My old friend Charlie Peace was a violin virtuoso. Wainwright was no mean artist."

Charlie peace

Perkins, Mr.   [3GAB]   Male dead   Young man killed by persons unknown outside the Holborn Bar. Steve Dixie maintained that he had nothing to do with the death and that he was training in Birmingham. Holmes was not convinced.

Perkins, the groom   [HOUN]   Male Alive   Groom at Baskerville Manor, collected Sir Henry Baskerville, James Mortimer and Watson from the train station and took them to the hall.

Address : Baskerville Manor

Paul Thiriat

B. Widman

Persano, Isadora   [THOR]   Male In a mental ward of a hospital   The third unsolved case worthy of note is that of Isadora Persano, the well-known journalist and duellist, who was found stark staring mad with a match box in front of him which contained a remarkable worm said to be unknown to science.

Peter, the groom   [SOLI]   Male Alive   It was a young fellow about seventeen, dressed like an ostler, with leather cords and gaiters. Groom employed by Carruthers Was taking Violet Smith to the train station when they were attacked, he was hit on the head and lay insensible, while violet Smith was taken away and forced to marry Jack Woodley. His injuries did not penetrated the bone.

Peters of Adelaide, Henry   [LADY]   Male Escaped   See Rev. Dr. Shlessinger

Peters, Holy   [LADY]   Male Escaped   See Rev. Dr. Shlessinger

Peterson, The commissionaire   [BLUE]   Male Alive   A very honest fellow. Official-looking person in uniform A very honest fellow. Saw Henry Baker being attacked by a little knot of roughs while returning from some small jollification and tried to help, but everyone ran off leaving a battered Bowler hat and a Goose. When the Goose was being prepared for cooking, the Blue Carbuncle was found in it's crop. Was in line for the £1000 reward for finding the Gem.

Josef Friedrich   *Sidney Paget*

Petrarch, Francesco [BOSC] Male dead (Real Person 1304 – 1374) Italian Scholar and poet during the early Italian Renaissance . Rediscovered Cicero's letter often credited with initiating the 14th Italian Renaissance and founding of Renaissance Humanism-century. On the train journey to Boscombe Valley Holmes wanted to read his Petrarch.

Sherlock Holmes Quote : "And now here is my pocket Petrarch, and not another word shall I say of this case until we are on the scene of action. We lunch at Swindon, and I see that we shall be there in twenty minutes."

Francesco Petrarch

Phelps, Percy   [NAVA]   Male Alive   A young man, very pale and worn. Watson had been intimately associated with him Similar age as Watson, although he was two classes ahead of him. He was a very brilliant boy, and carried away every prize which the school had to offer, finished his exploits by winning a scholarship which sent him on to continue his triumphant career at Cambridge. Extremely well connected, because his mother's brother was Lord Holdhurst, the great conservative politician. Teased at school, was chivvied about the playground and hit over his shins with a wicket. The Naval treaty, he was working on was stolen from his desk, while he was absent, which resulted in him having brain fever for nine weeks. Slept in a downstairs room, that had previously been used by his future brother-in-law, Joseph Harrison, who had stolen the treaty and had hidden in under the floorboards of the same room. Eventually Joseph Harrison was caught by Holmes when the room was vacated by Percy Phelps while the later was up in London with his old school friend Watson. We presented with the treaty by Holmes at breakfast the next morning, who hid it under a covered plate.

Address : Briarbrae, Woking

Sidney Paget   *William H. Hyde*

Phillimore, Mr. James   [THOR]   Male Among the unfinished tales of Holmes is that of Mr. James Phillimore, who, stepping back into his own house to get his umbrella, was never more seen in this world.

Pickwick, Mr. Samuel   [CHAS]   Male Fictional character from Charles Dickens' book The Pickwick Papers (1837) His character was loyal and protective toward his friends but was often hoodwinked by conmen.   Watson said about Charles Augustus Milverton that 2]There was something of Mr. Pickwick's benevolence in his appearance, marred only by the insincerity of the fixed smile and by the hard glitter of those restless and penetrating eyes. "

Joseph Clayton Clark (Kyd)

Pierot   [BRUC]   see Hugo Oberstein.

Pike, Langdale   [3GAB]   Male Alive   Watson said that Langdale Pike was Holmes' human book of reference upon all matters of social scandal. He spent his waking hours in the bow window of a St. James's Street club and was the receiving-station as well as the transmitter for all the gossip of the metropolis. He made, a four-figure income by the paragraphs which he contributed every week to the garbage papers which cater to an inquisitive public.

Pinkerton, Allan   [VALL, REDC]   Male dead (Real Person 1819 – 1884)
The American, a quiet, business-like young man, with a clean-shaven, hatchet face, flushed up at the words of commendation Spy during the American Civil war, then turned Detective and started the Pinkerton Detective Agency. [VALL] Birdy Edwards was a Pinkerton Man. [REDC] In the story, Mr. Leverton works for the Pinkerton's American Agency."

Allan Pinkerton

Pinkerton, Bruce   [RESI]   Male Benefactor to the Medical profession, who offered a prize and medal for outstanding articles in medicine. Mr. Percy Trevelyan was the recipient of this award for his monograph on nervous lesions.

Pinner, Arthur   [STOC]   Male Alive A middle-sized, dark-haired, dark-eyed, black-bearded man, with a touch of the Sheeny about his nose. He had a brisk kind of way with him and spoke sharply, like a man who knew the value of time. Clean shaven in the role of Harry Pinner. His second tooth upon the left-hand side had been very badly stuffed with gold Alias of one of the Beddington brothers. Financial Agent with the Franco-Midland Hardware Company. Franco-Midland Hardware Company was meant to have a "hundred and thirty-four branches in the towns and villages of France, not counting one in Brussels and one in San Remo." Also played the role of Harry Pinner promoter and managing director based up in Birmingham. Offered Hall Pycroft a salary of a beggarly five hundred a year to start with.

Address : 126b Corporation Street, Birmingham.

William H. Hyde   *Sidney Paget*

Pinner, Harry **[STOC]** **Male Alive** See Arthur Pinner

Pinto, Jonas **[VALL]** **Male dead** The man John McMurdo confessed to shooting and killing in Chicago in 1874. He helped McMurdo in his counterfeit operations by distributing the fake money, he said he would split, so McMurdo killed him and was wanted now in Chicago. Police Captain Marvin of the Chicago Central said he hadn't forgotten the shooting of this man, when he encountered McMurdo in McGinty's saloon.

Address : Lake Saloon, Market Street, Chicago

Pinto, Maria **[THOR]** **Female dead** See Mrs. Maria Gibson

Pitt, William 'The Younger' **[HOUN]** **Male dead (Real Person 1759 – 1806)** Prominent British Tory statesman of the late eighteenth and early nineteenth centuries. Linked to Sir Henry Baskerville, through Sir William Baskerville, "That is Rear-Admiral Baskerville, who served under Rodney in the West Indies. The man with the blue coat and the roll of paper is Sir William Baskerville, who was Chairman of Committees of the House of Commons under Pitt."

William Pitt 'The Younger'

Plunkett, St. Oliver   [HOUN]   Male dead (Real Person 1652 – 1681)   Irish Saint and martyr. Mr & Mrs Vandeleur (Stapleton/Baskerville) owned a private school called St. Oliver's, Stapleton said it was in Yorkshire and that an serious epidemic broke out and three boys died.

Sherlock Holmes Quote : "Here is a photograph of the couple taken in York four years ago. It is endorsed 'Mr. and Mrs. Vandeleur,' but you will have no difficulty in recognising him, and her also, if you know her by sight. Here are three written descriptions by trustworthy witnesses of Mr. and Mrs. Vandeleur, who at that time kept St. Oliver's private school. Read them and see if you can doubt the identity of these people."

St. Oliver Plunkett

Poe, Edgar Allen   [STUD,RESI]   Male dead (Real Person 1809 – 1849)
Watson says of Holmes "You remind me of Edgar Allen Poe's Dupin." [STUD]
American writer, poet, editor, and literary critic. Poe is best known for his poetry
and short stories, particularly his tales of mystery and the macabre.

Sherlock Holmes Quote : [STUD] "No doubt you think that you are
complimenting me in comparing me to Dupin," he observed. "Now, in my
opinion, Dupin was a very inferior fellow. That trick of his of breaking in on his
friends' thoughts with an apropos remark after a quarter of an hour's silence is
really very showy and superficial. He had some analytical genius, no doubt; but he
was by no means such a phenomenon as Poe appeared to imagine."
[RESI]"You remember," said he, "that some little time ago, when I read you the
passage in one of Poe's sketches, in which a close reasoner follows the unspoken
thought of his companion, you were inclined to treat the matter as a mere tour de
force of the author. On my remarking that I was constantly in the habit of doing
the same thing you expressed incredulity."

Edgar Allen Poe

Pollock, Constable [STOC] Male Alive   Together with Sergeant Tuson, captured Beddington as he tried to make off with a hundred thousand pounds' worth of American railway bonds, with a large amount of scrip in mines and other companies.

Pompey, the dog [MISS] Alive   a squat, lop-eared, white-and-tan dog, something between a beagle and a foxhound. Holmes and Watson did not have much luck following Dr. Leslie Armstrong's carriage until they used the dog Pompey from Jeremy Dixon, Trinity College. Holmes had walked into the doctor's yard that morning and shot his syringe full of aniseed over the hind wheel. The dog was tracking a aniseed trail left by Dr. Leslie Armstrong's carriage.

Sherlock Holmes Quote : Pompey is the pride of the local drag hounds, no very great flier, as his build will show, but a staunch hound on a scent.

Frederic Dorr Steele   *Sidney Paget*

Pope, Alexander [REIG] Male dead (Real Person 1688 – 1744) Regarded as one of the greatest English poets. The second-most quoted writer in the English language after Shakespeare. Translated Homer A copy of his translation of 'Homer' was stolen from Mr. Acton's house along with two plated candlesticks, an ivory letter-weight, a small oak barometer, and a ball of twine.

Alexander Pope

Porlock, Fred   [VALL]   Male Alive   His writing used the Greek e with the peculiar top flourish which was distinctive. Worked for Professor James Moriarty. Wrote to Holmes about a forthcoming Holmes wondered if he were led on by some rudimentary aspirations towards right, and encouraged by the judicious stimulation of an occasional ten-pound note sent to him by devious methods, he has once or twice given me advance information which has been of value—that highest value which anticipates and prevents rather than avenges crime. His message in this story was as follows.

534 C2 13 127 36 31 4 17 21 41

DOUGLAS 109 293 5 37 BIRLSTONE

26 BIRLSTONE 9 47 171

Unfortunately, in an later message from Fred Porlock, he says "DEAR MR. HOLMES (he says): "I will go no further in this matter. It is too dangerous—he suspects me. I can see that he suspects me. He came to me quite unexpectedly after I had actually addressed this envelope with the intention of sending you the key to the cipher. I was able to cover it up. If he had seen it, it would have gone hard with me. But I read suspicion in his eyes. Please burn the cipher message, which can now be of no use to you. FRED PORLOCK." Holmes was however able to work out what book to use to reveal the message.

Sherlock Holmes Quote : "Porlock, Watson, is a nom-de-plume, a mere identification mark; but behind it lies a shifty and evasive personality. In a former letter he frankly informed me that the name was not his own, and defied me ever to trace him among the teeming millions of this great city. Porlock is important, not for himself, but for the great man with whom he is in touch. Picture to yourself the pilot fish with the shark, the jackal with the lion —anything that is insignificant in companionship with what is formidable: not only formidable, Watson, but sinister—in the highest degree sinister. That is where he comes within my purview. You have heard me speak of Professor Moriarty?"

Porter, Mrs.   [DEVI]   Female Alive   Elderly Cornish cook and housekeeper at Tredannick Wartha. She had a young girl to assist her. On the night the tragedy she had gone to bed and had slept deeply and heard no sound during the night. She reported that nothing had been stolen or disarranged, and there is absolutely no explanation of what the horror could have been which had frightened a woman to death and two strong men out of their senses. She had fainted with horror upon entering the room in the morning and seeing that dreadful company round the table. She would not herself stay in the house another day and was starting that very afternoon to re-join her family at St. Ives.

Address : Tredannick Wartha

Pott, County Delegate Evans   [VALL]   Male Alive   A sly, little grey-haired rat of a man, with a slinking gait and a sidelong glance which was charged with malice. The County Delegate feared throughout the area. Held much power and knew much more of all the doings of the society. Had power over several different lodges which he wielded in a sudden and arbitrary way. Potts send a letter over to Boss McGinty about the arrival of two assassins who were being sent over to Vermissa to kill Josiah H. Dunn.

Address : Hobson's Patch

Prendergast Major   [FIVE]   Male   Was saved by Holmes in the Tankerville Club scandal. (untold story) Was wrongfully accused of cheating at cards Suggested to John Openshaw that he should ask Holmes for help.

Prendergast, Jack   [GLOR]   Male dead   He was a young man with a clear, hairless face, a long, thin nose, and rather nutcracker jaws. He carried his head very jauntily in the air, had a swaggering style of walking, and was, above all else, remarkable for his extraordinary height. Over six and a half feet tall. Had a face which was full of energy and resolution. He was a man of good family and of great ability, but of incurably vicious habits, who had by an ingenious system of fraud obtained huge sums of money from the leading London merchants. Stole nearly a quarter of a million, none of which was recovered. Leader of the prisoners who took over the 'Gloria Scott'. Managed to get his partner onboard as the Chaplain and had bought off two of the four wardens as well as the second mate Mereer. All went well to begin with but in the end apart for a few survivors, all were killed when the ship blew up.

Sidney Paget   *Sidney Paget*

Presbury, Edith   [CREE]   Male Alive   A bright, handsome girl of a conventional English type. Daughter of Professor Presbury and fiancee to Mr Trevor Bennett. She is in the habit of calling Trevor, Jack for some reason. Visited Holmes in baker street while Mr. Trevor Bennett was already there, explaining the situation to Holmes and Watson. She explained that she had been woken by the barking of Roy, the dog and when she looked at her Second floor bedroom window, she saw the face of her father staring in at her. She explained to Holmes "Mr. Holmes, I nearly died of surprise and horror. There it was pressed against the windowpane, and one hand seemed to be raised as if to push up the window. If that window had opened, I think I should have gone mad. It was no delusion, Mr. Holmes. Don't deceive yourself by thinking so. I dare say it was twenty seconds or so that I lay paralysed and watched the face. Then it vanished, but I could not—I could not spring out of bed and look out after it. I lay cold and shivering till morning."

Presbury, Professor   [CREE]   Male Alive   He had a grizzled and a pair of keen eyes under shaggy brows which Large horn glasses. He was a portly, large-featured man, grave, tall, and frock-coated, with the dignity of bearing which a lecturer needs. His eyes were his most remarkable feature, keen, observant, and clever to the verge of cunning. The famous Camford physiologist Had been twice attacked by his own dog. Widower with a single daughter, Edith. A man of very virile and positive, one might almost say combative, character. he became engaged to the daughter of Professor Morphy, his colleague in the chair of comparative anatomy. It must have been sometime in June that the professor disappeared for a fortnight and returned rather travel-worn. It turns out that he had visited Prague and had brought back a little wooden box. From that time on, the professor had become somewhat furtive and sly, as if he was under some shadow which had darkened his higher qualities. The professor requested that any Letters marked with a cross under the stamp were not to be opened by his secretary Trevor Bennett. On 2nd July, Trevor Bennett found the little wooden box in a cupboard and picked it up, much to the annoyance of Presbury, who got very angry and reproved him in words which were quite savage for his curiosity. Around this time his faithful dog Roy started attacking him, with attacks every nine days apart. On the night of the 4th September at around 2 am Mr. Bennett had seen the professor crawling down the passage, outside his bedroom. When Mr. Bennett asked the professor is he needed any assistance, the professor sprang up, spat out some atrocious word at him, and hurried on past him, and down the staircase. Watson suggested that the professor might be suffering from Lumbago, but this reason was dismissed by Holmes. Holmes and Watson visited the professor with the ruse that they had made an appointment on the 26th August to visit on the 7th September, hoping that the professor would be a bit hazy. Unfortunately, the professor was not fooled and would have attacked Holmes and Watson, had Mr. Bennett not interceded. He was taking a drug that he hoped would keep him young, that he learned about from H. Lowenstein, when he visited Prague. It was now being supplied locally by a man called Dorak on Commercial Rd. He took the drug every nine days and it's side-effects caused the professor to behave in his current manor. On the night of the 8th September, the professor, who had again taken his drug was roaming abroad, climbing walls and trees and teasing Roy, by throwing stones in his face and prodding the dog with a stick, when the chain holding the dog broke and the dog was upon him attacking the professor's throat. It was only the presence of Mr. Bennett voice and the obedience of the dog, in stopping his attack that saved the professor's life. This 'Elixir of life' was derived from Apes and lately from Langur, the great black-faced monkey of the Himalayan Slopes Roy had attacked thinking that he was attacking a monkey.

Sherlock Holmes Quote : "A man of very virile and positive, one might almost say combative, character.

Address : Camford

Howard K. Elcock   *Ralph C. Criswell*

Prescott, Rodger   [3GAR]   Male dead He was a tall, bearded man with very dark features.   Famous forger and coiner in Chicago. Killed by Killer Evans (AKA James Winter, Morecroft) in a nightclub in Waterloo Road, January 1895.

Address : once lived at 156 Little Ryder Street

Price, Mr   [STOC]   Male Alive See Dr. John H. Watson

Pringle, Mrs.   [SECO]   Female Alive The elderly housekeeper of Mr. Eduardo Lucas Retired early and slept at the top of the house, so she heard nothing.

Address : 16, Godolphin Street

Pritchard, Dr. Edward William   [SPEC]   Male dead (Real Person 1825 – 1865) English Doctor convicted of murdering his mother-in-law and wife by poisoning them. Might have killed the servant girl Elizabeth McGrain, who died in a fire which started in her room. Convicted after five day trial in July 1865 and was the last person to be hanged in Glasgow. Talking about Dr. Grimesby Roylott, he mentions Pritchard.

Sherlock Holmes Quote : "Subtle enough and horrible enough. When a doctor does go wrong he is the first of criminals. He has nerve and he has knowledge. Palmer and Pritchard were among the heads of their profession. This man strikes even deeper, but I think, Watson, that we shall be able to strike deeper still. But we shall have horrors enough before the night is over; for goodness' sake let us have a quiet pipe and turn our minds for a few hours to something more cheerful."

Address : 131 Sauchiehall Street, Glasgow

Dr. E. W. Pritchard

Proosia, King of (Prussia) [BLUE] Male Alive (Real Persons) Mentioned as Breckenridge gets annoyed at James Ryder who kept asking him about a goose. Breckenridge says "Well, you can ask the King of Proosia, for all I care. I've had enough of it. Get out of this!" We have a choice of two kings here depending on when the Blue Carbuncle was set. There was a change of king around the time that this story is set and there are a few options for the date of the story. if it was set in 1887 then the king would be Kaiser Wilhelm l (first photo) Reigned 1861-1888 If the story was set in 1890, then it was Kaiser Wilhelm ll (second photo) Reigned 1888-1918

Kaiser William l   Kaiser William ll

Prosper, Francis   [BERY]   Male Alive   Sweetheart of Lucy Parr, second waiting maid. Greengrocer Has a wooden leg.

Felix Juven

Pugilist the Horse   [SILV]   Male Horse Alive   Horse belonging to Colonel Wardlaw. Pink cap, Blue and black jacket. ran in the Wessex plate, not placed. Wessex Plate 50 Sovereigns each h ft. with 1000 Sovereigns added for four and five year olds. Second, £300. Third, £200. New course (one mile and five furlongs).

Pycroft, Hall   [STOC]   Male Alive   A well-built, fresh-complexioned young fellow, with a frank, honest face and a slight, crisp, yellow moustache. He wore a very shiny top hat and a neat suit of sober black, which made him look what he was—a smart young City man, of the class who have been labelled cockneys, but who give us our crack volunteer regiments, and who turn out more fine athletes and sportsmen than any body of men in these islands. Had a round, ruddy face which was naturally full of cheeriness, but the corners of his mouth were pulled down in a half-comical distress. had worked for Coxon & Woodhouse's for five years. The crash of the firm resulted in twenty-seven clerks being laid off including Hall Pycroft. Managed to get a position at Mawson & Williams'

Address : Hampstead way, 17 Potter's Terrace.

Stanley E. Armstrong

William H. Hyde

R is for the Red-Headed League

R

Rae, Andrew   [VALL]   Male dead   Senior partner of the Coal company of Rae & Sturmash. Division Master Windle of Merton County Lodge 249 stated in a letter that there was a job to be done on this person's coal company. McGinty asked for volunteers and Tiger Cormac and a young boy in his teens called Wilson, stepped forward. This job was to return a favour that the Merton County Lodge had tendered the previous fall in the matter of the patrolman.

Raffaello Sanzio da Urbino   [3GAB]   Male dead   See Raphael

Ralph, the old butler   [BLAN]   Male Alive   Seemed about the same age as the house. Had skinny hands. A little wrinkled old fellow. Wore a conventional costume of black coat and pepper-and-salt trousers, with only one curious variant. He wore brown leather gloves that had a curious tarry odour oozing from them. Ralph, the old butler at Tuxbury Old Park. His wife was said to look even older. In talking to James Dodd about Godfrey, he slipped up when he said "He was a fine boy—and oh, sir, he was a fine man.", which Dodd seized upon. Then he really put his foot in it, when Dodd asked if Godfrey was dead, he cried "'I wish to God he was!"

Address : Tuxbury Old Park

Howard K. Elcock

Frederic Dorr Steele

Ralph's Wife, Old Nurse [BLAN] Female Alive Seemed about the same age as the house, Wife of Ralph the old butler at Tuxbury Old Park. Said to have looked older that the house. Had been Godfrey Emsworth's nurse. Godfrey regarded her as a second mother.

Address : Tuxbury Old Park

Rance, John [STUD] Male Alive Policeman walking the beat from 10pm till 6am. at 11pm was at the White Hart pub. at 1am it began to rain. Discovered the body of Enoch J. Drebber and had a chance of arresting his killer . Was interviewed by Holmes at his home.

Sherlock Holmes Quote : "I am afraid, Rance, that you will never rise in the force. That head of yours should be for use as well as ornament. You might have gained your sergeant's stripes last night. The man whom you held in your hands is the man who holds the clue of this mystery, and whom we are seeking. There is no use of arguing about it now; I tell you that it is so. Come along, Doctor." "The blundering fool."

Address : 46, Audley Court, Kennington Park Gate.

George Hutchinson   *George Hutchinson*

Randalls, three [ABBE] Male Alive Collectively, the father and his two sons. Called the 'Lewisham gang of burglars'. The father was described as a broad-shouldered, elderly man with a beard, and the others young, hairless lads. Hopkins said "It's their work. I have not a doubt of it. They did a job at Sydenham a fortnight ago, and were seen and described. Rather cool to do another so soon and so near, but it is they, beyond all doubt. It's a hanging matter this time., but of course he was wrong.

Rao, Lal [SIGN] Male Alive   Indian Butler at Pondicherry Lodge, arrested by Athelney Jones. He was Jonathan Small's confederate in Pondicherry Lodge.

Raphael [3GAB] Male dead (Real Person 1483 – 1520)   Italian Renaissance Painter. Holmes speculated that the reason Mrs. Malberley's house and contents were so sought after was perhaps because of a Raphael or a first folio Shakespeare somewhere in the house.

ffaello Sanzio da Urbino

Ras, Daulat [3STU] Male Alive   A silent, little, hook-nosed fellow. Had rooms on the second floor. He was a quiet, inscrutable fellow, as most of those Indians are. He was well up in his work, though his Greek was his weak subject. He was steady and methodical. He was innocent.

Frederic Dorr Steele

Rasper the horse   [SILV]   Male Horse Alive   Horse belonging to Lord
Singleford. Purple cap, Black sleeves. ran in the Wessex plate, not placed. Wessex
Plate 50 Sovereigns each h ft. with 1000 Sovereigns added for four and five year
olds. Second, £300. Third, £200. New course (one mile and five furlongs).

Reade, William Winwood   [SIGN]   Male dead (Real Person 1838 – 1875)
British historian, explorer and philosopher who wrote the book 'The Martyrdom of
man' in 1872 Holmes recommends that Watson reads his book ' 'The Martyrdom
of man' Holmes later says, referring to the baker street irregulars "Winwood
Reade is good upon the subject," "Let me recommend this book,—one of the most
remarkable ever penned. It is Winwood Reade's 'Martyrdom of Man.'
Sherlock Holmes Quote : "He remarks that, while the individual man is an
insoluble puzzle, in the aggregate he becomes a mathematical certainty. You can,
for example, never foretell what any one man will do, but you can say with
precision what an average number will be up to. Individuals vary, but percentages
remain constant. So says the statistician

William Winwood Reade

Red King **[VALL]** **Male dead** See King William ll

Reilly, Brother. **[VALL]** **Male Alive** One of the two reckless youngsters, John McMurdo employed in helping him blow up Chester Wilcox's House. Might have been the Son of the Lawyer the Lodge used.

Reilly, Mr. **[VALL]** **Male Alive** The lawyer used by the Lodge to get members off charges. He managed to get John McMurdo and others off the assault charge on the Herald newspaper editor Sanger. Might be the father of the reckless youngster John McMurdo used to help him blow up Chester Wilcox's house.

Remington, Eliphalet **[HOUN]** **Male dead (Real Person 1793 – 1861)** Inventor of the 'Modern' QWERTY typewriter The typewriter used by Mrs Lyons, mentioned in the story was probably a model Type No.2 A maid showed me in without ceremony, and as I entered the sitting-room a lady, who was sitting before a Remington typewriter, sprang up with a pleasant smile of welcome.

Eliphalet Remington

Reuter, Paul Julius   [FINA]   Male Alive (Real Person 1816 – 1899)   World wide news organisation founded in 1851 by Paul Julius Reuter. Watson says that there have been only three accounts in the public press, concerning what happened between Holmes and Moriarty at the Reichenbach falls: that in the Journal de Genève on May 6th, 1891, the Reuter's despatch in the English papers on May 7th, and finally the recent letter to which I have alluded

Paul Reuter

Reynolds, Sir Joshua [HOUN] Male dead (Real Person 1723 – 1792)
English Painter who specialised in Portraits. Sir Henry Baskerville said "I know what is good when I see it, and I see it now. That's a Kneller, I'll swear, that lady in the blue silk over yonder, and the stout gentleman with the wig ought to be a Reynolds. They are all family portraits, I presume?"

Sir Joshua Reynolds

Richards, Dr. [DEVI] Male Alive   Doctor who met with Mr. Mortimer Tregennis early in the morning of the 16th and was on a most urgent call to Tredannick Wartha, where something had happened to the other three members of the Tregennis Family. Mr. Mortimer Tregennis joined the doctor on his travels and they arrived to find Brenda dead and the other two brothers, Owen and George out of their minds.

Richter, Johann Paul Friedrich   [SIGN] Male dead   German romantic writer best known for his humorous novels and stories. Holmes Quotes "How small we feel with our petty ambitions and strivings in the presence of the great elemental forces of nature!"

Sherlock Holmes Quotes : "How small we feel with our petty ambitions and strivings in the presence of the great elemental forces of nature!"
"That was like following the brook to the parent lake. He makes one curious but profound remark. It is that the chief proof of man's real greatness lies in his perception of his own smallness. It argues, you see, a power of comparison and of appreciation which is in itself a proof of nobility. There is much food for thought in Richter. You have not a pistol, have you?"

Jean-Paul Friedrich Richter

Ricoletti, Mr [MUSG] Male Inside a large box, Holmes opened were bundles of papers that detailed previous cases including the Ricoletti of the clubfoot, and his abominable wife. A story never revealed.

Sidney Paget

Roberts, Lord Frederick Sleigh [BLAN] Male (Real Person 1832 – 1914)
Field Marshall and one of the most successful British Commander of his time.
Highly decorated VC, KG, KP, GCB, OM, GCSI, GCIE, KStJ, VD, PC, FRSGS
(Victoria Cross, Order of the Garter, Order of St Patrick, Order of the Bath, Order
of Merit, Order of the Star of India, Order of the Indian Empire, Order of Saint
John, Volunteer Officers' Decoration, Privy Council of the United Kingdom,
Fellow of Royal Scottish Geographical Society) did he have space on his calling
card? Holmes said that Mr. Kents' was so impressed with meeting Sir James
Saunders, it was equivalent to meeting with this illustrious person.

Sherlock Holmes Quote : The prospect of an interview with Lord Roberts would
not have excited greater wonder and pleasure in a raw subaltern than was now
reflected upon the face of Mr. Kent.

Frederick Sleigh Roberts

**Robespierre, Maximilien Francois Marie Isidore de [VALL] Male Alive (
Real Person 1758 – 1794)** French Lawyer and statesman involved in the French
Revolution. In this story he is used as a comparison with Evan Potts, with Boss
McGinty being Danton. It might be thought that as a member, all the doings of
the society would be told to him; but he was soon to discover that the organisation
was wider and more complex than the simple lodge. Even Boss McGinty was
ignorant as to many things; for there was an official named the County Delegate,
living at Hobson's Patch farther down the line, who had power over several
different lodges which he wielded in a sudden and arbitrary way. Only once did
McMurdo see him, a sly, little grey-haired rat of a man, with a slinking gait and a

sidelong glance which was charged with malice. Evans Pott was his name, and even the great Boss of Vermissa felt towards him something of the repulsion and fear which the huge Danton may have felt for the puny but dangerous Robespierre.

Maximilien Francois Marie Isidore de Robespierre

Robinson, John   [BLUE]   Male Alive   See James Ryder

Rodney, George Brydges   [HOUN]   Male dead (Real Person 1718 – 1792)
While Sir Henry is showing Watson around Baskerville Hall, he mentions some of the paintings of his ancestors. "That is Rear-Admiral Baskerville, who served under Rodney in the West Indies. The man with the blue coat and the roll of paper is Sir William Baskerville, who was Chairman of Committees of the House of Commons under Pitt."

George Brydges Rodney

Ronder, Mr. **[VEIL]** **Male dead** A huge bully of a man, he cursed and slashed at everyone who came in his way. He had a dreadful face—a human pig, or rather a human wild boar, for it was formidable in its bestiality. One could imagine that vile mouth champing and foaming in its rage, and one could conceive those small, vicious eyes darting pure malignancy as they looked forth upon the world. Ruffian, bully, beast—it was all written on that heavy-jowled face. He was a man of many enemies. Detective Edmunds said, in so many words, that when he was drunk, he was horrible. Owner of Ronder's Circus. Would beat up his wife and when he found that she was in love with Leonardo the strongman, beat her more. They schemed to kill him using a club fashioned to resemble a lion's paw. Was struck down from behind by Leonardo and killed instantly.

Frederic Dorr Steele

Ronder, Mrs. Eugenia [VEIL] Female Alive Long years of inaction had coarsened the lines of her figure, but at some period it must have been beautiful, and was still full and voluptuous. A thick dark veil covered her face, but it was cut off close at her upper lip and disclosed a perfectly shaped mouth and a delicately rounded chin. she had indeed been a very remarkable woman. Her voice was well modulated and pleasing. Married to the owner of the famous Ronder Circus. Wanted to tell Holmes her story after the death of Leonardo the strong man. She started out as a poor circus girl brought up on the sawdust, and doing springs through the hoop before she was ten. When she became a woman Mr. Ronder loved me, if such lust as his could be called love, and in an evil moment she became his wife. From that day she was in hell, and he the devil who tormented her. There was no one in the show who did not know of his treatment. He deserted her for others. He tied her down and lashed her with his riding-whip when she complained. They all pitied me and they all loathed him, but what could they do? They feared him, one and all. For he was terrible at all times, and murderous when he was drunk. Again and again he was had up for assault, and for cruelty to the beasts, but he had plenty of money and the fines were nothing to him. The best men all left the circus, and the show began to go downhill. It was only Leonardo and she who kept it up—with little Jimmy Griggs, the clown. Poor devil, he had not much to be funny about, but he did what he could to hold things together. She and Leonardo came up with a scheme to Kill her husband, Leonardo fashioned a weapon that resembled a lion's claw, made from a leadened club with five long steel nails in it. Once evening Mr. & Mrs. Ronder went to give the lion, Sahara King his evening meal. Leonardo was waiting, club in hand at the corner of the big van, which would have to be passed in order to get to the cages. Leonardo swung his club and smashed Mr. Ronder's skull, then Mrs. Ronder opened the Lion's cage, but, maybe it was the scent of Human blood or some strange instinct within the creature, he attacked Mrs. Ronder, pushing her to the ground and his teeth met her face, destroying her beauty forever. She was finally rescued from the lion by the belated efforts of Leonardo and Jimmy Griggs. From that day, she had covered her poor face, so that none would see it, she was a poor wounded beast that had crawled into its hole to die. She intended to take prussic acid poison and end it all, but Holmes managed to talk her out of it.

Sherlock Holmes Quote : "Your life is not your own, Keep your hands off it."

Frank Wiles   *Frederic Dorr Steele*

Rosa, Salvator   [SIGN]   Male dead (Real Person 1615 – 1673)   Italian Baroque painter, poet, and printmaker. Thaddeus Sholto had some artwork that was supposed to have been by this artist.

Salvator Rosa

Ross, Colonel [SILV] Male Alive A small, alert person, very neat and dapper, in a frock-coat and gaiters, with trim little side-whiskers and an eyeglass. Sent a telegram to Holmes requesting help down at King's Pyland. Owner of the horse Silver Blaze and Bayard. Well-known sportsman Employed Ned Hunter, Edith Baxter and John Straker.

Address : King's Pyland, Dartmoor

Sherlock Holmes Quote : "The matter does not rest with Colonel Ross. I follow my own methods, and tell as much or as little as I choose. That is the advantage of being unofficial. I don't know whether you observed it, Watson, but the Colonel's manner has been just a trifle cavalier to me. I am inclined now to have a little amusement at his expense. Say nothing to him about the horse."

Sidney Paget   *The Courier-Journal*

Ross, Duncan [REDH] Male in prison Small man with very red hair. A pensioner of the Red Headed League Moved offices from Suite 4, 7 Pope's Court, Fleet 1st to 17 King Edward Street (except, he didn't), near St. Paul's, but the latter address turned out to be a manufactory of artificial kneecaps. Posed as a Solicitor. As organiser of the Red Headed League, he selected Jabez Wilson as the latest recipient of the league and organised his work, when he attended. Helped in the digging of the tunnel to the bank. Was caught attempting to rob the bank.

Address : Suite 4, 7 Pope's Court, Fleet 1st & 17 King Edward Street, nr. St. Paul's

Sidney Paget   *Paul Carrey*

Ross, Mr. [HOUN] Male Unknown Ross and Mangles, the Pet shop dealers in Fulham Road.

Sherlock Holmes Quote : "Having conceived the idea he proceeded to carry it out with considerable finesse. An ordinary schemer would have been content to work with a savage hound. The use of artificial means to make the creature diabolical was a flash of genius upon his part. The dog he bought in London from Ross and Mangles, the dealers in Fulham Road. It was the strongest and most savage in their possession. He brought it down by the North Devon line and walked a great distance over the moor so as to get it home without exciting any remarks. He had already on his insect hunts learned to penetrate the Grimpen Mire, and so had found a safe hiding-place for the creature. Here he kennelled it and waited his chance."

Roundhay, Mr. [DEVI] Male Alive He was a middle-aged man, portly and affable, with a considerable fund of local lore. Somewhat garrulous. The vicar of the parish of Tredannick Wollas, Cornwall. He was something of an archaeologist, and as such Holmes had made his acquaintance. Rented out the rooms to increase his scanty resources. Currently had Mr. Mortimer Tregennis staying with him. Brought Holmes news of the most extraordinary and tragic affair at Tredannick Wartha and so started the Adventure of the Devil's Foot.

Address : Vicarage in the hamlet of Tredannick Wollas

George Hutchinson

George Hutchinson

Roy, The dog [CREE] Male Alive Professor Presbury's wolfhound had started attacking him and Holmes has to investigate why. There was Monkey business afoot. Attacked the professor on the 2nd July, then the 11th and finally the 20th

Ralph C. Criswell

Frederic Dorr Steele

Roylott, Dr. Grimesby [SPEC] Male dead A huge man. His costume was a peculiar mixture of the professional and of the agricultural, having a black top-hat, a long frock-coat, and a pair of high gaiters, with a hunting-crop swinging in his hand. So tall was he that his hat actually brushed the cross bar of the doorway, and his breadth seemed to span it across from side to side. A large face, seared with a thousand wrinkles, burned yellow with the sun, and marked with every evil passion, was turned from one to the other of us, while his deep-set, bile-shot eyes, and his high, thin, fleshless nose, gave him somewhat the resemblance to a fierce old bird of prey. Descended from a very rich family. Took a medical degree and went out to Calcutta,. Established a large practice because of his professional skill and force of character. In a fit of anger, however, caused by some robberies which had been perpetrated in the house, he beat his native butler to death and narrowly escaped a capital sentence. As it was, he suffered a long term of imprisonment and afterwards returned to England a morose and disappointed man. When Dr. Roylott was in India he married Mrs. Stoner, Helen and Julia's mother. The twins were aged two. Moved back to England and Mrs. Stoner died in a railway accident. Shut himself up in his house and seldom came out save to indulge in ferocious quarrels with whoever might cross his path. Violence of temper approaching to mania has been hereditary in the men of the family and had been intensified by his long residence in the tropics. A series of disgraceful brawls took place, two of which ended in the police-court, until at last, he became the terror of the village, and the folks would fly at his approach, for he is a man of immense strength, and absolutely uncontrollable in his anger. Threw the local blacksmith over a parapet into a stream, and it was only by paying over a large sum of money that another public exposure was avoided. He had no friends at all save the wandering gypsies, and he would give these vagabonds leave to encamp upon the few acres of bramble-covered land which represent the family estate, and would accept in return the hospitality of their tents, wandering away with them sometimes for weeks on end. He has a passion also for Indian animals, which are sent over to him by a correspondent, and he has at this moment a cheetah and a baboon, which wander freely over his grounds and are feared by the villagers almost as much as their master. Burst into the chambers of 221b baker street and berated Holmes "I know you, you scoundrel! I have heard of you before. You are Holmes, the meddler." "Holmes, the busybody!" "Holmes, the Scotland Yard Jack-in-office!"

Address : Stoke Moran on the western border of Surrey.

Sidney Paget   *Paul Dufresne*

Rucastle, Alice [COPP] Female Alive   Daughter of Jephro Rucastle and his first wife. Put under pressure to give up her inheritance. Hidden away in rooms at the Copper Beeches after she had a brain-fever and given a short haircut. Violet Hunter was told that she had gone away to Philadelphia. Rescued by her fiancée, Mr Fowler.

Address : The Copper Beeches, five miles on the far side of Winchester

Ernest Flammarion

Rucastle, Edward [COPP] Male Alive   Dear little romper just six years old. His father loved him saying "Oh, if you could see him killing cockroaches with a slipper! Smack! smack! smack! Three gone before you could wink!' J Violet Hunter voiced "I have never met so utterly spoiled and so ill-natured a little creature. He is small for his age, with a head which is quite disproportionately large. His whole life appears to be spent in an alternation between savage fits of passion and gloomy intervals of sulking. Giving pain to any creature weaker than himself seems to be his one idea of amusement, and he shows quite remarkable talent in planning the capture of mice, little birds, and insects. "

Address : The Copper Beeches, five miles on the far side of Winchester

Ernest Flammarion

Rucastle, Jephro [COPP] Male Alive A prodigiously stout man with a very smiling face and a great heavy chin which rolled down in fold upon fold over his throat. Wore a pair of glasses on his nose. He was such a comfortable-looking man that it was quite a pleasure to look at him. Had two children a daughter , Alice, by his first wife and a son, Edward, by his second wife. Was trying to get the inheritance money from his daughter and keep her away from her boyfriend, Mr. Fowler. Hid her away in a disused area of the house and hired Miss Violet Hunter to impersonate her. Holmes visited the house when Mr & Mrs Rucastle were out for the evening, but they arrived back early and Jephro went to release the dog, Carlo, and was attacked by him. Watson shot the dog dead, but Rucastle was never the same man after this incident.

Address : The Copper Beeches, five miles on the far side of Winchester

Josef Friedrich   *Sidney Paget*

Rucastle, Mrs.   [COPP]   Female Alive   A silent, pale-faced woman Had been married seven years to Jespho Rucastle. Violet Hunter thought that "She seemed to be colourless in mind as well as in feature. She impressed me neither favourably nor the reverse. She was a nonentity. It was easy to see that she was passionately devoted both to her husband and to her little son. Her light grey eyes wandered continually from one to the other, noting every little want and forestalling it if possible. "

Address : The Copper Beeches, five miles on the far side of Winchester

Rudge, Daniel   [VALL]   Male dead (Real Person 1840 – 1880)   Rudge-Whitworth bicycle company, formed when Whitworth cycle company of Birmingham merged with the Rudge Cycle Company of Coventry The bicycle ridden by Ted Baldwin was made by the company Rudge-Whitworth, it was left behind and found by the police.

Daniel Rudge

Rufton, Earl of [LADY] Male dead Ancestor of the Lady Frances Carfax.
"Lady Frances is the sole survivor of the direct family of the late Earl of Rufton.
The estates went, as you may remember, in the male line. She was left with
limited means, but with some very remarkable old Spanish jewellery of silver and
curiously cut diamonds to which she was fondly attached.

Rulli, Signor [WIST] Male Alive See Mr. Lucas

Russell, William Clark [FIVE] Male Alive (Real Person 1844 – 1911)
English writer best known for his nautical novels. Watson was deep in one of
Clark Russell's fine sea-stories until the howl of the gale from without seemed to
blend with the text, and the splash of the rain to lengthen out into the long swash
of the sea waves.

William Clark Russell

Russian, Count [RESI] Male Alive   This character was played by either
Biddle, Hayward or Moffat, insufficient details in Watson's story means we cannot
say who actually played the father and son. Look up Bibble, Hayward and moffat
for more details. Gained entry to 403, brook Street posing as a Russian count with
catalepsy but they wanted to look around the home and find a man known as
Sutton. They returned later, held a kangaroo court and hanged Sutton.

Sidney Paget

Russian, Count's Son   [RESI]   Male Alive   This character was played by either Biddle, Hayward or Moffat, insufficient details in Watson's story means we cannot say who actually played the father and son. Look up Bibble, Hayward and moffat for more details. Gained entry to 403, brook Street with a father posing as a Russian count with catalepsy but they wanted to look around the home and find a man known as Sutton. They returned later, held a kangaroo court and hanged Sutton.

Sidney Paget

Ryder, James   [BLUE]   Male Alive

Called Jem , by his sister. Upper(Head)-attendant at the Hotel Cosmopolitan. Stated he Showed John Horner up to the dressing room of the Countess of Morcar, but was called away, upon returning he discovered that Horner had disappeared and that the bureau had been forced open, that the small morocco casket was empty upon the dressing-table. Blamed Catherine Cusack for making him steal the Blue Carbuncle. Brother of Maggie Oakshott. Hid he Blue Carbuncle in the crop of a goose, then lost hold of the goose and then took away the wrong one. Went to Breckinridge in Covent Garden, to try and find out what happened to the goose that contained the gem and met up with Holmes. Holmes interviewed him in Baker street and got the story and how the gem ended up in the crop of the bird. Holmes let him go.

Sherlock Holmes Quote : "that there is the making of a very pretty villain in you."
"it is just possible that I am saving a soul. This fellow will not go wrong again. He is too terribly frightened. Send him to gaol now, and you make him a gaolbird for life."

Sidney Paget

Josef Friedrich

S if for the Speckled Band

S

Sahara King [VEIL] Male Alive   A very fine North African lion. He was usually fed by either Mr. or Mrs. Ronder and sometime both together. Was part of the Circus Act. Attacked Mrs. Ronder as she opened his cage door to feed him, after Leonardo has brutally killed Mr. Ronder. He had eaten Mrs. Ronder's face and disfigured her for life.

Frederic Dorr Steele

Frank Wiles

Sahib, Nana   [SIGN]   Male dead (Real Person 1824 - 1858   Indian Peshwa of the Maratha empire, aristocrat and rebel. While Jonathan Small told his story he mentioned this man; "Well, there's no use my telling you gentlemen what came of the Indian mutiny. After Wilson took Delhi and Sir Colin relieved Lucknow the back of the business was broken. Fresh troops came pouring in, and Nana Sahib made himself scarce over the frontier. A flying column under Colonel Greathed came round to Agra and cleared the Pandies away from it. Peace seemed to be settling upon the country, and we four were beginning to hope that the time was at hand when we might safely go off with our shares of the plunder. In a moment, however, our hopes were shattered by our being arrested as the murderers of Achmet."

Nana Sahib

Saint-Clair, Neville [TWIS] Male Alive As Neville Saint-Clair he wore some dark coat, such as he had started to town in, he had on neither collar nor necktie. As Hugh Boone A crippled wretch of hideous aspect. Is a professional beggar, though, in order to avoid the police regulations, he pretends to a small trade in wax vestas. Works down Threadneedle Street, upon the left-hand side. A shock of orange hair, a pale face disfigured by a horrible scar, which, by its contraction, had turned up the outer edge of his upper lip, a bull-dog chin, and a pair of very penetrating dark eyes. Extremely dirty, but the grime which covered his face could not conceal its repulsive ugliness. A broad wheal from an old scar ran right across it from eye to chin, and by its contraction had turned up one side of the upper lip, so that three teeth were exposed in a perpetual snarl. A shock of very bright red hair grew low over his eyes and forehead. Is ever ready with a reply to any piece of chaff which may be thrown at him by the passers-by. Moved to Lee in Kent in May 1884 and appeared to have plenty of money. He took a large villa, laid out the grounds very nicely, and lived generally in good style Married a daughter of a local brewer in 1887 Had two children. Father was a schoolmaster in Chesterfield. Received an excellent education. In secret, for many years, he went up to London ever day and transformed himself into the Beggar Hugh Boone. As he was changing back into his normal cloths, he looks out and spies his wife going by outside, in panic, he changes back his Hugh Boone outfit, but his old clothes are found and he is arrested for his own murder. By profession he was a journalist, but found he could make more money as a beggar. On first day as Hugh Boone he received 26s. 4d. (£6 11s. 8d. a week), but as a hard working reporter only got £2 a week. His disguise was good enough to deceive all by Holmes and when his face is washed with a sponge, early one morning by him, Neville's true identity is revealed. He promises never to pose as a beggar again and is released. Mentioned in the Blue Carbuncle when Watson makes Holmes allude to his attempt to recover the Irene Adler papers, to the singular case of Miss Mary Sutherland, and to the adventure of the man with the twisted lip, all of which were entirely free of any legal crime.

Address : 'The Cedars' Near Lee, in Kent.

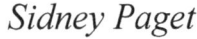

Sidney Paget   *Josef Friedrich*

Saltire, Lord Arthur   [PRIO]   Male Alive   Disappeared wearing his usual school suit of black Eton jacket and dark grey trousers. 10 year old son of Duke of Holdernesse, attending Priory School. Disappeared on the evening of Monday 13 may 1901. Left with Reuben Hayes, the land lord of the Fighting Cock, riding a horse wearing cattle track hooves. Was kept in the pub, against his will by James Wilder and Mr. & Mrs Hayes. Holmes tracks him down and gets him released.

Sherlock Holmes Quote : "Holdernesse, 6th Duke, K.G., P.C.'—half the alphabet! 'Baron Beverley, Earl of Carston'—dear me, what a list! 'Lord Lieutenant of Hallamshire since 1900. Married Edith, daughter of Sir Charles Appledore, 1888. Heir and only child, Lord Saltire. Owns about two hundred and fifty thousand acres. Minerals in Lancashire and Wales. Address: Carlton House Terrace; Holdernesse Hall, Hallamshire; Carston Castle, Bangor, Wales. Lord of the

Admiralty, 1872; Chief Secretary of State for—' Well, well, this man is certainly one of the greatest subjects of the Crown!

Address : Priory School and Carlton House Terrace; Holdernesse Hall, Hallamshire"

Sam, Uncle [LAST] Male Alive   Personification of the United States of America. He first appeared in 1816. In describing Altamont it was said that he had a general resemblance to the caricatures of Uncle Sam.

Uncle Sam

Samson of New Orleans [STUD] Male Alive   Holmes says that this person escaped hanging in New Orleans because Holmes' Blood test wasn't around.

Samuel [CROO] Male dead   Bible Reference Writer of the Book about King David, Uriah and Bathsheba.

Sherlock Holmes Quote : "Yes; David strayed a little occasionally, you know, and on one occasion in the same direction as Sergeant James Barclay. You remember the small affair of Uriah and Bathsheba? My biblical knowledge is a trifle rusty, I fear, but you will find the story in the first or second of Samuel."

Samuel

San Pedro, Tiger of   [WIST]   Male dead   See Mr. Henderson

Sand, George   [REDH]   Female dead (Real Person 1804 – 1876)   Referenced at the end of the story along with Gustave Flaubert. George Sands was the Pen-name of the French novelist, memoirist, and Socialist Amantine Lucile Aurore Dupin. Corresponded with Gustave Flaubert from 1863-1876.

Sherlock Holmes Quote : "Well, perhaps, after all, it is of some little use, 'L'homme c'est rien–l'oeuvre c'est tout,' as Gustave Flaubert wrote to George Sand."

George Sand

Sandeford, Mr. **[SIXN]** **Male Alive** An elderly, red-faced man with grizzled side-whiskers. In his right hand he carried an old-fashioned carpetbag, which he placed upon the table. Possessed the last of the Six Napoleon Busts. Holmes purchased it for £10. He was honest enough to say that he had purchased it for fifteen shillings. The bust he owned had the Black pearl of the Borgia hidden inside.

Address : Lower Grove Road, Reading

Frederic Dorr Steele

Sidney Paget

Sanders, Ikey   [MAZA]   Male Alive   Jeweller who cut diamonds but refused to cut up the Mazarin Stone and told Holmes all about the gem and Count Sylvius.

Sanger, Lord George   [VEIL]   Male Alive (Real Person 1825 – 1911)   He was an English showman and circus owner. Interestedly enough he was murdered with a hatchet by an old employee called Herber Charles Cooper, who later committed suicide, and nobody knows why. Mentioned by Holmes as he explained to Watson, who Mrs. Ronder was.

Sherlock Holmes Quote : "It will probably come back to your memory as I talk. Ronder, of course, was a household word. He was the rival of Wombwell, and of Sanger, one of the greatest showmen of his day. There is evidence, however, that he took to drink, and that both he and his show were on the down grade at the time of the great tragedy.

Lord George Sanger

Sarasate y Navascues, Martín Melitón Pablo de   [REDH]   Male Alive (Real Person 1844 – 1908)   Spanish Violinist and gifted composer of light, flashy music Spanish Violinist and gifted composer of light, flashy music. Holmes was a fan and suggested that he and Watson attend one of his concerts.

Sherlock Holmes Quote : "Sarasate plays at the St. James's Hall this afternoon, What do you think, Watson? Could your patients spare you for a few hours?"

Sarasate

Saunders, Miss **[DANC]** **Female Alive** Housemaid at Riding Thorpe Manor, Norfolk. Together with the cook, Mrs. King raised the alarm after discovering the bodies in the study. She and Mrs. King had adjoining rooms and were awoken by the sound of an explosion, which had been followed a minute later by a second one. They descended the stairs together and found that the door of the study was open and a candle was burning upon the table. They found their master face down in the centre of the room. He was quite dead. Near the window his wife was crouching, her head leaning against the wall. She was horribly wounded, and the side of her face was red with blood. Answered questions asked of her by Holmes and inspector Martin. Holmes was able to work out that the first bang was actually produced by two pistols going off at almost the same time.

Richard Gutschmidt

Saunders, Mrs.   [3GAR]   Female Alive   Caretaker of house at 156 Little Ryder Street and looks after Nathan Garrideb. Normally in the Basement until 4pm looked after Mr Garrideb after he had his nervous breakdown.

Address : 156 Little Ryder Street

Saunders, Sir James   [BLAN]   Male Alive   Was a leading specialist in tropical or semi-tropical diseases. Was beholding to Holmes, who had once been able to do him a professional service, was prepared to look at the patient Godfrey Emsworth as a friend rather than a specialist. He declared that Emsworth did not in fact have Leprosy, but a well-marked case of pseudo-leprosy or ichthyosis, a scale-like affection of the skin, unsightly, obstinate, but possibly curable, and certainly non-infective. He was so confident in his diagnosis that he was prepared to pledge his professional reputation.

Savage, Victor   [DYIN]   Male dead   Nephew of Culverton Smith. Poor Victor was a dead man on the fourth day—Was a strong, hearty young fellow, but died horribly. Victim of Culverton Smith. Holmes started looking into his death and almost ended up dead himself.

Sawyer, Mrs   [STUD]   Male Alive   Old Crone. a very old and wrinkled woman who hobbled. Actually a young friend of Jefferson hope who went to collect Lucy Ferrier's ring from Holmes Said he was the Mother of Sally Dennis

Address : 13, Duncan Street, Houndsditch

Richard Gutschmidt   *George Hutchinson*

Sawyer, Sally   [STUD]   Female Alive   See Sally Dennis

Scandinavia, King of   [SCAN, NOBL]   Male alive (Real Person 1829 – 1907)
[SCAN] The King of Scandinavia (von Saxe-Meningen) is the father of Clotilde Lothman von Saxe-Meningen Soon to be father in law to the King of Bohemia [NOBL] Mentioned again when Sherlock Holmes told Lord St. Simon that he already had a client of superior extraction than him, the King of Scandinavia.

King of Scandinavia

Scanlan, Brother Mike   [VALL]   Male Alive   A small, sharp-faced, nervous, black-eyed man. First Vermissa Lodge member to meet John McMurdo when he arrived in the Vermissa Valley. They met on a train and he advised McMurdo to see Boss McGinty. A good friend of John McMurdo. Took up lodgings with McMurdo at Widow MacNamara's on the extreme outskirts of the town. Was in the party that attacked the Herald newspaper Editor Stanger. Although a Scowrer, he was an inoffensive little man who was too weak to stand against the opinion of his comrades, but was secretly horrified by the deeds of blood at which he had sometimes been forced to assist. Probably escaped a prison sentence.

Address : Hobson's Patch

Scott, Bodymaster James H.   [VALL]   Male   Bodymaster of the Chicago Lodge 29. He was the Bodymaster of John McMurdo.

Scylla   [RESI]   Female Alive   In classical mythology, Scylla was a horrible six-headed monster who lived on a rock on one side of a narrow strait. Charybdis was a whirlpool on the other side. When ships passed close to Scylla's rock in order to avoid Charybdis, she would seize and devour their sailors. Watson says "The small matter which I have chronicled under the heading of "A Study in Scarlet," and that other later one connected with the loss of the Gloria Scott, may serve as examples of this Scylla and Charybdis which are forever threatening the historian." We would now say, "Caught between a rock and a hard place." or "between the devil and the deep blue sea".

Scylla

Selden, Convict. [HOUN] Male dead Was given Sir Henry's Cast-offs to wear. Selden, the Notting Hill murderer. Escaped from Princetown Gaol. Watson said "I remembered the case well, for it was one in which Holmes had taken an interest on account of the peculiar ferocity of the crime and the wanton brutality which had marked all the actions of the assassin. The commutation of his death sentence had been due to some doubts as to his complete sanity, so atrocious was his conduct." Younger brother of Eliza (Selden) Barrymore Mrs Barrymore said "We humoured him too much when he was a lad, and gave him his own way in everything until he came to think that the world was made for his pleasure, and that he could do what he liked in it. Then as he grew older he met wicked companions, and the devil entered into him until he broke my mother's heart and dragged our name in the dirt. From crime to crime he sank lower and lower, until it is only the mercy of God which has snatched him from the scaffold; but to me, sir, he was always the little curly-headed boy that I had nursed and played with, as an elder sister would." Was chased by the Hound and fell to his death.

Paul Thiriat   *Sidney Paget*

Selden, Mrs. Eliza [HOUN] Alive See Mrs. Eliza Barrymore

Shafter, Jacob [VALL] Male Alive Ran a boarding house that was recommended by a man John McMurdo knew in Chicago. Father of Ettie Shafter. Described as a honest a man as lives in this township. John Douglas says that he married Ettie Shafter in Chicago and that old Jacob Shafter was a witness of the wedding, but surely he was more likely to be the father of the bride.

Address : Sheridan Street, Vermissa

Shafter, Miss Ettie [VALL] Female dead She was young and singularly beautiful. She was of the German type, blonde and fair-haired, with the piquant contrast of a pair of beautiful dark eyes. Spoke with a pleasing little touch of a German accent. Mr. Jacob Shafter's daughter. Her mother was dead, She ran the boarding house with her father. Ted Baldwin thought she should be his girl, John McMurdo thought differently and so this was the start of their hatred for one another. Always called McMurdo Jack rather than John. First wife of person know as John McMurdo. Died some years before story takes place.

Address : Sheridan Street, Vermissa

Arthur I. Keller

Frank Wiles

Shakespeare, William   [3GAB]   Male dead (Real Person 1564 – 1616)   The world's greatest English language Writer and dramatist. Holmes speculated that the reason the house and contents were so sought after was perhaps because of a Raphael or a first folio Shakespeare somewhere in the house.

William Shakespeare

Sherman, Mr. **[SIGN]** **Male Alive** A lanky, lean old man, with stooping shoulders, a stringy neck, and blue-tinted glasses. Watson went to see him to pick up the dog Toby. Didn't want to answer the door to Watson and shouted down from his upstairs window "Go on, you drunken vagabone, If you kick up any more row I'll open the kennels and let out forty-three dogs upon you." then "Go on! So help me gracious, I have a wiper in the bag, an' I'll drop it on your 'ead if you don't hook it." "I won't be argued with! Now stand clear, for when I say 'three,' down goes the wiper." it was only when Holmes' name is mentioned that Watson manages to get Toby.

Address No. 3, Pinchin Lane, down near the water's edge at Lambeth

Thomas J. Nicholl   *The Bristol Observer*

Shlessinger, Mrs. Annie **[LADY]** **Female Escaped** Tall woman. Annie Fraser posed as Dr. Shlessinger's wife. Taking an active part in his schemes. She pawned Jewellery belonging to Lady Frances Carfax at Bovington's, but was followed by Philip Green back to her lodgings. When Holmes and Watson tried to search for Lady Frances at the house, illegally, she went off to get a policeman so that they would be removed before the Lady Frances was found.

Address : Baden and then No. 36, Poultney Square, Brixton

Alec Ball   Frederic Dorr Steele

Shlessinger, Rev. Dr.   [LADY]   Male Escaped   He had a jagged or torn ear, it had been badly bitten in a saloon-fight at Adelaide in 1889. A large, clean-shaven man of clerical appearance. A big, clean-shaven bald-headed man. He had a large red face, with pendulous cheeks, and a general air of superficial benevolence which was marred by a cruel, vicious mouth. A missionary from South America. Dr. Shlessinger had a remarkable personality and a whole hearted devotion to his missionary work. He was recovering from a disease contracted in the exercise of his apostolic duties. Lady Frances Carfax had helped Mrs. Shlessinger in the nursing of the convalescent saint. He was preparing a map of the Holy Land, with special reference to the kingdom of the Midianites, upon which he was writing a monograph. He had departed for London along with his wife and Lady Frances. In reality, he was one of the most unscrupulous rascals that Australia has ever evolved His particular speciality was the beguiling of lonely ladies by playing upon their religious feelings, and his so-called wife, an Englishwoman named Fraser, was a worthy helpmate.

Address : Baden and then No. 36, Poultney Square, Brixton

Alec Ball

Alec Ball

Sholto, Bartholomew   [SIGN]   Male dead   Identical Twin Brother of Thaddeus Sholto, (probably the eldest) Son of Major John Sholto. Said by his brother Thaddeus to be a clever fellow, who discovered where the Agra treasure was hidden in Pondicherry Lodge. Favourite son of Major John Sholto.(or so Thaddeus Sholto thought) Found dead in a third floor locked room with a horrible smile, a fixed and unnatural grin on his face. Had a long, dark thorn stuck in the skin just above the ear, that had poison on it. Probably some powerful vegetable alkaloid, some strychnine-like substance which would produce tetanus. [REDH] Referenced in the Red Headed League when detective Jones tells Mr Merryweather to place considerable confidence in Mr. Holmes because of the Sholto murder.

Address : Pondicherry Lodge in Upper Norwood

Richard Gutschmidt　　　　　*Charles Kerr*

Sholto, Major John [SIGN] Male dead Major of 34th Bombay Infantry. Friend of Captain Morstan. Stationed on Andaman Island in charge of prisoners there. Played cards with fellow officers, the surgeon and other prison officers, but kept loosing, until he was ruined. It was at this point that Jonathan Small proposed that the Agra Treasure could be shared, if the release was given to 'The Four'. Sholto double-crossed them and fled to England taking the treasure with him. He was visited by Captain Morstan, who died while arguing with Sholto. He hid the treasure in Pondicherry Lodge and died before revealing where he had hidden the gems. Died 28th of April, 1882 from shock at seeing Jonathan Small outside the window. [REDH] Referenced in the Red Headed League when detective Jones tells Mr Merryweather to place considerable confidence in Mr. Holmes because of the Sholto murder.

Address : Pondicherry Lodge in Upper Norwood

The Bristol Observer

Sholto, Thaddeus [SIGN] Male Alive A small man with a very high head, a bristle of red hair all-round the fringe of it, and a bald, shining scalp. He writhed his hands together as he stood, and his features were in a perpetual jerk, now smiling, now scowling, but never for an instant in repose. Too visible line of yellow and irregular teeth, which he strove feebly to conceal by constantly passing his hand over the lower part of his face. Thin, high voice Had grave doubts as to my mitral valve, which Watson listened to but found nothing for him to be concerned about. Wore a very long befrogged topcoat with Astrakhan collar and cuffs. This he buttoned tightly up, in spite of the extreme closeness of the night, and finished his attire by putting on a rabbit-skin cap with hanging lappets which covered the ears, so that no part of him was visible save his mobile and peaky face. Son of Major John Sholto. Identical twin brother of Bartholomew Sholto. He was partial to modern French school paintings and had a Corot, Salvator Rosa and a Bouguereau. Holmes and Watson got involved in this case when Mary Morstan asked them to accompany her when she visited his home. [REDH] Referenced in the Red Headed League when detective Jones tells Mr Merryweather to place considerable confidence in Mr. Holmes because of the Sholto murder.

Address : Cold Harbour Lane

Thomas J. Nicholl

Richard Gutschmidt

Shomu, Emperor   [ILLU]   Male dead (Real Person 701 – 755)   He was the 45th emperor of Japan. When Watson visited Baron Gruner in order to keep him busy, while Holmes tried to find the Baron's secret diary, he posed as Dr. Hill Barton, a collector of fine Chinese ceramics, but the Baron started to suspect him and said "Might I ask you a few questions to test you? I am obliged to tell you, Doctor—if you are indeed a doctor—that the incident becomes more and more suspicious. I would ask you what do you know of the Emperor Shomu and how do you associate him with the Shoso-in near Nara? Dear me, does that puzzle you? Tell me a little about the Northern Wei dynasty and its place in the history of ceramics."

Emperor Shomu

Shoscombe Prince [SHOS] Male Alive Sir Robert Norberton's only hope for getting out of debt, was for this horse to win the Derby. This horse was at long odds, too, since Sir Robert had his Half-brother out for trails. The horse belonged to the estate of Lady Beatrice Falder and would pass to her late husband's brother on her death. At the end of the story, the horse won and Sir Robert Norberton netted £80,000.

Address : Shoscombe Old Place

Frederic Dorr Steele

Shuman, Mr [VALL] Male Alive   Owner of an Ironworks in Vermissa Valley, who was forced to sell his business because of threats from the Scowrers. He sold to West Gilmerton General Mining Company.

Sigerson, Mr. [EMPT] Male Alive   See Sherlock Holmes Much Like Sherlock Holmes really. Sherlock Holmes' alias while travelling around the world after the death of Professor James Moriarty. Norwegian explorer who travelled to Tibet, Persia and Mecca.

Sherlock Holmes Quote : "I travelled for two years in Tibet, therefore, and amused myself by visiting Lhasa and spending some days with the head Llama. You may have read of the remarkable explorations of a Norwegian named Sigerson, but I am sure that it never occurred to you that you were receiving news of your friend. I then passed through Persia, looked in at Mecca, and paid a short but interesting visit to the Khalifa at Khartoum, the results of which I have communicated to the Foreign Office."

Silver Blaze, the Horse [SILV] Male Horse Alive   White forehead and mottled off-foreleg. Horse owned by Colonel Ross. Favourite in the Wessex Cup/Plate. Horse owned by Colonel Ross. Favourite in the Wessex Cup/Plate. Wessex Plate 50 Sovereigns each h ft. with 1000 Sovereigns added for four and five year olds. Second, £300. Third, £200. New course (one mile and five furlongs). First favourite for the Wessex Cup, the betting being three to one on him. He had always, however, been a prime favourite with the racing public, and had never yet disappointed them Killed his trainer John Straker, out on the moors, when Straker tried to make him lame.

Sherlock Holmes Quote : "From the Somomy stock, and holds as brilliant a record as his famous ancestor.
He is now in his fifth year, and has brought in turn each of the prizes of the turf to Colonel Ross, his fortunate owner.
He was the first favourite for the Wessex Cup, the betting being three to one on him.
He has always, however, been a prime favourite with the racing public, and has never yet disappointed them, so that even at those odds enormous sums of money have been laid upon him. It is obvious, therefore, that there were many people who had the strongest interest in preventing Silver Blaze from being there at the fall of the flag next Tuesday."

Address : King's Pyland, Dartmoor

Sidney Paget   *Martin Van Maele*

Silvester, Mr. [LADY] Male Unknown   Owner of the Silvester Bank. Lady Frances Carfax's Bank.

Sherlock Holmes Quote : "Single ladies must live, and their passbooks are compressed diaries. She banks at Silvester's. I have glanced over her account. The last cheque but one paid her bill at Lausanne, but it was a large one and probably left her with cash in hand. Only one cheque has been drawn since."

Simpson, Baldy   [BLAN] Male dead   Was a member of B squadron of the Middlesex Corps. Was in the morning fight at Buffelsspruit (Buffelspruit), outside Pretoria with Godfrey Emsworth and Anderson. They became separated from the others because it was very broken country. They were clearing brother Boer, but he was shot and killed along with Anderson and only Emsworth managed to escape on horse.

Simpson, Fitzroy   [SILV] Male Alive   Wore a Cravat. Carried a Penang-lawyer weighted with lead. He was a man of excellent birth and education, who had squandered a fortune upon the turf, and who lived now by doing a little quiet and genteel book-making in the sporting clubs of London. Charged with the murder of John Straker until Holmes managed to discover what really happened.

Sidney Paget   *Martin Van Maele*

Simpson, Master [CROO] Male Alive   small street Arab, who reported to Holmes. One of the Baker street irregulars.

Simpson, Mr. [LADY, ILLU] Male Alive   [LADY] Restaurant, in the Strand, that Holmes and Watson frequented. [ILLU] Holmes suggests going there at the end of the story, where Watson arrives to find Holmes sitting at a small table in the front window watching the world go by.

Sherlock Holmes Quote : [LADY] "When we have finished at the police-station I think that something nutritious at Simpson's would not be out of place."

Sinclair, Admiral   [BRUC] Male Alive   Sir James Walter was at the house of Admiral Sinclair at Barclay Square during the whole of the evening when the plans were stolen and Arthur Cadogan West was murdered.

Address : Barclay Square

Singh, Mahomet [SIGN] Male in prison   Tall, fierce-looking chap, was an old fighting-man who had borne arms against the British at Chilian-wallah Could talk English pretty well Slightly shorter and less fiercer of the pair of Sikhs (Mahomet Singh and Abdullah Khan) One of the Four. Was charged with murder of Achmet the Merchant, was found guilty and given penal servitude for life.

Richard Gutschmidt

Mahomet Singh

Singleford, Lord   [SILV]   Male Alive   Owner of the Horse Rasper. Purple cap. Black sleeves, which was entered into the Wessex Cup. Wessex Plate 50 Sovereigns each h ft. with 1000 Sovereigns added for four and five year olds. Second, £300. Third, £200. New course (one mile and five furlongs).

Singleton, Mr.   [SIXN]   Involved in some way with the Conk-Singleton Forgery case, but in what way is never revealed, but clearly he is linked in some way with Conk.

Sherlock Holmes Quote : "Put the pearl in the safe, Watson and get out the papers of the Conk-Singleton forgery case."

Slaney, Mr. Abe   [DANC]   Male In Prison   He was a tall, handsome, swarthy fellow, clad in a suit of grey flannel, with a Panama hat, a bristling black beard, and a great, aggressive hooked nose, and flourishing a cane as he walked. He swaggered up the path as if the place belonged to him. Said to be 'The most dangerous crook in Chicago.' by Wilson Hargreaves of the New York Police Bureau. Was in love with Elsie Patrick and had know her since she was a child. Had been engaged to Elsie, but she fled because she wanted nothing to do with crime and Abe wouldn't give up the life. Followed Elsie to England and pestered her with Dancing men messages, even sending one that said 'Elsie Prepare to meet thy God' Met with Elsie at Study window, when she tried to buy him off with money, but their meeting was discovered by Hilton her husband and in an exchange of gunfire, Hilton was killed and Abe ran off. Received a Dancing Men message that he thought had come from Elsie inviting him back to the Cubitt house, but it was actually sent by Holmes and he was arrested. Was condemned to death at the winter assizes at Norwich; but his penalty was changed to penal servitude in consideration of mitigating circumstances, and the certainty that Hilton Cubitt had fired the first shot.

Address : Elrige's Farm, East Ruston, Norfolk.

Sidney Paget

Frederic Dorr Steele

Slater, Stonemason [BLAC] Male Alive Reported that he had seen another person other than Captain Peter Carey in his Cabin two nights before the murder at around one O'clock in the morning. This man didn't have the same type of beard as the Captain, being short and bristled forwards in a way very different from that of the captain. His testimony was questioned firstly because he had been in the Public House for two hours and secondly because this incident took place two days before.

Sloane, Sir Hans [3GAR] Male dead (Real Person 1660 – 1753) He was an Irish physician, naturalist and collector noted for bequeathing his collection of 71,000 items to the British nation, thus providing the foundation of the British Museum, the British Library and the Natural History Museum, London Nathan Garrideb was happy that he might be inheriting five million dollars and said "Just think what I could do with five million dollars. Why, I have the nucleus of a national collection. I shall be the Hans Sloane of my age."

Sir Hans Sloane

Small, Jonathan   [SIGN]   Male Alive   Was a poorly-educated man, small, active, with his right leg off, and wearing a wooden stump which was worn away upon the inner side. His left boot had a coarse, square-toed sole, with an iron band round the heel. He was a middle-aged man, much sunburned, and had been a convict. Had a good deal of skin missing from the palm of his hand. He was a sunburned, reckless-eyed fellow, with a network of lines and wrinkles all over his mahogany features, which told of a hard, open-air life. There was a singular prominence about his bearded chin which marked a man who was not to be easily turned from his purpose. His black, curly hair was thickly shot with grey. His face in repose was not an unpleasing one, though his heavy brows and aggressive chin gave him a terrible expression when moved to anger. Keen, twinkling eyes. Was a Worcestershire man, born near Pershore. Was never much of a credit to the family, and I doubt if they would be so very glad to see me. They were all steady, chapel-going folk, small farmers, well-known and respected over the countryside, while I was always a bit of a rover. At last, however, when I was about eighteen, I gave them no more trouble, for I got into a mess over a girl, and could only get out of it again by taking the Queen's shilling and joining the 3rd Buffs, which was just starting for India. Lost his right leg, just above the knee, while swimming in the Ganges. (around the age of 20) Saved by company sergeant, John Holder. Next got a job with Abel White an Indigo-planter as overseer until the great mutiny broke out and he was forced to flee to the Agra Fort. Joined a volunteer corps of clerks and merchants to defend the Fort and was put in charge of two Sikh troopers to guard a gate. On the third night guarding a gate was 'forced' into helping his two Sikh trooper rob and kill Achmet the merchant when he arrived at the gate with Dost Akbar. The body was found and all four ended up in Prison Spent years in prison, escaped with the help of a native called Tonga and sought to recover the Agra Treasure that had been stolen by Major John Sholto. Sholto had hidden the treasure and died before he revealing the hiding place. Later Bartholomew Sholto found the treasure, Tonga, killed him and Tonga and Small escaped hoping to travel later on the vessel, the Esmeralda, at Gravesend, outward bound for the Brazils. Was captured on the steamboat 'the Aurora' by Holmes and party, Tonga was killed, but when the Agra treasure Chest was open, it is found to be empty, Small had thrown all the jewels into the Thames.

F. H. Townsend

The Bristol Observer

Smith, (Mortimer) [GOLD] At the start of this case, Watson was going over the three manuscript volumes that covered 1894 and mentioned the famous Smith-Mortimer succession case, but there are no further details. Referenced by Watson as to a possible story worth telling, but in the end he decides that the Golden Pince-nez was a better one. Not to be confused with Mortimer the gardener also mentioned in this story.

Smith, Culverton   [DYIN] Male in prison   Culverton Smith was a well-known Sumatran planter not a medical man. He was currently visiting London. While in Sumatra, he studied an outbreak of a tropical disease upon his plantation. His plantation was distant from medical aid, causing him to study it himself, with some rather far-reaching consequences. He was a very methodical person, and

Watson was asked to contact him after six o'clock and get him to come and attend Holmes. He killed his nephew Victor Savage with this tropical disease and when Holmes started investigating, Culverton Smith sent Holmes an ivory box with a sharp spring inside that was laced with the disease. Holmes pretended to be ill in order to make Culverton Smith admit to his guilt. He admitted his guilt in front of a dying Holmes and a hidden Watson and was arrested and taken away by Inspector Morton.

Address : 13 Lower Burke Street

Richard W. Wallace   *Walter Paget*

Smith, Horace   [VALL]   Male Alive (Real Person 1808 – 1893)   Partner in the American Firearms company Smith & Wesson. Jack McMurdo owned a Smith & Wesson revolver while he was living in Vermissa.

Horace Smith

Smith, Jack [SIGN] male Alive Curly-headed lad of six. Son of Mordecai Smith.

Sherlock Holmes Quote : "What a rosy-cheeked young rascal! Now, Jack, is there anything you would like?" He replied "I'd like a shillin'," Holmes then asked "Nothing you would like better?" To which he replied "I'd like two shillin' better,"

Address : Smith's Wharf, Opposite Millbank on river.

Thomas J. Nicholl

The Bristol Observer

Smith, James [SOLI] Male dead   Father of Violet Smith Had a brother called Ralph Smith Conducted the orchestra at the old Imperial Theatre

Smith, Jim   [SIGN]   male Alive   Eldest son of Mordecai Smith. Worked with father on Steam launch 'Aurora'

Address : Smith's Wharf, Opposite Millbank on river.

Smith, Joseph   [STUD]   Male dead (Real Person 1805 – 1844)   American religious leader and the founder of the Latter Day Saint movement (Mormons). "Do not jest at that which is sacred, We are of those who believe in those sacred writings, drawn in Egyptian letters on plates of beaten gold, which were handed unto the holy Joseph Smith at Palmyra. We have come from Nauvoo, in the state of Illinois, where we had founded our temple. We have come to seek a refuge from the violent man and from the godless, even though it be the heart of the desert."

Joseph Smith

Smith, Miss Violet [SOLI] Female Alive Young and beautiful woman, tall, graceful, and queenly. Had spatulated finger-end and a spirituality about the face. Country Complexion. Her father was dead and she lived with her Mother. The only other relative was Ralph Smith, an uncle who went to Africa twenty-five years previously and had never been in contact. She saw an advertisement in The Times inquiring for her whereabouts and on went to see the lawyer whose name was given in the paper. Met with two gentlemen, Mr. Bob Carruthers and Mr. Jack Woodley, who were home on a visit from South Africa. They said that her uncle was a friend of theirs, that he died some months before in great poverty in Johannesburg, and that he had asked them with his last breath to hunt up his relations and see that they were in no want. Went to work as a music teacher to Carruther's daughter. Went to see Holmes because she was being followed by a bearded cyclist as she made her way between Chilten Grange and Farnham Station. Was abducted and made to take part in a sham marriage with Jack Woodley conducted by Mr. Williamson. Rescued by Holmes, Watson and Carruthers. Inherited a large fortune from her uncle Ralph Smith. Married Clive Morton and set him up in his own Electrical company.

Sherlock Holmes Quote : "I nearly fell into the error of supposing that you were typewriting. Of course, it is obvious that it is music. You observe the spatulate finger-end, Watson, which is common to both professions? There is a spirituality about the face, however"—he gently turned it towards the light—"which the typewriter does not generate. This lady is a musician."

Address Chiltern Grange

Sidney Paget

Sidney Paget

Smith, Mordecai   [SIGN]   male Alive   Owner of Steam launch company and boat called the 'Aurora' Fresh painted, black with two red streaks. Funnel Black with a white band." The sides which were black. Was transporting Jonathan Small, when he tried to escape the police, but his steam launch wasn't quick enough. Jonathan Small, said he knew nothing of the murder or theft of the jewels. Father of Jim and Jack Smith.

Address : Smith's Wharf, Opposite Millbank on river.

Smith, Mrs.   [SIGN]   Female Alive   A stoutish, red-faced woman. Wife of Mordecai smith Mother of Jim and Jack Smith.

Address : Smith's Wharf, Opposite Millbank on river.

Thomas J. Nicholl   *Richard Gutschmidt*

Smith, Ralph   [SOLI]   Male dead   Uncle of Violet Smith Brother of James Smith, Violet's father. Ralph Smith, who went to Africa twenty-five years previously. Had amassed a fortune, by some means and left it all to Violet.

Smith, Willoughby   [GOLD]   Male dead   He was a decent, quiet, hardworking fellow, with no weak spot in him at all. Walked with a quick, firm tread. A very young man straight from the University The third secretary for Professor Coram in a year. Knew nobody in the neighbourhood. On 14 November 1894 was found stretched out upon the floor , by the maid Susan. He had blood pouring from the underside of his neck. His neck was pierced by a very small but very deep wound, which had divided the carotid artery. He had been stabbed by a small sealing-wax knife, one with an ivory handle and a stiff blade. His last words, before he died were "The Professor, it was she."

Address : Yoxley Old Place

Soames, Hilton   [3STU]   Male Alive   A tall, spare man, of a nervous and excitable temperament. Known to be restless in his manner. Tutor and lecturer at the College of St. Luke's. The story took place the day before the first day of the examination for the Fortescue Scholarship. His subject was Greek, and the first of the papers consisted of a large passage of Greek translation which the candidate had not seen. The passage was printed on the examination paper, and it would naturally be an immense advantage if the candidate could prepare for it in advance. For this reason great care was taken to keep the paper secret. Someone had managed to get into the Tutor's rooms and read the examination paper. The tutor's door was left unlock by Bannister. One of three students had entered the room, but which one?

Address : St. Luke's

Martin Van Maele   Sidney Paget

Soames, Sir Cathcart   [PRIO]   Male Alive   entrusted his son to Dr. Thorneycroft Huxtable and the Priory School

Address : Priory School, near Mackleton

Solomon, King [VALL] Male dead (Real Person 990 BC – 931 BC) King of Israel, noted for his wisdom When John McMurdo entered the Scowlers' lodged, the chairman greeted him saying that they had business here that wants a Solomon in judgement to set it right. It regards two murders called Lander and Egan, who both claim the head money given by the lodge for the shooting of old man Crabbe over at Stylestown. We never find out McMurdo's verdict, because he claims urgency.

King Solomon

Somerton, Dr. [SIGN] Male Alive The surgeon at Blair Island. A fast, sporting young chap, and the other young officers would meet in his rooms of an evening and play cards. Taking part in the card games were Major Sholto, Captain Morstan, Lieutenant Bromley Brown, Dr. Somerton and two or three prison-officials, crafty old hands who played a nice sly safe game.

Sotheby, John [3GAR] Male dead English auctioneer and a cofounder of the great auction house of Sotheby's Nathan Garrideb said that would drive down to Sotheby's or Christie's now and again, but really he never went out apart from these trips.

Southerton, Lord [COPP] Male Alive Owned the woods all-round The Copper Beeches.

Spaulding, Vincent   [REDH]   Male In Prison   Small, stout-built, very quick in his ways, no hair on his face, though he was not short of thirty. Had a white splash of acid upon his forehead. pierced ears (done for him by a gypsy when he was a lad) Regarded, by Holmes as the Fourth smartest man in London, and for daring third. Murderer, thief, smasher, and forger Grandchild of a royal duke. Attended Eton and Oxford. Brains as cunnings as his fingers. Mr Wilson thought he was interested in photography Notorious criminal. Associated with Duncan Ross to rob the City & Suburban Bank by digging a tunnel from the pawnshop of Jabez Wilson. He was a murderer, thief, smasher, and forger. He was a young man and at the head of his profession. Inspector Jones would rather have his bracelets on him than on any criminal in London. He was a remarkable man. He was able to crack a crib in Scotland one week, and be raising money to build an orphanage in Cornwall the next. Holmes had one or two little turns also with John Clay, and he agrees with the police that he is at the head of his profession. He was arrested by Sherlock Holmes and inspector Jones in the Coburg branch of the City & Suburban Bank. He was small, strong, quick of movement, has no beard, he is nearly thirty years old. He had on his forehead a white spot of acid. He was employed in the pay-day lending shop of Jabez Wilson as an assistant. He was not as young as you might think. He had worked there for about a month. He agreed to work at Jabez Wilson for half of a regular salary. He was a good worker. He had no vices. He was one of London's most daring and clever criminals.

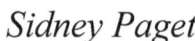

Sidney Paget   *Stanley E. Armstrong*

Spencer, Georgiana [IDEN] Female dead See Duchess of Devonshire

Spender, Rose [LADY] Female dead Had an aged and withered face. A worn-out wreck. She was a small woman. Dr. Shlessinger said that she was an old nurse of my wife's. They found her in the Brixton Workhouse Infirmary. They brought her to the home to die. She was a small woman in a very big coffin. She had died of senile decay. She was to be buried at eight o'clock the following day. But ended up sharing her coffin with Lady Frances Carfax. After Holmes found Lady Frances, her funeral was continued.

St. Clair, Mrs. [TWIS] Female Alive A little blonde woman who was clad in some sort of light mousseline de soie, with a touch of fluffy pink chiffon at her neck and wrists. Wife of Neville St. Clare. While picking up a parcel from the Aberdeen Shipping Company, she chanced to walking through Swandam Lane at 4:35 and looking up at a window, she saw her husband looking down at her and he suddenly disappeared from sight. She tried to get up to him on the first floor, but was stopped downstairs by the Lascar. She raced outside and managed to get a group of passing constables and together managed to gain access to the upstairs. It was inside this room that the beggar Hugh Boone was found, who swore that he was the only person here, but on searching the room, the discarded clothes of Neville St. Claire are found. Hugh Boone is arrested and now, some days later and her husband has still not return, so she asks Holmes to try and find him.

Address : 'The Cedars' Near Lee, in Kent.

Sidney Paget

Josef Friedrich

St. Simon, Lady Clara [NOBL] **Female Alive** The younger sister of the bridegroom, Lord Robert St. Simon. Attended the Wedding of Miss Hatty Doran and Lord Robert St. Simon. Daughter of the Duke and Duchess of Balmoral.

St. Simon, Lady Hatty [NOBL] **Female Alive** See Miss Hatty Doran

St. Simon, Lord Eustace [NOBL] **Male Alive** The younger brother of the bridegroom, Lord Robert St. Simon. Attended the Wedding of Miss Hatty Doran and Lord Robert St. Simon. Third son of the Duke and Duchess of Balmoral.

St. Simon, Lord Robert [NOBL] **Male Alive** A pleasant, cultured face, high-nosed and pale, with something perhaps of petulance about the mouth, and with the steady, well-opened eye of a man whose pleasant lot it had ever been to command and to be obeyed. His manner was brisk, and yet his general appearance gave an undue impression of age, for he had a slight forward stoop and a little bend of the knees as he walked. His hair, too, as he swept off his very curly-brimmed hat, was grizzled round the edges and thin upon the top. His dress was careful to the verge of foppishness, with high collar, black frock-coat, white waistcoat, yellow gloves, patent-leather shoes, and light-coloured gaiters. Had golden eyeglasses swinging from a cord in his right hand. Bit of a Snob. Second son of the Duke and Duchess of Balmoral. Arms: Azure, three caltrops in chief over a fess sable. Born in 1846. He's forty-one years of age. Was under-secretary for the colonies in a late administration. The Duke, his father, was at one time Secretary for Foreign Affairs. They inherit Plantagenet blood by direct descent, and Tudor on the distaff side. Wedding took place at St. George's, Hanover Square. Honeymoon would be passed at Lord Backwater's place, near Petersfield. First Met Miss Hatty Doran in San Francisco in 1885. Needed money, was this because he lost it playing cards with Ronald Adair and Colonel Moran, it would fit.

Address Grosvenor Mansions

Sidney Paget   *Josef Friedrich*

St. Simon, Lord Robert Walsingham de Vere   [NOBL]   Male Alive   See Lord Robert St. Simon

Stackhurst, Harold   [LION]   Male Alive   Lived half a mile away from the retired Holmes. Was Principle of the Well-known coaching establishment called 'The Gables' It was quite a large place, which contains some score of young fellows preparing for various professions, with a staff of several masters. He was a well-known rowing Blue in his day, and an excellent all-round scholar. He and Holmes became very good friends and as such they could drop in on each other in the evenings without an invitation. On the morning of the death of Fitzroy McPherson, he was on to join him for a swim. Remained with McPherson's body while Holmes went off and looked around for clues. 'Played' the part of Watson in this story. Helped Holmes drop a boulder on the Cyanea (Cyanea Capillata)

Address : The Gables

Frederic Dorr Steele   *Frederic Dorr Steele*

Stamford, Archie   [SOLI]   Male   Forger whom Holmes and Watson caught around Farnham, Surrey.

Stamford, Dr.   [STUD]   Male Alive   Met with Watson at the Criterion Bar. Watson invited him to lunch at the Holborn. Dresser under Watson at Barts. Said Holmes was a little queer in his ideas—an enthusiast in some branches of science, but he is a decent fellow enough. Also said Holmes' studies are very desultory and eccentric, but has amassed a lot of out-of-the way knowledge which would astonish his professors. Introduced Watson to Holmes.

George Hutchinson

Stamford, Edward [HOUN] Male See Edward Stanford

Stanford, Edward [HOUN] Male   Watson's error here, it should be Edward Stanford, not Edward Stamford. Leading map seller and sole agent for Ordnance and geological survey maps of England and Wales.

Sherlock Holmes Quote : "After you left I sent down to Stamford's for the Ordnance map of this portion of the moor, and my spirit has hovered over it all day. I flatter myself that I could find my way about."

Address : 26 Cockspur S, Charing cross.

Stanger, James   [VALL]   Male Alive Was an old man. He was respected in the township and the district. His paper, the Herald, stood for all that was solid in the valley. The Vermissa lodge decided that he needed to be taught a lesson, especially after he printed a piece that said waistcoat pocket. "LAW AND ORDER! "REIGN OF TERROR IN THE COAL AND IRON DISTRICT "Twelve years have now elapsed since the first assassinations which proved the existence of a criminal organisation in our midst. From that day these outrages have never ceased, until now they have reached a pitch which makes us the opprobrium of the civilised world. Is it for such results as this that our great country welcomes to its bosom the alien who flies from the despotisms of Europe? Is it that they shall themselves become tyrants over the very men who have given them shelter, and that a state of terrorism and lawlessness should be established under the very shadow of the sacred folds of the starry Flag of Freedom which would raise horror in our minds if we read of it as existing under the most effete monarchy of the East? The men are known. The organisation is patent and public. How long are we to endure it? Can we forever live—" Ted Baldwin was the leader of the group that attacked James Stanger. Others in the group were Gower, Mansel, Scanlan, the two willabys and John McMurdo, there were two others to guard the door. McMurdo stopped Baldwin from killing Stanger.

Frank Wiles

Stangerson, Elder [STUD] Male In PART II. The Country of the Saints section of the book. John Ferrier was provided with as large and as fertile a tract of land as any of the settlers, with the exception of Young himself, and of Stangerson, Kemball, Johnston, and Drebber, who were the four principal Elders. Elder Stangerson is the father of Joseph Stangerson.

Stangerson, Joseph [STUD] Male dead Was a high ranking Mormon in Utah. While in America he had four wives. He wanted to marry Lucy Ferrier to get her land and wealth. Friend of Enoch J. Drebber. Chased after John and Lucy Ferrier when they attempted to leave and while Lucy was returned and forced to marry Drebber, Stangerson killed John Ferrier. Left the Mormon church along with Drebber and they went travelling, forever followed by Jefferson Hope. Was killed at Halliday's Private Hotel about six o'clock this morning. Stabbed by Jefferson Hope when he refused to take one of the pills proffered to him.

George Hutchinson   *George Hutchinson*

Staphouse family   [VALL]   Male dead   Unknown members of the Vermissa lodge Scowrers blew up the Staphouse family for some reason.

Staples, Mr.   [DYIN]   Male Alive   Mr. Culverton Smith's butler. Was told off by Smith on being interrupted by Watson "Who is this person? What does he want? Dear me, Staples, how often have I said that I am not to be disturbed in my hours of study?" and he continued "Well, I won't see him, Staples. I can't have my work interrupted like this. I am not at home. Say so. Tell him to come in the morning if he really must see me."

Frederic Dorr Steele

Stapleton, Mr. Jack [HOUN] Male dead London Disguise. Around forty years of age, and he was of a middle height, two or three inches shorter than Holmes He was dressed like a toff, and he had a black beard, cut square at the end, and a pale face. Dartmoor description. He was a small, slim, clean-shaven, prim-faced man, flaxen-haired and lean-jawed, between thirty and forty years of age, dressed in a grey suit and wearing a straw hat. A tin box for botanical specimens hung over his shoulder and he carried a green butterfly-net in one of his hands. While he was in London he followed Dr. Mortimer and Sir Henry Baskerville around, Stole Boots belonging to Sir Henry Baskerville when they were left outside his room door at the Northumberland Hotel. Naturalist and butterfly collector. Using the name Vandeleur, he had been a school master at St. Oliver's Private School. entomologist, who had a moth named after him in the British museum. His wife Beryl, posed as his sister and befriended Sir Henry Baskerville. Promised Laura Lyons that he would marry her after you got her divorce. He purchased a giant dog and used the legend of the Hound of the Baskerville, to drive terror into old Sir Charles Baskerville and give him a heart attack. Tried to do the same to Sir Henry Baskerville, inviting him for a meal one evening and as Sir henry walked home over the moor, he released the hound onto his trail, but it was intercepted by Holmes, Watson and Lestrade and shot dead. Stapleton fled into the Grimpen mire and was never seen again, presumed dead.

Address : Merripit House, Dartmoor

B. Widman   *Sidney Paget*

Stapleton, Mrs. Beryl [HOUN] Female Alive one of the beauties of Costa Rica. she was darker than any brunette , slim, elegant, and tall. She had a proud, finely cut face, so regular that it might have seemed impassive were it not for the sensitive mouth and the beautiful dark, eager eyes. Maiden name Beryl Garcia. Used alias Beryl Vandeleur, while she and her husband were at St. Oliver's Private School.. Was devoted to her husband, but how much she knew of his plans in getting the Baskerville money is uncertain. She did try to warn Sir Henry Baskerville in London, sending him a note, which said "As you value your life or your reason keep away from the moor." When she met Watson for the first time, she thought that he was Sir Henry and again tried to warn him of the danger he was in. Befriended Sir Henry when she met him on the moor, but on the evening of his attendance at Merripit House, she was tied up in the bedroom and was only released after her husband had escaped into the Grimpen Mire.

Address : Merripit House, Dartmoor

Sidney Paget   *Raymond Pallier*

Stark, Colonel Lysander [ENGR] Male Alive A man rather over the middle size, but of an exceeding thinness. His whole face sharpened away into nose and chin, and the skin of his cheeks was drawn quite tense over his outstanding bones. This emaciation seemed to be his natural habit, and due to no disease, for his eye was bright, his step brisk, and his bearing assured. He was plainly but neatly dressed, and his age,. Nearer forty years old than thirty. Something of a German accent. Offered fifty guineas for a night's work to Victor Hatherley. Said that he was suing a hydraulic press to process fuller's-earth, but in reality was a coiner. Attempted to crush Victor Hatherley in the press, but he was pulled to safety by Elise. Lysander Stark did managed to cut off Victor Hatherley's thumb with a butcher's cleaver. Was a Coiner and murderer.

Address : he said Seven miles from Eyford station, in Berkshire, near border of Oxfordshire, but he lied.

Sidney Paget   *Josef Friedrich*

Starr, Dr. Lysander [3GAR] Male dead   Holmes invented this person in order to see if John Garrideb was honest, he said that Starr was a deceased doctor who was Mayor of Topeka in 1890 and had been in correspondence with Holmes in the past. Holmes knew John Garrideb was lying when he responded "Good old Dr. Starr! His name is still honoured."

Staunton, Arthur H.   [MISS] Male Alive   When asked, by Cyril Overton, if he knew a Godfrey Staunton, Holmes looked in the 'S' section of his Commonplace book and found Arthur H. Staunton, the rising young forger.

Staunton, Father of Mrs. [MISS] Male Alive   A rough-looking man with a beard who called with a note for Godfrey. He was not a gentleman, neither was he a working man. He was simply what was described as a "medium-looking chap"

Staunton, Godfrey **[MISS]** **Male Alive**   A three-quarter who played Rugby for Trinity College. An orphan and Lord Mount-James is his nearest relative —his uncle. Cyril Overton was worried about the following day's game against Oxford because Godfrey Staunton had gone missing. Cyril Overton said he was "simply the hinge that the whole team turns on" Cyril Overton couldn't believe that Holmes didn't know about Godfrey Staunton "I didn't think there was a soul in England who didn't know Godfrey Staunton, the crack three-quarter, Cambridge, Blackheath, and five Internationals." Godfrey Staunton Deserted his team mates to be at his wife's bedside while she died, causing his team's skipper Clive Overton to call on Holmes.

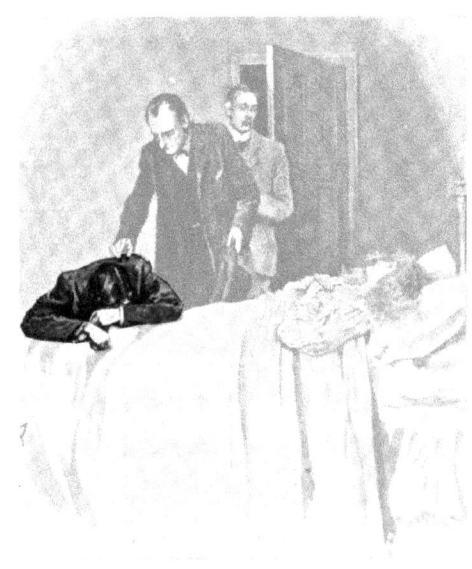

Frederic Dorr Steele   *Sidney Paget*

Staunton, Henry **[MISS]** **Male dead**   When asked if he knew a Godfrey Staunton, Holmes looked in the 'S' section of his Commonplace book and found Henry Staunton, whom Holmes had help hang.

Staunton, Mrs **[MISS]**   **dead**   Her calm, pale face, with dim, wide-opened blue eyes, looked upward from amid a great tangle of golden hair Godfrey Staunton's London Landlady's daughter. Married to Godfrey for just over a year. Dr. Leslie Armstrong said of her "She was as good as she was beautiful, and as intelligent as she was good. No man need be ashamed of such a wife." Died from consumption of the most virulent kind. Godfrey Staunton deserted his team mates to be at her bedside while she died, causing his team's skipper Clive Overton to call on Holmes.

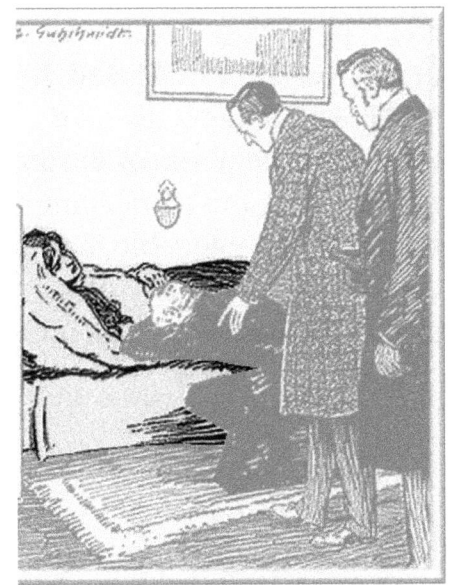

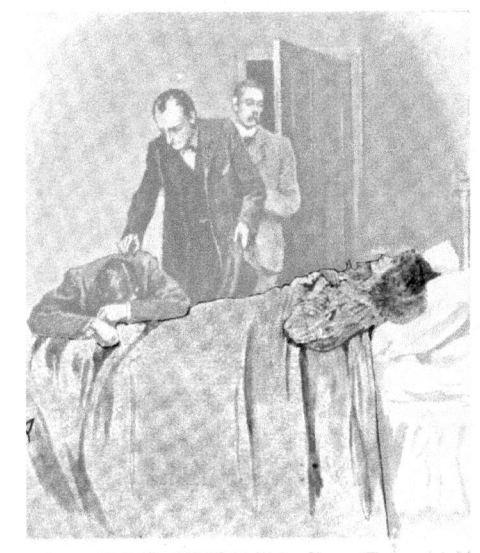

Richard Gutschmidt   *Sidney Paget*

Steele, Mr. **[3GAR]** **Male Alive** Junior partner in Holloway and Steele, who were the House agents for the Georgian house at 156 Little Ryder Street currently owned by Nathan Garridebs Told Holmes that Mr. Garrideb had been at the address for five years previously it had been empty for a year and before that a Mr. Waldron (Prescott) had lived there.

Steiler, Peter **[FINA]** **Male Alive** Landlord of the Englischer Hof inn and was an intelligent man, and spoke excellent English, having served for three years as waiter at the Grosvenor Hotel in London.

Address : Englischer Hof in the little village of Meiringen

Steiner, Mr. **[LAST]** **Male in prison** Spy working for Von Bork. The authorities had raided his store the previous night, and he and his papers were now all in Portsmouth jail. Steiner was the fifth man that Von Bork had lost since Altamont signed on.

Stendals family **[VALL]** **Male dead** Unknown members of the Vermissa lodge Scowrers murdered the Stendals for some reason

Stephens, Butler **[SHOS]** **Male Alive** Butler at Shoscombe Old Place, Reported that Lady Beatrice Falder's consumption of alcohol had increased from a glass an evening to often a whole bottle an evening. "Well, she took her glass, but now it is often a whole bottle of an evening. So Stephens, the butler, told me. It's all changed, Mr. Holmes, and there is something damned rotten about it. But then, again, what is master doing down at the old church crypt at night? And who is the man that meets him there?" Holmes rubbed his hands. "Go on, Mr. Mason. You get more and more interesting." "It was the butler who saw him go. Twelve o'clock at night and raining hard. So next night I was up at the house and, sure enough, master was off again. Stephens and I went after him, but it was jumpy work, for it would have been a bad job if he had seen us. He's a terrible man with his fists if he gets started, and no respecter of persons. So we were shy of getting too near, but we marked him down all right. It was the haunted crypt that he was making for, and there was a man waiting for him there.'

Address : Shoscombe Old Place

Sterndale, Dr. Leon   [DEVI]   Male Alive   He had a huge body, craggy and deeply seamed face with the fierce eyes and hawk-like nose. Had grizzled hair which nearly brushed the cottage ceiling. His beard—golden at the fringes and white near the lips, save for the nicotine stain from his perpetual cigar. As well known in London as in Africa, the great lion-hunter and explorer. he was as well known in London as in Africa, the great lion-hunter and explorer. Possessed may African curios including Devil's Foot Root, which was used as an ordeal poison by the medicine-men in certain districts of West Africa and was kept as a secret among them. He had a specimen, which he had obtained under very extraordinary circumstances in the Ubangi country. He had started his return journey to Africa, when he got a message from the Vicar about the death of Brenda Tregennis. He returned and tried to find out from Holmes whether he had any ideas regarding the incident at Tredannick Wartha Upon his Cornish mother's side he could call the Tregennis family cousins Killed Mortimer Tregennis out of revenge for killing Brenda Tregennis by inhaling the fumes given off by burning Devil Foot Root.

Address : A small bungalow buried in the lonely wood of Beauchamp Arriance

G. Dutriac   *George Hutchinson*

Stevens, Bert   [NORW]   Male   Holmes feared that he would not be able to help his client John Hector McFarlane from being found guilty of murdering Mr. Oldacre, Watson ask whether McFarlane's appearance would go far with any jury. Holmes' replied

Sherlock Holmes Quote : "That is a dangerous argument, my dear Watson. You remember that terrible murderer, Bert Stevens, who wanted us to get him off in '87? Was there ever a more mild-mannered, Sunday-school young man?"

Stevenson, Mr.   [MISS]   Male Alive   Player on Cambridge rugby team. Clive Overton said that "he was fast enough, but he couldn't drop from the twenty-five line, and a three-quarter who can't either punt or drop wasn't worth a place for pace alone. "

Stewart, Jane   [CROO]   Female Alive   The housemaid of Nancy Barclay, who brought her a cup of tea, on the night of the death of her husband, which was quite contrary to her usual habits. Along with the other maid and Coachman heard the argument between James and Nancy Barclay and eventually discovered James Barclay's body.

William H. Hyde   *Sidney Paget*

Stewart, Mrs. [EMPT] Female dead   Holmes believed she was killed by Colonel Sebastian Moran in 1887, but nothing could be proved.

Sherlock Holmes Quote : "You may have some recollection of the death of Mrs. Stewart, of Lauder, in 1887. Not? Well, I am sure Moran was at the bottom of it; but nothing could be proved. So cleverly was the Colonel concealed that even when the Moriarty gang was broken up we could not incriminate him."

Stimson, Mr. [LADY] Male   Owner of a Funeral Directors Stimson & Co. Dr. Shlessinger had booked them for an eight o'clock funeral. While the bearers were taking the coffin out of the house on the morning of the funeral, Holmes arrived and offered them money if they quickly opened up the coffin. When the coffin was opened, they discovered the Chloroformed body of Lady Frances Carfax inside.

Sherlock Holmes Quote : "Quick, Watson, quick! Here is a screwdriver !" he shouted as the coffin was replaced upon the table. "Here's one for you, my man! A sovereign if the lid comes off in a minute! Ask no questions—work away! That's good! Another! And another! Now pull all together! It's giving! It's giving! Ah, that does it at last."

Address : Kennington Road

Stockdale, Barney   [3GAB]   Male in prison   Barney Stockdale worked for Isadora Klein both in Italy and England. Employed Steve Dixie as the 'heavy'. His wife worked for Mrs Maberley. He and Dixie broke into 'the three gables' and stole Douglas Maberley's manuscript and gave it to Isadora Klein, who then burned it.

Sherlock Holmes Quote : "Barney, is a more astute person. They specialise in assaults, intimidation, and the like."

Frederic Dorr Steele

Stockdale, Susan   [3GAB]   Female Alive   Wife of Barney Stockdale, who took up the maid position at 'the Three Gables'. She past on the information that Holmes was going to be asked to aid Mrs. Maberley and this in turn lead to Steve Dixie's visit to Baker street. Was caught listening at the door, by Holmes after he heard her wheezing. He said "You breathe too heavily for that kind of work." Gave away a bit too much information to Holmes when he interview her. She was dismissed and left straight away.

Sherlock Holmes Quote : "Good-bye, Susan. Paregoric is the stuff... "

Address : The Three Gables, Harrow Weald

Frederic Dorr Steele   *Howard K. Elcock*

Stone, Rev. Joshua   [WIST]   Male Alive   An owner of a large house in the Esher area. His details were sent to Holmes by the Allan brothers, chief land agents in the village of Esher.

Address : Nether Walsling, Esher

Stoner, Helen   [SPEC]   Female dead   A lady dressed in black and heavily veiled, Holmes observed that she was shivering because of fear. she was indeed in a pitiable state of agitation, her face all drawn and grey, with restless frightened eyes, like those of some hunted animal. Her features and figure were those of a woman of thirty, but her hair was shot with premature grey, and her expression was weary and haggard. Lives with stepfather at Stoke Moran on the western border of Surrey. The Roylotts where at one time among the richest in England, but now had a horrible life of an aristocratic pauper. Her mother remarried when she was two years old and died eight years ago. Her sister Julia, had died two years ago. The night of Julia's death, she had mentioned that she had heard whistling during the night. In February/March Percy Armitage asked for her hand in marriage. She had now been moved o her sister's bedroom and the previous night she had heard, whistling. Holmes had been recommend to her by Mrs. Farintosh, so being in fear for her life, she had sought his help. Holmes arranged to visit Stoke Moran that afternoon and when he and Watson arrived, they had a good look around and asked Miss Stoner to leave her window unlocked, leave a light shining and move back to her old bedroom. In the middle of the night Grimsby Roylott send a snake into the room, and in the morning, her stepfather was dead and Holmes took her away to some place to shelter. Unfortunately she met with an untimely death a few months previously.

Address : Stoke Moran on the western border of Surrey.

Sidney Paget   *Josef Friedrich*

Stoner, Julia   [SPEC]   Female dead   Lived with stepfather at Stoke Moran on the western border of Surrey. The Roylotts where at one time among the richest in England, but now had a horrible life of an aristocratic pauper. Her last words were 'Oh, my God! Helen! It was the band! The speckled band!' Almost a locked room mystery, she died just outside her room in the arms of her sister Helen. Bitten by a Swamp Adder, the deadliest snake in India. (Proatheris superciliaris).

Address : Stoke Moran on the western border of Surrey.

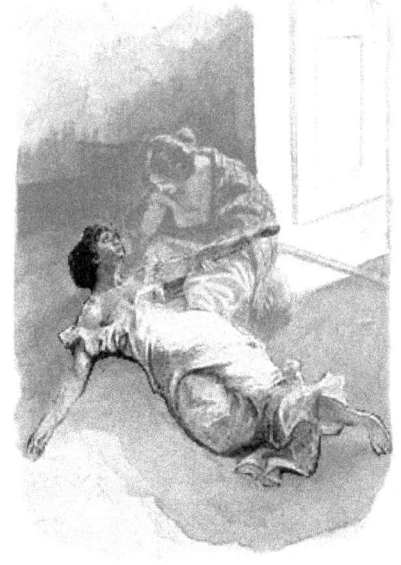

Josef Friedrich   *Martin Van Maele*

Stoner, Major-General   **[SPEC]**   **Male dead**   Husband of Mrs. Stoner. Father of Twins, Julia and Helen stoner. He was in the Bengal Artillery

Stoner, Mrs   **[SPEC]**   **Female dead**   Mother of Twins, Julia and Helen stoner. Maiden name Miss Westphail. Wife of Major-General Stoner, of the Bengal Artillery Married Dr. Grimsby Roylott around 1855 Died around 1875 in railway accident near Crewe and left a considerable sum of money-- not less than 1000 pounds a year-- and this she bequeathed to Dr. Roylott entirely while the twins resided with him, with a provision that a certain annual sum should be allowed to each of them in the event of their marriages.

Address : Stoke Moran on the western border of Surrey.

Stoper, Miss   **[COPP]**   **Female Alive**   Manager of Westaway's well-known agency for governesses in the West End. Violet Hunter met Jephro Rucastle at Westaway's agency, so was less than amused when Miss Hunter turned down the offer of employment. 'Well, really, it seems rather useless, since you refuse the most excellent offers in this fashion,' said she sharply. 'You can hardly expect us to exert ourselves to find another such opening for you. Good-day to you, Miss Hunter.' She struck a gong upon the table, and Miss Hunter was shown out by the page.

Josef Friedrich   *Sidney Paget*

Stradivarius, Antonio   [STUD,CARD]   Male dead (Real Person 1644 – 1736)
Italian Luthier and famous craftsman of string instruments like violins, cellos,
guitars, violas and harps. Holmes owned a Stradivarius, which was worth at least
five hundred guineas, and he purchased it at a Jew broker's in Tottenham Court
Road for fifty-five shillings.

Antonio Stradivarius

Straker, John   [SILV]   Male dead   Killed at the start of the story, his head had been shattered by a savage blow from some heavy weapon, and he was wounded on the thigh, where there was a long, clean cut, inflicted evidently by some very sharp instrument. A retired jockey who rode in Colonel Ross's colours before he became too heavy for the weighing-chair. He has served the Colonel for five years as jockey and for seven as trainer, and has always shown himself to be a zealous and honest servant. Had three lads working under him. Married and maybe bigamist or had a mistress. No children. Tried to nobble the Horse Silver Blaze, but the horse killed him in self-defence.

Address : A small villa about two hundred yards from King's Pyland

Martin Van Maele

William II. Hyde

Straker, Mrs   [SILV]   Female Alive   Wife of John Straker. didn't have a dove-coloured silk with ostrich-feather trimming. Was oblivious to the second life her husband was leading with a second wife or mistress.

Address : A small villa about two hundred yards from King's Pyland

Sidney Paget   *Martin Van Maele*

Straubenzee, Mr. [MAZA] Male Alive   old owner of a Gun workshop in the Minories area of London. Maker of Air-guns, Count Sylvius visited the shop and was followed by Holmes. Holmes thought that there might be one of Straubenzee's air-guns trained on 221b Baker street from the opposite window at that moment. Holmes had a dummy sitting by the window just in case.

Strauss, Herman   [VALL] Male Alive   Possible mine or ironwork owner who was not on the list to be murdered by the assassins Lawlers and Andrews.

Sturmash, Mr   [VALL] Male   Junior partner of the Coal company of Rae & Sturmash. Division Master Windle of Merton County Lodge 249 stated in a letter that there was a job to be done on this person's coal company. McGinty asked for volunteers and Tiger Cormac and a young boy in his teens called Wilson, stepped forward. This job was to return a favour that the Merton County Lodge had tendered the previous fall in the matter of the patrolman.

Sudbury, Student   [LION] Male Alive   A student at 'The Gables' coaching establishment. He and Blount found the body of Fitzroy McPherson's dog, dead on the very edge of the pool within which his master had swam. He may have been one of the students that joined McPherson in morning swims and had been saved by Ian Murdoch's algebraic demonstration.

Sumner, The Shipping Agent **[BLAC]** **Male Alive** He was the Shipping Agent in the Ratcliff Highway. Holmes sent him a Telegraph message saying "Send three men on, to arrive ten tomorrow morning.—Basil.", He sent three men, James Lancaster, Hugh Pattins and Patrick Cairns, the last being the murder of Peter Carey.

Sutherland, Miss Mary **[IDEN]** **Female Alive** large woman with a heavy fur boa round her neck A large curling red feather in a broad-brimmed hat which was tilted in a coquettish Duchess of Devonshire fashion over her ear. Broad, good-humoured face Short-sighted, sometimes wore a pince-nez Preposterous hat and vacuous face, but noble in simple faith. wore a slate-coloured, broad-brimmed straw hat, with a feather of a brickish red. Her jacket was black, with black beads sewn upon it, and a fringe of little black jet ornaments. Her dress was brown, rather darker than coffee colour, with a little purple plush at the neck and sleeves. Her gloves were greyish and were worn through at the right forefinger and had violet ink on glove and finger. She had small round, hanging gold earrings, and a general air of being fairly well-to-do in a vulgar, comfortable, easy-going way. Wore odd boots, one having a slightly decorated toe-cap and the other was plain. One was buttoned only in the two lower buttons out of five and the other at the first, third and fifth. Had double line marks a little above the wrists of plush jacket. Works as a typist earning 2d per sheet of copy and she can often do fifteen to twenty sheets per day. (earns around £32-£42 per year) She oscillated backward and forward, and her fingers fidgeted with her glove buttons while waiting outside 221b Baker street, then with a plunge, as of the swimmer who leaves the bank, she hurried across the road, and Holmes heard the sharp clang of the bell. Gets one hundred pounds a year from the interest on money left to her by her uncle Ned Sutherland in Auckland, New Zealand. Earns 4 1/2% interest on £2500 stocks, but can only touch the interest. She allows her stepfather to draw the interest every quarter. Met Hosmer Angel at the gasfitters' ball engaged after the first walk. Was to be married at St. Saviour's, near King's Cross and then have a breakfast afterwards at the St. Pancras Hotel. Mentioned in the Blue Carbuncle when Watson makes Holmes allude to his attempt to recover the Irene Adler papers, to the singular case of Miss Mary Sutherland, and to the adventure of the man with the twisted lip, all of which were entirely free of any legal crime.

Address : 31 Lyon Place, Camberwell.

Sidney Paget   *Josef Friedrich*

Sutherland, Mr. [IDEN] Male dead   Mr. Sutherland was the father of Mary Sutherland. He was a plumber in the Tottenham Court Road, and he left a tidy business behind him, which Mrs. Sutherland carried on with Mr. Hardy, the foreman until she remarried and her new husband ask her to sell it off.

Sutherland, Mrs. [IDEN] Female Alive   Mrs. Sutherland was the mother of Mary Sutherland. Widow of Mr. Sutherland, the plumber. She married James Windibank after the death of Mr. Sutherland. James Windibank made her sell the business because he was very superior, being a traveller in wines. Sold the Plumbing business after the death of Mr. Sutherland for £4700 for the goodwill and interest, which was a bit on the low side. Conspired with her new husband to keep her daughter Mary living at home and paying rent. Together they introduced her to Hosmer Angel, who brought her to the brink of marriage and they disappeared, having made her promise to keep faith with him.

Address : 31 Lyon Place, Camberwell.

Sutherland, Ned [IDEN] Male dead   Ned Sutherland was the uncle of Mary Sutherland. Mary Sutherland received, from his uncle Ned in Auckland, a New Zealand Stock, paying 4 1/2 per cent. Two thousand five hundred pounds was the amount, but she could only touch the interest.

Sutro, Mr. **[3GAB]** **Male Alive** Mary Maberley's lawyer, who lived in Harrow. When she showed him the document relating to the selling of her house, he warned her that it was a strange document and he said she would not legally take anything out of the house—not even her own private possessions.

Frederic Dorr Steele

Sutton, Mr. **[RESI]** **Male dead** See Mr. Blessington

Swain, John **[FIVE]** **Male dead** Mentioned in the remaining ledger page belonging to the KKK dated March 1869 7th. Set the pips on McCauley, Mr., Paramore, and John Swain of St. Augustine. 12th. Visited Paramore. All well. probably killed by the KKK

Swan, Sir Joseph Wilson **[HOUN]** **Male Alive (Real Person 1828 – 1914)** English physicist, chemist, and inventor. He is known as an independent early developer of a successful incandescent light bulb. Sir Henry Baskerville said "It's no wonder my uncle felt as if trouble were coming on him in such a place as this, It's enough to scare any man. I'll have a row of electric lamps up here inside of six months, and you won't know it again, with a thousand candle-power Swan and Edison right here in front of the hall door."

Joseph Swan

Swindon, Archie   [VALL]   Male Alive   Mine owner who sold out to the the State & Merton County Railroad Company "The old devil left a note for us to say that he had rather be a free crossing sweeper in New York than a large mine owner under the power of a ring of blackmailers."

Sylvius, Count Negretto   [MAZA]   Male in prison   The famous game-shot, sportsman, and man-about-town was a big, swarthy fellow, with a formidable dark moustache shading a cruel, thin-lipped mouth, and surmounted by a long, curved nose like the beak of an eagle. He was well dressed, but his brilliant necktie, shining pin, and glittering rings were flamboyant in their effect. Holmes believes that the count has stolen the one hundred thousand pound yellow Mazarin Stone and sets up a trap to catch him The Count arrived at 221b Baker street, just as Watson was leaving to fetch the Police, Watson leaves through a second exit. Holmes had told Watson the name and address of his would-be murder - Count Negretto Sylvius. The count is shown into Holmes room and sees what he thinks is Holmes seated in an armchair by the window. He creeps up with his thick stick raised to strike, when Holmes speaks from his bedroom asking him not to break his effigy. The count and Holmes talk for a while, then Sam Merton, The count's partner, is called up. Holmes leaves the room to allow them to discuss whether they want to return the Mazarin Stone and go free or not. They talk for a while and Merton demands to see the stone and when the count takes it out of a hidden pocket, the effigy leaps up and snatches it from him, Holmes had replaced the dummy and had been waiting to make his move. Holmes now holds a gun on them until Watson and the police arrive to take the felons away.

Address : 136 Moorside Gardens, N.W.

G. Dutriac

Alfred Gilbert

T is for The Problem of Thor Bridge

Tang-Ying [ILLU] Male dead (Real Person 1470 – 1524) Was a Chinese calligrapher, poet and painter of the Ming dynasty period. Lived in the Ming dynasty, but much of his work were illustrated with elements from pre-Tang to Song dynasty art. Holmes asked Watson to learn as much as he could about Chinese ceramics, so in the process, Watson learned of the hallmarks of the great artist-decorators, of the mystery of cyclical dates, the marks of the Hung-wu and the beauties of the Yung-lo, the writings of Tang-ying, and the glories of the primitive period of the Sung and the Yuan dynasties.

Tang-Ying

Tangey, Mr.   [NAVA] Male Alive Commissionaire at the Foreign Office. Remains all night in a little lodge at the foot of the stairs, and is in the habit of making coffee at his spirit-lamp for any of the officials who may be working overtime. Was fast asleep when Percy Phelps went downstairs to see what had happened to the coffee he had order previously. The Ringing of a bell woke the Commissioner up, the bell belonging to the room Percy Phelps had been working in, the room that had the Naval Treaty on the desk. Was in the guards and left with a good character.

Sidney Paget

Tangey, Mrs. **[NAVA]** **Female Alive** A large, coarse-faced, elderly woman, in an apron. Tall and elderly, with a Paisley shawl. Wife of the commissioner. Did the charring in the offices. Said to be a bad lot by Inspector Forbes. Said to Drink to excess. When Percy Phelps rang down to the commissionaire to order a cup of coffee, she turned up to see what he wanted. Left the offices in a hurry and was suspected of stealing the Naval Treaty. She was innocent.

Address : 16 Ivy Lane, Brixton

Sidney Paget

Tarleton murders   [MUSG]   dead   Inside a large box, Holmes opened, were bundles of papers that detailed previous cases including the Tarleton murders. A story never revealed.

Sidney Paget

Tarlton, Susan   [GOLD]   Female Alive   Maid at Yoxley Old Place She had worked there a couple of years and was a woman of excellent character. She was engaged in hanging some curtains in the upstairs front bedroom when she heard a commotion downstairs, going to investigate, she saw Willoughby Smith lying motionless on the floor of the study. She discovered that he had a deep wound in his neck and had been stabbed by a small sealing-wax knife His has words to her were "The Professor, it was she." The housekeeper, Mrs Marker arrived upon the scene, but she was just too late to catch the young man's dying words.   The professor is rather demeaning of her saying "Susan is a country girl, and you know the incredible stupidity of that class. I fancy that the poor fellow murmured some incoherent delirious words, and that she twisted them into this meaningless message." She did say that Willoughby Smith had gone out for a walk into town and been killed just half an hour after his return

Tavernier, Mr.   [MAZA]   Male Alive   French artist who made the effigy of Holmes. Holmes says that he was very good at waxworks and this is proved by Count Sylvius thinking the dummy was Holmes and trying to attack it.

Teddy the Mongoose [CROO] Male Alive A beautiful reddish-brown creature, thin and lithe, with the legs of a stoat, a long, thin nose, and a pair of the finest red eyes that ever I saw in an animal's head. Henry Wood's mongoose. "Well, some call them that, and some call them ichneumon," said Henry Wood. "Snake-catcher is what I call them, and Teddy is amazing quick on cobras. I have one here without the fangs, and Teddy catches it every night to please the folk in the canteen."

Thoreau, Henry David [NOBL] Male dead (Real Person 1817 – 1862) American Writer, essayist, Poet, philosopher, transcendentalist, naturalist, political dissident and human rights advocate. Henry David Thoreau wrote in Journal on 11th November 1850 " Some circumstantial evidence is very strong, as when you find a trout in the milk"

Sherlock Holmes Quote : "I have notes of several similar cases, though none, as I remarked before, which were quite as prompt. My whole examination served to turn my conjecture into a certainty. Circumstantial evidence is occasionally very convincing, as when you find a trout in the milk, to quote Thoreau's example."

Henry David Thoreau

Thucydides [3STU] Male dead (Real Person 460 BC – 400 BC) Greece general and historian who wrote his History of the Peloponnesian War between Sparta and Athens until 411 BC Proofs of the examination paper arrived from the printers. The exercise consists of half a chapter of Thucydides. They had to be read it over carefully, as the text had to be absolutely correct. The three sheets that comprised the examination were left on Soames' desk, while he went out to take tea with a friend and it was after this time, that someone entered his study and looked at these papers.

Thucydides

Thurston, Mr. [DANC] Male Alive   The only person Watson plays Billiards with at his club. Thurston had an option on some South African property (Gold Field) which would expire in a month, and which he desired Watson to share with him. Watson decided he didn't want to invest his money.

Sherlock Holmes Quote : "Here are the missing links of the very simple chain:
1. You had chalk between your left finger and thumb when you returned from the club last night.
2. You put chalk there when you play billiards to steady the cue.
3. You never play billiards except with Thurston.
4. You told me four weeks ago that Thurston had an option on some South African property which would expire in a month, and which he desired you to share with him.
5. Your chequebook is locked in my drawer, and you have not asked for the key.
6. You do not propose to invest your money in this manner."

Tobin, Mr.   [RESI]   Male dead   The caretaker at Worthingdon bank who was murdered.

Sherlock Holmes Quote : "You must surely remember the great Worthingdon bank business, five men were in it–these four and a fifth called Cartwright. Tobin, the caretaker, was murdered, and the thieves got away with seven thousand pounds".

Toby the dog   [SIGN]   Male Alive   Lived with Sherman at No. 3, Pinchin Lane, down near the water's edge at Lambeth. The third house on the right-hand side is a bird-stuffer's: Sherman is the name. You will see a weasel holding a young rabbit in the window. Proved to be an ugly, long-haired, lop-eared creature, half spaniel and half lurcher, brown-and-white in colour, with a very clumsy waddling gait. Was in Pen No. 7. Followed the smell of creosote from Pondicherry Lodge to (ultimately)

Sherlock Holmes Quote : "A queer mongrel, with a most amazing power of scent."

Address : No. 3, Pinchin Lane, down near the water's edge at Lambeth.

G. Grinham   *F. H. Townsend*

Todman, Mr   [VALL]   Male Alive   Mine owner, who had sold his mine to the State & Merton County Railroad Company and moved out of the area.

Toller, Mr   [COPP]   Male Alive   Servant and groom at The Copper Beeches along with his wife. A rough, uncouth man, with grizzled hair and whiskers, and a perpetual smell of drink. Part of an unpleasant couple. Looked after the dog Carlo the Mastiff.

Address : The Copper Beeches, five miles on the far side of Winchester

Ernest Flammarion

Toller, Mrs   [COPP]   Female Alive   Servant at The Copper Beeches along with her husband. A very tall and strong woman with a sour face, as silent as Mrs. Rucastle and much less amiable. Part of an unpleasant couple. Servant at The Copper Beeches along with her husband. A very tall and strong woman with a sour face, as silent as Mrs. Rucastle and much less amiable. Part of an unpleasant couple.

Address : The Copper Beeches, five miles on the far side of Winchester

Tonga   [SIGN]   Male dead   A little Andaman Islander, picked up by a convict-gang in the woods. He was sick to death, and had gone to a lonely place to die As venomous as a young snake, and after a couple of months Jonathan Small got him all right and able to walk. He took a kind of fancy to Jonathan Small. Very loyal. Could climb like a cat. Was a fine boatman, and owned a big, roomy canoe of his own and helped Jonathan Small escape from prison. Killed Bartholomew Sholto with a poison dart. Fired his last dart at Holmes and Watson as he was chased down the Thames in a Steam Launch. - Missed. Shot dead by either Holmes or Watson.

F. H. Townsend

Thomas J. Nicholl

Tosca, Cardinal   [BLAC]   Male dead   One of Holmes' 1895 famous investigation was that of the sudden death of Cardinal Tosca—an inquiry which was carried out by him at the express desire of His Holiness the Pope

Tregellis, Janet   [MUSG]   Female Alive   The daughter of the head gamekeeper. New girlfriend of Richard Brunton.

Martin Van Maele

Tregennis, Miss Brenda [DEVI] Female dead   She had been a very beautiful girl, though now verging upon middle age. Her dark, clear-cut face was handsome. Sister to Owen, George and Mortimer Tregennis. Her brother, Mortimer, killed her using Devil's Foot Root which he put onto the fire as he was leaving the room. Dr. Sterndale had a picture of her in his breast-pocket. For years she had been in love with Dr. Sterndale, but he had already married and could not divorce.

Address : Tredannick Wartha

G. Dutriac   George Hutchinson

Tregennis, Mr. George   [DEVI]   Male In a mental ward of a hospital   Brother to Owen, Mortimer and Brenda Tregennis. His brother, Mortimer, drove him insane using Devil's Foot Root which he put onto the fire as he was leaving the room. Was later taken to a hospital in Helston along with his brother Owen. It is difficult to know which person in the illustration is George and which is Owen, so please forgive me for repeating the same illustrations for both of these individuals.

Address : Tredannick Wartha

G. Dutriac

G. Dutriac

Tregennis, Mr. Mortimer   [DEVI]   Male dead   He was a thin, dark, spectacled man, with a stoop which gave the impression of actual, physical deformity. Strangely reticent, a sad-faced, introspective man, sitting with averted eyes, brooding apparently upon his own affairs. Was an independent gentleman, who increased the clergyman's scanty resources by taking rooms in his large, straggling house. Had two brothers, Owen and George and a sister called Brenda. Stole some Devil's Foot Root (Radix pedis diaboli{latin}) from Dr. Sterndale and used it to kill his sister and drive his two brother insane. Was killed by Dr. Sterndale, who used Devil's Foot Root in revenge.

Address : Vicarage in the hamlet of Tredannick Wollas

George Hutchinson   *G. Dutriac*

Tregennis, Mr. Owen   [DEVI]   Male In a mental ward of a hospital   Brother to George, Mortimer and Brenda Tregennis. His brother, Mortimer, drove him insane using Devil's Foot Root which he put onto the fire as he was leaving the room. Was later taken to a hospital in Helston along with his brother George. It is difficult to know which person in the illustration is George and which is Owen, so please forgive me for repeating the same illustrations for both of these individuals.

Address : Tredannick Wartha

G. Dutriac   *G. Dutriac*

Trepoff [SCAN] dead   Holmes was summoned to Odessa in the case of the Trepoff murder

Trevelyan, Doctor Percy   [RESI]   Male Alive   A pale, taper-faced man with sandy whiskers. His age may not have been more than three or four and thirty, Had a haggard expression and unhealthy hue told of a life which has sapped his strength and robbed him of his youth. His manner was nervous and shy, like that of a sensitive gentleman, and the thin white hand which he laid on the mantelpiece as he rose was that of an artist rather than of a surgeon. His dress was quiet and sombre—a black frock-coat, dark trousers, and a touch of colour about his necktie. The author of a monograph upon obscure nervous lesions, which Watson had read. His own hobby has always been nervous disease. Attended London University and afterwards devoted himself to research, occupying a minor position in King's College Hospital. Won the Bruce Pinkerton prize and medal by the monograph on nervous lesions. Was offered the post of Resident Doctor to a gentleman whose name was Blessington. Blessington would keep three-quarters of the Doctors fees, but would take the house, furnish it, pay the maids, and run the whole place.

Sherlock Holmes Quote : "Hum! A doctor's—general practitioner, I perceive, not been long in practice, but has had a good deal to do."

Address : 403 Brook Street, London

Sidney Paget

Martin Van Maele

Trevor, Justice of the Peace [GLOR] Male dead He was a man of little culture, but with a considerable amount of rude strength, both physically and mentally. He knew hardly any books, but he had travelled far, had seen much of the world and had remembered all that he had learned. In person he was a thick-set, burly man with a shock of grizzled hair, a brown, weather-beaten face, and blue eyes which were keen to the verge of fierceness. Was evidently a man of some wealth and consideration, a J.P., and a landed proprietor. Father of Victor Trevor, and also a daughter, who had died of diphtheria while on a visit to Birmingham. He had a reputation for kindness and charity on the countryside, and was noted for the leniency of his sentences from the bench. Threatened by knifing by a gang of poacher. Boxed in his youth. Did a good deal of digging in the gold fields of New Zealand, where he made all his money. Had visited Japan Had the initials J.A. tattooed on the bend of his elbow, but had made efforts to obliterate them. Was blackmailed, because of his past, by old sailor Hudson, who visited him. Died of Apoplexy, Nervous shock after receiving message from old friend Beddoes The message read 'The supply of game for London is going steadily up, Head- keeper Hudson, we believe, has been now told to receive all orders for fly-paper and for preservation of your hen-pheasant's life.' that was a code where you had to read every third word to reveal the message. So the actual message from Beddoes was 'The * * game * * is * * up * * Hudson, * * has* * told * * all * * fly * * for * * your * * life.' His original name was James Armitage and he 'borrowed' money that was not his own and before he could repaid it, an audit revealed the situation. He was sentenced to deportation to Australia aboard the 'Gloria Scott'. After a successful uprising by the prisoners and them taking over the ship, there was a falling out between the prisoner leader, Jack Prendergast over what to do with the Captain, Doctor and others. Was put in a painter along with four other prisoner and three sailors and set adrift on 6th November 1855 at N. Lat. 15 degrees 20', W. Long. 25 degrees 14'. Shortly afterwards, the Gloria Scott exploded killing all aboard except for a young seaman called Hudson, we they picked up.

Address : Donnithorpe, in Norfolk

Sidney Paget   *William H. Hyde*

Trevor, Victor [GLOR] Male Alive He was a hearty, full-blooded fellow, full of spirits and energy, the very opposite to Holmes in most respects, but they had some subjects in common, and it was a bond of union when Holmes found that he was as friendless as he. Finally, he invited me down to his father's place at Donnithorpe, in Norfolk, and I accepted his hospitality for a month of the long vacation. He invited Holmes down to his father's place at Donnithorpe, in Norfolk, and Holmes accepted his hospitality for a month of the long vacation. During Holmes' stay a sailor called Hudson arrived. Hudson blackmailed Victor's father and after leaving with ill feelings, Old Trevor received a message that Hudson had told all, which resulted in Old Trevor's death. Heartbroken at his father's death, he went out to the Terai tea planting, where he is reported to be doing well.

Sherlock Holmes Quote : "He was the only friend I made during the two years I was at college. I was never a very sociable fellow, Watson, always rather fond of moping in my rooms and working out my own little methods of thought, so that I never mixed much with the men of my year. Bar fencing and boxing I had few athletic tastes, and then my line of study was quite distinct from that of the other fellows, so that we had no points of contact at all. Trevor was the only man I knew, and that only through the accident of his bull terrier freezing on to my ankle one morning as I went down to chapel.

Address : Donnithorpe, in Norfolk

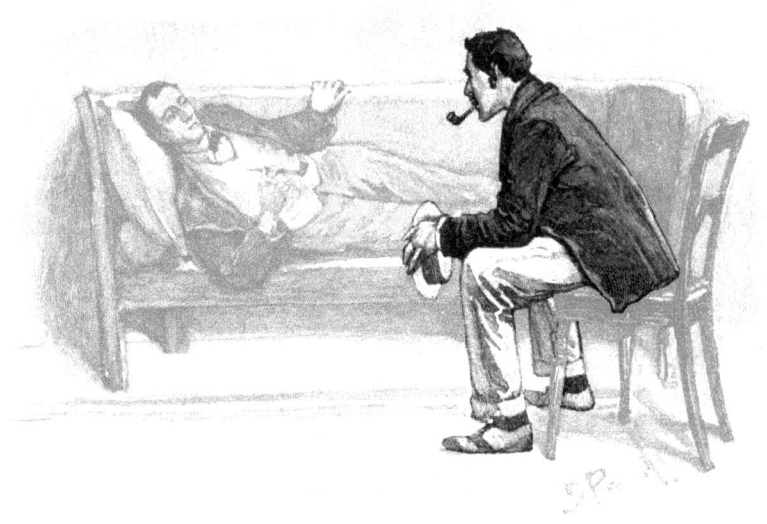

Sidney paget   *Martin Van Maele*

Trevor's (Victor) Dog GLOR Victor Trevor's bull-terrier attacked Holmes on his ankle, while Holmes was on his way down to chapel, this put Holmes out of action for ten days, but he was visited by the dog's owner, a first for a few minutes, but towards the end of the term, they were firm friends. This friendship drew Holmes into the Adventure of the Gloria Scott and the tragic outcome.(Holmes' first case). Is it this singular incident that lead to Holmes' 'dislike' of dogs, let's face it, he killed or let Watson kill, three dogs, He poisoned one himself in [STUD], shot at another in [HOUN] and got Watson to kill another in [COPP].

Marin Van Maele

Turkey, Sultan of [BLAN] Male Alive (Real Person 1842 – 1918) Sultan of turkey He was the 34th Sultan of the Ottoman Empire who reigned from 21 September 1842 to 10 February 1918. Was called the Red Sultan because of his massacres of Armenians during 1894-1896. Holmes says that he had a commission from the Sultan of Turkey which called for immediate action, as political consequences of the gravest kind might arise from its neglect and that he would not be able to go with James M. Dodd, down to Tuxbury Old Place for a few days.

Abdul Hamid II

Turner, John [BOSC] Male Alive Slow, limping step and bowed shoulders gave the appearance of decrepitude, and yet had hard, deep-lined, craggy features, and had enormous limbs showing that he possessed of unusual strength of body and of character. Had a tangled beard, grizzled hair, and outstanding, drooping eyebrows combined to give an air of dignity and power to his appearance. His face was of an ashen white, while his lips and the corners of his nostrils were tinged with a shade of blue. The largest landed proprietor in the Boscombe Valley area (not very far from Ross, in Herefordshire.) Made is money in Australia. Owned the Farm Hatherley that was let to Mr. Charles McCarthy. Kept half-dozen servants at least. Supposedly a Gold-miner in Victoria, Australia, but in fact a robber from Ballarat Tall Man, left-handed, limps with right leg, wears thick-soled shooting boots and a grey coat. Smokes Indian cigars (rolled in Rotterdam), uses a cigar-holder and carries a blunt penknife. Dying of some deadly and chronic disease (Diabetes). It should be pointed out that despite the fact that his status is alive at the end of the case, he died seven months later, sometime in January 1890. Leader of the Ballarat Gang.

Sidney Paget

Paul Thiriat

Turner, Miss Alice   [BOSC]   Female Alive   Most lovely young woman, Watson had ever seen in his life. She had violet eyes shining and a pink flush upon her cheeks Daughter of John Turner who hired Holmes to help prove the innocence of James McCarthy. Loved James McCarthy and was convinced of his innocents. Ran her father's estate.

Sidney Paget

Josef Friedrich

Turner, Mrs. [SCAN] Female Alive   Mrs. Turner brought up the tray of food. The landlady at 221b Baker street in all the other stories was Mrs Hudson, so there is some confusion about who Mrs. Turner is, she may of course have been a maid or someone who took over for Mrs. Hudson while she was away. The main point is she was only ever mention once in the Canon

Tuson, Sergeant [STOC] Male Alive   Sergeant in the city Police. Together with Constable Pollack, Arrested Beddington while the latter tried to rob Mawson & Williams of a hundred thousand pounds' worth of American railway bonds, with a large amount of scrip in mines and other companies.

Tussaud, Madame Anna Maria [MAZA] Female dead (Real Person 1761 – 1850)   French Artist know for the Madame Tussaud wax sculptures and museums. Sam Merton in talking about the Holmes effigy says "A fake, is it? Well, strike me! Madame Tussaud ain't in it. It's the living spit of him, gown and all."

Madame Tussaud

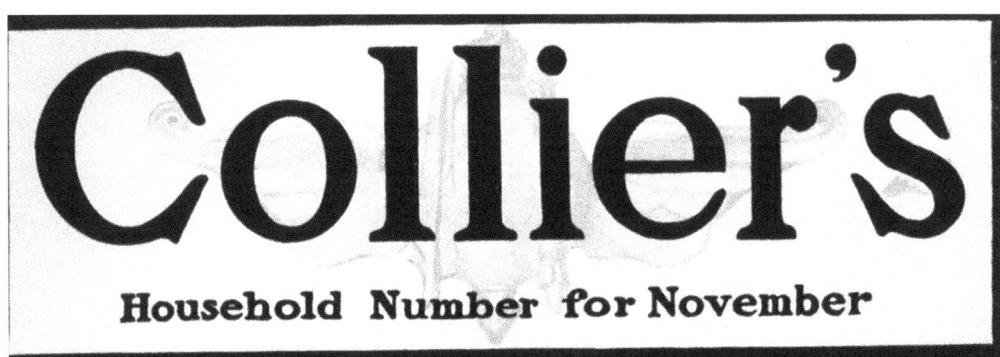

U is for Upper Norwood as in the Norwood Builder, unfortunately this was in Lower Norwood, rather than Upper Norwood.

U

Underwood, John and Sons [STUD] Male   Maker of hat found besides the dead body of Enoch Drebber. Gregson was surprised that Holmes had picked up on the maker's name from Drebber's Hat, Holmes did not pursue this lead, but Gregson did and was able to find out where Drebber had been living.

Address : 129, Camberwell Road

Upwood, Colonel [HOUN] Male Alive   Holmes had exposed the atrocious conduct of Colonel Upwood in connection with the famous card scandal of the Nonpareil Club

Uriah the Hittite [CROO] Male dead   Elite soldier in the army of King David. Sent to his death by King David so that he can claim Bathsheba, Uriah's wife. Nancy Barclay calls her husband 'David', since her husband had behaved like King David, sending Henry Wood on a suicide mission, so that he could court Henry's girl to be (then Devoy, now Nancy Barclay) Nancy Devoy would have been Bathsheba, Henry Wood = Uriah and James Barclay= King David

Uriah

V is for The Veiled Lodger

Vamberry, the wine merchant [MUSG] Inside a large box, Holmes opened were bundles of papers that detailed previous cases including the Vamberry, the wine merchant. A story never revealed.

Sidney Paget

Van Deher, Mr [VALL] Male Alive Owner of an Ironworks in Vermissa Valley, who was forced to sell his business because of threats from the Scowrers. He sold to West Gilmerton General Mining Company.

Van Jansen of Utrecht [STUD] dead Murdered person whom Holmes was reminded of when he saw the body of Enoch Js. Drebber. Murder took place in 1834.

Van Seddar, Mr. [MAZA] Male Alive The courier who Count Sylvius was going to use to take the Mazarin Stone out of the country to Amsterdam, where the gem was going to be cut into four pieces.

Van Shorst, Mr. [VALL] Male dead Unknown members of the Vermissa lodge Scowrer murdered this Mine or Ironworks owner.

Vandeleur, Beryl [HOUN] Female Alive See Mrs. Beryl Stapleton

Vandeleur, Jack [HOUN] Male Alive See Mr. Jack Stapleton

Vanderbilt [SUSS] As Holmes read through the 'V' section of his notebook looking for information about Vampires, he mentioned Vanderbilt and the Yeggman. (A yeggman is someone who breaks open safes.)

Sherlock Holmes Quote : "Voyage of the Gloria Scott, that was a bad business. I have some recollection that you made a record of it, Watson, though I was unable to congratulate you upon the result. Victor Lynch, the forger. Venomous lizard or gila. Remarkable case, that! Vittoria, the circus belle. Vanderbilt and the Yeggman. Vipers. Vigor, the Hammersmith wonder. Hullo! Hullo! Good old index. You can't beat it. Listen to this, Watson. Vampirism in Hungary. And again, Vampires in Transylvania."

Venner, Mr [ENGR] Male Partner in the Company Venner & Matheson. The well-known firm, of Greenwich. Victor Hatherley was apprenticed with them for seven years. Left them in 1887, using the inheritance from his poor father's death.

Venucci, Lucretia [SIXN] Female Alive She was the maid of the Princess of Colonna. She was involved in the stealing of the Pearl. She was the sister of Pietro Venucci, who was killed by Beppo. Like her Brother, probably came from Naples.

Address : Dacre Hotel

Venucci, Pietro [SIXN] Male dead He was a tall man, sunburned, very powerful, not more than thirty. He was poorly dressed, and yet did not appear to be a labourer. A horn-handled clasp knife was lying in a pool of blood beside him. There was no name on his clothing, and nothing in his pockets save an apple, some string, a shilling map of London, and a photograph, later found to be of Beppo. One of the greatest cut-throats in London. He was connected with the Mafia. He was sent to England to track down Beppo, who had broken the Mafia rules in some fashion and had taken the Pearl of the Borgia and hidden it in one of the Six Busts of Napoleon. He had a photograph of Beppo, so that he could track him down. He encountered Beppo at 131, Pitt Street, Kensington and had his throat cut on the steps of Horace Harker's house.

Nos loisirs

Verner, Dr. **[NORW]** **Male Alive** A young doctor, named Verner, had purchased Watson's small Kensington practice, and given with astonishingly little demur the highest price that Watson ventured to ask—an incident which only explained itself some years later when Watson found that Verner was a distant relation of Holmes', and that it was Waton's friend who had really found the money.

Vernet, Emile Jean-Horace **[GREE]** **Male dead (Real Person 1780 – 1863)** French artist and member of the Romanticism art movement. Famous for his battle painting and portraits Holmes' grandmother must be this Vernet's sister, if Holmes being born in 1854, if we go back two generations (2 x 30 years) we have a grandmother being born around 1894 making her this artist's older sister. And as if further proof is needed, this artist was a pipe smoker. Case Proven.

Sherlock Holmes Quote : "My ancestors were country squires, who appear to have led much the same life as is natural to their class. But, none the less, my turn that way is in my veins, and may have come with my grandmother, who was the sister of Vernet, the French artist. Art in the blood is liable to take the strangest forms."

Emile Jean Horace Vernet

Vibart, Jules   [LADY]   Male Alive   Boyfriend of the maid Miss Marie Devine. Worked as one of the head waiters at the Hotel National at Lausanne. He said that he thought the departure of Lady Frances Carfax from the Hotel, was due to the arrival of a tall, dark, bearded man. "Un sauvage—un veritable sauvage!"

Victoria, Queen   [SIGN]   Female Alive (Real Person 1819 – 1901)   her name was used in the arresting of Thaddeus Sholto by Athelney Jones "Mr. Sholto, it is my duty to inform you that anything which you may say will be used against you. I arrest you in the Queen's name as being concerned in the death of your brother."

Queen Victoria

Vigor **[SUSS]** As Holmes read through the 'V' section of his notebook looking for information about Vampires, he mentioned Vigor, the Hammersmith wonder.

Sherlock Holmes Quote : "Voyage of the Gloria Scott, that was a bad business. I have some recollection that you made a record of it, Watson, though I was unable to congratulate you upon the result. Victor Lynch, the forger. Venomous lizard or gila. Remarkable case, that! Vittoria, the circus belle. Vanderbilt and the Yeggman. Vipers. Vigor, the Hammersmith wonder. Hullo! Hullo! Good old index. You can't beat it. Listen to this, Watson. Vampirism in Hungary. And again, Vampires in Transylvania."

Villard, François Le **[SIGN]** **Male Alive** French detective Holmes helps out by refer him to two parallel cases, the one at Riga in 1857, and the other at St. Louis in 1871. regards Holmes as the teacher and himself as the pupil. Translating Holmes works into French, probably 'Ashes of the Various Tobaccos', 'Tracing of footsteps', 'influence of a trade upon the form of the hand'.

Sherlock Holmes Quote : "He has all the Celtic power of quick intuition, but he is deficient in the wide range of exact knowledge which is essential to the higher developments of his art"

Vittoria **[SUSS]** **Female** As Holmes read through the 'V' section of his notebook looking for information about Vampires, he mentioned Vittoria, the circus belle

Sherlock Holmes Quote : "Voyage of the Gloria Scott, that was a bad business. I have some recollection that you made a record of it, Watson, though I was unable to congratulate you upon the result. Victor Lynch, the forger. Venomous lizard or gila. Remarkable case, that! Vittoria, the circus belle. Vanderbilt and the Yeggman. Vipers. Vigor, the Hammersmith wonder. Hullo! Hullo! Good old index. You can't beat it. Listen to this, Watson. Vampirism in Hungary. And again, Vampires in Transylvania."

Vitus, St. **[STOC, GREE]** **Male dead (Real Person 290 – 303)** Martyred saint from Sicily. In the middle ages, people in Germany used to dance around a statue of him, this became very popular and this dancing became know as the St. Vitus dance. The Neurological disorder called Sydenham's Chorea produces rapid, uncoordinated jerking movements primarily affecting the face, hands and feet, much like the earlier German dancing and so is commonly called St. Vitus Dance. [STOC] Said that Mr. Farquhar suffered from St. Vitus Dance. [GREE] Mt Melas said James Latimer showed characteristics of St. Vitus Dance. "He pushed his face forward as he spoke and his lips and eyelids were continually twitching like a man with St. Vitus's dance"

St. Vitus

Von Bischoff of Frankfort [STUD] Male   Holmes says that this person escaped hanging in Frankfort in 1877, because Holmes' Blood test wasn't around.

Von Bork, Mr. [LAST] Male   Regarded himself a born sportsman. cigars smoker. A man who could hardly be matched among all the devoted agents of the Kaiser. His talents had recommended him for this English spying mission. Since he had taken on this mission his talents had become more and more manifest to the half-dozen people in the world who were really in touch with the truth. Was in a meeting with Baron Von Herling at the start of the story. Very sporting, yachting, hunting and playing polo. would match them in every game, his four-in-hand took the prize at Olympia. He would box with the young officers. Said to be a 'good old sport' 'quite a decent fellow for a German,' A hard-drinking, night-club, knock-about-town, devil-may-care young fellow, but the quiet country house of his was the centre of half the mischief in England, and the sporting squire the most astute secret-service man in Europe. When Baron Von Herling left, Altamont turned up and handed over the missing signals. Altamont tells him that the spies Jack James, Hollis and Steiner have all been arrested. Von Bork had a large safe with the combination that had been set four years previously to August 1914. Altamont hands over a package and receives £500 cheque. However the package is actually a copy of the book entitled Practical Handbook of Bee Culture, with Some Observations upon the Segregation of the Queen. Von Bork was then tied up and Watson and Holmes walk him to the car for transport to London. Von Bork was probably given Diplomatic immunity and would leave Britain for Germany

Frederic Dorr Steele   *Richard W. Wallace*

Von Goethe, Johann Wolfgang   [SIGN] Male dead (Real Person 1749 - 1832)
German write and statesman. Mentioned by Holmes

Sherlock Holmes Quote : "Wir sind gewohnt das die Menschen verhöhnen was sie nicht verstehen."
English Translation 'We are used to see that Man mocks what he never comprehends.'
"Goethe is always pithy."
"Schade, daß die Natur nur einen Mensch aus dir schuf, Denn zum würdigen Mann war und zum Schelmen der Stoff.
English Translation "Alas, that Nature made only one man of you, when there was material enough for a good man and a rogue."

Johann Wolfgang Von Goethe

Von Herder, Herr [EMPT] Male Alive Blind German Mechanic. Maker of the Admirable, unique, noiseless and powerful air rifle that belonged to Colonel Sebastian Moran. This gun was used to kill Ronald Adair in the story of the Empty House.

Sherlock Holmes Quote : "An admirable and unique weapon, noiseless and of tremendous power. I knew Von Herder, the blind German mechanic, who constructed it to the order of the late Professor Moriarty. For years I have been aware of its existence, though I have never before had the opportunity of handling it. I commend it very specially to your attention, Lestrade, and also the bullets which fit it."

Von Herling, Baron   [LAST] Male Alive He was a huge man, deep, broad, and tall, with a slow, heavy fashion of speech which had been his main asset in his political career. The chief secretary of the legation and spy who met with Von Bork before ,Holmes disguised as Altamont arrived. Drove a huge 100-horse-power Benz car Probably a 38/100hp.

Von Kramm, Count [SCAN] male Alive See Wilhelm Gottsreich Sigismond von Ormstein

Von Ormstein, Wilhelm Gottsreich Sigismond   [SCAN] male Alive Better known as 'The King of Bohemia', At least six feet six inches in height. Chest and limbs of a Hercules. His dress was rich with a richness which would, in England, be looked upon as akin to bad taste. Heavy bands of astrakhan were slashed across the sleeves and fronts of his double-breasted coat. Deep blue cloak which was thrown over his shoulders was lined with flame-coloured silk, and secured at the neck with a brooch which consisted of a single flaming beryl. Boots which extended Halfway up his calves, and which were trimmed at the tops with rich brown fur, Impression of barbaric opulence which was suggested by his whole appearance. He carried a broad-brimmed hat in his hand, while he wore across the upper part of his face, extending down past the cheekbones, a black vizard mask, From the lower part of the face he appeared to be a man of strong character, with a thick, hanging lip, and a long straight chin, suggestive of resolution pushed to the length of obstinacy. Client of Sherlock Holmes. Asked Holmes to recover a compromising photograph of him with Irene Adler. His future spouse was Clotilde Lothman von Saxe-Meningen, daughter of the King of Scandinavia. referenced in The story 'Case of Identity' presented Holmes with a snuffbox of old gold, with a great amethyst in the centre of the lid .

Address : Langham Hotel under the name of Count von Kramm.

Josef Friedrich   *Sidney Paget*

Von Saxe-Meningen, Clotilde Lothman   [SCAN]   Female Alive   Second daughter of the King of Scandinavia. The correct spelling is Saxe-Meiningen. Clotilde Lothman von Saxe-Meningen was the future spouse of the King of Bohemia. There is a real Saxe-Meiningen family, but no Clotilde Lothman belongs to it.

Von und Zu Grafenstein, Count   [LAST]   Male Alive   When the Nihilist Klopman tried to assassinate him, he was saved by Holmes. Was the elder brother of Von Bork's mother and so his uncle.

Von Waldbaum, Fritz   [NAVA]   Male   Holmes demonstrated the true facts of a case to this well-known specialist of Dantzig, who had wasted his energies upon what proved to be side-issues.

Von Wallenstein, Albrecht Wenzel Eusebius   [SCAN]   Male dead (Real Person 1583 – 1634)   Real military leader famous for being a bohemian general in the thirty years' war. Born in Hermanice, Bohemia, Assassinated in Eger (now Cheb) in BohemiaReferenced by Holmes, talking about the writing paper, the king had used.

Sherlock Holmes Quote : "Now for the 'Eg.' Let us glance at our Continental Gazetteer, Eglow, Eglonitz—here we are, Egria. It is in a German- speaking country—in Bohemia, not far from Carlsbad. 'Remarkable as being the scene of the death of Wallenstein, and for its numerous glass-factories and paper-mills.'

Albrecht Von Waldstein

**Von Zeppelin, Ferdinand Adolf Heinrich August Graf [LAST] Male Alive (
Real Person 1838 – 1917)** A German general and later inventor of the Zeppelin
rigid airships. In this story Baron Von Herling said "How still and peaceful it all
seems. There may be other lights within the week, and the English coast a less
tranquil place! The heavens, too, may not be quite so peaceful if all that the good
Zeppelin promises us comes true."

Ferdinand Adolf Heinrich August Graf Von Zeppelin

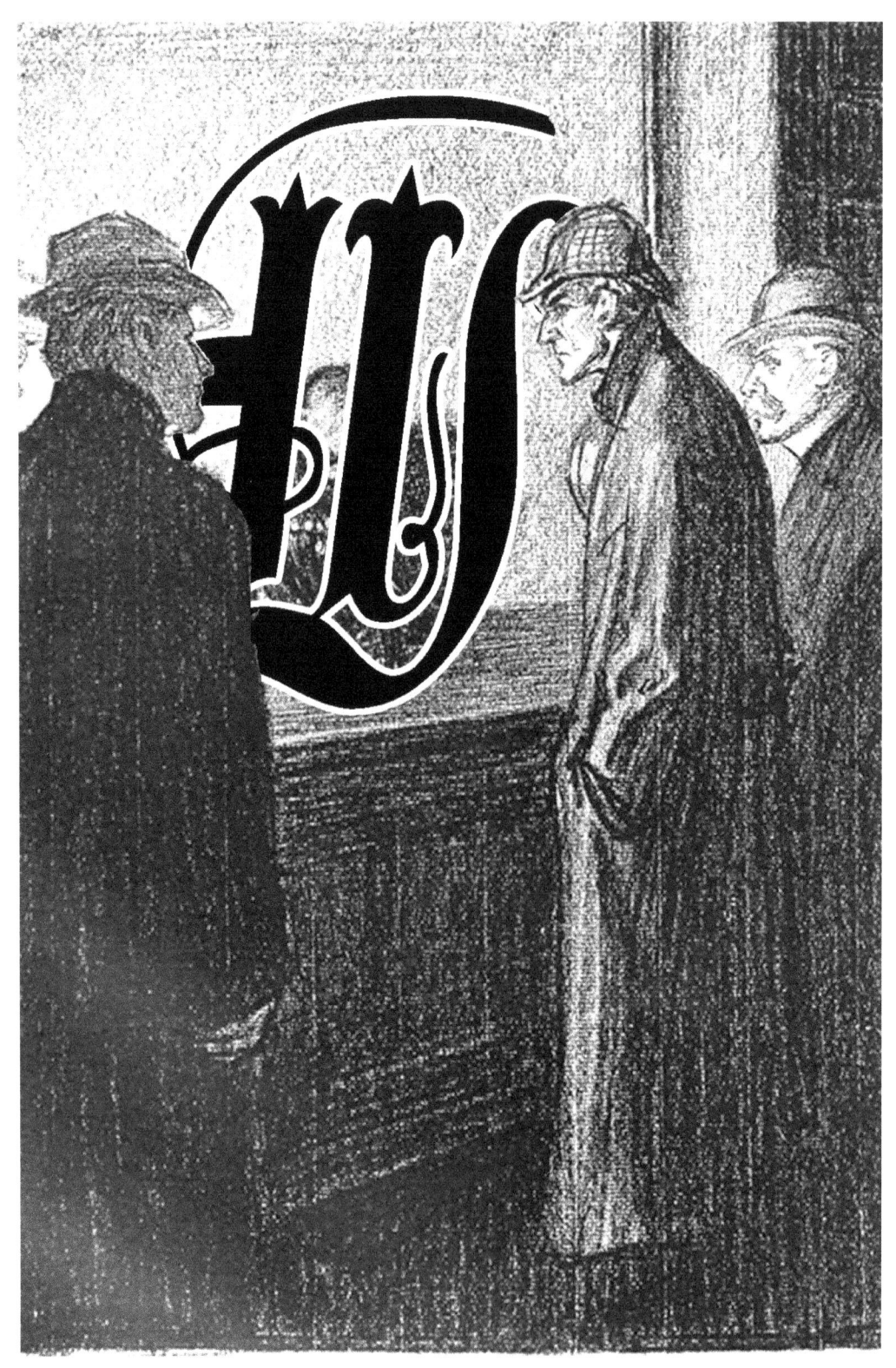

W is for Wisteria Lodge

W

Wagner, Richard   [REDC]   Male dead (Real Person 1813 – 1883)   German composer, theatre director and conductor.

Sherlock Holmes Quote : "Wagner night at Covent Garden! "Wagner night at Covent Garden! If we hurry, we might be in time for the second act."

Richard Wagner

Wainwright, Thomas Griffiths   [ILLU] Male dead (Real Person 1794 – 1840) English author, artist and suspected serial killer of various family members in order to get inheritance and insurance money. Holmes mentioned him when talking about Criminals and artists.

Sherlock Holmes Quote : "A complex mind, All great criminals have that. My old friend Charlie Peace was a violin virtuoso. Wainwright was no mean artist."

Thomas Griffiths Wainewright

Waldron, Mr. **[3GAR]** **Male dead** See Rodger Prescott

Walker, Brothers **[VALL]** **Male Alive** Brothers who owned a company in Vermissa valley who tried to pay a hundred dollars in protection money, but the treasurer, Carter, returned it and asked for five If Carter did not hear by Wednesday, their winding gear would get out of order. Carter stated that they had to burn their breaker last year before they became reasonable.

Wallenstein, Albrecht Wenzel Eusebius **[SCAN]** **Male dead** See Albrecht Wenzel Eusebius Von Wallenstein

Walter, Colonel Valentine **[BRUC]** **Male in prison** A very tall, handsome, light-bearded man of fifty. Younger brother of Sir James Walter. Was offered five thousand pounds for the plans. Made a copy or borrowed his brother's key and broke into the Woolwich Arsenal taking the Bruce-Partington Plans. However he was followed by Cadogen West, who trailed him until he met up with Oberstein in Caulfield Gardens, Kensington. As Oberstein opened the door to his house, Cadogen West rushed up and demanded to know what He and Oberstein were about to do with the papers. Oberstein had a short life-preserver, which he always carried it with him. Oberstein struck Cadogen West on the head, the blow was a fatal one and he was dead within five minutes. Together they placed Cadogen West's body onto a stationary Carriage roof from the back window. Was apprehended by Holmes who placed an advert in advertisement columns of The Daily Telegraph, supposedly coming from Pierot (Oberstein's alias) which read "Tonight. Same hour. Same place. Two taps. Most vitally important. Your own safety at stake. Pierrot." After capture, helped Holmes in getting the missing plans back by contacting Oberstein at the Hotel du Louvre, Paris. and arranging a meeting in the smoking-room of the Charing Cross Hotel. Colonel Walter died in prison towards the end of the second year of his sentence.

P. B. Hickling

G. Dutriac

Walter, Sir James   [BRUC]   Male dead   Had a brother called Colonel Valentine Walter. He was the actual official guardian of the Bruce-Partington papers. Famous government expert Had decorations and subtitles that filled two lines of a book of reference. He had grown grey in the service, was a gentleman, a favoured guest in the most exalted houses, and, above all, a man whose patriotism was beyond suspicion. He was one of two who have a key of the safe, the other key holder being Mr. Sidney Johnson. it was said by his brother Colonel Valentine Walter that "Sir James, was a man of very sensitive honour, and he could not survive such an affair. It broke his heart. He was always so proud of the efficiency of his department, and this was a crushing blow."

Walters, Police-Constable **[WIST]** **Male Alive** A Police constable told to be in possession of Wisteria Lodge. Rather nervous, complaining that "It's this lonely, silent house and the queer thing in the kitchen." He had seen a face at the window looking in at him. He described it's colour as "a kind of queer shade like clay with a splash of milk in it. Then there was the size of it—it was twice yours, sir. And the look of it—the great staring goggle eyes, and the line of white teeth like a hungry beast"

Arthur Twidle

Arthur Twidle

Warburton, Colonel **[ENGR]** **Male** A problem submitted to Holmes by Watson. One of only two. This case may have afforded a finer field for an acute and original observer Sadly Watson never writes about Colonel Warburton's madness.

Wardlaw, Colonel **[SILV]** **Male Alive** Owner of the Horse Pugilist. Pink cap. Blue and black jacket. Wessex Plate 50 Sovereigns each h ft. with 1000 Sovereigns added for four and five year olds. Second, £300. Third, £200. New course (one mile and five furlongs).

Warner, John   [WIST]   Male Alive   Late gardener of High Gable Had been sacked in a moment of temper by his imperious employer Mr. Henderson. Said that the gossip among the servants was that their master was terribly afraid of something. 'Sold his soul to the devil in exchange for money and expects his creditor to come up and claim his own.' Holmes employed him to be on guard at the gates of High Gable, Esher. Rescued Miss Burnett from Messrs Henderson and Lucas (Murillo & Lopez) while they attempted to take the train.

Warren, Mr.   [REDC]   Male Alive   Husband of Mrs Warner the landlady. Not well paid timekeeper at Morton and Waylight's, in Tottenham Court Road. Was abducted, by two men, as he stepped out of the house at around seven in the morning. They threw a coat over his head, and bundled him into a cab that was beside the curb. They then drove him around for an hour, and then opened the door pushed him out onto Hampstead Heath. It had been a case of mistaken identity, the abductors thought he was the lodger, but on realising their mistake has released him.

Address : A high, thin, yellow-brick edifice in Great Orme Street

Frederic Auer

Warren, Mrs.   [REDC]   Female Alive   Landlady of a high, thin, yellow-brick house in Great Orme Street. She asked Holmes for help regarding her current lodger of ten days. Nobody in the house had seen the lodger since his arrival at night ten days previously. The lodger was paying £5 a week instead of the normal fifty shillings (£2.50) a week, but with the proviso that he was to have a key of the house. and he was to be left entirely to himself and never, upon any excuse, to be disturbed. Meals were to be put on a chair outside his door when he rang a bell and the empty plates were to be removed when the bell was rang again. If the lodger wanted anything else he would print it on a slip of paper and leave it outside the door. Although the lodger spoke very good English, the messages left on slips of paper, showed a poor understanding. Further proof that a switch had taken place and that the original man was not actually the current lodger, was that, while the former was bearded and moustached, the cigarette stubs were so short that only a clean shaven man could have smoked them, in fact even a modest moustache would have been singed. Later Holmes visits Mrs. Warren and finds out the true identity of the lodger. Mrs Warren left a copy of the Daily Gazette every morning for the lodger.

Address : A high, thin, yellow-brick edifice in Great Orme Street

Richard W. Wallace

Warrender, Miss Minnie   [MAZA]   Holmes knew about Count Sylvius and knew the complete life history of Miss Minnie Warrender.

Watson Mrs.   [SIGN,SCAN]   Wife of Dr. John H. Watson. Maiden name was Mary Morstan, daughter of Captain Arthur Morstan. [SCAN] Mrs. Watson had given Mary Jane her notice as she was incorrigible. [TWIS] Mrs. Watson did needlework when Kate Whitney arrived at the Watson's home. Watson said that Folk who were in grief came to Mrs. Watson like birds to a lighthouse. She once called her husband James. (Hence the theory that the middle initial of H stood for Hamish, the Scottish for James) She was an old friend and school companion of Kate Whitney. Died after events of the Final problem (1891) and before the Empty House (1894)

Richard Gutschmidt   *Richard Gutschmidt*

Dr. John H. Watson

Watson, Dr John H   [ALL EXCEPT GLOR, BLAN, LION]   Male Alive   In the year 1878 took degree of Doctor of Medicine of the University of London. He played rugby for Blackheath. Then to Netley to go through the course prescribed for surgeons in the army. Attached to the Fifth Northumberland Fusiliers as Assistant Surgeon. Attached to the Berkshires. In battle of Maiwand and struck on the shoulder by a Jezail bullet which shattered the bone and grazed the subclavian artery. (27th July 1880) Returned home in the troopship "Orontes," and had to live on an income of eleven shillings and sixpence a day. Met Holmes in chemical laboratory of Saint Bartholomew's Hospital. Had an elder brother, H. Watson, now deceased.

Watson was middle-sized, strongly built man, square jaw, thick neck, with a moustache. He was quite handsome.

Was married at least twice, to Mary Morstan in 1889 , who died sometime between 1891 and 1894, causes unknown, and then to another woman, whose name is never mentioned.

He was about four years older than Sherlock Holmes, being born in 1850.

He was widely travelled and had been to Australia.

Was at school with Percy 'Tadpole' Phelps.

He looked up to Sherlock Holmes said of him that he would ever regard him as the best and the wisest man whom he have ever known.

Now some illustrations of Watson.

The first appearance of Watson in print in Beeton's Christmas Annual 1887

D. H. Friston

Then four years later, we get a chronologically earlier image of Dr. Watson, before he met Sherlock Holmes

George Hutchinson

ENGR

RETI

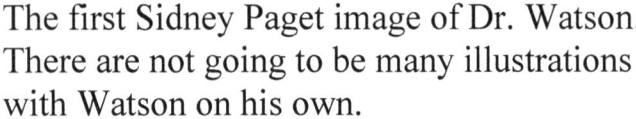

The first Sidney Paget image of Dr. Watson. There are not going to be many illustrations with Watson on his own.

Sidney Paget

Amberley in a rage, tears up the photo of his Wife

Frederic Dorr Steele

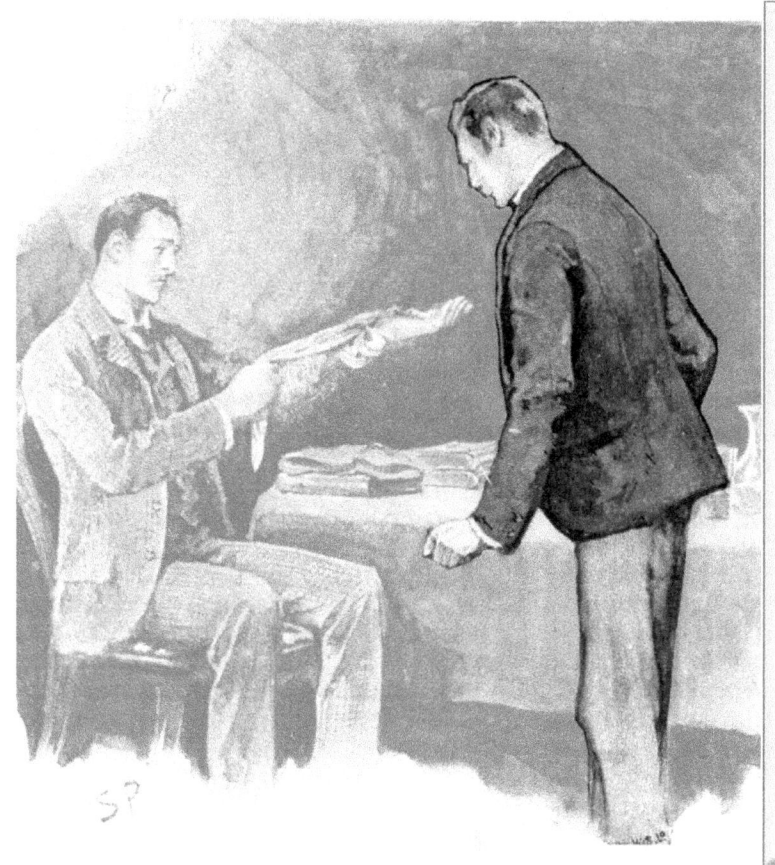

Is there a doctor in the House, Luckily, there is, and better yet, He know Sherlock Holmes

Sidney Paget

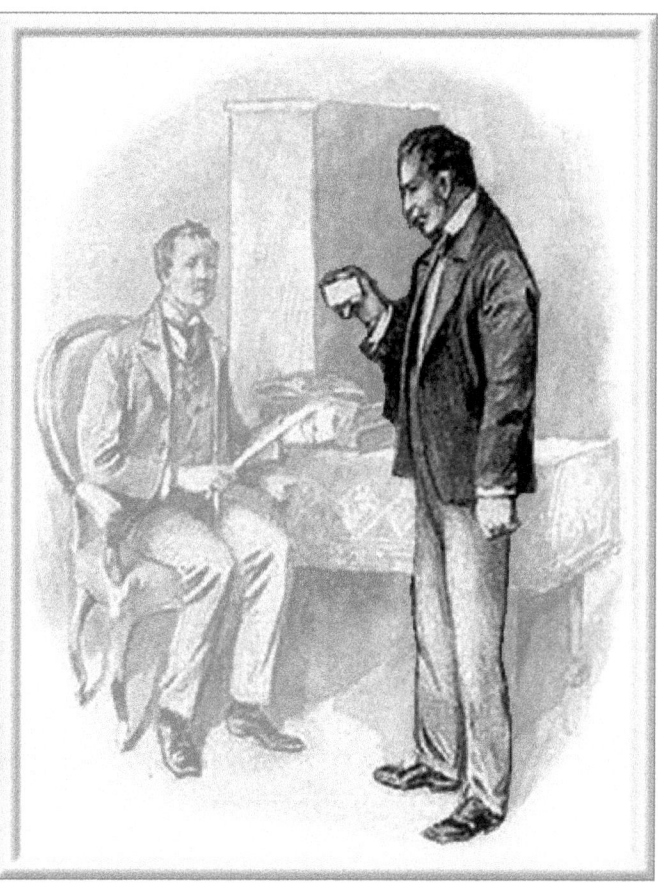

Watson treats Victor Hatherley's thumb after it was chopped off.

Josef Friedrich

BOSC

Watson takes the blame for spilling the fruit onto the floor and here is proof that it was Holmes all along

Sidney Paget

SILV

Watson lay upon the sofa and tried to interest himself in a yellow-backed novel.

Josef Friedrich

Watson and Holmes on their way to
Boscombe Valley, Note Sherlock's
headgear, the first Deerstalker image

Sidney Paget

Silver Blaze train trip this time, but same
clothes

Sidney Paget

Watson Helps Holmes restrain Von Bork in
their last ACD Adventure

Alfred Gilbert.

Watson returns to Reichenbach Falls, only
to find that Holmes is not there.

Sidney Paget

Watson gets the short end of the stick in this story as he has to interview Amberley and then travel to a remote village, to keep him out of the way.

Frederic Dorr Steele

One final image of Watson relaxing for once.

Watson lay upon the sofa and tried to interest himself in a yellow-backed novel.

Sidney Paget

Watson, H [SIGN] Male dead Elder brother of John Watson. Could also apply to John's father, as for the brother. Untidy habits, very untidy and careless. Had good prospects, but he threw away his chances. Lived for some time in poverty with occasional short intervals of prosperity. Took to drink and he died.

Sherlock Holmes Quote : "He was a man of untidy habits,—very untidy and careless. He was left with good prospects, but he threw away his chances, lived for some time in poverty with occasional short intervals of prosperity, and finally, taking to drink, he died. That is all I can gather."

Waylight, Mr.   [REDC]   Male   Junior Partner in the firm of Morton and Waylight's Employed Mr. Warren as a timekeeper in their Tottenham Court Road location.

Weiss, Mr   [SILV]   Probably Male   Owner of the company Weiss & Co., London. Maker of the ivory-handled knife with a very delicate, inflexible blade found in the possession of John Straker when he died. A cataract knife, a very delicate blade devised for very delicate work.

Wesson, Daniel B.   [VALL]   Male Alive (Real Person 1825 – 1906)   Partner in the American Firearms company Smith & Wesson. Jack McMurdo owned a Smith & Wesson revolver while he was living in Vermissa.

Daniel B. Wesson

Westaway, Mr   [COPP]   Male Alive   Founder of Westaway's well-known agency for governesses in the West End. This agency was managed by Miss Stoper. Miss Violet Hunter was interviewed for a position with Jephro Rucastle.

Westbury, Miss Violet   [BRUC]   Female Alive   white-faced young lady. Fiancée of John Cadogan West. They were on their way to the Woolwich Theatre (Barnard's Theatre), two dress-circle tickets were found on the dead body of Cadogen West. Knew her Fiancé was incapable of treason. Said "Arthur was the most single-minded, chivalrous, patriotic man upon earth. He would have cut his right hand off before he would sell a State secret confided to his keeping. It is absurd, impossible, preposterous to anyone who knew him."

Frederic Dorr Steele   *P. B. Hickling*

Westhouse, Mr. [IDEN] Male Senior partner in the company Westhouse & Marbank, the great claret importers of Fenchurch Street. The wine company has an office in Bordeaux, France. They employed Mr. James Windibank, Miss Mary Sutherland's step-father.

Westphail, Miss Honoria [SPEC] Female Alive Mrs Stoner's Maiden Sister and hence Helen and Julia Stoner's aunt. At Christmas in 1881, during a visit, Julia met a half-pay major of marines, to whom she became engaged.

Whitaker, Joseph [VALL] Male Alive There is a problem with the date this story takes place. Watson says that this story takes place at the end of the 1880s William Stuart Baring-Gould dates this story in 1888 while Jay Finley Christ dates it in 1889, both of these are correct as they are both at the end of the 1880s. The American section of this story takes place in 1875 and that was said to have been some twenty years previously, making the date around 1895, but Moriarty is killed in 1891, so rather than being twenty years ago, it has to be around fifteen. The reason this is explained here is because of further problems with the Porlock's cipher. It just doesn't decode in Whitaker's Almanac. The 1885 edition only goes up to page 472 1886 is no better with only 488, 1887 at least has enough pages, but 534 has a page on Orders of Chivalry, 1888 has a page on Chronological History of Astronomy, 1889 has a page on Celestial Objects and Phenomena for Observation, 1890 has a page on Foreign Countries - Tongking, Transvaal,

Tripoli. and 1891 only has 440 pages. thanks here to the Hathi Trust digital library, who have scanned numerous years of Whitaker's almanacs. Whitaker's Almanac originally published by J. Whitaker & Sons Watson suggested that an almanac was a possible source of the words in Porlock's message, Holmes agreed and suggested Whitaker's Almanac. Porlock's message was

"534 C2 13 127 36 31 4 17 21 41

DOUGLAS 109 293 5 37 BIRLSTONE

26 BIRLSTONE 9 47 171" From which Holmes deduced that it was page 534 and in column 2 that the words would be found. Finally the message was revealed, it read "There—is —Danger—may—come—very—soon—one—'Douglas'—rich—country—now—at—Birlstone—House—Birlstone—confidence—is—pressing."

Sherlock Holmes Quote : "Excellent, Watson! I am very much mistaken if you have not touched the spot. An almanac! Let us consider the claims of Whitaker's Almanac. It is in common use. It has the requisite number of pages. It is in double column. Though reserved in its earlier vocabulary, it becomes, if I remember right, quite garrulous towards the end." He picked the volume from his desk. "Here is page 534, column two, a substantial block of print dealing, I perceive, with the trade and resources of British India. Jot down the words, Watson! Number thirteen is 'Mahratta.' Not, I fear, a very auspicious beginning. Number one hundred and twenty-seven is 'Government'; which at least makes sense, though somewhat irrelevant to ourselves and Professor Moriarty. Now let us try again. What does the Mahratta government do? Alas! the next word is 'pig's-bristles.' We are undone, my good Watson! It is finished!"

White, Abel [SIGN] Male dead Mr. Abel White was an obstinate man. Was a kind man Indigo plantation owner located in Muttra near the border of the Northwest Provinces. Employed Jonathan Small as an overseer. Paid a fair wage. Often dropped into Jonathan Small's little shanty to smoke a pipe with him. he sat on his veranda, drinking whiskey-pegs and smoking cheroots, while the country was in a blaze about him. Died in the Indian Uprising.

Whitney, Elias [TWIS] Male dead Principal of the Theological College of St. George's Doctor of Divinity. Brother of Isa Whitney.

Whitney, Isa [TWIS] Female Alive He had a yellow, pasty face, drooping lids, and pinpoint pupils. Brother of the late Elias Whitney, D.D., (Doctor of Divinity) Principal of the Theological College of St. George's Addicted to opium because some foolish freak when he was at college. An object of mingled horror and pity to his friends and relatives. Frequented the 'Bar of Gold' opium den in upper

Swandem Lane. Watson rescued him from the Opium den and sent him home, so that Watson could join up with Holmes, who was also in the Opium den for another reason.

Whitney, Kate   [TWIS]   Female Alive   Clad in some dark-coloured stuff, with a black veil. Old friend of Mary Watson and she came to call on her to try and get help in locating her husband. He was addicted to Opium and so Watson volunteered to go to the 'Bar of Gold' den and bring him home.

Whittington, Lady Alicia   [NOBL]   Female Alive   Attended the Wedding of Miss Hatty Doran and Lord Robert St. Simon.

Whyte, Guliolmi   [STUD]   Male dead   Publisher of 'De Jure inter Gentes'—published in Latin at Liege in the Lowlands, in 1642. english translation being 'Of the law between men' Holmes was talking about a book he was reading, while he awaited the murderer of Enoch Drebber, this person was a previous owner of the book.
Sherlock Holmes Quote : "Philippe de Croy, whoever he may have been. On the flyleaf, in very faded ink, is written 'Ex libris Guliolmi Whyte.' I wonder who William Whyte was. Some pragmatical seventeenth-century lawyer, I suppose. His writing has a legal twist about it.

Wiggins   [STUD,SIGN]   Male Alive   Leader of the Baker Street division of the detective police force, more commonly known as the Baker Street Irregulars. spokesman for the six dirty little scoundrels or Street Arabs. [STUD] Asked to find the cabman Jefferson Hope [SIGN] Asked to find the steam launch Aurora.
Sherlock Holmes Quote : [SIGN] That wire was to my dirty little lieutenant, Wiggins"

George Hutchinson   *Richard Gutschmidt*

Wilcox, Chester   [VALL]   Male Alive   Was chief foreman of the Iron Dike Company. He was a hard citizen, an old colour sergeant of the war, all scars and grizzle. Twice the Lodge had tried to kill him, but they had no luck, and Jim Carnaway lost his life over it. Carnaway was around his house and was shot and killed by Wilcox. He was always armed and shoots quick and straight, with no questions asked. Had a wife and three children. John McMurdo blew up his house helped by Manders and Reilly, but Wilcox and family had moved out the day before. .

Address : house on Iron Dike crossroad

Wild, Jonathan   [VALL]   Male Alive (Real Person 1682/3 – 1725)   He was a Famous London underworld figure . He operated on both sides of the law. As a public-spirited crime fighter called the "Thief-Taker General" and simultaneously he ran a significant criminal empire, and used his crime fighting removed rivals and launder the proceeds of his own crimes when posing as a crime fighter. Became a powerful gang-leader, he manipulated the legal systems, collecting the rewards offered for valuables which he had stolen himself. He bribed prison guards to release his colleagues. Would blackmail any who crossed him. He was responsible for the arrest and execution of Jack Sheppard, a petty thief and burglar It became known by his men that he was duplicitous, so his men gave evidence against him. He attempted suicide, but was eventually hanged at Tyburn in front of a massive crowd.

Sherlock Holmes Quote : "Jonathan Wild wasn't a detective, and he wasn't in a novel. He was a master criminal, and he lived last century—1750 or thereabouts."

Jonathan Wild

Wilder, James [PRIO] Male Alive A very young man. He was small, nervous, alert, with intelligent, light-blue eyes and mobile features. Secretary to the Duke of Holdernesse. Illegitimate son of the Duke. Employed Reuben Hayes to kidnap the Duke's true heir, Lord Saltire, in order that he could force the Duke to recognise him. Unfortunately, Lord Saltire was seen leaving and followed by the German Master, Heidegger, who was then killed on the trail by Hayes. He was horrified by the death of Heidegger and confessed all to the Duke. In the end it was decided that he should seek his fortune in Australia, never to return.

Frederic Dorr Steele   *Sidney Paget*

**Wilhelm ll, Kaiser Friedrich Wilhelm Viktor Albert [LAST]   Male Alive (
Real Person 1859 – 1941)** The last German Emperor and King of Prussia. A
friend of the Assassinated Archduke Franz Ferdinand of Austria, he offered
support to help Austria-Hungary in destroying the secret organisation called the
Black Hand that had planned the murder. The Black Hand were believed to have
come from Serbia. The Death of the Archduke lead to Austria-Hungary declaring
war on Serbia, Russia mobilised to defend Serbia and because of all the alliances
of support between various countries, instead of a simple little war, Most of
Europe got involved. This Story takes place on the 2nd August 1914, Britain didn't
declare war until ten days later. Mr. Von Bork is said to be a devoted agent of the
Kaiser.

Kaiser Wilhelm II

Willaby, Arthur [VALL] Male Alive The two Willabys were men of action, tall, lithe young fellows with determined faces. Were involved in the attack on the Editor of the Herald newspaper James Stanger. The group was lead by Ted Baldwin and others in the group were Gower, Mansel, Scanlan and John McMurdo, there were two others to guard the door. Joined in on the entrapment of Birdy Edwards together with Boss McGinty, Baldwin, Harraway, Tiger Cormac and Carter. One of the brothers was called Arthur, the name of the other one is unknown. Escaped the scaffold and ended up in prison.

William ll, King (Refua) [VALL] Male dead (Real Person 1056 – 1100) William ll of England was called William Rufus, Rufus being the Latin for 'The Red', because of his red hair. Third son of William the Conqueror, he had two elder brothers, Robert Curthose and Richard. Richard died while hunting in the new forest. Robert inherited Normandy and William was crowned king of England in 1087. He died in a hunting accident in 1100, when an arrow hit him in the lungs Part of the ancient Manor House of Birlstone dated back to the time of the first crusade, when Hugo de Capus built a fortalice in the centre of the estate, which had been granted to him by the Red King.

King William II

William lll, King of Holland   [IDEN]   Male Alive (Real Person 1817 – 1890)
Reigning family of Holland   Standing at 6'5" (196 cm) he was an exceptionally
large and strong man by the standards of his age. Presented Holmes with a ring
though the matter in which he served them was of such delicacy that Holmes
could not confide it even to Watson. Now interestingly enough William III was
known to be a philanderer and had several dozen illegitimate children from
various mistresses, but perhaps not at the age of 71, but who can tell.

William lll, King of Holland

William lV, King   [3GAR]   Male dead (Real Person 1765 – 1837)   King of England from 26 June 1830 until 20 June 1837 Predecessor was George lll Successor William lV The Georgian Period Architectural style developed around the time of the first four Georges, 1714 - 1830, and sometimes William lV. Holmes asked Nathan Garrideb about his home, whether it was Queen Anne or Georgian period.

Sherlock Holmes Quote : "I am a bit of an archaeologist myself when it comes to houses, I was wondering if this was Queen Anne or Georgian."

King William IV

Williams   [SIGN]   Male Alive   prize-fighters in the employ of Major Sholto. He was once lightweight champion of England. Met with Mary Morstan, Holmes and Watson at the third pillar from the left outside the Lyceum Theatre

The Boston Observer

Williams, Charlie   [VALL]   Male dead   One of the victims of Lawlers & Andrews. They were prepared to talk until the cows come home about the killing of Charlie Williams or of Simon Bird

Williams, James Baker   [WIST]   Male Alive   An owner of a large house in the Esher area. His details were sent to Holmes by the Allan brothers, chief land agents in the village of Esher.

Address : Forton Old Hall, Esher

Williams, Mr.   [STOC]   Male Alive   Junior partner in the company, Mawson & Williams', the great stockbroking firm in Lombard Street. They were about the richest house in London. guardians of securities which amount in the aggregate to a sum of considerably over a million sterling. They advertised for a position and offered it to Hall Pycroft, sight unseen. But they almost lost a fortune when the person pretending to be Hall Pycroft, Nearly a hundred thousand pounds' worth of American railway bonds, with a large amount of scrip in mines and other companies, were discovered in the bag of the thief.

Williamson, Mr.   [SOLI]   Male in prison   Williamson was a white-bearded man Mr. Williamson was the name of the tenant at Charlington Hall. He was a respectable elderly gentleman. He lived alone with a small staff of servants at the Hall unfrocked clergyman. 'Married' Jack Woodley to Miss Violet Smith in an illegal ceremony and was later charged with abduction and assault, getting seven years in prison.

Address : Charlington Hall, Farnham

Martin Van Maele   *Sidney Paget*

Willows, Dr. [BOSC]   Male Alive   The doctor was treating John Turner. Said that Johm Turner was s a wreck and that his nervous system was shattered. Mr. McCarthy was the only man alive who had known John Turner in the old days in Victoria.

Wilson, Brother [VALL]   Male Alive   Boss McGinty said "You'll do, Tiger Cormac. If you handle it as well as you did the last, you won't be wrong. And you, Wilson." A teen who complained that he didn't have a pistol when he went to kill Andrew Rae. Not to be confused with the other three wilsons in this story, the Police Sergeant, the alias of Birdy Edwards (Steve Wilson) and the district ruler, Bartholomew Wilson.

Wilson, Canary-trainer [BLAC]   Male   Holmes ended a 1895 case with the arrest of Wilson, the notorious canary-trainer, which removed a plague-spot from the East-End of London.

Wilson, District Ruler Bartholomew   [VALL]   Male   Was the district ruler of lodges that included the one of which John McMurdo was a member.

Wilson, Jabez   [REDH]   Male Alive   Very stout, florid-faced, elderly gentleman with fiery red hair (Blazing) Tattoo of a fish with delicate pink scales on right wrist. small fat-encircled eyes looked like an average commonplace British tradesman, obese, pompous, and slow. rather baggy grey shepherd's check trousers A not over-clean black frock-coat, unbuttoned in the front, and a drab waistcoat with a heavy brassy Albert chain, and a Chinese coin dangling down as an ornament. A frayed top-hat and a faded brown overcoat with a wrinkled velvet collar lay upon a chair beside him. Arc-and-compass breast pin Previously had been a ship's carpenter. He takes snuff. He is a Freemason. He had been in China, Shiny right cuff for five inches and left one had smooth patch near elbow Had extreme chagrin and discontent on his face when being interviews by Holmes. arc-and-compass breast pin. Widower with no family. Was paid £4 per week for eight weeks by the Red Headed League. Copied out from the Encyclopaedia Britannica for eight weeks covering abbots, Archery, Armour, Architecture & Attica (hopefully not in that order) The Advert for the Red-Headed League was discovered in the Morning Chronicle on April 27, 1890 The Red-Headed League was dissolved October 9, 1890 (There is a problem with dates October 9 is not two months after April 27)

Address : Pawnbroker's Sax-Coburg Square

Sidney Paget

Josef Friedrich

Wilson, Mr. [HOUN] Male Alive District messenger offices Manager. Was helped by Holmes in a little case. He said "You saved my good name, and perhaps my life." Employed a lad called Cartwright.

Sherlock Holmes Quote : "Ah, Wilson, I see you have not forgotten the little case in which I had the good fortune to help you?"

Sidney Paget

Wilson, Police Sergeant [VALL] Male Alive A tall, formal, melancholy man. Policeman in charge of the Sussex Constabulary. The first alarm of the incident at Birlstone Manor House reached him at the small local station at eleven forty-five. Stood guard on the murder scene at Birlstone Manor House .

Wilson, Rev [GLOR] Male dead Partner of Jack Prendergast, who posed as the Ship's chaplain onboard the 'Gloria Scott'. Supplied the prisoners with guns and killed the Captain. Died in the explosion of the vessel when it blew up.

Sidney Paget *William H. Hyde*

Wilson, Sir Archdale   [SIGN]   Male dead (Real Person 1803 – 1874)   Soldier who distinguished himself in the British Indian Army. Was commended for his part in the capture of Delhi after a mutiny.   Mentioned in Jonathan Small narrative, when he said "Well, there's no use my telling you gentlemen what came of the Indian mutiny. After Wilson took Delhi and Sir Colin relieved Lucknow the back of the business was broken."

Sir Archdale Wilson

Wilson, Steve   [VALL]   Male dead   See John Douglas

Winchester, Mr. Oliver Fisher [VALL] Male dead (Real Person 1810 – 1880)
Known for founding the Winchester Rifle company. In the story, It was stated that a guard of police, armed with Winchester rifles, had been requisitioned for the defence of the Newspaper office.

Oliver Fisher Winchester

Windibank, James   [IDEN]   Male Alive   Five years and two months older than Mary Sutherland As James Windibank Sturdy, middle-sized fellow, some thirty years of age, clean-shaven, and sallow-skinned, with a bland, insinuating manner, and a pair of wonderfully sharp and penetrating grey eyes As Hosmer Angel He was a very shy man. He would rather walk with me in the evening than in the daylight, for he said that he hated to be conspicuous. Very retiring and gentlemanly he was. Even his voice was gentle. He'd had the quinsy and swollen glands when he was young, and it had left him with a weak throat, and a hesitating, whispering fashion of speech. He was always well dressed, very neat and plain, but his eyes were weak, just as mine are, and he wore tinted glasses against the glare. As Hosmer Angel five ft. seven in. Strongly built; sallow complexion, black hair, a little bald in the centre, bush, black side-whiskers and moustache; tinted glasses, slight infirmity As James Windibank Worked for Westhouse & Marbank, the great claret importers of Fenchurch Street. The wine company has an office in Bordeaux, France. As Hosmer Angel Worked as a cashier in an office in Leadenhall Street. Picked up letters addressed to him at the Leadenhall Street Post Office. His Step-daughter gave him money she received from an inheritance, he wanted to maintain that financial stream so he conspired with his wife to put their daughter Miss Mary Sutherland off men for years. Wooed his step-daughter as in the guise of Hosmer Angel, bringing her to the brink of marriage and then mysteriously disappearing.

Address : 31 Lyon Place, Camberwell.

Sidney Paget

Josef Friedrich

Windigate, Mr. [BLUE] Male Alive Ruddy-faced, white-aproned landlord at the Alpha Pub Instituted a Goose club at his pub, which, on consideration of some few pence every week, we were each to receive a bird at Christmas. Purchased two dozen geese from Mr Beckinridge in Covent Garden at 12s. each. Supplied the Goose to Mr Henry Baker.

Windle, Division Master J. W. [VALL] Male Alive Division Master of Merton County Lodge 249. who wrote to lodge 341, Vermissa as follows: "DEAR SIR: There is a job to be done on Andrew Rae of Rae & Sturmash, coal owners near this place. You will remember that your lodge owes us a return, having had the service of two brethren in the matter of the patrolman last fall. You will send two good men, they will be taken charge of by Treasurer Higgins of this lodge, whose address you know. He will show them when to act and where. Yours in freedom, J.W. WINDLE D.M.A.O.F. (Division Master Ancient Of Freemasonry ?) Windle had never refused requests from Lodge 341, Vermissa, when they had

had occasion to ask for the loan of a man or two, and they consider that it was not for us to refuse him.

Winter, James   **[3GAR]**   **Male Alive**   See John Garrideb

Winter, Miss Kitty   **[ILLU]**   **Female Alive**   A slim, flame-like young woman with a pale, intense face, youthful, and yet so worn with sin and sorrow that one could read the terrible years which had left their leprous mark upon her. Ex-lover of the Baron, who had discarded her, She know about the Baron's secret lust diary and wanted to get her own back on the Baron. "I'm easy to find," she said, "Hell, London, gets me every time. Same address for Porky Shinwell. We're old mates, Porky, you and I. But, by cripes! there is another who ought to be down in a lower hell than we if there was any justice in the world! That is the man you are after, Mr. Holmes." Tried to persuade Miss Violet De Merville of the error of marrying Baron Gruner, but ended up screaming 'You fool! You unutterable fool!' Went with Holmes to find the secret diary, but she carried a bottle of vitriol, which she throw into the face of the Baron as he followed Holmes into the garden. There were proceedings against Miss Kitty Winter on the grave charge of vitriol-throwing but Such were the extenuating circumstances that came out in the trial that the sentence, was the lowest that was possible for such an offence.

Howard K. Elcock   *Frederic Dorr Steele*

Wombwell, George   **[VEIL]**   **Male dead**   Owner of a famous Menagerie during the Regency and early Victorian. Founded Wombwell's Travelling Menagerie. Mentioned by Holmes as he explained to Watson, who Mrs. Ronder was.

Sherlock Holmes Quote : "It will probably come back to your memory as I talk. Ronder, of course, was a household word. He was the rival of Wombwell, and of Sanger, one of the greatest showmen of his day. There is evidence, however, that he took to drink, and that both he and his show were on the down grade at the time of the great tragedy.

George Wombwell

Wood, Dr. [VALL] Male Alive   A brisk and capable general practitioner from the village. Dr. Wood found a good-sized hammer which had been lying on the rug in front of the fireplace—a substantial, workmanlike hammer. They had hoped that John Douglas might have hit his assailant, but there were no signs of violence upon it.

Wood, Henry [CROO] Male Alive   The man sat all twisted and huddled in his chair in a way which gave an indescribably impression of deformity; but the face which he turned towards us, though worn and swarthy, must at some time have been remarkable for its beauty. He looked suspiciously at us now out of yellow-shot, bilious eyes, and, without speaking or rising, he waved towards two chairs. Corporal Henry Wood was the smartest man in the 117th foot. Barclay was sergeant in the same company The belle of the regiment and the finest girl that ever had the breath of life between her lips, was Nancy Devoy, the daughter of the colour-sergeant. Both Wood and Barclay loved Nancy Devoy, but she only had eyes for Wood, so Barclay arranged for Wood to be captured rebels in order to remove him. The rebels took him away with them in their retreat, he was tortured and tried to get away, and was captured and tortured again. He eventually managed to escape and wandered about for many a year, and at last came back to the Punjaub, where he lived mostly among the natives and picked up a living by the conjuring tricks that he had learned. At last he determined to see England before he died and ended up in Aldershot. Met up with Nancy Barclay and revealed who he was and what her husband had done. Followed her home and witnessed the altercation between husband and wife and when he appeared the shock to James Barclay was too much and he dropped down dead. "The bare sight of me was like a bullet through his guilty heart."

Sidney Paget

William H. Hyde

Wood, J.G. [LION] Male dead (Real Person 1827 – 1889) English writer of natural history. Holmes mentions that author and his work 'Out of Doors (the full title is Out of Doors : A selection of original article on practical natural history, published in 1874) and quotes from it. The actual quote is ' If the bather or shore wanderer should happen to see, either tossing upon the waves or thrown upon the beach, a loose, roundish mass of tawny membranes and fibres, something like a very large handful of lion's mane and silver paper, let him beware of the object, and, sacrificing curiosity to discretion, give it as wide a berth as possible. For this is the fearful stinger, scientifically called Cyanea capillata, the most plentiful and the most redoubtable of our venomous medusae." He goes on to describe the encounter. p.139 onwards. It is interesting to wonder whether Holmes also had another of Wood's book, called, 'Bees: Their habits, Management and Treatments (1860)

Sherlock Holmes Quote : "Here is a book, which first brought light into what might have been forever dark. It is 'Out of Doors', by the famous observer, J.G. Wood. Wood himself very nearly perished from contact with this vile creature, so he wrote with a very full knowledge. Cyanea capillata is the miscreant's full name, and he can be as dangerous to life as, and far more painful than, the bite of the cobra. Let me briefly give this extract. "'If the bather should see a loose roundish mass of tawny membranes and fibres, something like very large handfuls of lion's mane and silver paper, let him beware, for this is the fearful stinger, Cyanea capillata.'

John George Wood

Woodhouse, Mr [STOC] Male Alive Partner in Coxon & Woodhouse's, of Draper's Gardens. The Venezuelan loan had caused a crash and the company a nasty cropper. This resulted in twenty-seven clerks being laid off, including Hall Pycroft.

Woodhouse, Mr. [BRUC] Male Unknown Holmes was moaning about the weather and said how easy it would be to pounce on somebody. A villain, who would liked to have ended Holmes' life.

Sherlock Holmes Quote : "Suppose that I were Brooks or Woodhouse, or any of the fifty men who have good reason for taking my life, how long could I survive against my own pursuit? A summons, a bogus appointment, and all would be over."

Woodley, Jack [SOLI] Male Alive Coarse, puffy-faced, red-moustached young man, with his hair plastered down on each side of his forehead. Said that he was a friend of Violet Smith's Uncle, Ralph Smith and tried to get violet Smith to fall in love with him. Played cards on journey home to England with Bob Carruthers to see who would be violet smith's suitor. Violet Smith called him a bully to others, but had other intentions towards her. Fought with Holmes in pub and ended up being taken home in a cart. Abducted Violet Smith and forced her to marry him in a ceremony conducted by Mr. Williamson. Was shot by Bob Carruthers Was charged with abduction and assault, getting ten years in prison.

Sherlock Holmes Quote : "Woodley ended a string of abuse by a vicious back-hander which I failed to entirely avoid. The next few minutes were delicious. It was a straight left against a slogging ruffian. I emerged as you see me. Mr. Woodley went home in a cart,"

Address : Stayed with Mr. Williamson at Charlington Hall, Farnham

Sidney Paget   *Martin Van Maele*

Woodley, Miss Edith [EMPT] Female Alive Was engaged to Ronald Adair, but the engagement had been broken off by mutual consent some months before.

Wright, Theresa [ABBE] Female Alive A gaunt woman. "She has been with Mary Fraser all her life," said Hopkins. "Nursed her as a baby, and came with her to England when they first left Australia eighteen months ago. She was the kind of maid you don't pick up nowadays. She was an interesting person, this stern Australian nurse. Taciturn, suspicious, ungracious, it took some time before

Holmes' pleasant manner and frank acceptance of all that she said thawed her into a corresponding amiability. She did not attempt to conceal her hatred for her late employer.

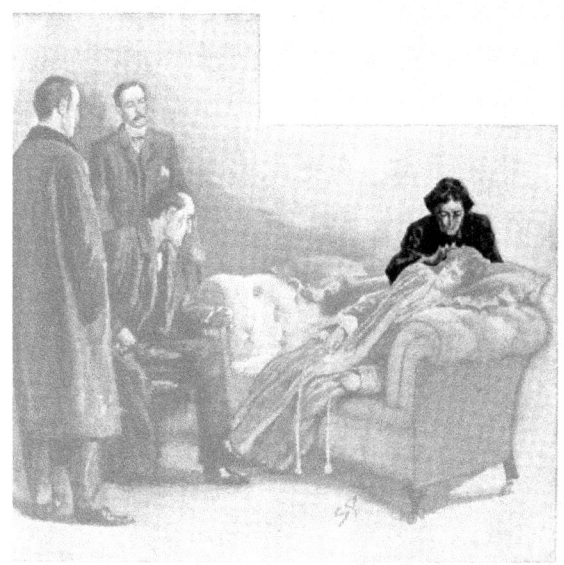

Sidney Paget

Richard Gutschmidt

Y is for The Adventure of the Yellow Face.

Z is for er, erm Zeppelin that Baron Von Herling threatened would fly over England

Y

Youghal [MAZA] Male alive Inspector of Scotland Yard of Criminal Investigation Department(CID). Holmes gave a note to Watson which he had to give to Youghal at Scotland Yard.

Young, Brigham [STUD] Male dead (Real Person 1801 – 1877) Elder Stangerson said "In a few days you will have recovered from your fatigues. In the meantime, remember that now and forever you are of our religion. Brigham Young has said it, and he has spoken with the voice of Joseph Smith, which is the voice of God." He went to visit John Ferrier and told him that Lucy Ferrier was to marry either Joseph Stangerson or Enoch Drebber and not the Gentile Jefferson Hope.

Charles William Carter

Richard Gutschmidt

Yuanzhang, Zhu [ILLU] Male dead See Hung-wu

Yung-lo [ILLU] Male dead   He was the third Emperor of the Ming dynasty (1368-1644), reigning from 1402 to 1424. Predecessor Emperor Jianwen Successor Emperor Hongxi   Holmes asked Watson to learn as much as he could about Chinese ceramics, so in the process, Watson learned of the hallmarks of the great artist-decorators, of the mystery of cyclical dates, the marks of the Hung-wu and the beauties of the Yung-lo, the writings of Tang-ying, and the glories of the primitive period of the Sung and the Yuan dynasties. So Watson was learning about early Ming items.

Z

Zamba, Mr. **[REDC]** **Male Alive** Junior Partner of the great firm of Castalotte and Zamba, who were the chief fruit importers of New York. Was an invalid and so much of the power resided in his partner's hands.

Zeppelin, Ferdinand Adolf Heinrich August Graf Von **[LAST]** **Male Alive**
See Ferdinand Adolf Heinrich August Graf Von Zeppelin

Zhu Di **[ILLU]** **Male dead** See Yung-lo

Edwards, Birdy [VALL], 150
Egan, Brother [VALL], 150
Eley, Charles [SPEC], 150
Eley, William [SPEC], 150
Elise, (friend of Lysander Stark [ENGR], 151
Elman, Rev J.C. [RETI], 151
Elrige, Mr [DANC], 152
Emsworth, Colonel [BLAN], 152
Emsworth, Godfrey [BLAN], 153
Emsworth, Mrs [BLAN], 154
Ernest, Dr. Ray [RETI], 154
Escott, Mr. [CHAS], 155
Etherege, Mrs. [IDEN], 155
Euclid of Alexandria [STUD,SIGN], 155
Evans, (Convict [GLOR], 156
Evans, Carrie [SHOS], 156
Evans, Killer [3GAR], 157
Evans, Policemen [VALL], 157
Faber, Johann Eberhard [3STU], 159
Fairbairn, Alec [CARD], 159
Falder, Hugo [SHOS], 160
Falder, Lady Beatrice [SHOS], 160
Falder, Norman [SHOS], 161
Falder, Odo [SHOS], 161
Falder, Sir James [SHOS], 161
Falder, Sir William [SHOS], 162
Farintosh, Mrs. [SPEC], 162
Farquhar, Mr. [STOC], 162
Ferguson, Baby [SUSS], 162
Ferguson, Captain [3GAB], 163
Ferguson, Jack [SUSS], 163
Ferguson, Mr [ENGR], 164
Ferguson, Mr. [THOR], 164
Ferguson, Mrs. [SUSS], 164
Ferguson, Robert [SUSS], 164
Ferrers, Mr [PRIO], 167
Ferrier, Bob [STUD], 167
Ferrier, Dr. [NAVA], 167
Ferrier, John [STUD], 167
Ferrier, Lucy [STUD], 168
Ffolliott, Sir George [WIST], 169
Fisher, Dr. Penrose [DYIN], 169
Flaccus, Quintus Horatius [IDEN], 169
Flaubert, Gustave [REDH], 169
Flowers, Lord [SECO], 169
Forbes, Inspector [NAVA], 170
Ford, Henry [LAST], 170
Fordham, Dr. [GLOR], 170
Fordham, Mr. [FIVE], 170
Forrester, Inspector [REIG], 171
Forrester, Mrs. Cecil [SIGN], 171

Fortescue, Mr [3STU], 171
Fournaye, Mme. Henri [SECO], 171
Fowler, Mr [COPP], 172
Frankland, Mr. [HOUN], 172
Fraser, Miss Mary [ABBE], 173
Fraser, the tutor [HOUN], 173
Freebody, Major [FIVE], 173
Gaboriau, Emile [STUD], 175
Gabriel, Archangel [VEIL], 175
Garcia, Beryl [HOUN], 176
Garcia, Mr. [WIST], 176
Garcia, Mr. Aloysius [WIST], 176
Garrideb, Alexander Hamilton [3GAR], 177
Garrideb, Howard [3GAR], 177
Garrideb, John [3GAR], 177
Garrideb, Nathan [3GAR], 178
Gelder, Mr. [SIXN], 179
George l, King [3GAR], 180
George ll, King [VALL, 3GAR], 181
George lll, King [3GAR], 181
George lV, King [3GAR], 182
Gibson, Mrs. Maria [THOR], 183
Gibson, Neil J. [THOR], 184
Gilchrist, Mr. [3STU], 186
Gilchrist, Sir Jabez [3STU], 186
Gladstone, William Ewart [TWIS], 186
Gold King, The [THOR], 187
Goldini, Restaurant [BRUC], 187
Gordon, Major-General Charles George
    [CARD,RESI], 187
Gorgiano, Giuseppe [REDC], 188
Gorot, Charles [NAVA], 189
Gower, Brother [VALL], 189
Graham, Mr. [NORW], 189
Gravelet, Jean Francois [SIGN], 189
Greathed, General Sir Edward Harris [SIGN], 189
Green, Admiral peter [LADY], 190
Green, Hon. Philip [LADY], 190
Gregory, Inspector [SILV], 191
Gregson, Inspector Tobias
    [STUD,GREE,WIST,REDC], 192
Greuze, Jean Baptiste [VALL], 193
Greyminster, Duke of [BLAN], 194
Griggs, Jimmy [VEIL], 194
Grimm, Jacob Ludwig Karl [SUSS], 195
Grimm, Wilhelm [SUSS], 195
Gruner, Baron Adelbert [ILLU], 196
Gyatso, Thubten [EMPT], 197
Hafiz [IDEN], 199
Haines, Mr. [3GAB], 199
Hales, William [VALL], 199

Table 1 List of stories in their Chronological order

Key	Full Title	Key	Full Title
GLOR	The Adventure of the Gloria Scott	FINA	The Final Problem
MUSG	The Adventure of the Musgrave Ritual	EMPT	The Adventure of the Empty House
STUD	A Study in Scarlet	GOLD	The Adventure of the Golden Pince-Nez
SPEC	The Adventures of the Speckled Band	3STU	The Adventure of the Three Students
RESI	The Adventure of the Resident Patient	SOLI	The Adventure of the Solitary Cyclist
NOBL	The Adventures of the Noble Bachelor	BLAC	The Adventure of the Black Peter
SECO	The Adventure of the Second Stain	NORW	The Adventure of the Norwood Builder
REIG	The Adventure of the Reigate Squire	VEIL	The Adventure of the Veiled Lodger
SCAN	A Scandal in Bohemia	BRUC	The Adventures of Bruce-Partington Plans
TWIS	The Man with the Twisted Lip	SUSS	The Adventure of the Sussex Vampire
FIVE	The Five Orange Pips	MISS	The Adventure of the Missing Three-Quarter
IDEN	A Case of Identity	ABBE	The Adventure of the Abbey Grange
REDH	The red-headed League	DEVI	The Adventures of Devil's Foot
DYIN	The Adventures of Dying Detective	DANC	The Adventure of the Dancing Men
BLUE	The Adventure of the Blue Carbuncle	RETI	The Adventure of the Retired Colourman
VALL	The Valley of Fear	CHAS	The Adventure of Charles Augustus Milverton
YELL	The Yellow Face	SIXN	The Adventure of the Six Napoleons
GREE	The Adventure of the Greek Interpreter	THOR	The Problem of Thor Bridge
SIGN	The Sign of Four	PRIO	The Adventure of the Priory School
HOUN	The Hound of the Baskervilles	SHOS	The Adventure of the Shoscombe Old Place
COPP	The Adventures of the Copper Beeches	3GAR	The Adventure of the Three Garridebs
BOSC	The Boscombe Valley Mystery	LADY	The Disappearance of Lady Frances Carfax
STOC	The Adventures of the Stockbroker's Clerk	ILLU	The Adventure of the Illustrious Client
NAVA	The Adventure of the Naval Treaty	REDC	The Adventures of Red Circle
CARD	The Adventures of the Cardboard Box	BLAN	The Adventure of the Blanched Soldier
ENGR	The Adventures of the Engineer's Thumb	3GAB	The Adventure of the Three Gables
CROO	The Adventure of the Crooked Man	MAZA	The Adventure of the Mazarin Stone
WIST	The Adventures of Wisteria Lodge	CREE	The Adventure of the Creeping Man
SILV	The Adventure of Silver Blaze	LION	The Adventure of the Lion's Mane
BERY	The Adventures of the Beryl Coronet	LAST	His Last Bow. The War Service of Sherlock Holmes

Table 2 List of stories in Canon Key order

Key	Full Title	Key	Full Title
3GAB	Adventure of the Three Gables	LION	Adventure of the Lion's Mane
3GAR	Adventure of the Three Garridebs	MAZA	Adventure of the Mazarin Stone
3STU	Adventure of the Three Students	MISS	Adventure of the Missing Three-Quarter
ABBE	Adventure of the Abbey Grange	MUSG	Adventure of the Musgrave Ritual
BERY	Adventures of the Beryl Coronet	NAVA	Adventure of the Naval Treaty
BLAC	Adventure of the Black Peter	NOBL	Adventures of the Noble Bachelor
BLAN	Adventure of the Blanched Soldier	NORW	Adventure of the Norwood Builder
BLUE	Adventure of the Blue Carbuncle	PRIO	Adventure of the Priory School
BOSC	Boscombe Valley Mystery	REDC	Adventures of Red Circle
BRUC	Adventures of Bruce-Parington Plans	REDH	red-headed League
CARD	Adventures of the Cardboard Box	REIG	Adventure of the Reigate Squire
CHAS	Adventure of Charles Augustus Milverton	RESI	Adventure of the Resident Patient
COPP	Adventures of the Copper Beeches	RETI	Adventure of the Retired Colourman
CREE	Adventure of the Creeping Man	SCAN	candal in Bohemia
CROO	Adventure of the Crooked Man	SECO	Adventure of the Second Stain
DANC	Adventure of the Dancing Men	SHOS	Adventure of the Shoscombe Old Place
DEVI	Adventures of Devil's Foot	SIGN	Sign of Four
DYIN	Adventures of Dying Detective	SILV	Adventure of Silver Blaze
EMPT	Adventure of the Empty House	SIXN	Adventure of the Six Napoleons
ENGR	Adventures of the Engineer's Thumb	SOLI	Adventure of the Solitary Cyclist
FINA	Final Problem	SPEC	Adventures of the Speckled Band
FIVE	Five Orange Pips	STOC	Adventures of the Stockbroker's Clerk
GLOR	Adventure of the Gloria Scott	STUD	tudy in Scarlet
GOLD	Adventure of the Golden Pince-Nez	SUSS	Adventure of the Sussex Vampire
GREE	Adventure of the Greek Interpreter	THOR	Problem of Thor Bridge
HOUN	Hound of the Baskervilles	TWIS	Man with the Twisted Lip
IDEN	ase of Identity	VALL	Valley of Fear
ILLU	Adventure of the Illustrious Client	VEIL	Adventure of the Veiled Lodger
LADY	Disappearance of Lady Frances Carfax	WIST	Adventures of Wisteria Lodge
LAST	Last Bow. The War Service of Sherlock olmes	YELL	Yellow Face

Table 3 List of stories in Publishing date order

Key	Full Title	Key	Full Title
STUD	A Study in Scarlet	SOLI	Adventure of the Solitary Cyclist
SIGN	The Sign of Four	PRIO	Adventure of the Priory School
SCAN	A Scandal in Bohemia	BLAC	Adventure of the Black Peter
REDH	The red-headed League	CHAS	Adventure of Charles Augustus Milverton
IDEN	A Case of Identity	SIXN	Adventure of the Six Napoleons
BOSC	The Boscombe Valley Mystery	3STU	Adventure of the Three Students
FIVE	The Five Orange Pips	GOLD	Adventure of the Golden Pince-Nez
TWIS	The Man with the Twisted Lip	MISS	Adventure of the Missing Three-Quarter
BLUE	The Adventure of the Blue Carbuncle	ABBE	Adventure of the Abbey Grange
SPEC	The Adventures of the Speckled Band	SECO	Adventure of the Second Stain
ENGR	The Adventures of the Engineer's Thumb	WIST	Adventures of Wisteria Lodge
NOBL	The Adventures of the Noble Bachelor	BRUC	Adventures of Bruce-Parington Plans
BERY	The Adventures of the Beryl Coronet	DEVI	Adventures of Devil's Foot
COPP	The Adventures of the Copper Beeches	REDC	Adventures of Red Circle
SILV	The Adventure of Silver Blaze	LADY	Disappearance of Lady Frances Carfax
CARD	The Adventures of the Cardboard Box	DYIN	Adventures of Dying Detective
YELL	The Yellow Face	VALL	Valley of Fear
STOC	The Adventures of the Stockbroker's Clerk	LAST	Last Bow. The War Service of Sherlock Holmes
GLOR	The Adventure of the Gloria Scott	MAZA	Adventure of the Mazarin Stone
MUSG	The Adventure of the Musgrave Ritual	THOR	Problem of Thor Bridge
REIG	The Adventure of the Reigate Squire	CREE	Adventure of the Creeping Man
CROO	The Adventure of the Crooked Man	SUSS	Adventure of the Sussex Vampire
RESI	The Adventure of the Resident Patient	3GAR	Adventure of the Three Garridebs
GREE	The Adventure of the Greek Interpreter	ILLU	Adventure of the Illustrious Client
NAVA	The Adventure of the Naval Treaty	3GAB	Adventure of the Three Gables
FINA	The Final Problem	BLAN	Adventure of the Blanched Soldier
HOUN	The Hound of the Baskervilles	LION	Adventure of the Lion's Mane
EMPT	The Adventure of the Empty House	RETI	Adventure of the Retired Colourman
NORW	The Adventure of the Norwood Builder	VEIL	Adventure of the Veiled Lodger
DANC	The Adventure of the Dancing Men	SHOS	Adventure of the Shoscombe Old Place